Lucky Girl

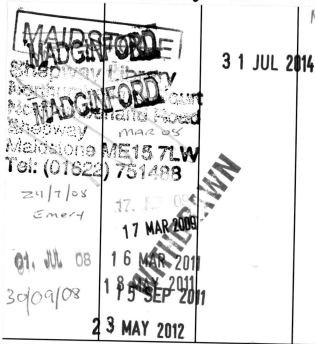

Please return on or before the latest date above.
You can renew online at *www.kent.gov.uk/libs*
or by telephone 08458 247 200

CUSTOMER SERVICE EXCELLENCE

Libraries & Archives

00884\DTP\RN\07.07   LIB 7

Lucky Girl

Fiona Gibson

LARGE PRINT
Oxford

First published in Great Britain 2006
by
Hodder & Stoughton, a division of Hodder Headline

Published in Large Print 2007 by ISIS Publishing Ltd.,
7 Centremead, Osney Mead, Oxford OX2 0ES
by arrangement with
Hodder & Stoughton, a division of Hodder Headline

British Library Cataloguing in Publication Data
Gibson, Fiona
    Lucky girl. – Large print ed.
    1. Fathers and daughters – Fiction
    2. Single women – Fiction
    3. Music teachers – Fiction
    4. Large type books
    I. Title
823.9'2 [F]

ISBN 978–0–7531–7778–5 (hb)
ISBN 978–0–7531–7779–2 (pb)

Printed and bound in Great Britain by
T. J. International Ltd., Padstow, Cornwall

For Cathy Gilligan with love

Acknowledgements

Huge thanks . . .

. . . to Tracy Short, for allowing me to pick her brain endlessly about flutes, Tom Grassie for flute-fixing know-how, Alison Munro for doc-type advice, Ann Hampsey for TV info, Gavin Convery for the perfect *tarte tatin*. My beloved writing group: Tania Cheston, Elizabeth Dobie, Amanda McLean, Vicki Feaver, Pam Taylor. For support all along the way: Ellie Stott, Liam Gilligan, Janine Wesencraft, Cheryl Zimmerman, Stephen Amor, Jenny Tucker, Kath Brown, Marie O'Riordan, Adele "Golden Hands" McGarry Watson. Sue and Chris at Atkinson Pryce. Keith Gibson, for being nothing like Frankie, and Margery Taylor, my lovely mum and ever-supportive friend.

Thanks to all at Hodder especially Sara Kinsella and Emma Longhurst. My wonderful agent, Annette Green. Enormous Lanarkshire-to-Isle-of-Wight hug to Wendy Varley for inspiration, unfailing gee-up emails and a treasured friendship. Love to Jimmy, for being with me always (and trawling charity shops for 1970s cookbooks, a nifty distraction from boxes of dusty old vinyl), and my darling nippers Sam, Dexter and Erin, for making life sparkly and so much more.

CHAPTER
ONE

Baked Beano

Take a can of luncheon meat, slice thickly and spread with French mustard. Fry until lightly browned. Heat one can baked beans, add a grated onion and dash of Worcester sauce. Arrange luncheon meat slices artfully around edge of a heatproof dish and pile bean mixture into centre. Sprinkle with grated cheese and grill until bubbling.

It's an easy dish, Stella. Even you can manage this one.

Regards,

Dad

Robert is seventeen minutes late. This doesn't count as properly late. Seventeen minutes can be lost while you're hunting for car keys, or reading on the loo. It's easy to forget, for seventeen minutes, that a friend is making you lunch.

This meal with Robert, it's nothing serious. It's a *light* lunch. He's been coming to me for flute lessons for two years, since before the birth of his twins and his break-up with Verity. He's drunk my coffee, my wine,

1

flicked through my CDs and once blurted out, "I don't think of you just as my teacher."

"Don't you?" I asked.

His brown eyes were steady and sad-looking. "I can *talk* to you, Stella," he added, as if he'd had to muster courage to say this.

"Come over," I said, "next Saturday. I'll make us some lunch. We could go for a walk, head down to the beach . . ."

"Are you sure? Don't want to put you to any —"

"You're not," I said, and hugged him as he left. He kissed me lightly on the cheek.

The smile was still hovering on my face when I glimpsed my distorted reflection in the kettle. It lingered there, an excited child's smile, even as I tried to swipe it away with the back of my hand. I couldn't remember the last time I'd invited anyone to anything.

I turn off the heat and scrape the bottom of the pot with a wooden spoon. I'm not making Dad's Baked Beano but wild mushroom risotto. I prowled around Roots and Fruits after work on Friday and bought fancy mushroom varieties: porcini, shiitake, oyster. They looked like curls of flesh in their brown paper bags, and smelt of damp forests. I also made chicken stock, some of which is left in the jug, and has a stagnant-dishwater look about it.

With risotto, timing is crucial. Already it's the wrong side of gloopy. You could imagine it setting inside you, clutching your vital organs, requiring an abdominal operation to remove it. I taste it, and it's still passable, although perhaps too pungently cheesy. Does Robert like risotto? I know he's a regular consumer of take-aways — the menu's Sellotaped to a kitchen cupboard — and drives a dented Fiat Panda with two oily-looking child seats jammed into the back. I know this vehicle is marred with spilt milk, gnawed plastic toys and two-handled baby cups flung down and forgotten, their contents yellowing under the seats. He prefers having lessons here now. He said, "I like your place, Stella. It's peaceful. Calm. It does me good, just being here."

I know all these details about Robert. But I don't know his feelings about Parmesan.

Through my kitchen window fine rain has darkened the descending tumble of slate roofs. The proud, red-brick houses look like they've been dropped randomly, then clamoured to grab their share of sea view. Wedged between them, more than a mile away, is my skinny sliver of sea.

Robert is twenty-nine minutes late. He's not hunting for car keys or even snared in Saturday traffic. Gluey rice has attached itself to the roof of my mouth. I push it off with my tongue, but my mouth still feels as if it needs cleaning with a high-pressure hose. The risotto looks like something you'd pour on to a garden path to stop weeds sprouting.

In the bathroom I inspect my face, which looks hot and damp from hanging over the bubbling pan. I blot myself with a flannel. My fingers stink of Parmesan. I squirt on lime-scented liquid soap — "Healing Garden", it's called — and scrub with the nailbrush, but the Parmesan smell won't go away.

3

My hair, which I blow-dried in a carefree manner, slumps dolefully round my face. I fluff it forward, which makes it look too bushy. I examine my teeth, baring them like a fierce dog. It's a cool September afternoon. The sky is pale grey, flat as a bedsheet. A small breeze sneaks in through the bathroom window, wafting the white gauze blind.

I check the street from the living room. A removal van struggles up the hill and judders to a halt in front of next door. On its side is a slogan: "Movers & Shakers". There's a picture of two men in dungarees, holding a sofa above their heads as if it's virtually weightless — a sofa-shaped cloud. The drawn men look infinitely capable. You'd trust them to move your entire life, even your precious things. They'd treat your possessions with respect.

A short man with a chunky body springs out of the van and marches along next door's path. He hammers on the door and steps back to peer at the upstairs windows. He bangs again, then shouts, "Hello?" into the sky, to the weaving seagulls.

A second man clambers out. "What's going on?" he yells. "Aren't they answering, or what?" He's wearing a green-and-white football top — Plymouth Argyle — and looks vaguely malnourished. Neither resembles the men on the side of the van. "Try the back," he instructs the other.

"Where's the back?"

"Round the *back*, where d'you expect?"

I'm itching to go out and direct these men into the alley that leads to the overgrown path at the bottom of

4

our back gardens. I want to quiz them — find out who my new neighbours might be. My mind conjures a pleasing image of an amiable young couple, both of whom — inspired by my playing, which drifts through our adjoining wall — block-book me for indefinite weekly flute lessons.

The chunky man is leaning against the van, smoking furiously. He directs his gaze into my living room window and narrows his eyes. I shuffle together an unwieldy pile of flute solos and duets, which I'm sorting for next week's private lessons. Dad's handwritten recipe lies beside its ripped envelope on the table. Years ago, when I'd just left home and he'd started to send them — perhaps fearing, rather belatedly, that I might be incapable of looking after myself — I noticed he always used the same kind of crinkly paper. The tiny type at the bottom of each sheet read, "finest onionskin". I imagined raw onions being churned up in some gigantic blender, spread thinly on wire racks and dried in a low heat. I nibbled the corner of a recipe — Baked Gammon with Tangy Marmalade Sauce — to see if it tasted oniony. It was just paper, lightly smoked by Dad's Café Crème cigars.

I tap out Robert's number. *Hello, we're not here right now. Please leave your name, number and time of calling . . .* The voice sounds like someone at work who leads teams, which is what Robert does (I've never quite figured out what his teams actually do). And he's still "we", even though Verity and the kids moved out just before Christmas. Robert joked, "She timed it to get out of buying me a present." He was laughing, but his whole body seemed crushed. He hasn't been a "we" for nine months. I bang down the phone without leaving a message, then fold the recipe over and over until it's a tiny square, thin as a fingernail. "Thanks, Dad," I murmur.

My father is Frankie Moon, front-man of 1970s show *Frankie's Favourites* and inventor of whizzy implements such as the Nine-nozzle Piper: an enormous syringe-like gadget that you could imagine being useful if you ever needed to tranquillize a buffalo. They're so long ago, the TV years, that sometimes I wonder if I've remembered it all wrong, and that Dad was something more ordinary, like a plumber, or worked for the council. It hardly seems possible that a broderie-anglaise bra with tiny pink rosebuds stitched between the cups was posted through our letterbox, accompanied by a fan letter scrawled in splodgy green ink. "Beware the green Biro," Dad would say, when stuff like that happened. "Bloody loonies and crazies." I knew, though, that he relished the attention. His cheeks would puff up, and turn slightly pink, as if they'd been inflated with my bicycle pump.

Robert is forty-eight minutes late, which counts as so late he's not coming. Anything could have happened — some child-related emergency. Aren't toddlers always falling over and damaging themselves? I've seen Robert in town, clutching the twins' reins, the boys tangling themselves up like wild puppies. That's it: Verity phoned him in a panic. They're at A and E with one of the boys dripping blood on to the waiting-area floor. Of course he's forgotten about our lunch. Anyone would, if

6

their screaming child was having his forehead repaired. They wouldn't be thinking, Stella cooked a whole blasted chicken on Saturday so she could boil up the carcass for stock. I must abandon my injured son for a wild mushroom risotto.

I pour the remains of the stock down the sink, and scrape the solidified rice into the kitchen bin, where it lands with a disappointed plop.

"Sorry to disturb you," says the man in the Plymouth top, hovering uncomfortably on my front step. His jaw is spattered with coarse hairs, which have sprung, black and defiant, from milky skin.

"That's okay," I say.

"Seen anyone next door, love? We're doing a removal. Woman's not shown up. We've got all her gear in that van." He exhales noisily through the gap between his front teeth.

"Sorry, I didn't even know there were new tenants. The house has been empty for ages."

He glances up at threatening clouds. "Christ, we'll just have to unload it into the garden. Haven't got time to hang about. We've another job at four."

"But it's raining," I protest. "You can't leave everything outside." It's the light, steady kind that doesn't feel like much but has a sly way of drenching you.

"Not my problem, love. That's what you get in this game — having to deal with that sort."

I frown at him. "What sort?"

"Imbeciles," he declares, strutting back to the van, where his accomplice is hauling a battered brown armchair, its overstuffed arms looking like mottled sausage rolls, on to the pavement.

Someone's things are out there, being drizzled on: more armchairs — one deep purple, another the pallid hue of an ill person's face — and a standard lamp with a faded pink shade, edged with a thick strip of Dalmatian fur. Rolled-up rugs have been propped against the house. A white Christmas tree has been bound tightly with rope to stop its branches escaping.

There are boxes and boxes of what look like books. Later, when I peer out again, one's been knocked over. They're not books but records, spilt from their sleeves on to the small square of pink gravel in front of the house. Mrs Lawrence, the previous tenant, had the gravel laid so it wouldn't need weeding, but dock leaves and dandelions still forced their way through.

To stop myself spying on the removal men I pick up the phone to call Robert again, then decide there's no point. He'll still be at A and E having his little boy's head fixed. In the kitchen I pile fancy mushrooms between slices of bread. They're so bouncy and light, it's like eating a foam sandwich.

A trace of sunlight struggles through the clouds. Rainbow weather. Mum used to say that rainbows were magical: "If you see one," she'd say, "it means something wonderful is about to happen." We'd spotted one the day my brother Charlie won cinema tickets in the *South Devon Echo*'s kids' quiz. Dad was away filming — he never came to the cinema with us anyway — so Mum took us to see *The Railway Children* at the Royale.

I'd put on my best pinafore with the huge purple flowers and picked a clashing buttercup yellow shirt to wear underneath. Going out with Mum felt special — almost birthday-special. In the plush foyer of the Royale, I noticed a man staring at her. He was surrounded by braying children demanding Butterkist popcorn and sweet cigarettes from the kiosk. Despite the mayhem around him, his gaze was firmly fixed upon Mum's pale brown bare legs. It was as if all of those kids had just melted away.

Mum didn't really look like a mum, I thought then. She looked like a long-limbed drawing from a Simplicity dress pattern: slender and tall, with surprised-looking eyes and a veil of shoulder-length honey-coloured hair. I clutched her hand, feeling the smoothness of her manicured nails, as she led Charlie and me into the dark.

The film was at least five years old. Charlie hadn't wanted to come. His schoolfriends were obsessed with *Star Wars* — all the boys fancied Princess Leia — but Charlie hadn't wanted to see that either. He preferred documentaries about real things, like the eerie fish that lurked at the bottom of oceans. "This film's for girls," he hissed, as we took our seats. "It's all kissing and *love*." He screwed up his face as if "love" smelt of bad things — ageing meat, perhaps, or blocked drains.

"Shush," Mum murmured back. "Stella and I have always wanted to see it."

Charlie chomped morosely on his popcorn with his chin thrust out. I wanted to say, "You won the tickets — would you cheer up, for God's sake, and stop spoiling this?" But the film had started. It wasn't a kissing movie at all. The man behind us — the one who'd been ogling Mum in the foyer — barked at one of his kids for dropping sweet cigarettes all over the floor.

Towards the end of the film I glimpsed Charlie's face. He was a year and a half older than me, old enough not to be scared of Dad's vexed stares and fraying temper, but still cried when the Railway Children's father came back from prison. The train pulled into the station, steam billowed and cleared on the platform, and there he was, their lovely dad, and my big brother's cheeks glistening wet. I was so horrified, I couldn't look at him.

As we walked home I wanted to hold Charlie's hand but I knew he would have shaken me off. He walked a little behind Mum and me, and kept stopping to peer into shop windows. "There's a trouser-suit pattern," Mum was telling me, "in *Golden Hands* magazine. I thought I'd make it for you for the concert — you're doing a solo this year, aren't you?"

"Yes," I said, finding it hard to focus as she discussed possible trouser-suit colours. My head was filled with the dad in *The Railway Children*, and my friends' fathers, and even the dads in the picture books I'd had when I was little — they'd let their kids wash the car and poke around with tools in the garage. We'd never done any of those things with our dad.

That evening I found Charlie curled up on his bed with an enormous book called *Mysteries of the Deep*, which he'd bought at a library sale. "What did you think of the film?" I asked, really wanting to know why he'd cried.

"Told you it'd be girly," Charlie said, without looking up.

I was nine years old and had figured that the dad part had got him. After all, I had Mum: I was a mini-her, everyone said, although I couldn't see the faintest resemblance. We did things together. We fitted, like spoons in a drawer.

And Dad? It felt like he wasn't there, even when we could hear him typing or banging his filing-cabinet drawers in his study. I didn't know any other dads who hid away in their study — who had a study at all, for that matter — or escaped to the garden in the midst of winter when there was nothing out there to be done.

Next door's front garden is all filled up. You can't see the gravel. It looks like a second-hand furniture shop with the shop bit removed. The path has been blocked by a plump sofa in such a fierce shade of fuchsia it's probably capable of sweating. The chunky man straddles the low wall that divides our meagre front gardens and bites into a pie. His mate perches daintily on the sofa's arm and tips Coke into his mouth.

A woman is running up the hill and lurches to a halt at the gate. "What the hell's going on?" she yells. Her circular face peeps out from a thick bale of magenta hair. Behind her I can see the indistinct shapes of two

11

scuffling children. The woman tries to force her way into the garden but is blocked by the sofa.

"Is this our new house?" a child trills behind her.

"I want everything inside," the woman thunders, "before it's *ruined*." The chunky man pops the last lump of pie into his mouth and sweeps his hands across his trousers.

"*Is* it?" the little girl asks. She's wearing a pea-green mac that sticks out like a capital A. Her head and shoulders are entirely covered by a dome-shaped transparent umbrella.

"Yes, Midge," the woman says, sounding defeated. The umbrella has antennae. It makes the child look like an alien, or how my younger pupils might draw an alien: triangular green body and a bubble for a head.

Behind her, hunched miserably on the pavement, a larger child loiters, shrouded in a hooded pink jacket. The alien steps daintily along the wall, then sees me at the window and starts waving madly. I wave back, then quickly turn away — I hate being caught spying — and slip Dad's folded-up recipe into the red-and-gold Mexican box on the bookshelf. Crammed into it are eighteen years' worth of meal solutions I've never cooked: Chicken Maryland, Duck à l'Orange, Pork and Apricot Casserole. Dishes requiring the uneasy pairing of meat and fruit. No matter how full the box looks when you take off the lid, there's always room for one more recipe. That's the thing about onionskin paper. It folds up to virtually nothing.

"It won't go up," a removal man shouts, "not round that bend in the stairs."

12

There's a dull scraping noise, and the woman's irate yapping. "She hit me three times," roars one of the kids. "She wants to *blind* me." Her accent isn't from round here — South Devon — but further north, maybe the Midlands. These children and that magenta-haired woman are my new neighbours.

"She hit me first!" the other child yelps. "She's a cow."

"Didn't!"

"Did!"

I spend my working days teaching primary-school children. I enjoy kids — love their spirit, the way everything's fresh and new to them.

"You stink of dog poo!"

But I don't want them living next door.

"You're stupid. I *hate* you." Someone's crying now, and I assume it's the small one — the alien — but when I step outside it's the older girl whose tearful face peeps out from a hood.

"Hi," I say, "I'm Stella, I live next —"

"Huh," the woman mutters. She's edging backwards out of the house, gripping one end of a salmon-coloured headboard.

"You're gonna drop that," the smaller child announces.

"Shut your face," the woman snaps.

"Can we unpack now? I want my toys. What did you do with my light sabre?"

"It's coming, easy now, easy," the woman says, as if she's assisting a birth and keeping her voice steady will

13

make everything all right. A faded denim jacket is buttoned tightly across her broad chest.

"Can I help with that?" I ask.

She flashes a quick, taut smile. "We'll manage, thanks."

"I wish she was never *born*," declares the bigger child. She's leaning against a scuffed melamine wardrobe, patting her tender eye.

"It'll have to go up," the woman announces. "You can't have a bed without a headboard."

I could point out that mine doesn't have a headboard, but now might not be the right moment to discuss our differing taste in home furnishings. "It's so old," the bigger girl complains, still snivelling. "You said we were getting a new house, not a horrible stinky *old* house."

"I like it," chirps the smaller one. "There's probably ghosts."

The woman props the headboard against the house and smoothes its velvet pile. "You could try hoisting it up," I suggest, "through the bedroom window. The stairs in these houses are so narrow — that's what I had to do with my bed when I moved in."

"Hoist it up," she says firmly. "Good idea."

I smile, offer a hand. "I'm Stella."

"Diane. Bloody nightmare, moving. Everything soaking wet, ruined." She rubs her small, pebbly eyes, ignoring my outstretched hand. I try to give the older girl a neighbourly smile but she glowers at me, and it sags.

14

"I'm Midge Price," shouts the alien, "and I'm seven and a quarter."

"And that's Jojo," her mother adds. "She's ten. Say hello to the lady, Jojo."

Jojo looks like she's trying to shrink into her hood. Diane fishes a squashed Benson & Hedges packet and a lighter from her jacket pocket. The lighter makes a rasping noise and won't work.

The men are upstairs now, hanging out of the open window and gripping the rope, which they've lashed round the headboard. The little girl waves some weapon of mass destruction with a light-up blade that she's unearthed from a binliner.

"Steady," Diane says, gazing up at the dangling headboard. She glances at me and says, "Cost me two hundred quid to have it re-covered, Cilla."

"Stella," I murmur. The headboard sways uneasily, like an aeroplane propellor. Perhaps it's just a temporary home: they'll discover that there are no other young kids at this end of Briar Hill — it's too quiet, too *dull* — and move back to wherever they came from.

The football-top man takes one hand off the rope. It springs from his grasp. The headboard's a living thing now, bouncing against the rendered front wall and living-room window to land in a heap of shattered glass, flattening the Christmas tree.

"Two hundred quid," Diane whispers. Dark wood shows through the ripped velvet.

"I want crisps," Jojo whines.

The alien, Midge, catches my eye. She's trying to keep her lips jammed together but a snort bursts out. She's laughing hysterically now, teetering on the wall in her bright yellow wellies, then falling and landing in a tangle of umbrella and light sabre on a heap of moist satin cushions.

Behind her, streaking the bruised lilac sky, is a rainbow.

CHAPTER
TWO

Bubble Gum

Paul Street Primary is a bright, airy school built on the site of the old Royale cinema. The music room, which doubles as the after-school club, has a row of acoustic guitars suspended from hooks on the wall, and another wall entirely made of glass, to which pupils have stuck drawings done in marker-pen on acetate (generally speaking, music lessons take place in school-furniture graveyards: seldom-used rooms filled with damaged tables and tremulous shelving).

Here, neatly seated and ready to play, is Sasha Rodgers, a delicate child with startling green eyes and the medical whiff of school soap. Here is Emily Catchpole, a talented flautist with speedy fingers that flick on and off keys like springing insects. Next to her, with grubby socks bunched at her ankles, is Laura Sweet. You can spot the children who'll soon decide they've picked the wrong instrument: they'll suddenly yearn to play drums, or bass guitar in a thrash metal band, deciding that music — at least, *this* kind of music — is for swots with troubled complexions and no friends. Laura is one of those kids. Right now, she's showing off the fake tattoo — entwined, spiky-stemmed roses — that circles her upper arm.

Willow Chambers thunders in and slams her tutor book on to the vacant stand. "Sorry," she gasps. "I thought it was Tuesday then realised I'd forgot."

"That's all right," I tell her. "Calm down. Take a few minutes to catch your breath. Now, everyone — Toby, could you at least *look* ready?" Toby is the lone boy here and is feasting hungrily on a fingernail. "Where's your flute?" I prompt him.

He continues to nibble the nail. *Ignore bad behaviour, if you can. Recognise and celebrate the good.* Jen the head teacher's mantra. "At Paul Street we focus on the positive," she says, at her introductory meeting with new children's parents. Second week of the school year, and I'm on at Toby already.

"Are you chewing gum?" I ask.

"No, Miss Moon." His jaw sets rigid.

"Okay, let's start with —"

"We always start with scales," Toby announces. A whiff of gum, synthetically sweet.

"Yes, we do, because it helps to warm up your flute, loosens the muscles . . . You *know* this."

He yawns dramatically. A flash of neon pink, embedded in a molar.

"Please get rid of that chewing gum. You know where the bin is."

"There's no chewing gum," he says airily.

"Do you want to leave this class? Stop lessons right now?"

A small smile tweaks his lips. Willow rolls her nose against her cardigan sleeve. I never thought I'd turn out like this, fizzing mad at things that don't matter. At college I'd visualised the kind of teacher I'd be: inspirational Stella, always addressed by her first name, capable of detecting the merest hint of musical ability and coaxing it from a child who'd been written off as hopeless. Music had done this for me: become *my* thing, then pretty much my entire life, after the bad thing had happened. It had nothing to do with my celebrity dad, or colossal-brained brother. I really thought music could rescue a person.

Toby lifts his flute and swoops through his scales. He plays beautifully, the notes flooding the room. But the moment he's finished he shrinks back into his chair, his face partially concealed by a shock of black hair. He behaves as if his talent has been draped round him like an embarrassing cape.

Willow launches into the Fauré piece. She starts at a steady tempo, gradually gathering speed and cantering onwards until, cheeks blazing, she charges to the finish like an out-of-control horse.

"Lovely, Willow," I tell her, "but try to play steadily next time, not so much of a rush."

Willow mumbles something like, "I wasn't Russian."

We discuss phrasing, how to take a breath so it doesn't sound like a gasp, as if you've been given an injection. Toby peers through his fringe at the acetate drawings on the window. "Okay," I say, as the kids put away their flutes, "remember to practise your minor scales for next week. And no chewing gum, Toby."

"It's not chewing gum, Miss. It's bubble gum." He hurtles out of the room, leaving a knocked-over stand and a chemical strawberry aroma.

Somewhere along the line, I've turned into the kind of teacher who loses her rag over gum.

My first flute teacher was an elderly lady called Mrs Bones. She had ivory skin and neat, closely packed teeth. The beads of her necklace were tiny black-and-white dice. "Breathing, Stella," she'd say, "it's all in the breathing." Sometimes she would devote entire lessons to breathing techniques. *Push down the diaphragm, fill up the cavity to the maximum, the absolute maximum.* I'd never thought of my angular nine-year-old body as having a diaphragm or a cavity. I pictured myself cross-sectioned in a medical book, filled with billowing air.

The building where Mrs Bones lived had oddly shaped windows, like circles and half-moons. The house had been split into four flats, and Mrs Bones lived at the top. From the outside you couldn't work out where one flat ended and the next one started, how they fitted together.

Mrs Bones was the only person I knew who lived in a flat. Our house was detached, with an assortment of sturdy outbuildings, wooden sheds and unruly herbaceous borders. Dad would try to tame them, digging up plants and shifting them, then moving them back to their original positions. I rarely saw him do anything practical in the house. Annoying things, like a wobbly shelf or a tap that couldn't be turned off, remained broken until we stopped noticing the wobbles and drips. Kids at school assumed I went home every night to a grand dinner, but Dad didn't even cook for us. Mum said, "Your father works very hard. He's had quite enough of food at the end of the day."

It was an ordinary Saturday afternoon when she came to collect me from Mrs Bones. Mum spoke quietly in the shadowy flat, as if she, too, was afraid of being told off for not using her diaphragm properly. "I'd like a word, Mrs Moon," Mrs Bones said. She ushered Mum into the kitchenette off the living room. I waited on the brocade armchair, breathing in old lavender and dust.

"Stella has an exceptional talent," Mrs Bones murmured, "which must be encouraged at all costs. It's imperative that this child is given full support to achieve her potential." Her voice grew louder until she sounded almost angry. "We're talking about her future, Mrs Moon," she added firmly.

"Yes, of course," my mother said. She trod softly into the living room. Pink patches were showing through the powder on her cheeks. She squeezed my hand as we stepped carefully down the twisting stone stairs. Instead of heading through the town centre she took me to Bay Street, where the shops had sagging, moss-covered roofs, and some rarely bothered to open. I knew this street. Mum and I had come here, to Grieves and Aitken, to buy my first flute.

"Where are we going?" I asked, as we approached the shop, but Mum didn't answer. A gilded harp stood in the music shop's window. My eyes followed the sweeping curve of its frame: it was beautiful.

I realised Mum was gazing at it too. "Isn't it lovely?" I asked.

"Yes," she said. She swallowed hard, then blinked at me, mustering a smile.

"What is it?" I asked.

"A harp," she said, deliberately misunderstanding.

"I wish I could play it. I bet it's really hard."

Mum turned away and pushed open the door. "Come on," she said, "let's see what we can find in here."

Inside the shop smelt of oiled wood. "Can I help you, Mrs Moon?" Mr Grieves asked. He had a shiny bald patch and a soft-looking grey moustache. I assumed he could play every instrument in the shop — I was convinced he did so the minute the "Closed" sign went up — and wondered if the moustache hindered his secret performances.

"Stella would like to try all your flutes," Mum announced. She was wearing a fitted trouser suit — a larger version of the one she'd made for me from *Golden Hands* magazine — in a colour she called burnt orange.

My face had flushed, and I was aware of a panicky sensation beneath my ribs. "I don't need —" I began.

"Just try them," Mum said.

Mr Grieves pieced together a selection and I played them in turn. They were ordinary, no better than the perfectly good flute I'd been playing for the past two years. "This," he said, when I'd finished, "is something special." He delved into a cupboard close to the floor and placed a slender black case on the glass counter.

He opened it, pieced the flute together and handed it to me. It felt weightier than my own instrument, and more precious than anything I'd ever touched. I wasn't grown-up enough to be let loose with something so special. I was sure I'd lose control of my hands, that they'd flop open and the flute would land with a terrible crack on the shop's cold tiled floor. "Just play, darling," Mum whispered.

I lifted the flute to my mouth. I never felt nervous playing in concerts but now my lower lip buzzed, as if an insect had landed upon it. Mr Grieves had brought through a spindly wooden chair from the back room for Mum to sit on. I took a breath. The sound poured out like water. Mum sat with her legs neatly crossed at the ankles, drinking me in.

"The headjoint is solid silver," Mr Grieves said, when I'd stopped playing. "I don't think you'll hear a richer, fuller sound." Richer, fuller: like the coffee adverts on TV. I played some more. I didn't want to stop. An old lady outside was gazing into the shop. Mr Grieves patted his moustache and had a conversation with Mum about money, which I pretended not to hear. I knew we weren't poor — we had just had our kitchen refurbished, complete with turquoise Formica-topped breakfast bar — but the price of the flute still made me feel dizzy. Mum wrote a cheque and I carried out the flute, snug in its case, in my arms.

Next door to Grieves and Aitken there was an Italian café where sorbets were served in hollowed-out fruits.

"Lovely Eleanor," announced Dino, the owner, touching my mother's arm. She chose lime sorbet. I had lemon. I didn't like sorbet — I'd rather have had raspberry ripple ice-cream — but I wanted to be grown-up and elegant like Mum. Our sorbets came with mint leaves on top. I opened the flute case on the table. "It's beautiful," I said.

"You deserve it. You've been practising so hard lately."

"What will Dad say?"

"It doesn't matter. This isn't about Dad."

"But it's not Christmas," I protested, "or my birthday, and Dad says —"

"Our whole lives revolve round him," she snapped. "What about you, me, Charlie? He's not interested in either of you, he —" She caught herself, and scraped a spoonful of sorbet from its shell. Usually she stuck up for Dad, pretending that we were a fully functioning family. Now she'd blown the housekeeping money on a flute. "I don't want you to miss out," she added, "on any chances in life."

I was going to ask, "What chances?" then noticed that her eyes were brimming with tears, which were threatening to spill into the lime shell. "He'll be mad," I said, "if he knows how much it cost."

Mum smiled unsteadily. "Then we won't tell him."

"Okay. We'll keep it a secret."

I felt warm inside, even though I'd wolfed down my sorbet. Mum stared down at the flute, gleaming in its purple velvet nest, and said, "Never tell your dad that this is anything special."

24

★　★　★

Jen sips her beer and asks, "And how was the delightful Toby today?"

"Grumbling about playing scales, refusing to spit out his gum . . ." Put that way, my gripes seem pathetic. He's just a child, an immensely talented child.

"You could kick him out of your group," Jen says, knowing I won't do that. We've been friends since we were fourteen. These damp planks we're sitting on now, at the far end of the jetty, are where we used to leap off into the sea.

"It's not serious enough to kick him out. You know how talented he is."

Jen rolls her eyes. "He's foul, Stella. Had to call in his parents last week. He's been bullying Alexander Holt — a year-two kid, for God's sake, four years younger than Toby. Pushed him downstairs, said he'd do worse if he told. That's the kind of monster we're talking about."

"Let's just give it a few more weeks," I say, draining my glass.

"He doesn't deserve it. There are lots of other kids who are keen to get started."

I stroll back along the jetty and jump down on to the sand. Seaweed is draped over beached boats like wet hair. A girl and a boy are grabbing handfuls to fling at each other. Jen lands on the beach behind me. "Still no word from Robert?" she asks, as we pick our way between the boats.

"Nothing. I've left a message — he hasn't even called back."

The girl scampers past, waving seaweed, the thick, slimy kind, like crimp-edged pasta. Water sprays off, hitting my shirt. "Sorry, Miss Moon," the girl shouts.

"That's okay, Laura."

"Doesn't he hang around after lessons," Jen continues, "saying what a 'good friend' you are?"

"I think he just wants someone to talk to."

"I can't believe he stood you up," she announces, kicking a stranded buoy out of her path. "What do you see in him?"

"He's a friend, Jen. He's kind, sensitive —"

"Gorgeous?" she cuts in.

"Well, yes." I don't tell her he's the first man I've noticed — really noticed — since Alex. Something about him tugs at my heart: the way he tries to be the best dad he can be, the way he flounders over his scales. I want to help him, hold him.

"Can he play?" Jen asks.

I shake my head, laughing. "He struggles, never seems to improve. At first I thought he only carried on with lessons to get a breather from the kids. But since Verity left —"

"He just wants to see you."

I shrug, batting off her suggestion.

"Has he ever pounced on you?"

The thought of Robert pouncing, panther-style, makes me splutter. "Of course not. He wouldn't dare, even if he wanted to."

"Why don't *you*?"

"What?" I ask, feigning innocence.

"Kiss Robert. Peel off his clothes . . ."

26

We smother our laughter, conscious of Laura, who's within earshot, stirring stagnant water in a beached rowing-boat with a stick. "I'm out of practice," I hiss. "Wouldn't know where to start."

"With the shirt," Jen suggests. "Not the socks."

"If it happens, I'll phone you. You can talk me through it."

"You think I remember?" She sniggers. "I don't undress Simon. He'd think I'd been reading some dumb sex manual . . ."

Alex used to undress me, piece by piece. "You have the perfect body," he said, the first time I stood naked before him. I wanted to laugh and point out the lack of what women's magazines refer to as curves. As a teenager I worried that I'd need an operation to become a proper woman.

"Still miss Alex?" Jen asks, reading my thoughts.

I could lie: *Of course not. He drove me mad with his crazes, his butterfly mind. I'm over him now, glad that he left. Life's so much better without him.*

The words are out before I can stop them. "Yes," I say, "I really do."

CHAPTER
THREE

Chewy Jewels

"Stella, can't believe I've done this . . . so embarrassed . . . something came up — it went right out of my mind . . ." Robert's voice limps from the answerphone, sounding tinny and hopeless. "Hope you didn't go to any trouble," the message ends.

I rifle the kitchen for acceptable edibles and find a jar of marinated peppers, which I bought in the fancy deli during a shopping day with Jen. She was trying to choose some food for her son Elliot to minimise the risk of starvation when he left for university. A "starter hamper", she called it. Jen was flapping in shops crammed with flavoured oils and pungent cheeses. She couldn't remember what he liked and disliked, and kept snatching non-starterish foods, like pickled walnuts and anchovy relish.

I drape the peppers over a hunk of French bread and eat on the sofa, over a dinner plate to catch the crumbs. There's a programme called *Dirty Business* on TV, about restaurants infested with rodents and bugs. "What you're ordering here," says a gaunt man in glasses, "is our little friend salmonellosis . . ." It sounds harmless — cute, even. Like something my brother

Charlie might have discussed in his PhD thesis: Agnostic Behaviour and Population Dynamics of Euphausiid Crustaceans. I flip channels to a gardening show in which a shiny-faced woman is helping to erect a hideous water feature. Distressed-looking cherubs cluster round a central plinth.

Before he moved out — before he announced that he didn't "feel right", whatever that meant — Alex decided that a water feature would act as a focal point in our back garden. I'd assumed that flowers were meant to be the focal point: wasn't that why people had gardens? He plonked a catalogue called *Aqua Designs* on my music stand, obscuring Mozart's Flute Concerto in G. I stared at a monstrous structure entitled Village Pump in Textured Resin. "It looks like a concrete penis," I said.

"Not that one," Alex retorted, flipping to the correct page. "See? It's a figure-of-eight." He jabbed at a bleak-looking structure, which looked like two dog bowls connected by a feeding trough.

"What's it for?"

"It's for aerating and energising water. We can use it to irrigate the garden, and bring oxygen to —"

"We don't need to irrigate," I pointed out. "This is Devon, not Africa."

He complained that I lacked imagination, wouldn't try anything new or different. Why else would I have left Devon to study in London, then scuttled back to my home town? I said, "If I hadn't, you'd never have met me."

Alex snatched the water-feature brochure and prodded the Mozart. "You're more interested in some bloke who died in 1870," he muttered.

"1791," I teased him.

After three years together — and, I assumed, thoroughly cheesed off with the air-filled void where my imagination should have been — Alex forced me to try something new and different, because he left me.

He still sneaks into my head when I least expect him. I don't want him there, don't want him back. "I don't *want* him," I tell the gardening woman and her dribbling fountain.

"Next week," she chirps, "we'll transform a dismal backyard into a Mediterranean-style courtyard with a few bits and pieces you'll have lying around your home." What does she mean exactly? An old clothes-horse, filing cabinet or deceased tumble-dryer?

I still wonder if things might have turned out differently with Alex and me if I'd agreed to a figure-of-eight water feature.

Midge, the younger girl from next door, is yelping from the front garden wall — *my* garden wall. I keep my gaze firmly fixed on the TV. "I'm *desperate*," she chirps, clutching her groin. By the time I reach the front door the older one, Jojo, is thumping rhythmically on the glass panel.

"Hi, girls," I say, half opening the door. "Isn't your mum —"

"We need the toilet," Jojo announces.

"Can't you use the one in your house?"

Midge leaps down from the wall, performing a desperate-for-bathroom wiggle. "She's still at work," she says.

"You mean you're locked out?"

"She didn't lock us *out*. She's just not *in*." She says this as if I have the comprehension of a cat flea.

"Okay, come in. Loo's upstairs, first door on the —"

"We know," Midge retorts. "Our house is the same as yours."

"But not as fancy," Jojo adds, following her sister as she thunders upstairs. The juddering sound of the bath's Jacuzzi setting comes from the bathroom. The multi-functioning bath was here when I bought the house — before Alex moved in — and has never done anything more useful than make a low rumble like an underground train. There's muffled giggling, the whir of loo roll being unravelled. "Everything okay?" I call up nervously.

"Yeah," they yell in unison. I hope they're not prying in the bathroom cabinet. This is my house; these are *my* things. I'm used to well-behaved pupils being here, not sniggering neighbours.

I pull out the music for tonight's lessons: Sophie at five, Jade at six thirty. I have taken on more private pupils since Alex left, nearly doubling my workload. My diary is packed with names and times, as if it belongs to someone with billions of friends and a dizzying social life.

Midge clatters into the living room and smears wet hands on the front of her skirt. She has springy pale gold hair and an old-fashioned face that belongs on a biscuit tin or a Pears Soap wrapper. "I like your house," she says, through a mouth crammed with sweets. "It's very tidy. But it smells funny."

"Does it? What of?"

"Don't know. Kind of *new*, like a shop."

Clean, she means. Alex despaired of my need for tidy surroundings. When he caught me pairing up his shoes in the hall, he said, "You're acting like my mother." After that I tried to stop tidying his things, because the last thing I wanted to be was his mother.

"One person doesn't make much mess," I tell Midge.

"You live in this massive house all by yourself?"

"It's not that big," I say, laughing. "Just the same size as yours."

Jojo stomps in, casting off her red school sweatshirt to reveal a grubby polo shirt and a necklace of pink plastic fairies joined by their outstretched arms. She perches on the sofa, her pale grey eyes flicking suspiciously around my living room. Midge examines the bookshelf with her head cocked to one side, trying to read spines. Make yourselves at home, I think.

"I like your hair," Midge announces. "How d'you get it like that?"

"Like what?"

"Kind of ginger."

"It's more . . . brownish, really. It's a colour you put on, called henna."

"You dye it," Jojo announces. "I said she did, didn't I, Midge? So does our mum. Last time she used the wrong sort of dye and it rained and ran down her face." She rests her upper body on the table, causing it to wobble dangerously, and flicks through the stack of sheet music. "What's this?" she asks.

"It's sheet music. You know I'm a teacher, don't you? Well, I teach flute . . ."

"Is this it?" She lifts the slender black case from the table and picks at the catch.

"Yes, that's it. Please leave it alone, Jojo."

The case opens. "Can I have a go?" she asks, prodding a key with her index finger.

"Not with that one. That's my special —"

"Just a *tiny* go," she insists.

"Mum says it's nice to share," Midge adds, smirking.

"Will your mum be home soon?" I ask, glancing at my watch.

"Could be ages," Midge declares. "I think she's going to the supermarket, then she'll maybe see her friend Gail what she works with."

I take the flute case from Jojo, shut it firmly and place it on top of the bookshelf. Sophie is due for her lesson in fifteen minutes. "Aren't you a bit young to be left waiting outside on your own?" I ask.

"No," Midge retorts. "I'm seven and a quarter, she's ten, and I'm starving."

"She ate all my sweets," Jojo adds accusingly.

All I can offer are tangerines, apples, grapes — "We don't like fruit," Midge informs me — and rice cakes, which the girls nibble at reluctantly, producing an impressive flurry of crumbs on their laps and the floor. "Look at this," Jojo says, extending a finger. A splinter peeps out from a small area of angry pink.

"It looks really painful. We should get it out."

33

"How?"

"Hang on a minute." I run up to the bathroom and fish tweezers from my makeup bag. A sweet packet — Chewy Jewels — lies crumpled in the washbasin. The toilet roll has been hastily wound back on to its tube.

I find Jojo trying to gouge out the splinter with grubby fingernails. "Let me try," I say, tweezing its end but feeling awkward — surely a mother should take charge of splinter removal?

"Ow!" she shrieks. "You're pushing it in. I'll get blood poisoning."

"Sit still," I mutter. Her breathing is noisy, chesty. I suspect that she's the kind of child who is always starting or finishing a cold. She rubs her damp nose against her non-splintered hand.

Midge peers intently over my shoulder, as if she's been allowed into an operating theatre to watch a complex surgical procedure. "Eugh," she mutters. The splinter slides out, leaving a tiny hole.

"Midge! Jojo!" yells Diane, from the street.

"Mum's home," Jojo says glumly.

"Christ, you two," Diane snaps, pushing past me as I let her in, "what are you playing at, bothering Cilla?"

"Stella," Midge corrects her.

"She pulled a thing out my finger with tweezers," Jojo announces. "It really hurt."

Diane frowns and squints at me. Her burgundy lipstick has meandered over her lip line. Beneath her denim jacket she is wearing a purple T-shirt depicting Freddie Mercury with a bare chest and multi-chained necklace. "I'm sorry," she mutters, although I'm not sure what for, as she ushers the girls over the low brick wall.

Jojo is telling her mother, "She gave us these horrible biscuits that smelt of sick."

I close the door, brush up rice-cake crumbs from the sofa and floor, and pluck more Chewy Jewel wrappers from between the cushions. The aroma of gummy sweets hangs in the air. Sophie's mother's car pulls up, and my pupil trips out, her blonde hair secured in immaculate plaits. "Be good now, play your best," her mother says, planting a kiss on the child's pale forehead.

"Hello, Miss Moon, how are you?" the child asks, like a mini grown-up. She fits her flute together and places her scales book carefully on the stand.

Music pounds through from next door. "Let's start by running through your arpeggios," I say, over twanging guitars.

Sophie starts to play, but her notes crumple beneath the sheer weight of "Killer Queen". She tugs anxiously at a plait. "What's that music?" she whispers.

"Just my new neighbours."

"Who are they?"

"Two girls and their mum. You might know Jojo and Midge Price from school."

She shakes her head quickly. "Where's their dad?"

"I don't know."

"Do they always play music this —"

There's an abrupt zipping noise — a needle being swiped across vinyl — then Diane's voice cuts through the wall as she roars, "Don't you go round there again, bothering that woman, do you hear me? She could be anyone."

CHAPTER
FOUR

How To Be Famous

Children didn't bang on our door when I was a child. The unspoken rule stated quite firmly that Stella and Charlie Moon weren't allowed to have friends round to play. "Your dad doesn't like being disturbed," Mum told us, even when he was engaged in nothing more taxing than dead-heading geraniums in the back garden.

"It's not fair," I protested.

"That's just the way he is, Stella. If you want to meet your friends, you'll have to play outside."

"What if it's raining?"

"You play at Lynette's, don't you?"

"I want to play here."

"Why?" she asked.

"Because it's my *home*," I yelled, flouncing up to my room where the special flute nestled in its open case on my bed, triggering instant guilt.

I could tell, from the way her cheeks flushed when he spoke sharply to her, that Mum was scared of Dad. Although small in stature, and prone to grunts and mumbles rather than shouting, Dad *was* scary. By the age of eleven I was a fervent nail-biter, despite Mum's star charts ("Five days without biting and I'll buy you a Sindy, sweetheart . . . a whole month and you'll have Sindy's bathroom!"). I couldn't break it to her that I'd outgrown Sindy, and developed a liking for the acrid anti-bite lotions she lovingly painted on.

Dad's show was now broadcast twice a week and repeated on Sundays. Fame, I'd realised, made someone not necessarily richer or happier than non-famous people, but appear bigger and more powerful than they really were. When fans clustered round Dad in the street, or stopped to talk to him over our front garden wall, they'd say, "You're not nearly as tall as you look on TV," or "You're really quite short!" as if they'd been expecting the towering persona who burst into their homes with his Stuffed Grapefruits and Savoury Rice Rings every Tuesday and Thursday teatime. They didn't realise that the Frankie they knew, or thought they knew — TV Frankie — didn't exist.

Like Mum, who'd secretly blown all that money on my special flute, Charlie and I gleaned a perverse pleasure from getting up to devious stuff behind his back. We'd sneak into his study — a boxroom with a frosted-glass window at the top of the stairs — and play with the manual typewriter on which he wrote cookery columns for the *Mirror* and *Woman's Life*. We'd rake through his drawers, filch coins from his jar, and stab at the buttons on his adding machine (calculators were still very new, and Dad didn't trust them to give the right answers). The only gadget we didn't fool around with was the guillotine, which Dad used to trim his hand-written recipes so they'd fit into Café Crème tins.

I'd glimpse its gleaming blade, like the flash of an eye, watching me.

"Want to watch the show being filmed?" Dad asked one morning during the Easter holidays.

"Why? When?" came my confused babble. Mum, Charlie and I were rarely invited to the studios. These rare flurries of attention — which Charlie and I referred to as "Dad Making An Effort" — usually followed a late-night row between our parents. The previous night I'd lain in bed, waiting for them to finish. "Is it any wonder," Mum had called out hopelessly, "when you don't care about us?" After these rows, Dad would behave as if he'd suddenly remembered he had a family and should involve himself with us.

"I've organised tickets for Thursday," Dad explained, as if this had required a supreme effort on his part.

"Thank you, darling," Mum said.

"Lynette's mum's taking us swimming on —" I began.

"Fine — you'd rather go swimming than see my show."

"No, Dad, we just had a plan . . ."

"Do *you* want to come, Charlie?" Dad asked.

My brother looked up from the table where he was using Letraset to caption the various bottom-feeding fish in his drawing. "Okay," he murmured.

"We'd all love to," Mum chipped in, with false gaiety. "Lynette could come too, couldn't she, Frankie? Could you arrange an extra ticket?"

"If I must," he growled, heading out to tend the less demanding young life currently sprouting in seed trays in the greenhouse's steamy warmth.

Dad drove swiftly towards Bristol, where *Frankie's Favourites* was filmed, speaking only when he needed Mum to light his cigars. Soon we'd left winding, tree-lined lanes and were passing through towns that looked grey and bleary, as if they were just waking up. Charlie was twelve, with a face that had arranged itself into smooth-skinned handsomeness. Lynette, my best friend, sat between us in the back, nibbling the liquorice stick from her Sherbet Fountain.

The inside of the car was thick with sweet, woody smoke, even though Mum had wound down her window. "I feel sick," Lynette complained, as we reached the fringes of Bristol. Everyone looked shiny and uncomfortable except Charlie, who was pretending to nap with his head resting on a bunched-up sweater.

"Enjoying the ride?" Dad asked, pretending he hadn't heard Lynette.

"Yes, Mr Moon," she said miserably. She had a thin line for a mouth, like a puppet's, and millions of peppery freckles. Her dad was in jail for hitting a man with a plank from a skip. Mum had suggested I replaced her with another best friend, preferably one whose dad wasn't locked up for GBH, but I'd pointed out that the plank incident was hardly Lynette's fault. I couldn't believe her dad had actually done it. I'd met him lots of times. He'd made tomato and salad cream sandwiches for us to eat in a tent in their garden. Until

40

his arrest, I'd nurtured a secret fantasy in which Lynette and I swapped dads for a weekend or even the rest of our lives.

"New car, Lynette," Dad told her. "Superior suspension. French." We had a white Citroën, which rose when you turned on the engine. Dad reckoned that French cars were the most stylish, and you couldn't buy that kind of style — although he had bought the Citroën, obviously.

Mum murmured gentle responses as he complained about *Woman's Life* refusing to increase his fee. Her fine, straight hair brushed against her bare shoulders like a thin curtain. "If you don't acknowledge your own worth," Dad ranted, "no one else will." I couldn't imagine Lynette's dad, banged up in Dartmoor, saying anything so pompous.

We arrived at the studios and glided into Dad's reserved parking space. A small, pillowy woman beetled across the car park towards him. "I must thank you," she said, breathing potent spearmint into Dad's face. "I had no confidence, never *dared* to make my own mayonnaise . . ."

Dad switched on his TV smile. "Well, thank you . . ." He raised his eyebrows, awaiting a name.

"Gloria."

"Mayonnaise really isn't that difficult, Gloria."

"I know that now." She wafted her eyelashes at him.

Lynette dug her toes into the gravel and kept stealing looks at Charlie. Mum stood primly in her mock-croc slingbacks, gripping her handbag as if it were a grenade she was about to throw. "You're not as big as you look

41

on TV, Frankie," Gloria blurted, then hurried away, her entire head flushed vivid pink.

The studios had too many corridors and reeked of powerful cleaning products. "Eleanor, kids," said Lisa, a production assistant, "we've got great seats for you today." She clopped briskly in red high heels to the centre of the front row. Most of the seats were occupied by chattering women in luridly patterned outfits: matching tops and skirts or summery dresses. The effect was like being presented with hundreds of clashing wallpaper samples at once.

The warm-up man lurched out to welcome us. He told half-baked jokes about cooking gone wrong: milk boiling over, cakes turning out as heavy as boulders. He wore a shiny navy blue suit with a yellow T-shirt underneath to make him look jaunty. "Recipe for disaster," he kept saying, and the well-behaved ladies behind us emitted short bursts of polite laughter.

Dad marched on to the set, feigning surprise at the clapping and cheering. He scanned the audience, pretending not to know us, and said, "Ladies and gentlemen, welcome to another great show! This evening" — it was ten a.m. — "we're creating a spectacular dinner party to astound your friends. We're cooking up chilled cucumber soup, pork in an apricot sauce, and finishing with a delicious meringue dessert, which will" — cue saucy eyebrow wiggle — "cause anyone who tries it to melt in your arms . . ."

More laughter. "I'm here," he boomed on, "to take the fear out of the kitchen. So," he swept grandly to his spot behind the red-and-white counter, "let's get cooking!"

Lynette picked liquorice from between her teeth. Charlie yawned, and Mum dug at him with her elbow. She despaired of him sometimes. All that time he spent alone in his room — it wasn't normal for a boy of his age. I once heard her saying on the phone, "He's turning out like his father. I just can't reach him."

Frankie's Favourites wasn't like how it looked on TV. It wasn't only Dad in the kitchen but a flurry of nimble assistants swooping in to wipe work surfaces and place finished dishes on the counter. Lynette began to giggle when Dad started on about best end of pork. As far as I could tell, the assistants did the real cooking. All Dad did with the pork thing was place little chefs' hats on the sticky-up bones.

The makeup artist dabbed Dad's face with her whippety hands and pink sponge. It was all stopping and starting. Even the polite ladies behind us were shuffling and fiddling with the contents of their handbags. As the show finished, at the part where the credits would roll, Dad beckoned Charlie, Lynette and me on to the set to try the dishes. The cucumber soup had a greasy film on top. Dad offered Lynette a knobble of pork. She grinned into the camera lens, a parsley leaf gummed to her bottom lip.

I was embarrassed to eat with the cameramen's equipment zooming too close, like glowering eyes. I imagined my classmates, in their normal homes, snorting at Stella Moon trying to nibble meringue in a delicate manner. My mouth felt too mobile, my lips unwieldy. I'd lost control of my face.

We drove home clutching goodie bags containing plastic aprons with the *Frankie's Favourites* logo on the front — two entwined Fs on a plate, straddled by cutlery — to join our vast collection of Dad-related paraphernalia, and a pamphlet entitled *Buffet Recipes in Full Colour*.

"You're so lucky," Lynette whispered, as we pulled up outside her house.

Perhaps she was right. Dad had spent an entire day with his family, which meant, I decided, that he *did* care about us. Most of the time he was busy being famous, which was hardly his fault. In many ways, we all breathed more easily when he wasn't around.

Back at school after the holidays, Lynette bragged about how exciting it had been, appearing on telly with millions of people watching. I didn't tell her that she'd have to wait weeks to see herself on TV.

We had a summer holiday that year. A proper one, requiring Hawaiian Tropic coconut oil and all of us being flung together. We flew to Alicante and stayed in a tiny apartment filled with fried-food smells and whining mosquitoes. Charlie and I spent every day ploughing through the warm turquoise sea. One evening I noticed Dad stroking Mum's knee under a restaurant table. I was shocked, not to witness this display of affection but at the realisation that I'd never before seen my parents touch each other.

44

A woman in a loosely crocheted dress strode over to our table. "Isn't this amazing?" she said. "Here we are on our holiday, and Frankie Moon's sitting six feet from our table!" She had that crackle-glazed skin that comes from decades of intense sunbathing. You could see her flesh-coloured bra through the holes in the crochet.

Dad dabbed his lips on a white napkin and shook the woman's hand. Mum seemed to have shrunk into her spotted sundress. She hated being bothered in public. She pulled that face — swooped-down lips, guarded eyes — while the woman delved in her handbag for a scrap of paper for Dad to autograph. "You make everything look so easy," she gushed. Mum had pushed Dad's hand from her thigh and was gazing down at her steak in its pearly sauce.

Each evening after dinner I'd sit on the small concrete balcony and write my holiday diary in meticulous script. Charlie must have crept out — I hadn't heard him — and suddenly read aloud: "'The best thing is Mum and Dad have stopped arguing'." I tensed, anticipating mocking laughter, but instead he said, "It's just normal, you know."

"What's normal?"

"Parents rowing. They all do it. You take it too much to heart — you're too sensitive."

"Lynette's parents never fight."

"How can they? He's in jail."

I managed a smile and said, "D'you think we're lucky, being rich?"

"We're not that rich."

"We're in Spain, aren't we? Who else do you know who comes to Spain?"

"Okay," he said. "I suppose we're lucky."

"I wish we weren't. I wish we were just normal." I shut my diary firmly.

Charlie leaned over the concrete balcony to gaze down at the street, where a young couple had emerged hand in hand from the Banana Moon bar. "Yes," he said softly. "Me too."

Then our luck changed. *Frankie's Favourites* was cancelled. Dad's viewing figures had slumped dramatically: it seemed that no one wanted to make Grand Marnier soufflés any more. His slot was replaced by *Lite Bites*, a breezy show filmed on location with the emphasis on low-fat cooking. Yogurt replaced cream. Artificial sweeteners took the place of sugar in pastries and cakes. It was, Dad asserted, "just a fad. It'll flop, wait and see." *Lite Bites* spawned its own spin-off magazine and range of low-calorie desserts ("not naughty . . . just nice").

"What will happen to us?" I asked Mum.

"What do you mean, darling?"

"Now we've got no money."

"We'll be fine," she said, mustering a wide smile that didn't quite reach her eyes.

Charlie and I had to make do with our old uniforms until the end of the school year, although his sweaters were unravelling and my pinafore had an indelible ink blot on the front. I noticed that, if we didn't finish our orange squash, Mum would pour it into a jug, which she'd place in the fridge. One newspaper nicknamed Dad "Frankie Coronary" and ran a cartoon depicting two ambulance men carrying a stretcher. One speech bubble read, "Did you hear Frankie Moon's been sacked?" The other man said, "Damn, that'll put us out of a job."

My move to secondary school coincided with Lynette terminating our friendship abruptly. I'd hear her in the playground, singing, "What's the recipe, Frankie?" Although I'd try not to look, I knew she was honking away with her new best friend Victoria Nixon and the boys with whom they sneaked to the bottom of the hockey field. I had no desire to be taken to the bottom of anywhere by a boy. I certainly didn't want to return to class with bits of dandelion leaf stuck in my hair. "Hey, swot!" Lynette yelled across the playground. "Been to *orchestra practice* lately?" At the word "orchestra" her new cronies yowled with laughter. She might as well have said, "Had the inside of your *bottom* inspected lately?"

"You're worth fifty Lynettes," Mum said later. "She's just jealous."

"Jealous? Of what?"

"Your playing, of course. Your talent. And was that a lovebite I saw on her neck the other day?"

"I want to stop playing the flute," I said dully.

"I'm sure it was. A purple mark, right here . . ." She indicated the hollow above her collarbone.

"Mum, I'm sick of being different."

She folded her thin arms round me and said, "Be proud of what you are, Stella. Don't give up."

I thought of all the money she'd spent on the flute. "Okay," I managed.

"You'll find a new best friend, I promise."

As usual, Mum was right. I was scooped up by Jen, whose fine-boned beauty allowed her to get away with gaining top marks in spelling tests *and* owning a viola. I'd assumed she was too blessed with looks and talent to bother with me, until our school trip to London. She was sharing a room with Linda Dewy, a fragile girl who cried for her mum and tried to barricade herself into the hotel lift.

Jen was mesmerised by the sprinkling of stars in the Planetarium. She blurted out, "We're so lucky, being here, but Linda's up all night crying and spoiling it." For the rest of the week we were inseparable. Jen said, "What I like best about you is that you're so unhomesick." We wondered what the opposite of homesick might be, and decided there wasn't a word for it.

I took photos of things, not people: a stuffed bat, suspended by a clear plastic thread, and an enormous speckled turtle shell in the Natural History Museum; swans in St James's Park; celestial globes at the Planetarium. The other kids photographed each other in front of landmarks — Big Ben or Tower Bridge — or messing around in bath-towel togas and complimentary shower caps in the hotel. I'd been thinking about Charlie and tried to take the sort of photos he'd like, although I could visualise him already, flipping through my pictures at breakneck speed, pausing only to study the turtle shell.

48

I loved being away from the clouds of tension that hovered between my parents. I felt so free from Dad's ill-humour and Charlie's sullenness that I even forgot to miss Mum. Jen didn't care who my dad used to be. She was the only person outside our family who knew how bad things had become. I returned home feeling as light as the air that Mrs Bones urged me to suck into my lungs.

Dad made a new series eventually — *Frankie's Feasts* — which was described by one newspaper as "ludicrously overblown", and was canned after six episodes. The *Mirror* had ditched Dad's column, although *Woman's Life* limped on for another year or so. No one wrote fan letters any more, not even in green Biro, and no bras were pushed through our letterbox. Dad looked exhausted. His face appeared to have flattened, and turned beige — the colour of envelopes containing final demands. He spent long, tense evenings in his study, shuffling papers around in a Café Crème fog.

Mum confided, "If *Woman's Life* drop him, I'm going to start looking for work." She'd dropped her "It'll be fine" act and grown gaunt and pale, which made her startling blue eyes look bigger than ever. I was shocked by the concept of her doing anything other than gliding around, looking pretty.

She was offered a job as an orderly at the hospital but gave it up after something bad happened involving one of the doctors and a cupboard. He'd "tried it on", apparently. She came home, eyebrows knitted with tension, and told Dad, "I can't do this any more."

Instead of buying new clothes, or even the fabric to make them, she wore the burnt orange trouser suit until it went thin and finally transparent at the knees, and stopped having her hair trimmed in a sharp line. I heard Dad telling her, "For God's sake, Eleanor, you're letting yourself go."

I wanted to help her but didn't know what to do with a worried grown-up. While I waited for her to come home from work — she'd taken a waitressing job at the Golden Egg — I'd blast Crispy Pancakes under the grill to be served with thick slabs of beef tomato. Mum didn't seem to enjoy food any more. I raided Dad's coin jar to buy *Lite Bites* magazine, but was forced to improvise as we never had the red peppers or mangetout that the recipes required. Mum picked at my offerings, growing even thinner, and would sparkle only when she talked to her friends on the phone.

"What's wrong with Mum?" I asked Charlie, finding him sprawled, belly down, on his musty eiderdown.

"She's just tired," he said. "She'll be okay when Dad gets a proper job again." Both of us knew that Dad had never had a proper job.

"Don't you care?" I snapped at him.

Charlie looked up from the books that were spread all over his bed and said, "Of course I do. I just don't worry like you do." He must have felt bad for being so dismissive because he appeared in my room later that evening with a folder covered with sticky-backed plastic in which I could store my loose pieces of sheet music.

I started to spend as much time as possible at Jen's pebble-dashed semi, which smelt not of cigar smoke and worry but of her mother's freshly baked scones. I'd really believed I was lucky when Lynette told everyone at school about our trip to the Bristol studios. Being Frankie Moon's daughter was, I'd reckoned, the best thing that could happen to a person.

And then I grew up.

CHAPTER
FIVE

New Friends

Robert wants things to be civilised. He pushes back nut-coloured hair and says, "She keeps going over stuff I should have done after the boys were born — how she felt trapped in the house with two babies. Like I can do anything about that now."

We're sitting at opposite sides of my living room table. My hands feel like new accessories that I'm not sure what to do with. I fill them with wads of sheet music and my coffee mug, but that makes them feel unbalanced. "I'm sure things will get easier," I say.

"It's been nine months. She's still finding new things to be mad about."

"Like what?"

"I feed the boys the wrong things — when I take them back she inspects their mouths to make sure their teeth haven't crumbled. And I don't do enough with them. Or I do too much and bring them back exhausted."

Verity was the reason he hadn't shown up for lunch last Saturday. She'd been calling him all morning, spitting anger into the phone, blaming him for Jack's nappy rash and for leaving the buggy outside to be splattered with rain and seagull droppings. He'd gone for a walk along the seafront to shake off the bad feelings. Our lunch thing had blown right out of his head.

Robert opens his flute case. It's an ebony instrument, its silver keys dull with neglect. Through the wall from Diane's house blares "Bohemian Rhapsody". There are more sounds: girls' yelps, like a real fight's going on, involving fists and maybe some frantic hair-pulling. Diane is smoking a cigarette in a deck-chair in her front garden. Her jeans are rolled up to her knees, her putty-coloured calves on display, feet resting in a plastic washing-up bowl of sudsy water.

No one on Briar Hill uses their front gardens to lounge in. Even if I was overcome by an urge to soak my feet, I'd never loll out there with strangers wandering past and gawping. "I'll have to speak to her," I tell Robert, "about this noise. It's only been a week, and it's driving me —"

"I've never seen you angry," Robert says, smiling.

"It's not funny." I peel Cellophane from the thin bunch of petrol-station carnations he'd brought to say sorry, and stuff them into a vase. They're a bleached peach colour, browning at their frayed edges. They *look* sorry.

Outside Diane dries her feet on a gaudy pink towel and saws at her toenails with an emery board. "Bohemian Rhapsody" climaxes and, mercifully, fades. I finish my coffee and lift my flute, about to play.

Another track starts: "Fat Bottomed Girls". "For Christ's sake," I snap. "This happened on Wednesday night. I'm trying to teach Sophie — a lovely girl, who's progressing so well — when this *music* starts up . . ."

Robert peers through the window, clearly fascinated as Diane hauls up a foot on to the opposite thigh and starts painting her toenails. She has positioned herself to take maximum advantage of a thin slice of sunlight. "I had to finish Sophie's lesson upstairs," I rant on, "which was quieter, but felt . . . wrong. I don't want pupils in my bedroom."

"No, of course you don't." Robert colours slightly. Diane's music has stopped. There are no cars straining up Briar Hill, no murmurings from lawnmowers or TVs. I join Robert at the window. Diane has produced a razor now, and is briskly skimming her legs.

I stare down at Robert's hand. He has placed it across mine, making a lattice of fingers. I'm aware of my internal organs, heart, lungs, and diaphragm, rising and falling in the correct manner. Robert smells of honey. His hand is warm over mine. My other hand grips the special flute, the one no one else ever plays.

"We should go out some time," he says.

"Yes, I'd like to."

He lifts my hand, and for a moment looks as if he might do something alarming — maybe kiss it — but instead lets it drop like a sweet wrapper. "Stella," he says, "you're a wonderful friend."

Charlie sounds his usual Saturday lunchtime self: barely woken, perhaps not alone. "We should visit Dad," I say.

"Mmm, some time." He yawns into the phone.

"I mean for his birthday. It's only two weeks away. Shall we club together for a present?"

"Oh, God," he says, and I'm not sure whether he's horrified by the prospect of shopping for Dad, or the schlep to Cornwall.

There's someone else, a girl's voice in the background. "Sorry," I say, "you've got company."

"It's just me," he protests.

"Still seeing that girl — Phoebe, is it? — with the beach hut?"

"Maybe," Charlie says, and I can hear his smile.

"So . . . Dad's present. We could look round the antiques market . . ."

"I'll trust you to pick something," he says — then, to make amends, "Let's meet up tomorrow for a swim," which we often do on Sundays anyway. Charlie's the only person I know who loves to swim as much as I do.

"We could buy him a grandfather clock," I add.

"Fine."

"Or a stuffed moose."

"Whatever you say."

"Want to come in on this present or what?"

He laughs and says, "Yes, Mum."

Later, as Diane drags her deck-chair inside, I'm still thinking, *Don't call me that.*

Next morning I'm woken at eight twenty by Midge rapping at my front door.

"Coming to play?" she asks pleasantly.

"Play?" I repeat.

"Yeah. I've got no one to play with."

"But it's Sunday, I'm still in my —"

"Pyjamas. Yeah, I can see that." She waltzes past me in her mud-caked boots and starts swinging on the living-room door. She manages this by gripping the handles on each side and pulling her knees up to her chest. Then thuds to the floor and skips across the room to plink-plonk on my piano. "I'll get dressed," I say wearily.

"Be quick," she commands.

"Yes, boss."

Jojo is lounging on the top bunk in the girls' shared bedroom. The room has been halved by a wobbly line of masking tape stuck to the stained, porridge-coloured carpet. "Look," Midge says, dragging a scuffed metal tray from beneath the lower bunk. It's piled high with necklaces and bracelets made from sweets threaded on fuzzy green string. "They're for wearing," Midge says, "but she just eats them. She's a pig."

"Shut up!" Jojo snaps.

"You two behaving up there?" Diane shouts from the foot of the stairs. Her habit of playing Queen at full volume doesn't seem to have impaired her hearing.

"This is my best one," Midge continues, plucking out a bracelet of ruby-coloured jewels, which have been dulled by a fine coating of hair and fluff. "I could get a lot of money for this. But you can have it."

"No, you keep it. It's part of your collection."

"It's for you," she insists.

"You never give *me* anything," Jojo complains. She has arranged herself so her head and shoulders are hanging down from the bunk. Her thin brown hair covers her face like a funnel.

"You want tea, Stella?" Diane calls up.

"Yes, please." The girls trip downstairs after me. Diane is unpacking glasses and ornaments from a tea-chest. Every cupboard is crammed haphazardly. She's behaving as if she's been forced to take part in a house-swap programme and can't figure out where to put anything.

"Make Stella a cup of tea," Midge prompts her.

Diane pulls the newspaper wrapping from a pottery mug tree and says, "The girls say you teach at their school."

"Yes, just part-time — I'm a music teacher. Peripatetic."

"My dad gets peripatetic drunk," Midge mutters.

Diane throws her a sharp look and rests a cut-glass vase on top of the hamster cage, which fills the windowsill. She abandons her unpacking project, pushes past Jojo, who's lounging in the doorway with a packet of Monster Munch, and leads me into the living room. There are so many places to sit — on the fuchsia sofa or one of three mismatched armchairs — that I can't decide where to park myself.

"Sit with me," Midge demands, perching on a chair arm.

I push aside an assortment of weaponry to make space for myself. "Are these your daggers?" I ask.

"No — that's a scabbard, these are daggers, and this is a cutlass what pirates use. Do you like war?"

"I usually try to avoid it."

Diane hands me a mug of biscuit-coloured liquid and says, "Girls, scram."

Midge slides off the chair arm and marches out of the room. Jojo pretends to leave, but lurks behind the living-room door, crunching Monster Munch.

"They're giving Jojo extra help," Diane murmurs, leaning forward, "like there's something wrong with her."

"Who?" I ask.

"*Them.*" She means teachers. Parents often forget we're ordinary people who shop in Roots and Fruits and go to the toilet. It's as if we shouldn't exist outside the classroom, but quietly fold ourselves up at the end of the school day, and slide into cupboards.

"What's she having trouble with?" I ask.

"Reading, writing. Basic stuff. Keeps bringing home extra worksheets."

"It'll be learning support. Her form teacher, Miss Barnes, is just trying —"

"She's been singled out," Diane blusters. "Midge is rubbish at maths and no one's forcing special anything on her."

"Lots of kids have learning support. You could make an appointment with Miss Barnes, or with Mrs Summer, the head teacher . . ."

Diane's plump hand lands on my knee. "It's been rough on them, leaving their dad. We had this dog — the girls loved him to bits — and had to leave him behind because pets aren't allowed here."

"That's such a shame."

"I had no choice, Stella. I'd had it up to here." Her arm shoots up in a salute.

With your husband, I think, or the dog?

"You don't have kids," she continues, "so you won't understand. But I'm a mum, right? A bloody good mum. And I bent over backwards for him. You know what happens when you do that?"

"What?"

"You get taken for granted. You're just a big old lump of ugly furniture."

"Diane, of course you're not a big —"

"In the early days, before kids, he'd whisk me away."

"Where to?"

"Restaurants, nightclubs. Went to a club on a riverboat once . . ."

"And what happened?"

Her face sags. "He stopped whisking. Stopped noticing me, basically. Unless he was out of his brain — paralytic — and then, ugh . . ." She lies back on the sofa, pushes away an invisible body.

"We all feel like that sometimes."

"Not you," she declares. "Look at you — single, successful . . . God, you're lucky."

"I don't feel lucky."

"You've got your head screwed on, Stella. That's why the girls like you so much."

"Do they?" I ask.

"They think you're the bloody bee's knees," she says, with a rich, rounded laugh, showing clusters of pewter-coloured fillings.

★   ★   ★

Midge watches me step over the wall as if I might be incapable of finding my own way home. "Stella," she calls after me, "why do you live all by yourself?"

I pause on my doorstep. "I like it."

"Don't you get lonely?"

"I don't really think about it."

"D'you want a boyfriend? Husband?"

"Not at the moment," I say, aware of hotness creeping up my neck.

"There's men's shaving things in that cupboard in your bathroom."

"You've been looking in my cupboards?"

"Just a little look," she says, flicking pink gravel with the toe of her trainer. "Whose is it?"

"My old boyfriend's," I mutter, as Jojo wanders out to aid her sister in the interview process.

"Maybe he's going to come back," Midge adds. "That's why he didn't take his man's razor."

"I don't think so." I grip my door handle.

"He might. What if he still likes you and —"

I unlock the door, relieved to escape interrogation, and shut it firmly behind me.

The crunch of feet on gravel, a light tapping sound. A small head appears briefly through the door's frosted-glass panel. "You forgot this!" Midge shouts through the letterbox. She feeds through a small, inky hand, clutching the bracelet. It drops to the floor.

"Thanks," I tell the letterbox.

"You can be our friend," she yells, her mouth jammed against the slot.

I feel cornered in my own home. The letterbox snaps shut. Midge's Chewy Jewel bracelet clings to my skin as I slide it on.

The first section of the antiques market is housed in a dank-smelling warehouse filled with dark, looming furniture. I wander past grandfather clocks with speckled faces and rusting hands. An agitated man is trying to decide whether to buy a glass-fronted bookcase while his child — a whirlwind of fuzzy black hair and fluorescent dummy — attempts to open the grandfather clocks' doors and manhandle their inner workings. Children and fragile objects don't mix. I have already had to ask Midge to use my doorbell instead of banging her fist on the glass panel.

"Now, Sebastian," the man says, tugging the child away from delicate timepieces and out to the open-air market. Stallholders are sipping steaming drinks from polystyrene cups. Tables are laden with chipped enamel kitchenware and wooden tools, their edges worn smooth as driftwood. One table is filled with nautical equipment: mysterious dials encased in mahogany and brass. There are binoculars, which I chose for Dad's last birthday. I'd thought he'd enjoy watching soaring cormorants, but he just peered through them briefly, out of his grimy living-room window — then, unnervingly, directly at me — and placed them at the top of his bookshelf where they appear to have remained ever since. He said, "Very thoughtful of you, Stella, but you shouldn't have."

The nautical stallholder lights a strong-smelling cigarette and gives me a lazy smile. "Know what this is?" he asks. He offers me a circular brass object with a dial and ornate markings that read, "Dry, Fair, Change, Rain, Stormy."

"It's a barometer," I say.

He takes quick puffs of his cigarette and asks, "D'you know how it works?" Across the market a lean figure peruses the old-tools stall. "It depends," the nautical man says, "whether we're talking the *mercurial* barometer, which contains a column of mercury — self-explanatory, really — or the *aneroid* barometer, which . . ."

The man looks like Alex, but is skinnier and has shorter hair. I haven't seen him since he walked or, rather, *strolled* out — kissing my cheek, and climbing into his friend Mo's yellow van like it was an ordinary day. As if they were going fishing, or to a gig.

The nautical man holds the barometer too close to my face. "The metal cells," he continues, "respond to atmospheric pressure, moving closer together . . ." The person turns, and it *is* Alex. Something jolts inside me. He's had his hair trimmed to chin-length, gone lean and angular. I try to swallow, but my throat feels scratchy and dry. The stall man's cigarette makes a sizzling noise as he drops it into his cup.

Alex has moved to the bookstall to flick through wooden boxes of paperbacks. "You'll be amazed," the stall man says, "by this barometer's sensitivity."

I watch as Alex drifts towards racks of old postcards. A girl is walking beside him. She has a pale, dainty face and glossy black hair that snakes down her back. Is she with him? No, far too young. Early twenties, maybe. She's wearing a chunky sweater — it looks like a man's — with a short tweedy skirt. Her legs are outrageously long. Alex and the girl wander to a caravan, the Snackmobile, which sells tea, coffee and hot dogs in an oniony haze.

"Falling pressure," the stall man rabbits on, "indicates a period of unsettled weather."

"I'll take it."

"Present or for yourself?"

"It's for my dad's birthday."

"A very lucky man. I'm sure he'll enjoy it."

I glance back at the Snackmobile where Alex and the girl are laughing. Clearly they are strangers, who have experienced hunger and thirst simultaneously and are sharing a joke in the queue. I remember that Alex isn't a joke-sharing person.

He and the girl with outrageous legs take napkin-wrapped bundles from the Snackmobile man. Then they stroll out of the market, nibbling the ends of their hot dogs, their arms linked.

CHAPTER
SIX

Mrs Bones

Charlie peers at the barometer. "It's different," he says.

"I thought you'd like it."

"I do like it. I'm just wondering what he's going to say."

I rewrap it, and we change for swimming in the beach hut. It's rented by Phoebe, Charlie's current love interest, and is painted searing blue inside and out. Her flip-flops, garnished with diamanté flowers, lie close to my feet.

We wade out between boats until the sea is uncluttered and perfectly clear. Charlie is far too tanned and healthy-looking for someone who spends ridiculous hours holed up in the university's biology faculty, where he lectures. He has inherited Dad's skin, which holds on to its brownness. Mine is paler — virtually transparent — like Mum's.

He's ahead of me now, his sleek shoulders rising like seals. "Heard Dad's news?" he shouts. It's unusual for my brother to talk while he's swimming. Despite possessing a brain jammed with crustacean-related facts, he is incapable of doing more than one thing at once.

"What news?" I yell back.

"An offer. *Friday Zoo*, some regular slot."

"You're kidding." *Friday Zoo* is a mishmash of a show fronted by three wacky presenters who pretend it's spontaneous but you know it's scripted. I rarely see *Friday Zoo* because I teach Katy Salmon when it's on.

Charlie grabs the bow of an anchored fishing-boat, which lurches uneasily. "I'm surprised you hadn't heard."

"Is he going to do it?" I ask, kicking through the seaweed, which tickles my ankles.

"Think so. It's the first real offer he's had for years."

"How will Dad fit into that kind of show? I hope it's not just a piss-take . . ."

Charlie laughs, pushes away from the boat and heads back to shore. "We should be pleased for him," he calls back. "Might cheer the old bugger up."

"I *am* pleased for him. I just worry —" I clamp my mouth shut. I should be more like Charlie and stop fretting.

We towel ourselves in Phoebe's hut, and drink the beer I've brought. The hut is sparsely furnished with a small table, a worn rattan mat and two folding chairs. "Are things going well with her?" I ask. I could be referring to a frail elderly relative or a pet.

"Yes, thank you," Charlie says, mock-serious. "How about you?"

"What about me?"

"*Men*," he says, feigning drama.

I'm about to tell him about seeing Alex with the black-haired girl, but he has already wandered out of the hut and back on to the beach. I don't know why I bother to quiz him about girlfriends. He reveals little, snapping himself shut like a clam; a trick learned, I suspect, from Dad.

Late-afternoon sun has forced its way through the clouds. A gaggle of kids splosh in the shallows. "You going back in?" I call after Charlie.

"Race you," he says, kicking up sand as he runs.

I come home from the beach to find Robert's white Fiat parked crookedly outside my house. He climbs out and says, "Hi there, Stella. Is this a good time?"

For what? I wonder. "Of course it is. Come on in."

He follows me up the path. "Can't stay long. I realised I'd forgotten to pay you for my last lesson."

"You didn't have a lesson. We just talked."

"I feel bad about taking up your time." His grey eyes look anxious. Fine hair flops uncertainly round his face.

"For God's sake, stop apologising."

"Sorry," he says, and we laugh, as if we've been given permission to breathe again.

I make him coffee, which he barely touches before he has to leave. Verity needs him to look after the boys during her leg-waxing appointment. As he drives away I notice he's left money on the shelf in the hall.

Fifteen pounds for holding my hand. I feel cheap, yet ridiculously overpriced.

"Was *that* your boyfriend?"

"No, Midge, he's . . . someone I know." She's dragged an enormous terracotta plant pot across her back lawn. Balancing on it enables her to quiz me over the fence.

"He looked cross," she adds.

"He wasn't cross. He's just a bit serious."

"Serious boyfriend," she cries triumphantly.

"He's my pupil, Midge."

"I saw you kissing him."

"I didn't! Well, I might have, but only on the cheek."

"That's still kissing," she retorts.

"Yes, the kind of kiss mums give to show they love you. Doesn't your mum kiss you?"

Midge blows away the wisp of hair that's drifting across her face. "Of course," she says firmly. "All mums do that."

Mum was a kisser, a holder of hands, a warm arm that felt as light as chiffon round my shoulders. Occasionally, though, there would be no kiss, no "how was your day?" when I came home from school. The house would feel cooler, and smell slightly stale, the way it does when you come back from holiday.

I'd head upstairs to find Mum in bed, the rumple of blankets suggesting that she'd lain there all day. She looked lazy, dishevelled. She'd flick through women's magazines — the kind filled with patterns for crocheted shoulder bags, or little bonnets to keep boiled eggs warm — and glance up at me as if I were a hospital visitor who showed up too often.

Dad once roared, "She's not as perfect as you think!" which confused me, because either a person was perfect or they weren't. I knew she took tablets — pale yellow pellets — although I couldn't figure out what for, and she wouldn't tell me. "They're for when I'm not feeling good," was all she would say.

I once heard her sobbing fervently upstairs. I crept into her bedroom, terrified of what I might find. I didn't want her to be like this. I wanted my warm, capable mum back — the mum who took me to Dino's and let me choose new sheet music at Grieves and Aitken.

She was perched on the edge of the bed, trembling and glossy with sweat. No one cooked dinner that night. Charlie and I went out for chips and hung about at the end of our road, wondering when it might be safe to go home. "What's wrong with her?" I asked him.

"I think it's some nerve thing women get."

"Will I get it?" I asked anxiously.

"Bound to. You're just like her. That's why you're her favourite."

"I'm not!" I protested.

"Don't deny it," he said, screwing up his chip-wrapper and kicking it into the path of an oncoming car. His handsome face was twisted, not like my brother's at all. And he was wrong about Mum, I knew it. Dad was the problem, not some mysterious fault with her nerves. If she'd married an ordinary man — with an office job, and family photos cluttering his desk — she'd be happy now. She wouldn't be shivering on an unmade bed.

"It's okay," Charlie said airily. "I know it's not your fault."

"You're talking crap," I snapped.

"And you're full of it." He flicked a strand of damp hair out of my eyes.

I managed a smile. "Think it's safe to go home now?"

"It had better be," he said. "I'm still famished."

"Mum's come off her tablets," Dad told us later. I didn't understand why this would make her sweaty and shaky and not want us near her. I thought tablets were supposed to make people better.

Mostly, though, Mum took her pills obediently and seemed to like being with me. After my flute lesson on Saturdays we'd often go shopping to the covered arcade, spinning out our time together. Elders' perfume hall had a bigger make-up selection but Mum preferred the arcade's old-fashioned chemist, filled with sparkling bottles of scent. "Let's have some girl time," she'd say, and I'd begun to realise what Charlie had meant. It wasn't that she preferred me, just that we got on. We shared jokes, secrets, a liking for lounging in cafés and testing lipsticks on the backs of our hands. I felt lucky, as we strolled around town, to be her daughter — to be me.

One Saturday morning Mum and Dad had an argument about how much she'd been spending, even though she only seemed to buy herself the occasional lipstick or pair of tights. "You need to face up to reality," Dad bellowed. "You can't have everything you want."

"I don't *want* everything," she protested, her voice wavering as if she were caught in a gale.

"Why was Dad cross?" I asked, as we hurried through town to Mrs Bones's flat. The argument had made us late for my lesson.

"Just silly grown-up stuff," Mum said, squeezing my hand.

I wanted to ask, "Are you getting divorced?" but didn't have the nerve. I'd heard that Lynette's mum was going to divorce her dad when he came out of prison. She'd started dating the man who'd fixed loose bits of wood in her garden fence.

Dad didn't love Mum, I was certain of that. For one thing he never looked at her — at least, not properly, the way I did. He must have been the only man alive who hadn't noticed how lovely she was. It would be embarrassing if they got divorced — Lynette had been teased at school about the fence man — but I was confident that I'd cope admirably. I imagined overhearing her talking on the phone, saying, "Stella's been a pillar of strength. I don't know how I'd have got through this without her."

My divorce fantasy involved Mum, Charlie and me exchanging our tawdry old house with its sinister corners for a cheery cottage by the sea. Instead of being papered with a lurid floral design, my bedroom would be pure white with warm sunlight beaming in through its numerous windows. Charlie and I would still visit Dad, and he'd be so pleased to see us that he'd take Charlie crab hunting, make ridiculous puddings for us (involving hot chocolate sauce) and sit in the front row to watch me play at school concerts. He'd be a regular dad.

"Come *on*, Stella," Mum said, tugging me by the arm as we hurried along the path and into Mrs Bones's building. She ran up the stairs ahead of me and rapped on the door. "Must hurry back," she said. "I've promised to help Dad with his accounts." During their squabble I'd heard Dad mention some scary-sounding person called the tax man, and imagined a man with fierce-looking eyebrows and a sharp-cornered briefcase.

Mrs Bones was standing there, waiting for me to come in. I glanced at Mum. Her eyes, I noticed, were pink-rimmed and sore-looking. She was wearing Jean Patou perfume, which Dad bought her every Christmas and birthday, and an ageing shift dress in a colour she called ochre (Mum never used ordinary words for colours). I wanted to wrap my arms round her and tell her I didn't want pocket money any more — she could send it straight to the tax man — but Mrs Bones cleared her throat and I followed her inside. "Bye, darling," Mum said. She kissed my forehead, then turned and ran, her slingbacks smacking against the cold stone stairs.

Towards the end of my lesson Mrs Bones said, "I think you have a future in music, Stella. You should discuss it with your mother when you're older. You're what? Thirteen now?"

I nodded. She told me the name of the college in London where she'd studied. She described its courtyard — a leafy oasis in the middle of the city — and said, "You'd have a wonderful time there. You have the talent to make it happen."

I still wore a Snoopy vest and spent my pocket money on Blackjacks and Fruit Salad chews but the thought of being grown-up and living in London made my insides fizzle like sherbet. I didn't want to wait until I was older to talk it over with Mum. I kept glancing at Mrs Bones's clock on the mantelpiece — a gold-rimmed face trapped in a glass dome — desperate for the hour to be over and Mum to collect me so I could tell her what Mrs Bones had said. I was an ordinary-looking kid with teeth that seemed too big for my mouth, but I didn't feel ordinary that day.

"It's not like your mother to be late," Mrs Bones said, as I packed away my flute. "Perhaps she's caught up in traffic."

"Mum doesn't drive," I reminded her.

Mrs Bones frowned, then checked her watch and the clock, as if one of them might be tricking her. "I have another pupil in twenty minutes," she added.

"I'll wait for Mum outside."

"Don't be silly," Mrs Bones said gently. "I'll make us some tea."

We couldn't call Mum as our phone had been cut off. Mum had explained, "It's just a fault on the line, a man will soon come to fix it," but I knew phones stopped working when you didn't pay the bill. It had happened to Lynette's when her dad went to prison. I nibbled Mrs Bones's shortbread and drank her salmon-coloured tea, watching the carriage clock's rotating gold balls.

"Perhaps she's forgotten," Mrs Bones said, peering out of the window that overlooked the flats' communal garden.

"Maybe," I replied, although I knew she wouldn't forget. I just knew. I stared out at the lazily shifting clouds, willing her to come.

There was a rap at the door. I leaped up from the chair, slopping hot tea on to my knee. I reached the front door ahead of Mrs Bones.

Elona stood there. She lived in the upstairs part of the house next to ours and came from Czechoslovakia. I was wary of her clipped accent and startling green eyes. "I'm taking you home," she announced gripping my hand. Hers was chilled, on a warm summer's morning.

"Why?" I asked. "Where's Mum? What's happened?"

"Just come with me," she murmured. Mrs Bones handed me my flute case, which I tucked under my arm. I could feel tea trickling down my leg. Elona was wearing a brown crocheted sweater, which was starting to unravel at the neck.

All the way downstairs she wouldn't talk or even look at me. I felt sick, filled with shortbread and fear. Elona grasped my hand with her papery fingers. "Something terrible's happened, my darling," she said, as we stepped outside. I was really scared then. Elona usually called me "Stilla", not "my darling".

"What?" I whispered.

"Your mother has been knocked over."

I'd known something like that would happen. Her skinny legs weren't built for rushing about. She'd been so worried about the tax man that she'd tripped over and broken something. "Is she in hospital?" I asked, as an awful feeling of dread flooded through my stomach and chest. I pictured her beautiful face, pallid without its customary makeup, on a white hospital pillow.

Elona was wearing a necklace of cloudy glass beads. She stopped on Mrs Bones's path and pulled me to her bony chest. The beads pressed into my cheek.

Ordinary things went on around us. Dogs barked, cars pulled into driveways, a yellow bus stopped at the bus shelter. "No!" I screamed. "No! You're lying!"

I pushed Elona away and started to run. Kids hurtled along the pavement on bikes, madly ringing their bells. The clouds were shifting too quickly, swilling above my head. Elona caught up with me at the gate, and I dissolved into the scratchy wool of her sweater.

I never got the chance to tell Mum about the exciting things Mrs Bones had said.

CHAPTER SEVEN

Goulash

Brown pork in a casserole and remove from dish. Soften onions and peppers, add 1 oz flour and cook for a minute. Put pork back into dish with 1 tin tomatoes, 1 pint beef stock, 1 tsp paprika and bouquet garni. Cook in moderate oven for two and a half hours. Garnish with chopped parsley and a swirl of sour cream.

Silverdawn Cottage is perched at the furthest tip of Penjoy Point. It looks stranded out there, with its drooping roof and precarious chimneys, as if a particularly violent gust might send it toppling over the cliff. "How long are we staying?" Charlie asks from the passenger seat, as he always does.

The pot-holed lane twists its way down to the point. "Only a night," I say, although he knows this. Charlie mimes winding a noose round his neck. I'm glad I cajoled him into coming, relieved that I'm not on my own.

The Silverdawn Cottage sign is peeling so badly it's barely legible. Beneath it, on another hastily constructed wooden sign, Dad has painted "NO CALLERS NO

TRESPASSERS DANGEROUS DOGS". While he's made no visible improvements to the house, he has created a lush garden from the battered ground on which there once lurked just an ancient cracked bath and a decaying hut. Turf, the more docile of Dad's dogs, lies on the cobbled path, lapping at a hind paw.

It's Dad's partner Maggie who bustles out to greet us. "*Here* you are," she says, dispensing kisses on cheeks as if we're terribly late and she's been fearing for our safety. She leads us into the kitchen, patting her loosely curled auburn hair as if it's a cake. Dad is sniffing the contents of a pot on the stove. "Lunch is nearly ready," he announces.

I think, Yes, Dad, we had a good journey, thanks.

"Aren't they looking well, Frankie?" Maggie prompts him. "So good of you both to come."

"Happy birthday, Dad," I say.

"Well, thank you," he says, with a small chuckle, as if he's astounded that anyone's remembered the occasion, let alone made the effort to visit.

"What's cooking?" Charlie asks.

"Goulash. Not still vegetarian, are you?"

"No, Dad," Charlie says. "I *love* goulash. It's my favourite thing in the world."

"That's good — can't be doing with faddy eaters," Dad says, as if we're seven and prone to spitting out our food. Surf, Turf's wayward brother, biffs hopefully around Dad's ankles. The kitchen smells of gravy and wet fur. "Maggie was threatening to make her famous vegetable casserole," Dad adds.

"I only offered, dear," Maggie says pleasantly.

"Ah, Maggie's vegetable casseroles," he teases. "One of the great mysteries of the modern world. What goes into them, dear?"

"*You* know," she says, stacking the Café Crème tins on the kitchen table into a tidy pile. Dad still trims his recipes with the old-fashioned guillotine so they fit into the tins. Each tin is labelled with a white rectangular sticker on which he's written a food category: "soufflés", "cold desserts" or, mysteriously, "sauces/rescuing".

Maggie places the stack on the top shelf of the dresser. Neither Charlie nor I is sure how they met. She just seemed to sneak into his life, to sort onionskin squares into orderly piles, ready for filing. He's cared for — loved, I suppose — which makes me feel marginally less guilty about the unfavourable feelings that swill around in my head.

Dad dollops rice and goulash on to plates and pours on sour cream in a decorative spiral. He has already opened our present, dumping the barometer on the kitchen dresser without comment. He never changes. I don't know why I keep expecting him to say, "I love this!" or even "Thanks." There's a murky splash on the front of his navy blue polo-necked sweater. He's wearing rust-coloured cords, which hang loosely like ageing curtains, and a signet ring, which pinches his middle finger.

Charlie pours the wine, looking like some long-limbed circus performer in the low-ceilinged room. We all take our places. Maggie has fixed herself a slice of withered quiche. "Your dad's always wanted a barometer," she says.

"Have I?" he asks, through a mouthful of meat. He is impossible to buy for. He reckons he has everything he needs, and no room for things he doesn't need. And he's right: the kitchen feels too full, like the parts of my house that are still cluttered with Alex's possessions. The dresser's shelves sag beneath chipped earthenware bowls and storage jars. The top shelf is strewn with cookbooks, all shedding their spines.

"I thought you'd like an old-fashioned radio," I tell him, "but I found the barometer in the antiques market —"

"Radios are distracting," Dad says, stirring more cream into his goulash.

"And barometers aren't?" Maggie says brightly.

"Because they don't do anything," Dad adds. "Sure it's working, Stella? It's still pointing to stormy. It doesn't look very stormy from where I'm sitting."

"It *predicts* the weather," I explain, "for the next twenty-four hours. It's all to do with pressure."

"I see," Dad says.

I turn to Maggie so I don't have to look at his face. He wants us to visit — complains that we don't come to Cornwall often enough — then acts like he wants us to leave. "Finished working for the year?" I ask Maggie.

"Yes, thankfully." Several years ago she bought the field behind Saltwinds Bay, a sweeping arc of ivory sand, and put up a sign inviting tourists to park on the grass. Dad assembled a hut in which she sits for eight hours a day, from May until the end of September, nibbling quiche and taking the money. On Sundays she pays the local surfies to man the car park because, as she once pointed out, "Spending the whole summer in a shed can get a bit much."

The kitchen table feels too big, even with me and Charlie helping to fill space. Maybe Dad intended to do lots of entertaining, to cram Silverdawn Cottage with the friends he'd make when he moved to the north Cornish coast. But he has only one friend that I know of — Harry Sowerbutt, the vet — and they meet for drinks at the Smugglers Inn.

After lunch we arrange ourselves in the cramped living room. It's furnished with mismatched easy chairs, their floral patterns faded by the sun, and a towering bookshelf, which dwarfs the room. The binoculars I bought for Dad's last birthday are perched on top. It's a gusty afternoon, just tipped into October. The Monet calendar above the fireplace is still open at February. I have never seen a fire in the grate, although occasionally Dad plugs in a small fan heater, which sends out a stench of burning dust.

"Charlie told me about *Friday Zoo*," I say. "That's great news, Dad."

"Just a five-minute slot. One day's filming a week." He talks as if this is quite ordinary.

"That's better than nothing."

"It's live," Maggie says, handing out squares of peppery dark chocolate. "Never done live, have you, dear?"

"Of course I have," Dad says quickly. "I had my own show — two shows — for nearly a decade, remember?"

"Yes, dear," Maggie murmurs.

Frankie's Favourites was taped, but I don't remind him of that. "What will you be doing on the show?" I ask, determined to make an effort. It's quite exhausting. Charlie seems happy to sit mutely, sipping tea. "I'll be cooking, of course," Dad says, as if there hasn't been so much as a blip in his brilliant career.

Unshakeable confidence. Sometimes I wish I could siphon off a little for myself. I'd demand that Alex comes round to pick up the rest of his things, shock Robert with a kiss on the lips.

"Take it, dear, you need feeding up," Maggie says, pressing the last square of chocolate into my palm. Detecting illicit foodstuff, Surf lunges for my lap, a scramble of barking and drool.

Dad and I stride across the concrete slipway and into the dunes where he unclips the dogs' leads. Surf tears off, reappearing as brief flashes of ear or tail. Turf, who can't see the point of tearing anywhere, mooches beside us.

Charlie has brought assignments to mark. I left him with papers spread all over the floor in the spare room where we'll sleep tonight. Maggie was clearing away after lunch, making a foil parcel of the remaining quiche.

Soon the dunes give way to slabs of rock, their crevices filled with water and languorous weed. Two boys are crouching at the edge of the biggest rock pool. "Cool," one murmurs. "It really moves sideways." The boy has skinny, goose-pimpled arms. He nudges the crab with a fishing net.

"That's what crabs do," Dad says, startling the boys. I want to tell them that my brother knows everything there is to know about crabs — that crabs are his *life* — but they'd think I'm some crazy lady who marches around making up stories.

"Why?" the skinny boy asks.

"They just do," Dad says, shrugging.

"But *why?*"

Dad marches on, unable to handle small children demanding information. I assumed that was why he started to spend more time in the allotment after Mum's accident, where no one pinged questions: *Where is she now? Can she see us, do you think? How can she see us, if she was put in a fire?* "Stop it!" Dad roared. The subject was closed.

We're at the cliff's edge now, higher than swooping gulls and the waves, which from here look like small splashes in a bathtub. The sky has darkened, swathed with watery ink. "Looks like a storm's coming," I say.

"I think it'll blow over."

"No, Dad, the barometer's right."

"Maybe." He pulls a tight smile. I want to ask him, "Do you ever think about Mum?" But I can't: we don't talk about her. We pretend that it — she — never happened.

I remember Dad greeting my uncles, sallow middle-aged men whom I remembered vaguely from distant Christmases, when they arrived in the small tarmacked car park before the funeral. During the service Charlie lurked at the back, away from everyone. Dad sat with my uncles — Mum's brothers — who all looked the same with their black suits and gaunt faces. Jen gripped my hand. Elona kept trying to hug me but I shook her off. There was faint music, which sounded as if it came from a badly tuned radio, then a tinny buzzing noise — the mechanism that caused the wine-coloured curtain to close round the coffin. I wanted to push through the people, grab that curtain and rip it to shreds.

After the service everyone came to tea at our house. A ragged assortment of vaguely known aunties arranged plates of finger rolls and cold meats. Dad mingled, talking seriously with his jaw set hard, as if discussing programme proposals with TV executives.

Jen rescued me from hovering aunties. "Everyone means well," someone said, patting the top of my head as if I were a dog. I didn't know what meaning well meant. I felt crushed, barely able to form proper words, and kept pushing between the chattering groups to find Charlie. Across the room I saw him coil his fingers round Uncle Dave's sherry glass and tip the contents down his throat.

"Why was she cremated?" I asked Dad later, when the guests had finally tumbled back into their cars. Charlie had locked his bedroom door and refused to open it, even when I'd banged and banged with my fist.

Dad looked up from his slumped position in the green velour armchair. "It's what Eleanor wanted," he said, "and it's what I want, when it's my time to join her."

I didn't make any noise, even though sheets of wetness were pouring down my face. Dad's eyes were soft and watery, as if he really wanted to get up from the chair and hold me the way I needed him to, but didn't know how.

It's starting to rain now. Dad is gripping Surf's lead as he snuffles close — too close — to the cliff's edge. "Charlie works too hard," he announces. "Comes here for my birthday, spends half the time in the bedroom . . ."

"He can't help it." I want to add, "He didn't have to come."

Dad stomps back to the dunes, freeing Surf. The dog lurches ahead, barking wildly. "Damn dog," Dad snaps. "Can't do a thing with him."

Surf lunges out of a copse at the far end of Harry Sowerbutt's field. Burrs are embedded in his muddy fur. Dad grips him as we try to pick them off, but Surf writhes free and scampers ahead towards the house, leaping haphazardly as if trying to bite flying bugs.

"Ever think of getting yourself a dog, Stella?" Dad asks, stooping into the drizzle.

"Definitely not. I don't have the time or the space."

"You can trust them," he adds. "That's what I like. A dog won't let you down."

"I'm not really a dog person, Dad."

"I just wondered," he continues, "if it might keep you company, living all on your own."

"I don't need company. I'm fine as I am."

"Are you?" he asks, stopping on the narrow path and squinting at me. The wind has lifted his damp hair into meringue-like peaks.

"Yes," I say, "I really am," but my words are blown out to sea.

Next morning Charlie and I find the crab boys huddled over the rock pool with a magnifying glass. We left Dad and Maggie still sleeping and Surf gnawing the sofa's loose cover in the living room. The house smelt of yesterday's goulash.

Charlie is telling the boys that hermit crabs don't have homes of their own: they hide in the discarded shells of other species. "It's blocked the hole with its claws," the skinny boy says.

"That's hermit-crab language," Charlie says, "for leave me alone." He's wearing his wetsuit and carrying a faded blue surfboard. Everything felt wrong the time Charlie tried to teach me to surf: my skewed feet, never at the right angles, my ungainly body, which couldn't even ride, belly down, on the board. He said, "You need to *go* with it," whatever that meant.

We leave the boys trying to trap the crab in their net. I strip off to my swimsuit and plunge into the water. It's shockingly cold, but quite bearable by the third stroke as I push through the waves.

A bunch of surfers usually gathers here, even in October, but today there's only me, Charlie and the crab boys, who are paddling now. When my arms start to ache I wade back to the beach and get dressed, shrouded in a towel. Charlie rises and falls on scooping waves, where no one can reach him.

Dad checks his watch and says, "I'm due to meet Harry at the Smugglers. We're figuring out a training programme for Surf."

"About time," Maggie says briskly, looking up from her cross-stitch sampler at the kitchen table. Surf disgraced himself this morning by lunging for a plateful of bacon she'd placed on the hob. We breakfasted on stale corn flakes. Dad lights a Café Crème, clouding the kitchen, then heads upstairs for our bags. He places them at the front door, where they wait like expectant dogs.

"Well, I suppose we should be going," Charlie says brightly.

Maggie's kiss is feathery, her shoulders fragile as I hug her. Sensing a walk, some kind of adventure, Surf springs out of his basket and up at me, scraping my hand with his paw.

"Surf!" Maggie cries. "Bad, bad dog."

I stare down at my hand. Three ragged lines are oozing blood. It looks too vivid, like joke blood from a bottle. "Frankie, look what Surf's done," Maggie cries.

Dad is tapping the barometer with a fingernail, trying to make it do something. He was right: the threatened storm had come to nothing. "Just a scratch," he murmurs. "Give it a wash."

Water floods over my hand, cold as the sea. "It still says stormy," Dad adds. "You sure this thing's working?" He raps the barometer's glass with a knuckle.

They trail out after us, Maggie trying to wrap a dank-smelling tea towel round my wounds and Dad thrusting his hands into his pockets. I kiss his plump cheek, and try for a hug, but he flinches and steps back into the doorway — which, as any crustacean expert will tell you, is hermit-crab-speak for "Leave me alone."

"Why do we bother, Charlie?"

"It was your idea," he says, swirling the steamed-up passenger window with a finger.

"I thought he'd be pleased to see us. I feel bad, you know, not coming more often, when he goes to the trouble of sending all those recipes . . ."

"What recipes?"

"His own, of course. The ones he handwrites on those little crinkly squares."

"Not still sending them, is he?"

I glance at Charlie. "At least a couple a month. Don't you get any?"

He shakes his head and laughs softly. "He sent a few when I'd just left home. That first house I lived in had a coal fire. Crinkly paper makes great firelighters, did you know that? Burns like you wouldn't believe."

"Charlie, you didn't."

"What d'you do with yours? Stick them lovingly in an album?"

"I keep them in a box, in case I'm ever stuck for dinner-party ideas."

"What you need," Charlie sniggers, "is a lovely rich goulash, with piped . . . What do you call those piped potatoes?"

"*Fondante,* I think."

"*Avec les pommes de terre fondantes . . .*"

We construct ludicrous menus until it's dark and we're pulling up outside Charlie's house. He rents the lodge that guards the entrance to Hurleigh House, a bleak manor that has been reinvented as a hotel, country club and conference centre, and now lies eerily vacant. "Take care of that hand now," he says, unloading his bag and surfboard.

"I'm sure it'll be okay."

He bends to kiss my cheek. Someone opens the lodge's front door and steps out to greet him. My brother hurries towards her without looking back.

Instead of driving home I turn down to the new marina. The boats appear grey under the streetlights but are really gleaming white, like Hollywood teeth. I park and walk along the seafront to the end of the damp wooden jetty. The scratches on my hand have formed three raised wiggly lines as if they've been drawn with a glue-pen. Midge had those pens: they spurted out glittery glue in fluorescent colours to be smudged on to curtains and T-shirts, and Diane eventually confiscated them. She stuffed them into the everything-drawer in the kitchen.

I stroll away from the seafront and through town until the roads widen and have names like Primrose Avenue and Camellia Grove. Pampas grass sprouts like startling haircuts from groomed lawns. There are bird tables, wishing wells, a figure-of-eight-shaped pond.

The bungalows' windows beam rectangles of pale yellow light or bluish flickers from TVs. Here's a burgundy three-piece suite, a glass-fronted cabinet filled with crystal glasses, every detail visible in the stark centre light. Staring into other people's houses is a bad habit of mine. Mum used to tug my arm sharply when she caught me spying. "Come *on*, Stella," she'd say. "It's so rude to stare. Your head will stick like that." We'd march onwards with me twisting my neck, trying to steal glances into other people's lives. I wanted to see what it would be like to live with an ordinary dad. Despite those risks I took, fearful of my head freezing in its prying position, there was never anything remarkable in those houses. No matter which grove or crescent you found yourself in, everyone owned similar things: plump sofas and chairs, mantelpieces dotted with ornaments, framed landscapes with fake-looking clouds skittering across impossibly blue skies.

Now the bungalows have made way for cramped Victorian terraces, whose front doors open on to the street. Dock Lane smells of vinegar from the chip shop on the corner. I'm nearly at his road now, where there are no gardens or views, just a dismal pub, the Old Admiral, and a junk shop with faded lampshades stacked messily in its window.

A doorbell with two names beneath it: ground-floor flat, Brown. No lights on there, nothing to see. Top flat: Alex Carson, and the dim glow from a table lamp. "This doesn't feel right," he had told me. "I'm sorry,

Stella, I've got to move out." He had already found himself the flat and asked Mo-with-the-van to move his important stuff (he promised to collect the rest as soon as he'd got himself sorted).

I had gone to the back beach and ploughed back and forth, thinking that the harder I swam, the better I'd feel, but it hadn't worked that time. I had come home and stared at odd spaces where his things had been. My house had looked burgled.

Jen was convinced he'd come back. "It's just one of his fads," she spat angrily. "I can't believe he's putting you through this." She was familiar with Alex's short-lived passions for fishing, poetry, classical guitar. She wanted to come round: that's what you do when a friend's in crisis. But it didn't feel like a crisis. I sat in the garden, in the plum-coloured evening light, wondering how long it would take me to get used to being without him.

He'll look out in a minute, and notice me standing there. He'll be so damned pleased to see me he'll hurry downstairs to let me in. Inside his flat there'll be a table, a couple of worn chairs, a TV borrowed from Mo and unwashed coffee cups everywhere. The guitar, in which he lost interest after the E string broke, will be propped against a wall. The floor will be strewn with dirty clothes. Clearly, the person who lives here is falling apart without his girlfriend.

He'll examine the scratches on my hand. Casually, I'll mention seeing him at the antiques market with that girl. "She's Mo's little sister," he'll say, or "She's just a girl I work with." He has rent to pay now. He's had to get a job. This job requires him to work alongside stunning girls with outrageously long legs. "I made a mistake," Alex will tell me. "I still love you, Stella."

I blink away the wetness from my eyes. The doorbell is so close, so touchable. I'll decide whether to leave or to stay the night. Even if I stay, it won't mean a thing. I might just crave warm limbs wrapped round mine, the feeling of being wanted. I'll shower in the morning — his shower dribbles pathetically, unlike the power-shower I have at home — then watch him watching me get dressed. He'll behave like we never broke up.

I walk back to the harbour, and wait until the raven sky becomes streaked with orange — burnt orange, the colour of dawn and old-fashioned trouser suits — without noticing it happen.

CHAPTER
EIGHT

Bonkers Hound

Midge flings her light sabre on to my sofa. "Where's your bracelet?" she asks.

"What bracelet?" I hand the girls a glass of lemonade each (I have started to buy lemonade, and iced biscuits called Party Hoops, instead of organic sesame rice cakes).

"The one I gave you," Midge retorts, drumming on my table impatiently. "The ruby one that took me ages to make. The *special* one."

"Oh, made of sweets. I put it somewhere safe. I'm sure it'll turn up."

She frowns at me as if to say, Yeah, like in the bin, and fishes out a Chewy Jewel packet from her school-bag. The girls had been lurking in my front garden, swiping at each other with sticks, when I came home from work.

"What's up with your hand?" Jojo asks.

"Just a scratch from my dad's dog."

"It looks horrible," she says, shuddering dramatically.

"Is that where you were at the weekend — at your dad's?" Midge cuts in. "We called for you five times, didn't we, Jojo? We even climbed into your garden and checked your shed. You weren't there."

"I do go out sometimes," I say, feeling cornered.

"You can get blood poisoning from dog scratches," Jojo continues. "You could go blind or even die. Mum told me." She picks insipid pink icing from a biscuit and observes me with foreboding eyes. "Or maybe that's dog poo," she adds.

"I'm sure I'll live, Jojo."

"Is this your special flute?" she asks, prodding the open case on the table with her sugary finger.

"No, just my everyday one. The one I use for teaching."

"Can I have a go?"

"Sure, when you've finished your biscuit." She gulps it down, wipes her mouth on her cuff and picks up the flute. I don't mind her having a try — she won't be able to play it — and at least it'll take her mind off the state of my blood and imminent death. I start to explain where to place her fingers, and how to position her mouth, but she's already standing up, filling her lungs. A sound — a wavering yet powerful note — fills the room.

She stops suddenly, cheeks blazing, and falls back on to the sofa. "Jojo," I say, "you didn't tell me you could play."

"I can't. I haven't ever." She sounds shocked. She dumps the flute on her lap and reaches to the table for a third Party Hoop.

"Are you sure? Not just a little bit?"

"Not a bit," Jojo says, puffing out crumbs.

No one picks up a flute for the first time and just plays. There are hollow sounds until a note struggles through, then more notes as the mouth and fingers find their way, and the flute stops being a cold, scary metal thing. It's all in the muscle control — the mouth — and, of course, the breathing. At first I didn't understand what Mrs Bones meant. Eventually, I managed to breathe the way she described, with the diaphragm, filling myself up. I felt powerful, full of air, as if I could take off and soar.

Not even Toby Nichols played a true note straight off.

Jojo brings the flute back to her mouth. I show her where the fingers go to play a B. "I want a go!" Midge announces, swiping the light sabre excitedly.

"In a minute, Midge. Let your sister —"

Jojo plays a clear B. "That's lovely," I say. "Now try taking a bigger breath, and holding the note for longer . . ."

"*My* turn," Midge insists.

Jojo places the flute gently on the table. "She's putting me off," she declares, pulling out her pink scrunchie. Buff-coloured hair bushes round her chubby face.

"You could learn how to play properly," I tell her. "Read music and everything."

"My reading's not good," Jojo murmurs.

"Music's different. I'm sure you could do it. I'll help you."

"I haven't got a flute."

Of course she hasn't, and Paul Street Primary doesn't have instruments to lend. Kids like Toby and Willow have parents who can afford to buy them. Laura Sweet has a top-notch Yamaha, bought last Christmas, which she's on the verge of giving up.

"You could borrow this one," I say, "just for a few days, to see if you like it."

Jojo eyes the flute warily, as if it's a crocodile that's likely to snap at her fingers. "It's not your special one," she says.

"No, but it's still very expensive and delicate. You'd have to keep it in its case and take care of it."

"What's special about your other flute?"

"The headjoint — the top section — is solid silver." That's not why it's special, but I don't tell her the rest.

Midge has forgotten that she wanted a turn with the flute and instead demands junk for modelling. I have several empty Evian bottles, ready for recycling, and let her bind them together with Sellotape to make a missile. "I want to paint it," she announces. All I have is white emulsion left over from decorating the living room (Alex despaired of my liking for white). I cover the table with newspaper, then hand her a brush and the half-empty can. "Next time," she retorts, following the bottles' ridges with the brush, "get better colours."

Diane is home now. "Killer Queen" thumps through the wall. Midge stomps out, with Jojo following her, hugging the flute close to her chest as if a sudden temperature change might cause it to shatter. I watch them clamber over the garden wall. Jojo might break the flute, damage its delicate springs, use it to battle Midge with her light sabre. They could move away, as abruptly as they arrived, and I'd never see it again.

Jojo flings their door open. "It's really important to take care of it," I call after her.

"Like your ruby bracelet," Midge yells back.

Jojo was right. Something is festering inside my hand. I arrange myself in bed so it's untouched by any other part of my body or the duvet. I still sleep on my side of the bed, not Alex's. It doesn't feel right, sleeping where he slept, even though the bed's all mine now — was always mine. The window is open a fraction but I'm still shivery-hot.

By morning my hand feels like it's trapped in a tight rubber glove. I try to shower but this involves keeping the poorly hand out of the spray, as if I'm performing some weird, one-arm-out dance. I feed it gently through a shirtsleeve and pull on a pale grey sweater. I waggle fingers over invisible keys.

As I'm leaving for work Diane stumbles out of her house, tugging on a denim jacket over a bulky mohair sweater. The jacket has golden sparkles shaped like shooting stars on the pockets. "Late again," she mutters, banging the door behind her.

"Me too. Been trying to get hold of the doctor, but they're constantly engaged."

"What's wrong?"

I show her my hand. "That looks awful," she says. "Come on in — I've got bandages, magic cream. Midge

95

is always falling off walls, cutting herself, bloody liability."

"It doesn't need bandaging," I protest.

Diane stabs a key into the door and tugs me into the kitchen. The table is scattered with runaway Coco Pops. I tread in a puddle of brownish milk. Next to the open cereal packet lie an overflowing ashtray, shaped like glossy pink lips, and a brush that's matted with so much aubergine hair, it looks as if a small rodent's trapped on it. "Bloody Beirut," Diane huffs, "every morning."

The room smells of wet washing and hamster bedding. "What you don't want," she continues, lifting down an ice-cream carton from a wall cupboard — the tub still bears its Neapolitan Softie label — "is it blowing up and going pussy." She flashes a reassuring smile. "That happened to Midge after her jab. Her arm puffed up, all this stuff oozing out . . . Impetigo, as it turned out." Sometimes I wonder if it's just as well that Alex and I never got round to the business of having children.

The carton is crammed with squashed tubes and bottles of liquid in varying shades of pink, all of which appear to have crystallised. "No bandages," Diane announces. She pulls out a kitchen drawer and slams non-medical items on to the worktop: rusting spanners, a screwed-up Chinese takeaway menu, Midge's confiscated glitter pens. "Here," she says, unearthing a small pot of antiseptic cream and a strip of grimy-looking cloth. She dabs on the cream gently, winds the cloth round my hand and secures it with a gigantic safety-pin from the drawer. My hand throbs even harder.

"There," Diane says, patting my knee as if I, too, am a child who's turned out to be a bloody liability.

My first lesson is at Greenhills Primary, a neat little cottage of a school, close to the sluicy grime of the docks. The children are learning to sight-read, pencilling letter names beneath the notes on the stave. Diane's homespun bandage bites into my skin. In a far corner of the classroom, I unfasten the pin and drop the grubby strip into the wastepaper bin. When I turn back, six pairs of curious eyes are assessing my wound. "What?" I ask brightly.

No one speaks. The children are poised on their chairs, as if awaiting some startling announcement. I draw notes on the whiteboard: crotchets, quavers, semiquavers. I remind the children of their various lengths, and the lengths of the rests that fall between them. Sweat tweaks my forehead. "Can anyone remember this note's name?" I ask, pointing to a crotchet.

"Breve?" asks one girl hopefully.

"Semi-breve," chirps the boy next to her.

I lower myself on to the nearest chair, still clutching the black marker pen. *It's okay. This will pass in a minute. Breathe slowly, deeply. Focus.* "Demi-quaver?" another child offers, her gaze firmly fixed on my hand. I want to be home, in my cool, quiet bedroom, far away from these kids with their gawping eyes. I need to lie down.

Sarah Pengelly shrinks away from me, as if crotchets and quavers have left a sour taste in her mouth, and festering hands might be contagious.

In the surgery's waiting room a cluster of squalling toddlers tussles over a plastic fire engine. Its siren wails each time someone presses its light. The chairs are all occupied by the children's mothers and a small clump of elderly people, who are conducting discreet chats about ailments and medication.

"Doctors are running late," the receptionist announces through the glass partition. This means I'll probably miss my first afternoon class at Greenhills, where I should be right now, on top of the woodwind group's practice.

As all the seats are taken I loiter beside an enormous clear plastic bubble. There's a slot through which you can post money for charity. I fish out a coin from my purse and push it in. It rolls round on an invisible helter-skelter, finally dropping through a hole to join the rest of the coins at the bottom. I feed in another coin, and another, watching them spiral. "Here, have mine," says a man who's been studying the noticeboard. His pale brown hair and the shoulders of his sweater are speckled with light rain.

From his pocket he produces a small pile of change. He has elongated green eyes and a soft Scottish accent. I hold out my left hand, the undamaged one. His fingertips graze my palm as he hands me the money. "Thanks," I say.

He smiles and says, "Glad to get rid of it."

I post in the coins one by one, and we watch them roll. When they're all gone I delve into my bag and rummage among Chewy Jewel wrappers and Diane's tub of antiseptic cream, plus a spare strip of material and more safety-pins, which she insisted I took for emergency bandage repair. My fingers come out from my bag dusted with ivory powder. My compact hasn't shut properly since Jojo asked for a go with it, and patted it all over her face and neck, lost in a world of fairy pink.

After a few moments' hush the toddlers have started squabbling again. "*My* fire engine," yells a red-headed boy, gripping the toy tightly. He slaps a little girl hard on her back, which sets her screaming wildly.

"Ryan! It's *everyone's* fire engine," snaps his exhausted-looking mother.

"Why?" the boy bellows.

"It's for sick children, to make them happy."

"No, it's not. It's mine." Ryan tries to deconstruct the fire engine by removing its flashing light and ladder, but succeeds only in activating its siren again. The girl he smacked has peed on the carpet. A pregnant woman in denim dungarees lurches for the bathroom and emerges with fistfuls of paper towels, then scrubs at the small, dark pool that is creeping along a join in the carpet tiles.

The Scottish man catches my eye and smirks. "Your turn," I say, handing him the rest of my coins.

He touches the skin near Surf's clawmarks. "What happened?" he asks.

"My dad's dog scratched me. He's just excitable — Dad's made no effort to train him."

The siren wails over and over. Something's gone wrong with its workings: it won't turn off. The receptionist glowers at the red-headed kid but, unlike most adults, he is unafraid of the fierce-looking women who bristle behind glass partitions in doctors' waiting rooms. "Poor you," the Scottish man says.

"I'm sure I'll survive."

There's a pause, and I can sense Ryan, still clutching the fire engine, fixing his beady gaze upon us. "Doctors are running at least fifteen minutes late," the receptionist tells an elderly man through her partition.

Good, I think. Be late, late, late.

"Live round here?" the Scottish man asks.

"Pretty close. Briar Hill, do you know it?"

"No, I've just moved —"

"Stella Moon?" calls Dr Marsden, at the door that leads to the surgeries.

"Interesting name," the stranger says.

"What's yours?"

"Ed. Very ordinary."

I mean to say it's not ordinary, but it comes out as "You're not ordinary." Hotness creeps up my neck.

"Miss *Moon*?" Dr Marsden calls out impatiently.

I look at Ed. Sand-coloured flecks, like speckles in amber, are trapped in his eyes. The smile floods his face as he says, "Beautiful woman savaged by bonkers hound."

★ ★ ★

I have cellulitis, an infection of the blood. "Keep it clean and dry," Dr Marsden says, "and take a couple of days off work. You're running quite a temperature." He scribbles a prescription for an antibiotic and adds, "See the nurse at the end of the corridor. She'll dress it for you."

"Will I be able to go swimming?" I ask.

"Of course not," Dr Marsden mumbles, turning his tweed-jacketed back to me. I'm wondering, as the nurse parcels up my hand, if Ed will still be waiting by the charity box. But when I come out there's only Ryan and his mother — he's lost interest in the fire engine now — and a frail-looking man huddled over the *Telegraph* crossword, crunching lemon-scented sweets.

That lovely face, lovely voice — it's as if I dreamed them up.

Wednesday must be Diane's day off because Queen comes thick and fast all morning: "The Show Must Go On", "We Will Rock You", "I Want To Break Free". Over and over, with Diane's squawking lead vocal and her Hoover providing a whining accompaniment. The record stops, and the Hoover stops, and she rattles out to the back garden, singing flamboyantly.

She stabs at the hardened soil with a garden fork, then looks up and beckons me outside with a flapping hand. "How are you feeling?" she asks.

"Ropy. I'm taking a couple of days off work."

She stamps on the fork. Her slippers have ears and doleful-looking eyes and are meant to be puppies. "D'you like Queen?" she asks.

101

"They're okay."

"Rock's not really your thing, is it?" she says, delving into a pocket in her fleece and extracting a custard-cream biscuit, which she nibbles, rodent style. "More . . . orchestra-ish, aren't you? Stuff that chunders on for hours — violins and all that — with no lyrics or choruses."

"That kind of thing," I say, laughing. "How's Jojo getting on with the flute?"

Diane shrugs. "Plays it all hours, till God knows when. Nice of you to lend it. Looks expensive."

"She can keep it for longer if she's enjoying it. I could teach her, if it's okay with you."

"We can't afford stuff like that."

"That's okay. I'm happy to do it."

"What about your flute? Don't you need it back?"

"She can hang on to it for now. I have another anyway."

"Don't let her think I'll be buying her one," Diane adds firmly. "I don't want her getting any ideas."

"I'm sure she won't —"

"Because it's not like all this schoolwork she's having trouble with, is it? I'm happy for her to have a little hobby, as long as that's all it is."

"She'll have to practise, if I'm going to teach her. It shouldn't interfere with her schoolwork. She has a natural ability, Diane, like I've never —"

"I enjoy my music," she cuts in, "we all do — but it's not *important*, is it?"

"Well, it can be. It might help with her confidence, bring her out of herself . . ."

"Are you saying there's something wrong with her?"

"No, of course not —"

She sucks in her lips, then her face softens, and she says, "Thing is, Stella, the flute's not the instrument I'd choose for a strapping girl like our Jojo. She might bust it."

"I hope she's playing it, Diane, not sitting on it."

She throws back her head, laughs a deep, rich laugh and says, "Don't suppose you've an electric guitar you could lend her, do you?"

CHAPTER
NINE

Unwanted Goods

Smart Shopping, as Diane calls it, enables her to whip round the charity shops — RSPCA, Sue Ryder, Oxfam, Cancer Research — in minimal time without doubling back on herself. "You need an eye," she tells me, "for smart shopping. I've got the eye. It's a rare gift, Stella."

Her hands are large and powerful-looking, her nails the colour of dried blood. In Oxfam her eyes scan shelves bearing butter dishes, colour-enhanced photos of piers and winter gardens, and huge cookie jars shaped like teddy bears — stuff that serves no purpose apart from filling space. Diane had insisted I come shopping. "It'll take your mind off your poisoned hand," she declared. She selects an onyx sphinx ornament, a nightie covered with dancing fairies for Jojo, and a battered book entitled *Mercury Rising: The Untold Queen Story.*

I never know what to do with myself in charity shops, and rarely find anything I'd want to take home. Like Diane, Alex enjoyed burrowing among strangers' unwanted goods. He'd drag me from one junk shop to the next, collecting gnarled books that he intended to resell to antiquarian bookshops in Exeter. They would pile on his bedside table, acquiring dried coffee rings.

Diane has drifted towards the clothes rails. There's an over-abundance of dark brown knitwear, and the occasional splash of garish colour that my mother might have called "nasturtium" or "aquamarine". A handwritten sign above the bookshelves reads, "Quality clothing, books, magazines and bric-à-brac gratefully received". I scan the books' spines: *Hors d'oeuvres Made Easy, Dinner Parties In Colour, 1001 Pasta Recipes*. Rather bruised, its jacket frayed at the edges, is *More Frankie's Feasts*. Dad beams from the cover, his broad hands resting on a table bearing plates of unreal-looking food. Everything looks too shiny, as if it has been glazed. A trout is garnished with apple slices and a gloop of something resembling hair-conditioner.

Diane crunches a free Glacier mint from the dish on the counter. "Buying that book?" she asks.

I slide Dad back on to the shelf. "Just browsing," I say.

Back in the Midlands, before Diane left George — she refers to him as "their dad" — she had the easiest job ever invented. "Worked in the visitors' centre at a honey farm," she says, plucking chips from a paper bag. "Never advertised, so hardly anyone came. We were lucky if we had four visitors a day."

"What did you do?" I ask.

"I had to let them taste the honeys — that was the downside, sticky bloody fingers all over the shop — and make candles. Midge, of course, she'd make wax guns and torpedoes and blast the hell out of anyone who'd dared to wander in." She laughs and flumps on to a bench on the seafront, dumping the carton of chips on her lap.

Carrier bags are bunched round her feet. I can't figure out where she's going to put all this stuff. When Mrs Lawrence lived next door, the house felt sparse and eerily still. Occasionally I'd help her in with shopping and she'd make a pot of insipid tea. Entire rooms contained just an old wooden chair, a small table and billions of swirling dust particles.

"I'm in bedding now, factory work," Diane continues. "Just short-term to tide me over. It's all right. You get to bring offcuts home. I make stuff with them, my sideline."

"What things?" I ask, prodding at my chips. They've gone cold already, and loll in their paper like slugs.

"Rag rugs," she explains. "You cut your fabrics into strips and hook them through the backing material. I'll show you. Your place is a bit plain, isn't it?"

"*I* like it . . ."

"Could do with brightening up," she concludes, marching over to the railings to tip our unwanted chips into the bin.

We wander along the breezy seafront. A woman is showing her son where to put money into the toy-grabber machine. She manoeuvres the silver claw — the grabber — until it appears to be gripping a cuddly tiger. But at the critical moment the claw goes limp and the tiger remains in the glass box with all the others. The little boy bangs on the glass and shouts, "Again, again!" until his mother stuffs in more money.

Diane throws her a sympathetic look, the way women do with fellow members of their club — the mothers' club. "Did you speak to Jojo's teacher?" I ask, lugging a bag of vases in my good hand.

"I went to school, like you said. Met that snooty headmistress."

"What did she suggest?"

We're climbing Briar Hill now. Diane's breathing is ragged; she's tugged off her jacket and stuffed it into the terrier-tray bag. "Gave us this pile of books — stupid stories for kids of Midge's age. *And* extra maths work for Midge, like I've got time for that."

"I'm sure she's just trying to help."

"You would say that," Diane huffs, meaning, You're *one of them*, aren't you? "You stick together," she adds, "like doctors."

"What do you mean?"

"We had a spot of bother at the girls' old school. I went in, not looking for a fight. You know me, Stella — reasonable. And, of course, it's our Jojo's fault. Not Mr bloody Henderson's fault."

"What had happened?"

"He made her read out loud in class, and she just couldn't — not at the front of the classroom with everyone staring."

"And he forced her to? That's terrible —"

"My little girl," Diane continues, her eyes glimmering now, "went and wet herself in front of the class."

"Diane, no one would treat her like that at Paul Street."

"So you can see why I'm not very keen on teachers."

We dump the carrier bags at her front door. Diane swipes her eyes with the flat of her hand and rummages in her shoulder-bag for keys. "We're not all like that," I add.

She sighs and says, "Remember to take your antibiotics."

"Yes, Miss." Diane tries to give me a stern look, but the smile flits across her round pink face, like a bird escaping.

Alex subscribed to specialist magazines: *Trout and Salmon, Caged and Aviary Birds, Poetry Now*. He'd never get round to cancelling subscriptions so they'd keep rolling in, long after his brief interest in poetry had given way to canoeing.

Quality clothing, books, magazines and bric-à-brac gratefully received.

They're stacked tidily on top of the bookcase. Occasionally, when a heavy vehicle roars up Briar Hill, one slips from its pile and lands on the floor with a resounding slap. There, at my feet, lies an article entitled "Tried and Tested: a New Generation of Softbaits".

I find a box in the shed, bring it into the living room and fill it with the magazines. Upstairs I haul out bundles of Alex's shirts from beneath my bed. They still smell of him, like warm bread, even though they've lain there for months. There's his party shirt — dazzling orange with a black floral pattern — bought when he wanted to create a stir at Jen's thirty-fifth birthday celebration. But most are pale blue, cream or washed-out yellow: faded and wilting and not, I suspect, the "quality clothing" required by the charity shops.

Here is his zip-up bag, pushed so far under the bed I have to slide on my stomach to retrieve it. It's filled with summery things: battered Birkenstocks, flip-flops, cheap sunglasses, a raffia mat for the beach. Alex enthused about travelling to Goa, Mexico or Guatemala — he'd buy the *Rough Guides* — but could only get it together to come on one holiday with me, to Nice, and several solo excursions to his aunt Gina's boarding-house in Weston-super-Mare. I pile his stuff in the corner of my bedroom, like some challenging art installation entitled My Ex-boyfriend's Old Crap, then wish I'd left it under the bed where I wouldn't be able to see it.

There are more of his things in my bottom drawer: a cracked leather wallet and a pair of miniature binoculars in a rigid case, the only remaining evidence of his bird-watching fad. And here's something that isn't Alex's but Mum's: a quilted cream bag sprigged with daisies. Inside is a black kohl pencil with a silver lid, and two colours of eye-shadow — shimmery cream, for highlighting the brow bone, which women did then, plus chestnut brown. Her lipstick is frosted pink, Elizabeth Arden's Rose Blush, her face powder Cussons' Palest Ivory. There's a black mascara, a tiny bottle of Jean Patou perfume, and a tortoiseshell comb.

109

I lay out her things on my duvet, all her colours and smells. A few pale brown hairs are attached to the comb. The lipstick is barely used. I touch its smooth silver case and twist it up to its full length. Years ago, feeling sorry for me without a mother, Elona bought me copies of *Jackie* magazine. One issue had a feature about the shape of your lipstick revealing your hidden personality. If yours wore down to a sharp angle you were inquisitive and enjoyed new challenges. I grabbed Mum's lipsticks from the dressing-table drawer, which Dad hadn't got round to emptying, and pulled off all their lids.

They were perfectly rounded. "On the surface you're loving and giving," the *Jackie* article said, "but tend to nurture a secret side." Suddenly it felt wrong to be examining her private things, and I stuffed them back into the drawer.

I pack her makeup back into the quilted bag and lift the bedside phone. "Hey, Stella," Alex says, "how's things?" It sounds like a voice I don't know.

"Fine, Alex. I'm just . . . clearing out. Going through your old stuff."

"Not moving, are you?"

"No, of course not. I just need the space." My voice is emotionless, flat as cardboard.

"Okay," he says gently. "What have you been up to, anyway?" I want to get off the phone and bundle the rest of his stuff into bags. The art installation glowers at me.

"Working lots," I say briskly.

110

"Nothing's changed, then." Alex once said I was too busy for him: "You're so full of your damn flute and your music," he announced, and stormed upstairs, perhaps to write a poem entitled "My Girlfriend Loves Mozart More Than She Loves Me". I found him later, fully clothed and asleep, as if he'd been waiting for me to come up and say sorry but I'd taken too long.

"I have to earn a living," I remind him.

"Are you going out much?"

"Of course I go out! I'm not a recluse." My heart quickens. *Don't be defensive. Just make the arrangements and finish the call.*

"We could meet up," Alex adds. "Haven't seen you in months."

"Of course you haven't. That's what happens when people break up."

"We could still have a drink, when you're not working. It'd be good to catch up."

"Maybe," I say carefully.

"I've been past your place," Alex adds. "Saw a couple of girls sitting on your doorstep."

"My new neighbours. I'm teaching the older one flute. She's amazing —"

"Stella," he says, "it's lovely to hear your voice."

I could give his stuff to Midge to add to her Evian-bottle missile. The Birkenstocks could be leathery wings.

"Have you met anyone?" Alex asks.

"I need you to collect your stuff."

"Well, have you?"

"No, Alex."

A pause. "Are you sure?"

There's a face, indistinct apart from the eyes, which are startling green with pale flecks like sand. *Beautiful woman savaged by bonkers hound.*

"Of course I'm sure. What about you?"

"I was . . ." he pauses ". . . seeing someone for a while. Nothing special."

Was Nothing Special the reason he left me? "That's nice for you," I murmur.

"Don't be like that."

"I've got to go, Alex."

"Listen, I read something about your dad joining *Friday Zoo.*" Alex always enjoyed Frankie stories. Dad's kind of job — seemingly easy, not quite real — appealed to his dubious work ethic.

"I can't really believe it. Never thought he'd work in TV again."

"Remember that time we went to Cornwall, and his fence — the one he'd just put up — blew right across the fields?"

I remember, and a small laugh escapes. "Dad was chasing bits of stick in his dressing gown . . ."

"And his girlfriend . . ."

"Maggie."

"Maggie with the veggie casseroles . . . She was scared he'd get pneumonia."

"They liked you," I tell him. Alex had come to Silverdawn Cottage several times, and charmed Dad with his knowledge of sea-fishing, which he'd picked up from *Coarse Angler* magazine.

He sighs, then says something that sounds like "I miss you."

And he waits for me to say, "I miss you too."

CHAPTER
TEN

Friday Zoo

"... And a huge welcome to Dirk, Chuck and Johnnie, our fabulous wildmen ... Let's unleash them, open the cage now ... it's *Friday Zoo!*"

At the word "zoo" the cage opens and the presenters tumble out. "Tonight," says the one with swathes of silken dark hair, "we have some *incredible* guests ..." He names an ex-porn actress who's launched her own underwear range, an elderly actress who plays a fearsome café owner in a soap, and a young singer, who grins tensely as he's steered towards a pink leather sofa that looks like a vast, squishy bottom.

Katy was due for her lesson at seven but hasn't shown up. The presenters fire questions and the boy singer can't respond quickly enough. He keeps tugging at his fringe. He's outnumbered three to one. "I know the female contingent here," the ginger-haired presenter says, "is dying to know if young David is available ..."

"I've been too busy," he manages, "for a girlfriend."

The ex-porn star is showing her collection of gel-filled bras, designed to give "oomph" to the cleavage. I could do with one of those. My cleavage lacks oomph. When I'm not working I don't even bother with a bra. "Even flat-chested women should wear bras," the girl chirps, "or your boobs will be hitting the floor by your thirties."

She's an unsettling combination of highly tanned face and silver hair. She looks unreal, as if she's made of plastic or wax. You might expect her to pop, or start melting under the studio lights. Dad used to alert Charlie and me to the dangers of the lights' fierce heat. "It's tough out there," he said, as if preparing Beef Cobbler before two hundred well-behaved housewives posed similar risks to maintaining oil rigs in the North Sea. To guard against embarrassing damp patches, he wore a strong anti-perspirant, which claimed to shut the pores completely.

The soap actress reveals that the man she lives with is precisely half her age. "You're as young as the man you feel," she says, cackling, and her outsized hoop earrings collide with her cheeks. I check the street, but there's still no sign of Katy's mum's car. I want to turn off *Friday Zoo* but can't force myself to press the button on the remote. I try to look away but my eyes keep sliding over. Like peering into other people's houses, I just can't help myself. I lose control of my eye-swivelling muscles.

I peel a cherry-flavoured Chewy Jewel off the rug and pick up my flute to play, but can't focus with the presenters guffawing with the ex-porn star. She's pretending to love the attention but is only there to sell gel-filled bras and highly flammable camisoles. The soap actress has just published an autobiography;

the boy singer has released a solo album of ballads. Dad has nothing to sell except himself. Maggie has confided that the *Friday Zoo* fee will enable them to have the roof fixed.

"Put your hands together," says the startlingly handsome presenter — he looks like someone who'd be rude to waiters and barmen, "to welcome our new regular guest. He's responsible for clogging millions of arteries, wrecking billions of hearts . . ."

The audience roars. The ex-porn star is clapping, like she knows or cares who he is.

"A big hand," the presenter commands, "for the kitchen sensation of yesteryear . . ."

Dad's eyes seem more bulbous than usual, as if they might actually fall out and roll like marbles along the worktop. Maybe he always looks like this — startled and moist-lipped — and TV just emphasises everything. It's been so long since I've seen him on screen. "Thank you," he says, as the applause fades. "Tonight, ladies and gentlemen, we're cooking up a forgotten classic."

Forgotten classic, like Dad himself. Only he's not forgotten. Occasionally, at the doctor's or dentist's, I'll flip through a magazine and come across an article called something like "Where Are They Now?" *After several failed attempts to revive his career, Frankie Moon retired from television and lives quietly in a ramshackle cottage on the north Cornish coast with his partner Maggie and their two mongrel dogs . . .*

Dad is making Baked Alaska. "Something nice and chilling for winter," the ginger presenter jibes, peering over his shoulder.

Dad is wearing a pale blue shirt, a darker blue tie and a red-and-white PVC apron emblazoned with the *Friday Zoo* logo, the words bursting through the bars of a cage. "What I'm doing," he continues gamely, "is placing the ice-cream on the sponge, which I made earlier —"

"Which we bought, actually," the presenter cuts in. "Ninety-nine pence for three. Special offer at Tesco."

"And I'm covering it thickly with meringue, which will act as an insulating layer so the ice-cream . . . um . . . Does everyone know how to make meringue?"

"Eggs, sugar?" suggests the presenter.

"Beat the egg white until it's stiff, fold in the —"

"Ever been to Alaska, Frankie?"

"Can't say I have, Dirk."

"Johnnie," the presenter corrects him. "Dirk's the good-looking one. Know what they used to call me at school, Frankie? Gingernut. Gingersnap. Did you ever bully ginger people at school, Frankie?"

"I, um, can't, um . . ."

"Course you didn't," Johnnie cuts in, "nice guy like you."

Dad forces a tight smile. His hair looks freshly cut, clippered into respectability. I imagine Maggie watching on their ancient TV, trying to feel proud. He swirls on the meringue with a palette knife. The screen is filled by the top of his head where his hair's thinning. "Sure it won't melt?" Johnnie asks. "Like, run out all over the oven and start burning? Is this a fire hazard, Frankie? You're worrying me now."

Dad tries for a quick response but is left hanging, his lips undulating wildly. Years ago he'd known what to say when strangers stopped him in the street and said, "I thought it was you. It *is* you!", blinking at him as if they were expecting him to do something terribly clever with aspic.

"We'll come back to Frankie," Johnnie announces, "at the end of the show. Can't *wait* for a taste of that Baked Alaska."

"So sorry," Katy's mum pants into the phone. "Car won't start. We're walking to your house. Hurry *up*, Katy — we're already late. Sure you can still fit her in, Stella?"

"No problem," I say.

"Hope we haven't messed up your evening."

"No, not at all." I can still hear Johnnie's braying voice rattling out of the TV. I try to busy myself by wiping out the fridge, even though it's perfectly clean. When I peek back into the living room Johnnie is saying, "We've had a bit of an incident here." He peers into the oven, as if it's a cave from which a ferocious bear might burst out. It's a set-up, of course. A joke. Anything can happen on *Friday Zoo*. That's the whole point. Dad probably knew, and why should he care? He's working again. He's *somebody*.

The camera closes in on the Baked Alaska. It looks like a smouldering slipper. Johnnie pokes it, then bashes it with his fist. The handsome one strides on to the set, clutching a chisel and mallet. He whacks the pudding, sending it bouncing off the worktop and skidding across the floor like shrapnel. The audience is laughing, and Dad's laughing too. His mouth has formed the right shape, at least.

The doorbell sounds. I let in Katy, who is pink-cheeked and gasping from being marched up Briar Hill by a vexed mother. "Can I stay while she has her lesson?" her mum asks. "I'll just read my magazine. I won't get in the way."

"Of course you can stay," I tell her.

Friday Zoo's credits are rolling. The presenters are jostling with the ex-porn star and her armful of bras. "What are you watching?" Katy's mother asks.

It's so awful, seeing Dad's big, fake face, watching him trying to bluster through it — really *trying*, the way he'd occasionally attempt to be a good dad to Charlie and me.

"Just some rubbish," I say.

"Oh, it's *Friday Zoo*. Isn't that your father, Stella? Brought him out of retirement, have they?"

"Yes, that's my dad."

"I remember him from when I was a kid. You must have had an amazing time as a child, with him being so well known and respected."

I nod, and busy myself with extracting Katy's pieces from the pile of music on the table.

"Weren't you a lucky girl?" she gushes, beaming at the screen.

"Yes, I was." I fix on my widest smile and click off the TV. Dad's hollow laughter still rattles between my ears.

CHAPTER
ELEVEN

Moon Pie

When Dad tried to be Good Dad, Charlie and I started to worry. We'd grown used to rattling along in our own cackhanded way. We didn't welcome interference.

"Good news," Dad announced, one morning over breakfast. "I've found someone to look after you." I thought he meant somewhere else — that Charlie and I were being sent to a home or a distant relative's house.

"Where?" I asked, picturing an attic filled with scuttling spiders and a growling water tank.

"Here, of course. We'll have to clear out the spare room because the nanny will need it."

"We don't need a nanny," Charlie retorted. He was fifteen and sprouting so fast he'd taken to having daytime naps in his room with the door locked. I was tall like Charlie — the loftiest in my class — but conscious of too much energy buzzing inside me, sabotaging any hope of concentrating on my work. My head felt as if it was full of bees.

"There's no point arguing," Dad said. "Someone's got to cook, clean, take care of the house. She'll make life easier for all of us."

I realised then that it was our house or — more accurately — Dad who needed nannying. She must be coming cheap, I decided, because he was hardly making any money by then. *Woman's Life* had replaced him with a chef-cum-nutritionist, who grinned from her page in a scoop-necked top. "*I* cook," I protested. "*I* clean the house." It was true. Around twice a year I'd drag the Hoover round and maybe extract a soggy hairball from the plughole in the bath.

"It's all arranged," Dad said. "She's very efficient. She's starting on Monday and I'll expect you both to be nice to her."

I stared at him, gulping air. What would Mum think? I wondered, certain that she would have been proud of the way I'd run things during the past year. Yes, the sink was perpetually piled high with dirty crockery, but none of us was starving, or running around naked. We were *managing*. "Tell her she can't come," I begged Dad.

"It's too late, Stella." He pulled on his old corduroy jacket and headed out to the allotment, leaving the prospect of Efficient Nanny lingering in the air, like milk on the turn.

"What d'you think?" I asked, tipping my untouched Rice Krispies into the bin.

Charlie shrugged. "It's up to him."

"You really want someone — some stranger — living with us?"

"Of course I don't. She won't last long, you'll see. She won't be able to stand it."

"We're not that bad."

He laughed bitterly. "Aren't we?"

"We're fine," I snapped at him, just like Mum used to say, *Nothing to worry about, darling, okay? No, we're not poor. We're just going through a difficult patch.* Charlie pulled on his blazer, picked up his grubby Adidas schoolbag and headed for the front door. "What shall we do," I called after him, "when this woman starts on Monday?"

Charlie paused in the doorway. "Don't know about you," he replied, "but I'm going to do whatever I like."

So Melody Hunt — age undetermined, but probably between eighteen and thirty-five; distinguishing feature, a vast, pale forehead that reminded me of an ice rink — came to live with us. She had faint body odour and engaged in energetic Jane Fonda workouts in her bedroom.

Charlie and I went to great lengths to avoid her. We paid ourselves pocket money from the coin jar on the shelf in Dad's study, awarding bonuses for doing our own laundry, as Melody refused to acquaint herself with our temperamental washing-machine. I'd try to iron my clothes dry and hurry to school with steam rising from my box-pleated navy skirt.

Melody did, however, cook our dinners. Her Bolognese quivered with raw-looking lumps, and her fried eggs could be dissected only with our sharpest steak knives. Charlie and I would delve into the chest freezer in the garage, unearthing Black Forest Gâteaux that we'd defrost on a chair in front of the blazing gas fire.

"Bloody loonies," Melody muttered, hurrying up to her bedroom. "Feel the burn," we could hear. "Feel the burn."

"We need something sharper," Charlie muttered, stabbing the cake with a fork. He crept down to the cellar and emerged with dust-frosted hair and an old-fashioned hand drill. Even the sharpest bit couldn't penetrate the gâteau's icy core.

Dad used Melody's arrival as an opportunity to virtually move to the allotment. Our house was just somewhere to sleep, change his clothes and make the occasional sandwich. Yet nothing resembling a vegetable ever found its way home — not even a radish. Charlie reckoned he didn't really grow things but locked himself in a shed — we assumed there were sheds — where he was designing a covered walkway to link the allotment to his study window, thus minimising any risk of coming into contact with his offspring.

He knew nothing of our gâteau consumption, or that our school grades had slipped. Charlie's form teacher had written on his report that "a *laissez-faire* attitude is beginning to erode his performance". My reports were less exotic. I tried to cultivate a *laissez-faire* attitude of my own, but fretted about falling even further behind in maths, which I struggled with anyway. Being *laissez-faire* was proving stressful, which, surely, wasn't the point.

Anyway, did it really matter what my teachers thought of me when Charlie, I reckoned, knew more than the entire bunch put together? I hung out with my brother as much as he would allow, which was surprisingly often. Being left to our own devices had forced us together: the two of us, united against critical teachers and Melody's Bolognese. Of all the places we could have chosen to hang out — the beach, with its reddish sand and faded huts, or the park, from which the smugglers' tunnel led steeply down to the furthest bay — we favoured an expanse of concrete littered with deceased vehicles, called the Slab. Its owner, the fearsome Mr Syrup, rarely put in an appearance. He would just dump the odd car there to crumble slowly to rust.

Although Charlie and I were really too old for such antics, we would climb into a dented Beetle through the driver's door — the passenger door had rusted shut — and go for imaginary drives. Usually Charlie would let me take the wheel. I'd speed along, yelping at invisible pedestrians to get out of the way. Sometimes Lynette and her friends would loiter at the edge of the Slab, willing Charlie to climb out and notice them. "She fancies you," I hissed at him.

"Drive on," he commanded, and I banged my foot on the accelerator, heading straight for Lynette's mottled thighs.

One day Charlie had been "driving" the Beetle by himself. He tried to force open the door but it wouldn't budge. "Let me out!" he yelled, but I couldn't open it either. He tried to climb out of the passenger window, but his limbs wouldn't fit through. He was man-sized by then, a good four inches taller than Dad.

The window was edged with shattered glass. "I've cut myself," Charlie cried.

"How bad is it?"

"Really bad."

I peered in. Blood was dripping down his arm and starbursting the front of his white T-shirt. His eyes were filled with tears and fear. I hadn't seen him cry since the part in *The Railway Children* where the dad comes home. "I'll get help," I said. I ran home and all through our house, shouting for Melody.

In her bedroom the Jane Fonda book was lying open at the sit-ups page. "Where *are* you?" I shouted, imagining Charlie's arm bleeding and bleeding until it looked like a drooping sausage balloon.

Melody staggered into the kitchen, laden with Chelsea Girl carrier bags. "Charlie's hurt himself," I announced. "We've got to help him."

"Jesus," she muttered. "What's *wrong* with you two? You're not normal."

We ran to the Slab where my brother was gazing miserably through the Beetle's back window, steaming the glass with his breath. Melody found a lump of concrete and smashed it through the windscreen, battering away enough of its shattered edge to make a Charlie-sized hole. He looked far too big to be playing in cars as he struggled through it. The remains of the windscreen glimmered in the sunlight, like millions of jewels.

We waited for Dad, desperate to show him Charlie's injury. We wanted to see him angry, as if Charlie's arm really mattered. He'd storm over to see Mr Syrup and rant about the dangerous vehicles and his poor, damaged son.

Melody had waltzed out wearing a Chelsea Girl dress printed with a repeat pattern of lightning bolts. Charlie and I waited some more, then searched the freezer for gâteaux but could find only a curious ice-cream log, which tasted of chalk. We watched a horror movie about kids trapped in a basement by a crazy man who wanted to conduct weird brain experiments on them.

"This is spooking me out," I said. I mooched off to play with the adding machine in Dad's study and filch more coins from the jar.

By midnight Dad still hadn't come home. Perhaps he was out with Lindy Richards, a woman he'd met at the Social who wore catsuits with no zips, buttons or discernible openings. Charlie and I couldn't figure out how she went to the toilet. Dad denied that she was his girlfriend, complaining, "That woman's plaguing me again." He made her sound like an infectious disease.

I lay in bed, listening as Charlie rummaged about in his room, unable to sleep for his bad arm. I wished I could go in there, just to talk to him, and we could be sleepless together.

"You two are running wild," Dad declared next morning over breakfast. "Can't you find better things to do than hang about on that Slab? Shouldn't you be studying your extra maths, Stella? Using your *brain*?"

"We were only playing —"

"Playing? At your age?"

"What does it matter?" I countered, shocked by the rage in my voice. "You're never here, you don't care what —"

"It wasn't Stella's fault I got hurt," Charlie cut in. "It was *my* fault. Just leave her alone."

Dad reddened and opened his mouth to speak, then clamped it shut as Melody strode into the kitchen.

"I'm leaving," she announced.

I blinked at her, wondering if this was just an empty threat, or a joke. "Great," Charlie muttered under his breath.

"But you can't," Dad protested. "We need someone to —"

"I'm not spending another day in this filthy house with you nutters." Melody stormed out with a carrier bag of LPs and a bulging bin-liner of clothes, banging the front door behind her.

She was replaced by Gayle, a girl only three years older than Charlie, with a face as flat and unwelcoming as a paving slab. At least Gayle prepared edible meals: meat pies that came in round, flat tins, and fruit cocktail (also tinned), which she'd divvy between us. She always kept the cherry for herself.

One day after school, while Charlie pored over his biology notes at the breakfast bar, I opened a can of fruit cocktail, fished out the cherry and popped it into my mouth. It tasted more like marzipan than cherry. Gayle drifted in, her face that nondescript buff colour you see on hospital walls. "Stella," she said, "did you open that tin?"

"No." I poked out my tongue with the cherry perched on it.

Gayle's hand came hard and fast, burning my cheek — like when you're burrowing into a freezer and graze bare skin on ice.

No one replaced Gayle. Dad decided we'd manage better by ourselves. One evening, in the dusty gloom of our living room, he said, "I've been asked to write a book about French cuisine. It'll probably lead to TV."

"Great," Charlie said flatly, over the TV's dull mumble.

"I've been paid an advance," Dad continued, "so I might as well take you two on holiday."

Charlie and I stared at him in disbelief. We thought he'd forgotten that going on holiday was something families did. "Where are we going?" I asked.

"France, of course. Home of great cooking — real cooking. We'll take the ferry, rent a cottage . . . When do your summer holidays start?"

"We break up next Friday," Charlie murmured.

"Really? That soon?" Dad looked scared, then blustered, "I'm sure we'll find something."

I wasn't sure about France, and I certainly didn't relish the prospect of being trapped with Dad in a cottage for two weeks. Without an allotment to escape to, how would he fill the days? We'd have to fit together, the three of us, a feat that seemed virtually impossible. "I don't want to come," I said firmly.

"Why not?" His cheeks flushed angrily.

"I was thinking of getting a summer job."

I saw it then — a terrible hopelessness hazing his pale grey eyes. He had tried the nanny option, which had been a dismal failure. This holiday was his way of trying to make things better. "I won't force you to come," he said quietly.

Something twisted inside me. I wanted to put my arms round him, bury my face in his soft nest of chins. "Dad," I said, "of course I'll come."

I decided, right then, to try to make things better too.

We drove to Plymouth to board the ferry to Brittany. In a quayside pub Charlie and I practised our French. "*Je voudrais,*" he announced grandly, "*une tasse de café.*"

"*Mais bien sûr!*" I replied. "*Prenez-vous le sucre?*"

"*Oui merci!*"

Dad sipped his pint and gazed through the window. He looked worried, as if unsure how he'd survive two vast, virtually *endless* weeks with a couple of teenagers he hardly knew. Rain dribbled down the window's dimpled glass.

On the ferry Charlie discovered an upper lounge filled with reclining pink seats and long-haired French teenagers with edible accents. One girl kept peeping through a gap between the seats and grinning at him. She said something, but too quickly for us to understand. "*Je voudrais une tasse de café,*" Charlie said, and we creased up laughing.

We arrived at the cottage in the early hours and tumbled into the musty living room, breathing in spores. "Charlie, you can sleep here," Dad said, indicating a decrepit brown sofa. We hauled it open. A speckled sheet was stretched tightly like skin across the thin mattress.

Dad marched upstairs with Charlie and me in pursuit. This was exciting, an adventure, like the Railway Children arriving at their crumbling house on the moors in the middle of the night. Dad marched from room to room, clicking on lights. The bulbs were the dim low-wattage kind. "This can be your room," Dad told me, indicating a boxroom with dark yellow walls. Ochre, Mum might have called it.

"It's lovely," I said, and it really was.

"I'm starving," Charlie complained. We hadn't brought any food. Dad, who was exhausted from the drive, lay fully clothed on the double bed in the biggest room, and was soon snoring throatily. He hadn't even taken off his shoes.

I tripped downstairs and peered into the fridge. As we'd neared the cottage Dad had said, "I'm sure the owner will have left a few basics — a hospitality package." I wasn't sure what that was. I'd imagined a medical kit with plasters and the smelly antiseptic cream that Melody had dabbed on Charlie's cut arm.

We couldn't find a hospitality package. The fridge contained only fuzzy blue crumbs. Charlie wrapped himself in a blanket on the pull-out bed, looking like a giant swiss roll. "*Bonne nuit,*" I called from the stairs.

"*Je voudrais une tasse de café,*" he murmured back.

"*Avec du sucre?*"

"*Oui, merci bien!*"

★ ★ ★

Sunlight poured, warm and golden, into the ochre room. We'd never been anywhere since before Mum had died, and now I'd woken up in France. "Get dressed!" Dad shouted up. "We're not lying around the house all day."

I pulled on yesterday's clothes and hurried downstairs. Dad bustled Charlie and me into the car and drove at around seventeen miles per hour along the narrowest roads I'd ever seen. Bushes were thickly laden with blowsy pink and blue flowers. "They're hydrangeas," Dad said. "What's interesting about hydrangeas is . . ."

I had already decided that there wasn't a single fact I wished to learn about hydrangeas.

". . . so it's their environment, the acidity or alkalinity of the soil," Dad burbled on, "that determines the colour of the blooms."

I winced every time Dad veered too close to a creamy stone wall. I wished he'd stop wittering about hydrangeas and keep his mind on the road. But as the day unfolded, and we ambled around ancient, sun-dappled towns, I realised that something was happening to Dad — it was as if he, too, was changing, because he was on a different part of the earth. The Slab and our chest freezer might have been on some distant planet.

Everything looked freshly painted in colours I had never seen in Devon. The town hall was a dazzling blue, adorned with hanging baskets overflowing with tomato-red geraniums. I blinked at the brightness. In the market, which sprawled through the streets of our nearest town, Dad pressed unfamiliar notes into our hands and said, "You two, go and buy dinner. It's time you learned about food instead of that rubbish you eat."

"Aren't you coming with us?" I asked.

"No, I'm going to pop into a couple of restaurants, talk to the chefs, see what's going on around here. Stick together, use your French — isn't that the point of learning it?"

I wanted to ask, "Why don't *you* speak French?" then remembered that Dad only knew food words, like *boeuf bourguignon* and salmon *en croûte*.

Charlie and I slipped into the throng of the market. We peered at fat, glossy cherries and crusty cheeses, which looked like they had fallen off the underside of cars. We wandered and sniffed and touched things. Strangers smiled at us. Two girls at the cooked-chicken stall whispered and pointed at Charlie. "This way," he said, pulling me by the arm into a *pâtisserie*.

"What shall we buy?" I asked him.

He grinned. "Whatever we want."

We stared at the glossy tarts in the display cabinet. "*Je voudrais . . .*" Charlie began. I felt a giggle starting deep in my belly.

The shop lady smiled expectantly. She had a soft, plump face and dazzling red lips.

". . . *une tarte tatin*," Charlie said, his accent perfect. The woman placed it in a shallow box, tied a thin golden ribbon round it and presented it to him like a gift.

132

"It's not quite what I had in mind," Dad said later, back at the house. The three of us gazed at the design on the box lid: a crest with fish, a fleur-de-lis, and three stars. Stars like Stella, my name.

The tart was deep and filled with soft pieces of apple. Charlie poked in a finger and licked it. "Don't do that," I said. I didn't want him to spoil it.

Dad cut us each a thin slice. "This," he said, his mouth full, "is something very special." It was what Mr Grieves had said when he'd shown me the silver flute.

I could still taste the tart when I woke up at around two a.m. in the ochre room. I slipped out of bed and crept downstairs in my pyjamas. There it was, uncovered on the table, with a quarter missing. I snapped off a fragment of pastry and popped it into my mouth.

Charlie stirred on the pull-out bed. "What are you eating?" he whispered.

I couldn't remember the tart's proper name. Through the living-room window I could see the moon: full, round and golden. "Moon pie," I whispered back.

"*La tarte de la lune. C'est bien?*"

"*Oui,*" I said, "*c'est très bien.*"

I crept back to my room and lifted the special flute from its case. Dad had never found out how much it had cost, hadn't even realised I owned two flutes. I could have told him how Mum's hand had trembled as she'd written the cheque: she wasn't here any more so she couldn't have got into trouble. Even Charlie assumed it was just ordinary. That made it even more special. It had nothing to do with my colossal-brained brother, or Dad being famous a lifetime ago.

I no longer cared what Dad really got up to at the allotment, or that I was incapable of being *laissez-faire*. I felt warm inside and ridiculously happy as I slid back into bed. Here we were, the three us, on holiday together. Just like any ordinary family.

Eight twenty-five a.m. Dad whirled into the ochre room and snatched my *Advanced Flute Solos* book, which, having forgotten to bring my music stand, I had propped up on the windowsill. "Same piece," he boomed, "over and over. Can't you play something else?"

I placed my flute carefully on the bed. "Mrs Bones said I should practise over the holidays, and this is the piece we've —"

"You, you, you," Dad ranted. The bedroom seemed to slump into gloom.

"I didn't know," I murmured, "that you minded me practising."

Dad paused. "There are limits," he said. I realised then that Dad was usually out when I played, back at home.

"Well, I *can't* stop," I said firmly.

His eyes met mine. "Why not?"

"I . . . I can't explain it. It's like —"

"Love?" Dad cut in.

I nodded, unable to form words. That was it exactly. Playing made me soar like nothing else could. I had yet

134

to fall in love, but this was exactly how I'd imagined it would feel. How did Dad know?

"You could show some thought for others," he blustered, embarrassed now.

"For you, you mean."

"Everyone likes some peace and quiet on holiday."

"So you're banning me from playing?"

He dropped the music book on the bed. It landed on top of the flute. "Until we're home," he added brusquely. "Then you can do as you please."

I watched him as he marched out of the room, and stared at the space he'd left. Four days until I would be allowed to play.

I was fuelled then with a fury that rose up my throat and burnt my ears. I snatched my flute from the bed. I would never again be scared of Dad. I would do as I pleased, just as he'd said. The mouthpiece was still warm as I brought it back to my lips. I filled myself with air, and the note poured out, flooding the huddled French cottage. I propped *Advanced Flute Solos* on the windowsill and resumed playing the piece, expecting Dad to yell up, or thunder into my room again, but there was nothing.

I played on, knowing that Mrs Bones would say, "That's it, Stella! That's lovely," and wishing that Mum could have heard me. She would never have banned me from playing, not for a second, let alone four days.

Dad didn't shout up to the ochre room, but even if he had, I'd have carried on playing right into his face. I

135

wasn't scared any more. The special flute was about Mum and me. She had gone, but it was still our secret.

We would always have that.

CHAPTER
TWELVE

Log-Log

Saturday, nine-fifteen a.m. A rap at my door. Midge's pale cheek flat against the glass. I open the door a fraction. She shoves it fully open and wedges it with her booted foot. "It's a bit early, girls," I say.

"We thought you'd like to play," Jojo announces behind her.

"Sorry, a friend's coming round. We're —"

"You're still in your pyjamas," Midge observes. "I like them better than your others."

"Thank you, Midge."

"Is it a boyfriend what's coming?" she asks brightly.

"No, not a boyfriend — a pupil, actually, the man who —"

"The one you kissed?"

"Well, yes."

Robert is skipping his lesson today: we're taking the boys out instead. "It'll be fun," Robert insisted. "The boys will love you being there."

"Why?" I asked. Because I was female? Or a teacher and, allegedly, good with children?

"Is that him?" Midge shouts, hopping on my path and jabbing her light sabre in the direction of an elderly man hauling a wheeled shopping basket up the hill.

"No, Midge, you *know* that's not Robert."

"Is he handsome?" Jojo enquires.

"Not bad. Yes, I suppose so. I like him."

"Whooo," Midge says, grinning. Her foot is still firmly planted over the threshold of my house. Behind her, Jojo blows her nose loudly on what looks like a close relative to the strip of fabric Diane used to bandage my hand.

"Okay," I say, "come in for a few minutes. You can draw at the table while I get dressed."

They troop in, glancing around suspiciously as if I might be hiding my mysterious male friend under the table or behind the piano. I lift down the box of paper and felt pens from the bookshelf, and Midge spills them on to the table. By the time I'm dressed they've produced a fantastically detailed drawing of a lanky henna-haired woman who would certainly benefit from a gel-filled bra. "It's lovely to see you two doing something together," I say, "and not squabbling."

"We're trying to be good," Midge murmurs.

"God," Robert says, "those girls aren't exactly friendly. And their mother's the one with the Queen fetish? Don't know how you put up with them."

His Fiat is struggling up the hill, whining like an impatient child. When I glance back Midge is standing in the middle of the street, a splodge of pea-green mac, flapping her light sabre mournfully. "They're just shy with people they don't know," I say.

"They were sizing me up," Robert adds, "as if I were a job candidate."

"I think you failed your interview."

"I'm devastated," he says, chuckling.

Verity lives at the end of a row of mock-Tudor semis perched high above the road. It's a temporary home until Robert redecorates their flat so it can be sold for maximum profit. These houses' gardens slope so steeply that any attempts to make sense of them — creating rockeries or stepped flowerbeds — have failed to take away their cliff-like appearance.

"Does she know I'm coming?" I ask.

"She knows I'm seeing someone," Robert says — then, flustered, adds, "I mentioned that I'm bringing a friend."

"But does she know who —" I begin, but Robert has already climbed out of the car and is hurrying up the steps. Verity's new boyfriend — Robert calls him the Twit — is taking her to Barcelona for three days. Having kept Robert waiting for several minutes, she appears at the door. She has a thin, vexed face and bobbed hair, which looks freshly blow-dried. She was stiffly polite when Robert had his flute lessons at their flat. Once, when she gave me coffee in which the milk floated on the surface in sour flakes, I wondered if she'd made it that way on purpose.

Verity peers down at Robert's car. She's wearing sandals with spindly heels and a short, skinny-strapped navy blue dress. It's not a mother-of-twins outfit. It's a going-to-Barcelona-for-breathtaking-amounts-of-sex outfit. Robert is talking urgently to her, pushing back his hair distractedly. The boys appear like a whirlwind around Verity's legs. Robert pecks her cheek, takes their reins and guides them down the steps.

They're yelping toddler words, "Dadda!", "Juice!", "Mamma!" and are dressed identically in denim dungarees and red jackets. The only way to distinguish one from the other is that Finn — or is it Jack? — is clutching a ginger monkey. Both boys eye me warily as they reach the bottom of the steps.

"This is Stella," Robert says, "and she's very nice." He makes me sound like an unfamiliar dish — something lacking obvious child appeal, like braised liver — that he wants them to try. I wind down the window and try to rearrange my face to look friendly and caring. Robert starts bundling one of the boys into his car seat while gripping his brother's reins.

I should get out and help but Verity is glowering down at us with her arms firmly crossed, as if they are glued in place. Robert could have picked up the children first and brought them to my house. He *chose* to bring me here. He wanted Verity to see me. It's important for her to know that while she swans off to Barcelona with the Twit he, too, will be enjoying the company of a young(ish) person of the opposite sex. He glances up at Verity. I can almost see him mouth, *So there*.

Robert tries to hoist in the second child, whose hands are clamped round the car door's handle. I suspect that my smile says neither "friendly" nor "caring". It feels too big, as if it might fall off my face and be lost among the crushed juice cartons and

140

cracked polystyrene coffee cups that litter the area around my feet. Verity is still gazing down at us, making mental notes: *See? Robert can't even lift our sons safely into a vehicle. Is it any wonder I left him?*

Both boys are strapped into their seats now, and are wailing heartily. "Fucksake," Robert mutters, starting the engine. I try to soothe them but they scream harder. I'm spending too much time in the company of small people with their unpredictable demands. Jojo and Midge visit nearly every day, banging on my door, demanding biscuits and drinks and switching on the Jacuzzi function in the bathroom. Soggy towels are strewn on my bathroom floor. I've found a child's stray sock in there, and a pink glitter pen, slowly leaking on to my cream bathmat.

It's not quite the life I'd planned for myself, as I watched the endless grey sea during our ferry trip home from France. Ignoring Dad's warning, I had continued to play my flute each morning. He hadn't complained again. I assumed he had given up on me, as I had on him. When I grew up, I decided, as the boat cut through the thrashing waves, I'd have a clean, tidy house, proper food in the fridge, and no interference from anyone.

At least the girls seek out my company, which is vaguely flattering. Younger kids seem to find me horrifying. For a short time Charlie was seeing a wispy young thing called Caitlin, who had a baby. The child, who had been nestling peacefully in her mother's arms, started howling as I walked into Charlie's living room. It was as if she'd been stabbed with a pin. I tried sitting

141

where she couldn't see me, and not talking, but she could still sense my presence, and sobbed into Caitlin's lambswool sweater until I left the room.

The engine eventually lulls Robert's children into calm. We're driving to Butterfly Land, an oversized greenhouse out in the country filled with free-flying butterflies. "Finn, tell Stella your monkey's name," Robert says brightly.

"Kilty," he mutters.

Robert explains, "Verity bought it. I said it was a guilty present because she's going away, and he heard me."

"Kilty!" Finn pipes up from the back.

It takes longer than it should to reach Butterfly Land because Robert's Fiat keeps stalling at junctions and roundabouts. It's a cool, breezy morning. Butterfly Land is filled with damp plants and butterflies with enormous fragile wings, which the boys try to swipe at while piling Maltesers into their mouths. Verity doesn't allow them sweets or chocolate. I suspected that Robert bought them to spite her.

He has brought a tiny digital camera and wants a picture of me with the children. "No," I protest, "I can't stand having my photo taken."

"Come on, you look lovely."

I'm aware of my cheeks flushing as I crouch beside the children on the fake cobbles. I look up at the grey-blue eyes and the nut-coloured hair, which always looks wind-blown even on calm days, and I smile at him.

142

Robert takes a picture, then another. I can feel him observing me through the camera, moving closer, and I put my arms round the boys to stop them escaping. A woman stops and says to Robert, "Aren't you lucky to have such a photogenic family?"

She walks on before I can say that they're not mine, that I'm just an impostor mother. Robert winks at me and says, "Yes, I am."

The children sleep in their car seats all the way home. We carry one each into Robert's flat and place them, still snoozing, on the sofa. "Thanks for helping me today," he says.

"I didn't help at all. It was fun."

"Well," he says, "you're really natural with kids."

He starts to prepare the boys' supper in the kitchen. We're planning to eat later when they are in bed. I've brought wine, which he knows about, and my toothbrush, spare knickers, moisturiser and deodorant, which he doesn't. The flat starts to smell of tinned spaghetti hoops, the sort of tea I'd knocked together while Charlie ploughed through his homework.

Finn's eyes flick open. "Kilty," he murmurs.

"Kilty? Oh, your monkey." I scan Robert's living room and check under the cushions.

"Kilty!" repeats Finn, scrambling off the sofa.

Robert fetches the boys and lifts them into their high chairs in the kitchen. The phone rings, and the answerphone clicks on. "Hi," Verity says, "just got to the airport — could you call me, please, Robert?"

143

She's sensed that I'm here. Both boys are banging their high-chair trays. Finn is whimpering now, his mouth wilting like a flower.

"Verity just called," I tell Robert.

"Yes, I heard."

"Maybe Kilty's in the car, or at Butterfly Land."

"Oh, God," Robert says. Jack has dunked his hands into his dish of spaghetti hoops and is now slathering sauce up his arms. Finn hurls his rubber spoon at me. Robert hurries out to check the car, but there's no monkey. He stumbles back in, announcing, "I'll have to drive back and get it."

"Will they still be open?"

"I'll make it, if I go now. I'll put on a video for the boys. You'll be okay, won't you? I'll drive as fast as I can."

"Okay," I say, panic welling in my stomach. He's leaving me in sole charge of children who think you wear spaghetti instead of eating it. I suspect that Verity might not approve of this arrangement.

Robert frees the boys from their chairs, wiping sauce from their hands and arms with a tea towel. He leads them to the TV and stuffs a video into the player. Teletubbies scamper eerily across fake grass.

"Won't be long," Robert says. His kiss is so light on my lips, it might have been a butterfly landing there.

Laid out on the kitchen worktop are the ingredients for our grown-up meal: onions, mushrooms, salad, fancy bread with cranberries nestling like gems inside. Robert is planning to cook steaks. There's also an opened box of vanilla-scented candles on the worktop. I check the boys, who are mesmerised by the TV, and freshen my makeup in the bathroom.

"Want dink," Finn says at the door. "Want Dadda."

"Drink? Come on, let's get you a drink." I lead him to the kitchen, find a beaker in the cupboard and fill it with water. Repulsed, he shoves it away.

"Want Kilty," he mutters.

"Daddy will be back in a minute," I say, trying to steer him back into the living room, where a machine with a corrugated tube is squirting out pink stuff called Tubby Custard.

"Want log-log," Finn adds.

"Log-log?"

"*Log*-log!" he roars. Does he mean a toy, something to eat, or a person? A rich odour is eking out from his dungarees. I have never dealt with a child's soiled bottom — anyone's soiled bottom, for that matter — and have no idea where Robert keeps nappies or the log-log. This feels like some kind of terrible test.

I check all cupboards and drawers in the kitchen. Finn assists by opening a freezer drawer, extracting an opened pack of frozen peas and stuffing a handful into his mouth. Peas ping across the kitchen like bullets. "Let's pick these up," I suggest, "before Daddy comes back."

"Want Daddy," he bleats, tipping out the rest of the peas.

I search the fridge for some foodstuff to offer instant contentment but find only our steaks, some ancient green beans, like withered fingers, a bottle of neon pink

145

medicine and a pile of out-of-date yogurts in unappealing flavours named Strawberry Fizz and Toffee Delight.

The phone rings, and Verity's faraway voice drifts out of the machine: "Robert, just about to get on the plane. Wanted to remind you about Finn's medicine . . . might need to pick up another bottle on Monday . . . don't need another prescription . . ."

Jack thunders towards the phone. ". . . and don't forget that special cream for Jack's bottom," she continues.

I block the boys from grabbing the receiver and informing their mother that they've been left in the care of a woman who doesn't know where log-logs or nappies are kept. Frozen peas are embedded in Finn's hair. He swipes at me with an icy fist. I offer toys from the wicker basket in the corner of the living room, and try to read *The Cat in the Hat*. They don't want toys, *Teletubbies* or even Dr Seuss. They want Dad, who's been gone for just thirty-five minutes, although it feels like a month. The sky has darkened, as if a grey sheet has been draped over everything.

The phone rings again, and Robert says, "Stella — can you hear me? Please pick up the phone."

I grab it and ask, "What's wrong?"

"Damn car broke down just after I left Butterfly Land. Conked out at a roundabout, the way it always does. I've called the garage. They'll be here within an hour."

"An *hour*?"

"Look, I'm sorry. We'll still have our meal. Is everyone okay?"

I peer into the kitchen where his kids are now lying flat on their bellies, flicking peas at each other. "Of course," I say. "We're having great fun, aren't we, boys?"

I check the bathroom, then the larger bedroom, for bottom-cleansing supplies. Compared to the rest of the flat, which is littered with sticky toys and gnawed picture books, it's very orderly. The bed is smoothed over, and vanilla candles have been arranged in glass bowls on each side of the bed. Candles, freshly made bed. My stomach shifts uneasily.

One nappy lies in a plastic box on the floor, but no wipes. I position Finn so that he can watch a programme about people who've found valuable items in their attics and unpopper his dungarees. I peel off the dirty nappy, wipe away as much of the damage as I can with loo roll, and fix on the clean one. Both boys are whimpering meekly. No wonder Verity started to lose it after giving birth. She felt trapped, Robert told me, as if she'd been put in a bubble and no one could hear her.

A car door slams, followed by hurried footsteps. The boys scramble towards the front door like wild cubs. "No Kilty," Robert mouths at me, then asks, "Have you had a lovely time with Stella?"

"Bad lady," Finn mutters.

"Verity called again," I say. "She left a message about Finn's medicine."

"Right." He glances into the kitchen.

"Sorry about the mess. I changed Finn's nappy, and he wanted log-log, but I didn't know —"

"Log-log's yogurt."

"Oh, of course."

"What did she say? Did she want me to call back?"

"She'll ring you when she's landed."

I watch from the doorway as he wanders past me into the kitchen, where he pulls out a brush from the tall cupboard and starts to sweep up the peas. I've messed up, proved myself incapable of keeping two toddlers relatively clean and content. I don't belong here. "Story!" Jack chirps, waving *The Cat in the Hat.*

"Later, darling," Robert says. He's thinking about Verity and the Twit in their hotel room.

"Robert?" I say.

He carries on sweeping, his head filled with his wife and his boys and that damned lost monkey. He thinks he wants me — wants someone, at least — but there's no room for anyone else.

"I think I'll go home," I tell him.

He doesn't say, "Stay." He doesn't even say, "I'll call you." I kiss his cheek, and feel the boys' eyes boring into the back of my head as I pick up my bag and jacket. "Take care," Robert says, as I leave.

Outside, the air feels heavy and damp. The pub in Robert's road is glowing inside. I could murder a drink, but I know a couple of teachers who live in this street and I don't want them to think I make a habit of sitting in the White Mare all by myself on a Saturday night.

Most of the houses have lights on and it's so tempting to peek in. People are busying themselves in kitchens, preparing special meals. Girls are getting ready for pub crawls. Some are setting out already. They clatter along the pavement, their sleek hair shining in the streetlights. One says, "Hi, Miss Moon," and I realise it's Amber, whom I used to teach until she decided that boys and a part-time dish-washing job at the Beachcomber left little opportunity for practising scales.

Robert was wrong. I'm not good with children. Toby Nichols played beautifully on Monday, but as soon as his moment was over he started fidgeting and telling Laura jokes about the toilet parts of donkeys. Willow kept stumbling over her notes and looked as if she might cry. I sent Toby back to his class. After he'd gone the room felt lighter, as if clouds had parted.

The following day I popped into the Cancer Research shop. Midge had added various accessories to her Evian-bottle missile and I thought I'd pick up some bits for her. I found a hairy grey coat with enormous silver buttons, and felt someone watching me. The woman moved away to the display of Christmas cards and tree decorations. "See her in the grey sweater with the long hair?" she hissed.

I examined the coat on its hanger. Its buttons were just right for the missile's control panel. "That's the music teacher I told you about," the woman continued. "The one who picks on our Toby."

"Oh, her," her companion muttered.

"No kids of her own," Toby's mother added. They seemed unconcerned that I might be able to hear them. I walked out of the shop, leaving the coat on the rail with all the other blankety garments, and the two women agreeing that Miss Moon didn't know the first thing about children.

I call Jen on my mobile and leave a message: "I know you'll say it's okay, but I'll be coming on my own to your Christmas party." I'm apologising for having no one to bring, as if Jen would mind. Like Robert with his candles, I'd made a plan: I'd intended to ask him to come to Jen's party with me.

I walk faster now, moist air filling my throat. I call Dad, but as usual Maggie answers: "Of *course* he's fine, dear. That's the whole point of having him on the show. It's a sort of pastiche. Didn't you think he came across well?"

"As long as Dad's not upset . . ."

"Not a bit, dear. We're both delighted."

"Can I speak to him?"

"He's in the garden."

"But it's dark," I protest, like a child.

"He's just pottering with the dogs." There's a catch in her voice, like elastic across her throat. "I'm at the end of my tether with Surf," she continues. "Drank the toilet water after I'd put bleach in. Sick everywhere, Stella, terrible mess."

"Oh, that's awful. Will he be okay?"

"I expect so. Wretched mutt has nine lives. Anyway, I can hear you're rushing off somewhere. Enjoy your night out."

150

I arrive home just after eight and glance through Diane's window: they're all watching TV through a smoky haze. Diane's arms are draped round the girls' shoulders like scarves. Midge is wearing a camouflage dressing gown and some kind of headgear resembling a Second World War helmet.

Their Christmas tree never recovered from being crushed beneath the headboard. Its crooked branches are strewn with thick ropes of pink and red tinsel. Diane hasn't bothered to put it into a pot, and it doesn't appear to have its own stand. It's just propped in the corner, like an awkward party guest, next to a picture of a Spanish girl with enormous circular eyes.

We had real Christmas trees every year before Mum died. She'd drive the Citroën all the way to Somerset to choose one from Patrick Lowey's farm. After she'd gone, we didn't bother with trees any more, not even a fake one. Dad said, "What's the point?"

I let myself in and fish out the toothbrush, moisturiser and knickers from my bag. Clearly, I shouldn't have taken them to Robert's. Interesting things happen only when you're unprepared. The day I met Alex — he'd been trying, unsuccessfully, to windsurf off the back beach — we talked until the sea shivered under silvery streetlights. He took me back to his flat where there were no candles or wine or spare knickers, and none of that mattered.

I throw my bag on to the sofa. It still looks too bulky, even without my overnight kit. I pull out a packet of sequined butterfly postcards and there, bundled up at the bottom, lies a monkey called Kilty.

"Robert?" I say to his answerphone. "I'm so sorry, Finn's monkey was in my bag all the time. I'll drop him off, or you can come over and pick him up." I must be reasonably child-friendly if I refer to a soft toy as "him" and not "it".

It's ridiculous, of course, to suspect that Robert asked me to come to Butterfly Land to make Verity jealous. And the bedside candles — they're probably there all the time. Candles are relaxing. Sometimes I light one — lavender-scented, for its soothing properties at the end of a Toby Nichols day. Candles don't mean "I want us to go to bed."

Robert will be bathing his sons now, or reading *The Cat in the Hat*, too busy being a good dad to pick up the phone.

CHAPTER
THIRTEEN

Here Boy

Diane tried to burn George. She removed the back of a photo frame, pulled out the picture and snipped it in two with her pinking shears. She put her gold lighter to the George half and waited for him to go up in smoke, but he refused to burn. He beamed at her, in that sly, lazy way of his, and she grew madder, convinced she could hear his mocking laugh. The photo crinkled and blackened at the edges, but you could still see his face. Diane ended up flinging George into the bin.

"She must have been really mad," I say.

Midge hurries along beside me, relating the story. "She *is* mad," she declares. "She's not like other mums."

"What are other mums like?"

"Normal. Nice. Like you."

The girls have started to call for me on my Paul Street days so we can walk together. I assume this is at Midge's instigation because, as we near school, Jojo starts to lag slightly behind us, presumably to avoid being spotted associating with a teacher.

She's wearing a love-heart badge on her coat. It came free with her favourite comic, *Fairy World*. The

153

badge has a jagged cut down the middle and can be worn open or closed. When I asked her about it she explained, "You wear it just above your heart. Closed if you're in love, open if you're single." At Jojo's age the concept of being in love or single hadn't entered my brain. Apart from my music, I was interested only in ferreting in Dad's study and pretending to drive the old Beetle. Dad once told Mr Bazrai, his friend from the allotment, that I was a late developer, and they both snorted into a tray of tomato plants.

By the time my first lesson starts Jojo has transferred the love-heart badge from her coat to her sweatshirt. She has taken Laura's place in the group. The badge has been snapped shut, into its "in love" position. She keeps glancing at Toby, who has barely spoken today. Whenever he looks at her, she dips her head and her cheeks turn feverishly pink. I can smell apple bubble gum, but don't mention it. I'm determined to make things better between Toby and me.

Jojo plays the simple piece we've been practising, and afterwards Willow says, "You're so good, Jojo. I can't play like that and I've done it for ages."

"Can you believe," I say, "that until three months ago, Jojo had never picked up a flute?"

Jojo prises a drawing-pin from the sole of her shoe. I wish I hadn't said that. No one knows I teach her at home, or that the flute she's clutching is mine. I don't want to be accused of favouritism. "Toby," I say, "do you think you and Jojo could play a duet? I've got some pieces here . . ."

154

I flick through the pile of music, and when I look up he's staring out at the skidding clouds, his eyes blazing.

He has always been my top pupil, a reluctant star. And he knows that's all over.

Christmas cards have started to arrive. I place them on the bookshelf in the spaces between Midge's weapons of mass destruction and an invitation to Jen and Simon's Christmas do. It came by post, even though Jen and I see each other several times a week. On the front is a picture of them — Jen and her husband Simon — in a circle of feathers and twigs. Empty-nest syndrome. Elliot started university in September but she's still conscious of the space he left. "I'm still waiting," she said, over drinks at the Anchor, "for it to feel normal."

Jen had her baby shortly after leaving school. She and Simon lived with her parents while she studied for her degree. Everyone said it wouldn't last. Eighteen years later, Jen and Simon are sending out beautifully hand-made invitations that read, "Come Fly With Us".

The last week of term passes in a blur of carol concerts, church services and the Christmas concert at St Mary's. The year-six boys writhe on their front row chairs, trying to peek up Hilary Bullock's skirt as she plays her cello. As the orchestra skids through the Bach piece I fear it's all going to unravel, like loose knitting. The kids battle onwards, careering towards a chaotic climax, and the mums and dads — the dutiful parents who show up at every school-related event — are clapping and dabbing faces on tissues and sleeves.

Each day of the final week I come home laden with cards and presents: a candle decorated with pansies, a mouse-shaped pumice, cheap bubble bath with a leaky stopper and a pen that lights up and plays "Greensleeves". Toby Nichols gives me heady gusts of Lemon Hubba Bubba as he skids past me, giddy with freedom.

Jen and a cluster of Paul Street teachers have drifted down to the Anchor for drinks. I slip off to town to avoid the inevitable "What are you doing for Christmas, Stella?", which leads seamlessly into "Going to your dad's? How is he these days? Still doing that . . . *thing* on *Friday Zoo*?"

Earlier this week, I'd wandered into the staff room with my coffee and flapjack from the baker's. Stephen, the deputy head, looked up from his copy of *Q* magazine and said, "Hey, Stella, how's your father?" Everyone laughed. I forced myself to join in, until Stephen shifted uncomfortably in his seat and turned back to his magazine.

In the town centre people are surging into pubs in their party clothes and tinsel tiaras. I wander through the quieter back-streets, looking for presents. Charlie and I have a hazy plan to spend Christmas Day together. He, like Dad, is impossible to buy for. Doesn't care about clothes, never reads novels or spruces up his house. You wouldn't, for instance, buy him a cushion.

In Grieves and Aitken I buy a book of duets for Jojo and Toby to play in the new term. "Met a friend of yours," Mr Grieves says. "Young girl — your next-door neighbour."

"That's Jojo. Her playing's amazing. I've never met anyone who's picked it up so easily."

Mr Grieves chuckles. His moustache is white now, like the fuzz of hair above each ear. "She's certainly keen. Came in with her mother, persuaded her to buy lots of music, quite advanced pieces — they had a squabble, actually. Made some deal about the girl promising to keep her room tidy."

"I'm surprised Diane gave in."

"You know, Stella," Mr Grieves adds, "that girl reminded me of you, when you used to come in here with your mother." He catches himself, touches his moustache.

"I remember that too," I say.

The sign next to Grieves and Aitken still says "Dino's" even though the café is long gone. Thin white paint has been swirled over its windows. At the far end of Bay Street there is a new shop called Feathers 'n' Fur. There's no sign of it being open — no lights on, no one inside — but the door pushes open. I am greeted by the low mumble of a radio in a back room, and the faint odour of rodents' bedding, reminding me of Diane's kitchen.

Towards the back of the shop fish tanks glow with eerie pale blue lights. An olive-skinned man is transferring fish from a black bucket into a tank with the aid of a miniature net. "Looking for something?" he asks.

"Yes — a present. Something for a dog who's quite . . . excitable."

He places the net across the bucket and ambles to the front of the shop. "Gift set?" he suggests, indicating a shelf of wicker baskets containing dog chews and rubber hedgehogs. Below the baskets are packets of pigs' ears and a wonkily written cardboard sign, which reads, "Delicious Treats For Your Dog. Eat Whole Or Cut Into Strips For Smaller Dogs."

"I'd like something," I explain, "to help to train him. His behaviour's quite . . . challenging." I could be talking about Toby Nichols. I wonder how he'd respond to a Good Doggie Gift Set.

"You want a training whistle," the man says. He rummages on a shelf and hands me a slender gold object, its cap attached to the main whistle part by a gilt chain.

"Do they work?"

"I don't sell anything that doesn't work," he retorts, plucking a leaflet from the box:

HEREBOY DOG WHISTLE

* Adjustable frequency
* Tune according to your dog's hearing
* Ideal for close or distant work
* Our products have been used with a wide range

of animals including dolphins, killer whales and giraffes.

Hereboy whistles: bringing dogs to heel since 1936.

I put the whistle to my lips and blow, but of course there's no sound. The door dings open, and a voice says, "Stella Moon, don't tell me you've bought yourself a dog."

Between the woollen hat and bunched-up scarf I see Alex's face, and Alex's smile. "It's you," I say, stupidly.

He smiles, and I try not to smile back, but can't keep it down. I'm horribly conscious of my blinking and breathing. "Good to see you," he says.

"You too." There's an awkward pause. I feel a pang of sadness.

"You're buying a whistle?" he says.

"For Dad's dog. Remember Surf, the mad one, who was always getting injured?"

"So he's still crazy." I don't know if he means Surf, or Dad.

I pay the shop man, and he slips the whistle into a waxy bag. "Use it wisely," he says. "You need to show him who's boss."

"I'll do that," I say, feeling Alex's eyes on me. He's standing very close, as if he's waiting for me and we're going somewhere together. "Coming for a drink?" he asks.

"Okay. Just a quick one."

"Be firm, love," the shop man adds. "Don't stand for any nonsense." He strides away to attend to the bucket of fish at the back of the shop.

Alex follows me out. "What are you doing for Christmas?" he asks. All that time we spent together, and we fill our small silences by asking about Christmas.

"Probably spend it with Charlie. I haven't decided."

"Me neither."

Our pale breath fills the space between us. "What were you in the pet shop for?" I ask.

"You," he says.

Alex sets our drinks on the table in the darkest corner of the Mariner Bar. "So," I ask, "are you working these days?"

"Not at the moment, but I had an . . . unusual job towards the end of last summer."

"What were you doing?"

"Ever seen a crop circle?" he asks, settling into the opposite chair.

"In pictures, yes. Something to do with ley lines or aliens." I think of Midge and her antennaed umbrella.

"I met a guy who needed help on his farm over in Somerset. The previous year he'd made three times as much from crop circles as he did from farming."

"How?"

"Believe it or not, people pay to tramp round them with their dowsing sticks, all that hippie mumbo-jumbo . . ."

"You were interested in dowsing," I remind him. "You went all summer-solsticey and did that aura-reading course."

He touches my hand and says, "I've done lots of stupid things."

I look down at his arm. It's fuzzed with fine golden hair. I'm itching to ask about that girl, the one he replaced me with. "Nothing special," he said on the phone. I want to know her name, age, occupation, favourite perfume, whether she's the type to plough into the sea or prefers to arrange herself in an aesthetically pleasing position on a beach towel. Whether she was the girl with outrageous legs in the antiques market. Questions flit round my head like tiny darting fish.

"Alex, are you still seeing that girl?"

"I told you, that was nothing. I'm not really looking." I try not to seem pleased. He studies me, narrowing his eyes. The pub's filling up now. A cluster of friends or maybe work colleagues is presenting a birthday girl with novelty gifts: handcuffs with pink fur attached, chattering false teeth. There are bursts of high-pitched laughter.

"How did you help with the crop circles?" I ask.

"I made them," Alex says.

"You mean you *faked* them?"

"Sure. If you look at a genuine crop circle — if there is such a thing — the corn's flattened in the same direction as if it's been blown down or rolled on. It's not difficult to —"

Laughter bubbles inside me. "I can't believe you did that."

"Why not?"

"It's just so, so . . . you."

He gazes at me quizzically. "You should come with me next summer. We could do with the extra help."

I snort into my glass. "What?" he says, laughing too. He looks like the Alex I first met, trying to windsurf off the back beach, lurching from one project to the next, just to see what would happen. It frustrated me, eventually — the way he filled our home with barely touched guitars and fishing tackle. But it had been the reason I'd loved him. His keenness to try everything. The very opposite of me.

"I don't think I'm cut out to be a crop-circle faker," I say, draining my glass.

"That's a pity. Another drink, Stella?"

"No, I'd better get home."

Without thinking, I bend to kiss his cheek. I can feel him watching me as I head for the door. "Don't forget this," he calls after me.

He stands up, squeezes through the birthday girl's party and hands me the bag bearing the Feathers 'n' Fur logo.

"Thanks."

"Call me, if you want to."

"Okay."

The smile surges across his face like a wave. "Or," he says, "you could whistle."

CHAPTER
FOURTEEN

Turkey Mousse

This recipe is ideal for using up leftover turkey. Dissolve 2 oz packet aspic powder in 1 pint chicken stock. Add 8 oz cooked turkey, 1 tbsp tomato purée, 8 fl oz double cream and a generous splash of brandy. Liquidise — do you own a liquidiser, Stella? — and pour into a fancy mould. When set, garnish with satsuma segments.

Dad's on the phone, sensing that I've filed his recipe for future non-use. I figured out a long time ago why he sends them. He needs to remind me of who he was, who he *is* — that he knows things I haven't the faintest chance of getting my head round. "Any plans for Christmas?" he barks into the phone. No pleasantries. No "How are you, Stella? How's your hand?"

Surf is growling fretfully in the background. I'm about to launch into a detailed run-down of the many glittering events to which I've been invited (my sole invitation, to Jen's Come Fly With Us party, eyes me from the bookshelf) when Dad continues, "We have a problem here, Stella. Blasted radiator in the big bedroom. Fell off the wall, can you believe it? Water

163

pouring through the living-room ceiling. Plumber's in, and we're being replastered . . ."

"Dad, that's terrible."

"We're staying at Harry's so I'll have to be quick." Dad regards phone calls as an outrageously expensive indulgence. When Maggie calls I often hear him in the background, muttering at her to get off the phone.

"What will you do for Christmas?" I ask.

"That's the issue. Harry's expecting a houseful, and Charlie can't help us — he's booked a last-minute holiday with some woman."

I assume he means beach-hut Phoebe. Charlie hasn't mentioned anything about going away. "You're welcome to come here," I say.

"Can you accommodate dogs?" he asks, as if I'm a hotel.

"Of course, it's no problem."

"We'll go home on Christmas Eve. Ceiling should be fixed by then. We don't want to intrude."

"Dad, you might as well spend Christmas Day here."

He sighs, as if I've forced the situation upon him. "Don't go buying me presents," he adds. "You know there's nothing I need. That barometer still said stormy last time I looked, and we've had clear skies all week."

"What I want for Christmas," Midge announces, "is a gun with real pellets — *pew! Pew!*" She extends two fingers, aiming at Jojo, who's a few bars into Schumann's "Traumerei".

"Shush, Midge," I hiss at her.

164

"Or a crossbow," she rattles on, "or one of them things that pings boulders at baddies, like in the olden days . . ." She turns back to her work in progress: several cardboard tubes swathed in tin foil, which she intends to strap to her body with a pair of tights and use as a portable torpedo-shooter. She'll blast people like Toby, who called Jojo "Piggy" in the dinner queue. "Or a bike," she adds. "I've always wanted a bike."

Jojo stops playing abruptly. "Midge," I say, "you'll have to keep quiet while Jojo's having her lesson."

She dumps the torpedo-shooter on the table and stomps upstairs. I hear the bathroom door creak, and the slosh of water as she fills the basin. "What happens," Jojo asks, "when you need your flute back?"

"Perhaps your mum could treat you to one. I'd hate to think of you having to give up."

"How much are flutes? More than twenty-five pounds?"

"They're a lot of money. At least, good ones are. I won't need mine back for ages."

"Mum says Santa's only bringing us one Christmas present each," Jojo says firmly.

I'm surprised that, at ten years old, she still believes in Santa. She adjusts her alice band, which is covered with silver beads, like cake decorations. Midge is padding around on the landing now. I need to speak to Diane — explain that these are real lessons, and I can't have Midge chatting incessantly, demanding tin foil and poking around in my house. "I want a dressing-table," Jojo continues, "with lights round the mirror like what film stars have."

"I'm sure you'll get lovely things." Midge is directly above us now, creeping around in my bedroom. Diane has gone out. She said she'd be home by the end of the lesson, but how long does she think lessons go on? It's eight thirty. They've been here for two hours. A rhythmic thudding is coming from my bedroom.

I hurtle upstairs and into my bedroom where Midge is bouncing on the bed, her pale hair flying. Pink and brown warpaint is smeared all over her face. "I'm a Red Indian!" she squawks, then catches the horror on my face. She staggers off the bed and lands in a ragged heap on the floor.

It's not warpaint. It's eye-shadow and lipstick. Mum's quilted bag lies on my pillow, its contents scattered all over the bed. I try to speak but my mouth is stuck, frozen open. It's her make-up, Mum's make-up. The lipstick and eye-shadow she used to wear, which I took with me when I left home, without telling Dad.

Midge stares up at me from the floor. "I'm sorry," she whispers. She says it over and over, wanting me to tell her it's okay — that some ancient, half-used make-up doesn't matter. *Sorry, sorry, sorry.* I stare at her, watching her mouth form the words. "I didn't mean it," she adds desperately.

Something snaps inside me. "How *dare* you? Did you go through my drawers, Midge? Get out of my room, do you hear me?"

She stumbles to her feet, crying now. The lipstick and kohl are lidless on the bed. I can smell Jean Patou

166

perfume. Loose powder has been scattered like finest sand on my duvet and pillowcase.

Jojo sniffs loudly behind me. Midge mumbles something, which doesn't quite make it out of her mouth.

"What?" I yell at her.

"It was a joke. I wanted to make myself look funny so you'd laugh. I just wanted you to laugh."

I snatch the frosted-pink lipstick from the bed. It's mashed, ruined. Midge makes a lame attempt to brush mud from the duvet.

"Just leave it, Midge." I hate it that my voice wobbles, that tears are spilling down my cheeks in front of a seven-year-old kid who knows nothing. It's only a bag, after all. Only make-up. Midge tries for a hug, winding her thin arms round me, but I shake her off. On the back of her hand is a skull and crossbones drawn with the kohl pencil.

"I'll tell Mum what you've done," Jojo announces. "She'll kill you, Midge. Stella's our *friend*."

They clatter downstairs after me, and by the time we're in the hall Midge's sobs have turned into hiccups. "You won't like me any more," she says, struggling into the pea-green raincoat, which is too small for her now. Its sleeves finish above her wrists.

Diane is clanking about in her house. She didn't come to collect them as soon as she arrived home; clearly, she was hoping to wangle the maximum amount of free childcare. "Don't forget the flute," I remind Jojo, "and the duets book. Make sure you keep practising over the Christmas holidays."

"Okay," she says warily.

"Because I thought we'd take a break from lessons," I continue, not liking the brittleness that has crept into my voice.

"Why?" Jojo asks. Her face is pale, moon-like, in the shadowy hall.

"My dad's coming to stay for a few days. I'll be really busy."

"Oh," she says softly.

Midge's upper lip is damp and sore-looking. "She's your favourite," she whispers.

"Don't be silly. Of course she's not."

"I'm sorry about your make-up."

I hold open the door and say, "It wasn't mine."

I don't bother with make-up for Jen's party. I just shower, pull on jeans and an ancient black sweater. I find high-heeled boots that I've hardly worn — heels make me feel ungainly, like a kid in her mother's footwear — and tie back my hair in a ponytail. I called Charlie several times to ask if he'd come with me, but no one answered. Looks like he's already gone on that last-minute holiday.

Outside the air feels like a cold drink in my throat. I walk briskly down Briar Hill towards the new houses by the marina where Jen and Simon live. A smart-looking couple with a carrier bag of clinking bottles is marching towards the house; I realise I've forgotten to bring wine.

I step into the heat and the noise and say hello to the teachers from Paul Street, Jen's friends from college, and a scattering of schoolfriends with whom I meet up occasionally. Some of the women are dancing already, clacking on the polished floor. Jen's Christmas tree is, as ever, colour-co-ordinated: a voluptuous pine adorned with silver and purple baubles.

The back garden is strung with fairy-lights shaped like miniature lanterns. "Hi, I'm Lionel," a man says, offering me a deep-red drink I didn't ask for. It looks like watered-down blood.

"Stella," I say, and take a sip: it's spicy and citrussy, laced with cloves and maybe Cointreau.

"I'm in oil," Lionel says. "Food-importing. Supply oils to restaurants and the baking industry."

"Oh," I say, suddenly wanting to escape from Lionel and his potted CV.

"And you?" he prompts me.

"I'm a teacher." He nods, awaiting more information. "Music," I add. Donna Summer is playing "Hot Love".

"Classical music?" Lionel asks.

"Yes, mostly."

"More of a rock man myself. AC DC, Hawkwind, Marillion." He grins, exposing large, protruding teeth.

Simon's colleagues from the architectural practice have gathered round the barbecue where Simon is grappling sausages with an outsized pair of tongs.

"So if you're after a particular oil," Lionel continues, "I can source it for you, Stella, because I travel the world, looking for . . ."

Elliot, Jen's grown-up son, is introducing his new girlfriend, Ruby, to his parents' friends. Her narrow, widely spaced eyes give her a serene look. She is wearing a slippery red dress, and is so lovely I have to force myself not to stare. I focus on the hairs between Lionel's eyebrows.

". . . not forgetting walnut and sesame oils," he goes on, excitedly. He delves into a jacket pocket and hands me a card: Lionel Rashley, Food Importer.

"I'll be in touch," I say, "if I ever need oil."

"You do that," he says.

The architects are trying not to gawp at Ruby. "Meet Mum's friend Stella," Elliot says. "She's an incredible flute player." He sloshes more red liquid into my glass from a jug. He tours the decked area of the garden, offering crudités and bowls of pale beige dip — the colour I imagine Dad's turkey mousse would turn out — as if he's just returned from a crash course in manners.

"I love your dress," I tell Ruby. I must be the only person out here who's thinking, Poor girl must be freezing.

As she can't really comment on my black sweater, she says, "I didn't know what to wear. I was so nervous about this — I've never met Elliot's parents before."

"They're really scary," I say, and she giggles.

Two of the architects wander over and say, "Hi, girls," as if Ruby and I might be of the same species.

"So, Stella," Lionel asks, "which of these lucky men is your husband?" The architects look uncomfortable, although thankfully not aghast.

"My husband's at home," I tell him. "He doesn't like parties."

"Off the leash, then?" he says suggestively. "Bit parky out here, isn't it? Shall we go inside? Have a boogie?" He places a hand on my waist and tries to steer me into the house, as if I am incapable of manoeuvring my own body. I look around for Jen, Simon, anyone. The night air feels dry in my throat.

"I'm just talking to Ruby," I say, then realise she's gone, and the architects have gone, and it's just me and Lionel, whose flattened hand is pressing into the small of my back.

"I'm sure I know you," he says.

Jen appears with her hair all undone and pulls me into the house. "New neighbour," she hisses. "Bloody creep. Are you going to dance or what?"

"Maybe later." My sweater feels heavy and itchy. I can't take it off because, stupidly, I didn't put on anything underneath. I wish I was wearing lipstick; I might feel more here, more party-spirited. I keep trying to edge into conversations, but when someone says, "I hear you and Alex aren't . . ." all I can manage to say is, "No." And they shift uncomfortably, pick at a plate of rolled-up slivers of smoked salmon and ask, "So are you . . . okay?" as if I look faintly ill, or might still be grieving.

I glimpse my unadorned face in the mirror above the fireplace. I look as if I've wandered in here by accident. Despite being a rock man, Lionel is making flamboyant moves to Sister Sledge. Debbie, a girl Jen and I went to school with — who stole my Snoopy pencil case, if I remember rightly — weaves unsteadily towards me and retorts, "Nice of you to dress up, Stella."

"It's my best jumper," I tell her.

"You look hot."

"Thanks." I tip the rest of my drink down my throat. I have a sudden urge to drink more, to be just the right side of drunk. An image of Mum's powder scattered over my pillow drifts into my head.

"Only teasing," Debbie says. "Come and sit with us, if you're all by yourself."

"She's *dancing*," cuts in Lionel, tugging my hand.

I'm beginning to place him. Father of a girl I taught briefly, until the flute was sold and the child bought the rollerblades she'd really wanted.

I try to dance but my arms and legs feel like new body parts I'm breaking in. The boots are constricting my feet. Lionel has decided that dancing together has to mean holding hands. "Aren't you Blair's dad?" I ask, pulling away from him. "I used to teach her, remember? You'd come to pick her up. Or sometimes your wife did."

He laughs falsely, then turns away and gyrates, less enthusiastically now, to "We Are Family".

I step out into the small front garden where Elliot and Ruby are kissing. His hands are moving all over her long, smooth hair. She's wearing teetering heels, but still has to rise on tiptoe to reach his lips. They don't notice me slipping out through the gate.

The main lights have been switched off in the Anchor. In the darkened lounge a fibreoptic tree changes eerily from yellow to blue. A young couple totters back from the end of the jetty. The girl walks crookedly, as if one of her heels has come loose and is likely to snap off, or maybe she's drunk. They climb into a waiting cab, clutching each other and laughing. Maybe they came here by taxi just to walk to the end of the jetty and back. It's the kind of thing new couples do, before they start squabbling over paint colours.

I pull off my boots, roll up my jeans and jump down to the sand. It feels cold and damp, gradually becoming mushy and squelching between my toes. I step into the sea, and it's so bitingly cold I can't feel it. Reflections of blue-white streetlights tremble on its surface.

I wade further out with my jeans pulled up to my knees. If Charlie were here we might dare each other to strip off to our underwear, pile our clothes on to one of the rowing-boats, and swim. We've done it before in the middle of winter: plunged in and raced each other until it wasn't cold any more.

The figure who's striding along the jetty looks a bit like Charlie. But he's in the Canaries, Dad reckons, where plunging into the sea in December is no trouble at all. And this man is more powerfully put together: broad-shouldered with long, striding legs.

At first I think he's wearing a wetsuit but when I wade closer I can see it's just trunks. He reaches the end of the jetty, pushes hair away from his face and stands at the edge, as if he's waiting for something. The right moment.

He stands tall and raises his arms. I still can't make out his face. I wade closer, soft sand giving way with each step. There are no stars, just a slice of pale yellow

173

moon, and small transparent clouds smudged over the blackness.

It's Ed, I recognise him now. Ed, the man with the soft Scottish accent at the doctor's. If he sees me, he doesn't show it. I will him to look down, to focus on my face. I want to call out, "I'm Stella, remember me?" but I'm frozen in shyness.

He raises his heels, like Ruby reaching up for her kiss, then pushes up further with his arms, tensing his entire body. He is beautiful — graceful yet strong. I stand very still, and realise I'm holding my breath. Ed springs up and falls, cutting into the sea like a spear.

He comes up further out than I'd expected. I wait for him to swim back to the beach but he heads round the jetty and out of sight. I want to run out of the sea and along the front and wait for him. But he'll think I'm drunk or crazy.

I wade back to the beach, perch on the edge of an overturned boat, and pull down my sweater to dry my chilled feet. I manage to blot away most of the water, but can't wipe the smile off my face.

It's gone one a.m. by the time I'm home. Midge's torpedo shooter still lies on the table. I file Dad's turkey mousse recipe in the Mexican box. Upstairs, I try to de-Midge my bedroom. The eye-shadow compact is too crumbled to rescue. The kohl is flattened but I replace its lid anyway. I try to mould the lipstick back into shape with my finger but all that's left is a small mound of shimmery pink.

The Jean Patou bottle lies on the floor with its stopper off. A tiny puddle of perfume fills a dent in the floorboard. I stuff Mum's things back into the quilted bag, zip it up firmly and slip it into the drawer. The loose powder has left a creamy smudge on my pillow.

I open the window to let out her perfume, then strip off and try to sleep. My feet are sandy — I've forgotten to wash them. There's grit in my bed.

Some time later I'm woken by gusts of cold air from the window, or maybe the smell of Mum. I can see the two of us eating sorbet in Dino's. She's reminding me to use the paper napkin to wipe my mouth. "Good girl," she says.

I slide back into sleep, breathing her in. Then it's not her but him: the diver, falling in a sleek curve. I've never learned to dive. We were forced to try during school swimming lessons. The diving boards scared me so much I was sick into the drain in the shower area.

I'm doing it now: standing tall at the end of the jetty. Springing up, like a cat pouncing. My fingers and arms, then the rest of me — so fast I can't separate the parts — shoot into the deep. It feels so right, like those distant days before Mum died, when the world was perfect as long as the lady in the old-fashioned chemist could produce the right shade of lipstick from her secret drawer.

CHAPTER
FIFTEEN

Hiding From Children

Maggie and Surf tumble out of the car as if relieved to escape from Dad's ill-humour and cigar fumes in the confined environment of an ageing Lada. Since his move to Cornwall Dad has conducted casual, rather grudging relationships with a series of decrepit Eastern European vehicles. It's more than twenty years since he drove the Citroën, which rose up like a hovercraft, as if preparing itself to brave the sea.

Surf lollops into my house and bounds upstairs, lashing his woolly tail. Turf settles beneath the shelf in the hall, looking like a hairy sweater. "Still all white, I see," Dad says, peering into my living room.

"I'm not planning to change it," I say.

"Oh. Last time we came I assumed it was an undercoat."

"Well," Maggie says, "I think your house is lovely."

"So do I," I mutter, as I carry their threadbare tartan bags up to my room where they'll be sleeping. On the landing — which is also white — ghosts of other colours show through the paint. Alex kept urging me to agree to bright yellow or green; he bought Matchpots to splash on to the walls and demonstrate how great they'd look. The roughly painted squares jarred my eyes every time I walked past them. One Sunday afternoon, while he had his guitar lesson across town, I whited everything over.

"You mustn't give up your room for us," Maggie protests, following me into my bedroom. She has immaculate pearly fingernails, and her shoulder-length auburn hair is set in springy waves. I wonder how she maintains such a high standard of grooming, living at Silverdawn Cottage.

"It's no trouble," I tell her. "Just make yourselves at home." I have changed my bed and left the window open for the past three days but Jean Patou still lingers, like faint breath. I wonder if Dad will notice, and start remembering.

"What about the dogs?" he asks, huffing up the stairs. "Surf gets anxious away from home. He likes to know where he is." The dog has jumped on to my bed and is nuzzling into the pillows.

"Surf!" Maggie cries. "Off Stella's bed immediately." He shifts his head to the other end of the pillow, leaving a spillage of drool.

"They can sleep up here with you," I say, "if they'd be happier."

"That's probably best," Dad says, tossing his jacket on to the bed.

"It's good of Stella to have us," Maggie says, "isn't it, Frankie?"

Dad glances around my bedroom, as if checking that the amenities match the high standard to which he's accustomed at home. An oily dog smell has mingled with Mum's perfume. "Don't understand why you didn't sell up when that boyfriend moved out," he says. "Could have got yourself a nice little flat."

To avoid feeling pressurised to cook one of his recipes, I take Dad and Maggie out for dinner. We leave Surf barking urgently at the living-room window, smearing the glass with saliva, and Turf dozing under the table.

Maggie clutches Dad's arm, as if afraid that she'll topple down the hill in her dainty heels. Windows are decorated with fake snow and tufts of cotton wool. I wouldn't have bothered with a Christmas tree but Midge pleaded, "Please, Stella, it'll look so sad in here without one. You *must* have a tree."

I bought a small pine from Ripley's garden centre and dressed it with white lights and frosted silver baubles. It still wasn't right. "Not sparkly enough," Jojo complained. "Christmas trees shouldn't be green. And you don't even have a fairy."

The restaurant is called Coq au Vin. Its tables are festooned with too many glasses, pink napkins folded into elaborate fans and glass dishes filled with corrugated curls of butter. I have never eaten here, but imagined it might be Dad's sort of place: pretentiously ornate, with perfectly enjoyable food messed up with too many sauces and garnishes. The woman who shows us to our table has mauve shadows beneath her eyes. She looks exhausted from the effort of making everything so fancy.

Our table is jammed too close to the window. I feel conscious of my elbows and knees. "I'm sorry," the woman says — I'm hoping she'll say, "I'm sorry, but the cooker's broken, you'll have to eat somewhere else," but she explains, "The veal's off, and I only have one portion of langoustine."

"That's quite all right," Maggie says.

The woman hands us enormous laminated menus and disappears into the kitchen. The place smells fishy, and not in a good way. The menu lurches in and out of French like someone who's beginning to learn the language but keeps losing confidence and tripping over their tongue. There's a *terrine de* duck, pork fillets served with *pommes au gratin*, and *chateaubriand de boeuf* accompanied by a *julienne de* vegetables.

"What's a *julienne*?" I ask Dad, knowing that this will delight him.

"Ah," he says, and I faze off and watch what looks like an office party tumble past the window. There's an abundance of Santa hats with flashing lights strung round their brims.

"Because a meal's appearance," Dad rambles on, "is just as important as the taste, and so with your classic *julienne*, you're talking a mixture of colours — carrots, beans, maybe some celery, all cut into very fine strips . . ."

Dad's lemon sole is accessorised with a salad comprising limp leaves and tomatoes, which look as though they've been cut with pinking shears. Maggie tucks into *legumes au gratin*, which seemed the closest thing on offer to a vegetable casserole. My pasta slips down my throat to form a gloopy lake in my stomach. "How's *Friday Zoo*?" I ask, then regret it as Dad proceeds to enthuse about the show's rising ratings and the positive feedback he's received from the production crew and viewers.

"If I say so myself," he says, "I'm coming across very well to a new, younger audience."

"Are they renewing your contract?"

"That's not finalised, but it's looking good. I'm hoping, of course, for a show of my own."

"I'm sure it'll happen, Dad."

"Of course it will," Maggie says firmly, patting his hand.

No one else comes into the restaurant. The woman keeps emerging from the kitchen to replenish our glasses. Dad fills the room with the sound of enthusiastic chewing. I wonder what Surf's doing to my house — whether he's gnawed the cushions, or done his business on the rug. "He has the occasional accident when he's overexcited," Maggie warned me.

Although we haven't ordered dessert, the woman appears with a large silver platter piled high with profiteroles. They're filled with something yellow and squidgy, like the kind of paint that offers excellent coverage with only one coat. The chef marches out of the kitchen and says, "Everything fine for you?" I thought he'd be French, but he has a South London accent.

"Excellent, thank you," Dad says.

"I knew it," the chef announces. "Heard your voice, thought, No — it can't be."

Dad beams at him. The chef has trembling cheeks and a mass of wild black hair, which bushes out from under his hat. "You're the one," he continues, "who got me into this game, all them years ago."

"Well," Dad says, "I'm honoured to hear that."

Maggie gazes at him proudly. Dad lights up a Café Crème. I noticed a line at the bottom of the menu: "No Cigar Smoking Please." Perhaps Café Crèmes don't count as cigars, or the rule doesn't apply to someone as important as Dad. He could probably set his hair on fire and no one would ask him to leave.

The chef rests a ham-coloured hand on Dad's shoulder. Pale smoke hazes the space above our heads. It's the sweet, woody smell that filled the Citroën and Dad's study. The smell of TV Frankie, who's glowing now as he and the chef discuss the finer points of choux pastry, just like it's 1979.

Robert phones as I'm tipping the remains of Dad's boiled egg into the kitchen bin. "Stella?" he says, sounding anxious.

"Robert, what's wrong?"

"They're getting a place together," he blurts out. "One of those new flats by the marina. He'll be living with my children, and there isn't a damn thing I can do about it."

"Stella?" Dad booms from the living room. "Stella, there's a —"

"That's awful," I manage, trying to blot out Dad's voice.

"One good thing," Robert adds, sniggering bitterly, "is that the Twit — her boyfriend — was mugged in Barcelona. Some guy ripped off his moneybelt. My wife's moving in with the kind of man who wears a *moneybelt*, for Chrissakes."

"Stella!" Dad shouts. Surf hurtles into the kitchen, as if he had been sent to fetch me.

"Who's that?" Robert asks.

"Just my dad, he —"

"Verity wants to formalise things," he cuts in, sounding calmer now. "See a solicitor, make arrangements. She wants custody, as if I'm not a good enough father —"

"But you're a wonderful —"

Dad looms in the kitchen doorway, a fragment of egg white stuck to his lip. "Stella," he snaps, "there's a child playing around on your property. What does it want?"

"Let's speak soon," I tell Robert.

"Thanks," he says. "It's good to talk to someone who's not — you know — a mother. You're not biased."

I hurry through to the living room where Midge's face is pressed against the window like malleable plastic. "Can I come in and play?" she shouts through the glass.

"Who *is* it?" Dad blusters behind me.

I let her in. She looks tiny, standing there gawping at Dad. Her antennaed headband bounces lamely. Dad has shrunk back into the chair, as if afraid of contamination from this small person with blackcurrant-lolly-stained lips. "Midge," I say, "this is Frankie, my dad. Midge is my friend from next door."

"Hiya," she says nonchalantly, rummaging in her jeans pocket. She fishes out a length of hairy green string on to which she's threaded green Chewy Jewels.

"I made you this," she says, "because you lost the other one. This one's emeralds."

"It's lovely, thank you." I slip on the bracelet, which is warm and clammy from being in her pocket.

"Don't eat it," she warns me, "even if you get really hungry."

"I promise."

Maggie comes down from her shower swathed in a velour dressing gown. "Hello, dear," she says, peering down at Midge.

"Are you Stella's mum?" Midge asks brightly.

"No," I say quickly, "Maggie's my dad's . . . partner."

Midge screws up her nose, trying to make sense of the word. "Can I finish my model?" she asks, meaning the torpedo-shooter.

"Not now, Midge. Come round some other time."

"You want me to go?"

"We're a bit busy . . ."

Dad stares at the living-room door, as if willing her to vanish through it. "When are they going home?" she asks loudly.

"We're not sure exactly. Soon after Christmas."

Midge ambles into the hall and mutters, "You're still mad at me for spoiling your makeup."

"No, I'm not. That's all forgotten."

She gnaws a grubby fingernail. "I can tell you're mad. You're different."

"I'm just the same, Midge," I say, but we both know I'm lying.

★   ★   ★

Dad says it's too wet to go out. Rain seeps into his bones, making them ache; this always happens when he comes back to Devon. Something to do with dirty rain. It's why he left this town: the filth, the noise, the traffic fumes. You'd have thought he was talking about Athens, not a fading seaside town with a groomed bowling-green and Saturday tea-dances at the Ritzy Hotel.

Maggie is immersed in her cross-stitch sampler. "What about the dogs?" I ask. "Won't they need to be walked?"

"Stopped on the way," Dad says.

"That was yesterday," I remind him, but he's turned back to study the newspaper.

By early evening Surf has taken to scraping madly at floorboards by the front door. Dad and Maggie are snoozing in the living room, their snores drifting out like bees' hums. I hook on the dogs' leads, and usher them out.

While Turf ambles lazily, Surf lurches ahead, straining to be free. He's the unruly brother, dismissive of rules and leads and pavements. I climb Briar Hill towards the leafier edge of town, where we used to live. Roads broaden and houses become widely spaced, not with doors opening on to the street but glossed railings and driveways.

Here's Lark Avenue — number fifteen, our old house. So many bits have been added: a porch, a small conservatory, and a double garage where Dad had a compost heap. It looks like someone's gone crazy with Lego.

There's no Slab any more. The old cars were towed away, the concrete smashed up by growling diggers, and the area turned into a landscaped park. Mr Syrup must have made a fortune because suddenly he had a permanent tan and a huge onyx ring.

There are dense shrubs where the Beetle used to be, and a skateboarding area where Lynette and her friends used to hang out and pretend they weren't stealing glances at Charlie. I let the dogs sniff around the wet hedges and call Charlie on my mobile, expecting his answerphone. "Yes?" snaps a real voice.

"I thought you'd gone away."

"Plans changed," he says curtly.

"What happened?"

"Don't want to go in to it." He sounds like a boy, a boy who doesn't want to talk.

"Why didn't you tell me?" Turf is peeing against a fountain made from shards of aqua-coloured glass.

"Should I have?"

"No, of course not. But Dad and Maggie are staying, and if you're going to be on your own . . ."

"I don't want to get roped into this."

"Roped into what?" Surf is sniffing a small mound of chips.

"The big family Christmas."

"It's not a big anything!"

"I can't face it."

"Please, Charlie, you can't be on your own at —"

"It's what you want, isn't it? The happy family, all together at Christmas."

"I just thought, seeing as Dad's here —"

"You want us to be normal."

"No, I don't," I snap, blinking back tears. He's right, of course. For us to be a proper family is all I've ever wanted.

I cook Christmas Eve dinner — my famous mushroom risotto — which Maggie enthuses over and Dad shunts round his bowl as if waiting for it to morph into something more interesting. We're eating at the living room table and trying to ignore Midge, who's brandishing a bat and ball joined by elastic in the drizzly street. "Your bedroom's awfully cold," Dad says. "I've managed to get the window shut, finally."

"You could have asked me," I say.

"And isn't your allergy flaring up, Maggie?"

She shakes her head and says, "It's nothing."

"It's that perfume smell," Dad continues. "Does something to Maggie's sinuses."

"I spilt a bottle," I explain, but Dad has lost interest and is narrowing his eyes at Midge.

"What's that child up to now?" he asks.

"She's not doing any harm, Dad."

Midge is waving and shouting something. Maggie smiles weakly and forks in the last of her risotto. "What?" I mouth through the window.

She pulls out a scrap of paper, a sweet wrapper maybe, from her jeans pocket and hunches on my wall to scribble on it. "Doesn't she bother you?" Dad asks.

"Not really. She's a pretty good kid." I don't add that I've lain on my bed, waiting for their insistent knocking to stop. One evening I peeped out and saw two droopy figures in the street. Jojo glanced up. I'm sure she saw me as I hurried away from the window. Later, when she asked where I'd been, I pretended I'd been napping and not heard them.

"In my day," Dad adds, "children knew discipline. You didn't stand for any nonsense. It's all different now."

"She's not doing anything wrong!"

"You're too soft, that's your trouble. Can't imagine how you keep control of a class."

I march through to the kitchen loaded with plates. In the hall I find a crumpled note that's been pushed through the letterbox. It reads, "*Don't eet the braslet.*"

Next morning we open our presents. Dad and Maggie have given me a set of multi-storey vegetable steamers, which fit on top of a stainless-steel pan. Dad tosses aside the chocolate brown sweater I'd bought him, as if he's examined it in a department store and decided it's not his colour. He turns the dog whistle slowly between his broad fingers. "It's for training Surf," I explain. "The pet shop man said these things never fail."

"They're just a gimmick," he says. "Frankly, I'd say Surf's untrainable."

"Anything's worth a try, dear," Maggie says, fixing on the pearl earrings and necklace I've given her.

Jojo and Midge flood into the room bearing homemade gifts: a photo frame constructed from the kind of polystyrene container that holds chicken portions, and a shoebox with smaller boxes glued inside to form separate compartments. "It's a jewellery box," Midge explains, "to stop you losing your bracelets."

"Thank you," I say, swamped by their hugs.

Jojo pores over the presents I've given her: a story called *Fairy Wishes* — its page corners are perforated to tear off, fill in with your own wishes and place under a pillow — and a book of Debussy sonatas. "Wow, thanks," she gushes.

"Cool!" Midge cries, ripping the paper from her spud gun.

Maggie picks up its discarded box and reads: "'One potato can provide hundreds of pellets.' Did you have one of these, Frankie, when you were a boy?" But Dad has willed himself into sleep, to some other place; a cliff top, perhaps, populated only by untrainable dogs, and no children or spud guns.

Charlie shows up as Dad is loading the tartan bags into the boot of the Lada. They shake hands, like work colleagues at the start of a meeting. Charlie kisses Maggie's cheek, then hugs me and whispers, "She went with somebody else."

Dad is peering into the boot as if at a particularly difficult puzzle. "Who?" I ask.

"Phoebe. So, no holiday." He shrugs, making light of it.

"Oh, Charlie, that's awful."

"Sorry for being such a shit on the phone."

"That's okay." I squeeze his arm.

He crouches to ruffle Surf's belly, sending him into a quivering ball of delight. Turf has already curled up on the back seat like a dense brown cushion. "Well, we'd best get going," Dad says. "I don't like driving in the dark, not these days, with those crazy boy racers . . ."

"Good to see you, Dad," Charlie mutters.

"You too. Thanks for having us, Stella," he adds stiffly. No one mentions that it's dark already — that the streetlights came on two hours ago.

Something pulls inside me, a knot that won't come undone. "Thanks," I say into the moist air, "for the steamers."

"They bought you *ships?*" Charlie whispers.

Dad and Maggie climb into the car. He winds down the driver's-side window and says, "Make sure you have a word with those children."

"I told you, Dad. They're quite sweet really."

"You and Charlie," he continues, "didn't go around bothering neighbours. You were well brought up. You *behaved.*" A loud snort of laughter explodes from my mouth. "What's funny?" Dad asks, frowning.

"You had no idea what we did. You didn't know us."

He turns the key, starts the grumbling engine. His voice wavers as he says, "Of course I knew. I'm your father."

CHAPTER
SIXTEEN

Fireball

Splosh whisky, vodka and Cinzano into a receptacle such as an empty Sodastream bottle. Pour in some fizz — lemonade, cream soda or dandelion and burdock. You might like to add some of the more unusual drinks that have lain untouched in the cabinet for years: Pernod, sloe gin or advocaat. Stealing a little from each bottle is unlikely to arouse suspicion. Shake it, add ice if desired, and drink.

NB The fireball cocktail is best made when there are no adults present.

Charlie and I had tired of delving in the freezer for gâteaux and turned our attention to concocting liquid refreshments. I enjoyed the mixing and shaking — the swirling of colours, the soft *pfff* as we unstoppered the lids — but was less keen on the drinking part. For hours afterwards I'd be conscious of a sourness in my throat. Charlie, however, devoured our cocktails with gusto (the only discernible after-effect was a potent whiff of Wrigley's, which Dad never commented on).

It was a clammy summer's afternoon. We weren't long home from school but already Charlie had slugged enough Fireball to fuel an idea. "Where's Dad?" he asked.

"Still at the allotment, I think." I was lying on the living-room carpet, dabbing my earlobes with wet cotton-wool balls. Cheryl Havers had pierced my ears on the hockey pitch at lunchtime and they still felt scalded.

"Let's go," Charlie said. "See what he gets up to."

"You mean *spy* on him?"

"Come on, it'll be a laugh. We could make weird noises. Spook him out."

"Know where it is?" I asked. It was a childish idea, but anything Charlie wanted to do, I was keen to be part of.

"Of course," he said, grinning. "It's round the back of the old match factory."

By the time we set out, the day was tipping into dusk. Charlie walked purposefully, humming to himself. I was thinking about the small navy blue box I'd found in the desk drawer in Dad's study. I'd opened it, expecting to find nothing more enticing than rubber bands or paperclips. A gold heart-shaped locket nestled inside.

For a moment I thought he'd bought it for me. I shut the box quickly, wishing I'd never seen it and not spoiled my birthday surprise. By the time I'd come downstairs I'd figured that Dad would never buy me anything so special. I felt so stupid, I didn't even mention the locket to Charlie.

191

We headed into town, past the docks and through a small housing estate, its gardens littered with paddling pools containing dregs of murky water. We crept along a damp-smelling alley and gazed up at the fire-escape stairs that zigzagged above us. The alley ended unexpectedly at a small square of parched grass. It looked as if someone's lawn had been stolen from its proper place and hidden there between towering factories.

"Here it is," Charlie announced. The lawn was bordered on one side by a looming brick wall.

"How d'you get in?" I asked.

"Through that little green door. But we're not going in. We're going to spy."

I was fifteen — long and narrow, like a chimney — but still couldn't see over the wall. Charlie crouched down and I clambered on to his shoulders. He straightened up unsteadily. I gripped the top of the wall and peered over.

"Wow," I whispered. I'd imagined neat rows of vegetables being prodded by men in acrylic shirts and fawn-coloured slacks. It hadn't occurred to me that there might be flowers: swathes of clashing yellows and purples, and hydrangeas laden with deep pink globes. Sweetpeas surged across the far wall. There were flowers whose names I didn't know, and sunflowers taller than the neat row of sheds. It was secret and lovely, as if someone had gone wild with different inks. No wonder Dad spent so much time here. He barely used his study any more. He didn't even complain if the paper roll from his adding machine had been

192

unravelled from its spool and left strewn across his desk.

"What is it?" my brother hissed from beneath me.

"It's beautiful, Charlie."

"Can you see him?"

"No, I don't think so." A girl with coppery streaks through her hair was crouching at a neat row of lettuce. Someone was sitting on a bench wearing a bottle-green corduroy jacket like Dad's. It *was* Dad. A woman was resting her head lightly on his shoulder.

"Jesus, Stella, you're killing my back," Charlie whined. "I'll have to put you down."

"Just a minute. There's someone . . ." She had delicate shoulders and was wearing a red-and-white spotted headscarf. Her feet were tucked neatly under the bench. It wasn't Lindy Richards. Lindy was always trying out different perms — from tight curls, like pan-scourers stitched together, to bouffant waves — and wouldn't have been caught dead in a headscarf. Dad had stopped seeing her anyway. He'd even given up going to the Social.

I didn't know this woman. I could only see the back of her: the thin brown arms, and the scarf tied at the nape of her slender neck. Charlie lowered me to the ground. I stood there, trying to find words.

"What is it?" he asked, frowning. He was still chewing spearmint gum to mask the Fireball smell.

"Dad's there," I said quietly. "He's with someone. A woman."

Charlie pulled himself up and peeked over the top of the wall. We walked home slowly, without talking. My earlobes were still leaking where Cheryl's needle had gone through. Charlie didn't seem happily drunk any more — just deflated, as if something had shrivelled inside him.

It was nothing really. Just two people sharing the tail end of the day. But both of us realised that we'd never seen Dad sitting like that — so close, so intimate — with anyone else. "She's probably just a friend," Charlie ventured as we reached the end of our road. "Someone who helps him with weeding and stuff." I knew he was only trying to make us feel better.

"No she's not. He's in love with her, Charlie."

"How can you tell?" He was seventeen, could correctly identify more than thirty species of crab and been offered a place at three universities, yet he knew nothing.

I didn't say what I was thinking: that he had never bought Mum a gold heart-shaped locket. It had been Jean Patou year after year. I rammed my key into the lock. "I just know," I said, thinking, *It's not fair, it's not fair, it's not fair*.

"It's not fair," Midge says, when I won't agree to take her to Aquasplash. "I never get to go swimming." She's tired of firing potato pellets at my kitchen window. The Christmas holidays are stretching too long — for Diane, at least. I've heard her shouting, "For God's sake, get out from under my feet. Go and play — *do* something! Go and see Stella."

"Sorry," I tell Midge, "I just want some time by myself. I'll take you swimming another time."

"Why do grown-ups like being by themselves?"

"I just want to swim, Midge."

"Well, *I* can swim. I've got my own stroke." She rotates her arms, demonstrating a curious crawl/doggy-paddle hybrid.

"I'll give you a knock when I come back. You can come round for a special tea." She screws up her face, as if that couldn't possibly compensate for my meanness. "I'll make jelly," I add.

"Okay," she says grudgingly.

"Raspberry jelly."

"Yeah, all right."

I can't understand how this child of seven, who ruined my mum's makeup — and regularly trashes my house — can activate my guilt mechanism with just one little wrinkle of her upwardly pointing nose.

I stroll out of the changing room, through the showers and into the chlorine-filled air of the pool area. Despite all the kids yelping, splashing and balancing precariously on lilypad-shaped floats, I spot him immediately.

The diver. Ed. Not diving now, but pulling himself out of the deepest pool — the lagoon — then striding across the wet tiles towards me. "Stella," he says, my name tripping off his tongue. He's all long brown limbs, all smiles.

"Hi, Ed, come for a swim?" I'm a tongue-tied fifteen-year-old with simmering cheeks.

"Thought I might while I'm here," he says, teasing me.

195

"It's so busy. I don't usually come here, especially in school holidays."

"I know," Ed says. "You prefer the sea. I've seen you at the back beach."

"And I've seen you diving."

Droplets trickle down his chest. I try to keep my gaze fixed on his face.

"Can you dive, Stella?" he asks.

"No, I've never been able to."

"Like to try?"

I shake my head firmly. "I've got a . . . kind of fear of it."

"Really? Which part scares you?"

"Falling in. Letting myself go."

"Come on," he says, taking my hand and leading me to the deep end of the main pool.

"Ed, I can't do it."

He stops at the pool's edge, still holding my hand. Honey-coloured hair clings to his broad back. "Believe you can do it," he says, "and you won't be scared."

"You don't understand. I really can't."

"Why not?" he asks gently.

"Our teacher used to take us to the old pool, before this place was built. It was one of those Victorian pools, with three diving boards at one end. This teacher forced us on to the first one — it was much higher than this — then the next, and finally the highest board . . ."

"Why?" Ed asks.

"If you wanted to be in the swimming club you had to learn to dive. I was desperate to be in — I was the strongest swimmer in my class — but every time I stood on those boards I'd freeze. Mrs Clegg would send me out early to get changed."

"That's nuts," Ed says.

"And it's why I can't dive."

"You don't start on boards. You start like this." He comes down to his knees and topples in headfirst, surging out of the water to face me.

I copy him, and we tumble over and over. It's just a game we're playing, like a couple of kids.

"Okay," Ed says, clambering out, "stand up now, just bend at the waist." I pull myself up and stand next to him at the poolside. His hands hover at my middle, but don't touch. Goosepimples prickle my entire body. "Now fall forwards," he says.

I'm about to say, no, let's do more tumbling, or swim lengths — but I'm standing at the pool's edge, toppling in. I come up spluttering, but alive.

"See?" Ed says. "You can do it."

"It felt good. I could do that again."

"Want to try the diving board?"

"Okay."

"I'm joking," Ed says.

"No, I really want to."

He frowns and says, "Are you sure?"

Something surges inside me, something stronger than fear. I say, "Yes."

Me and Dad. The two of us are jammed into his study with my maths homework scattered all over his desk. "At your age," Dad thundered, "I can't believe you can't long divide." I imagined my whole body split lengthways, exposing a substandard brain that couldn't figure out numbers. I couldn't do maths, couldn't dive. I played the flute, but what good would that be when I was grown up? Charlie could do anything. I was useless.

Dad was occupying the leather swivel chair. I'd had to bring up an orange vinyl-covered stool from the kitchen. My pencil scratched at the paper. I'd bitten off the rubber from its end, plus the silvery metal band that had attached it to the pencil. My mouth tasted of wood.

Dad had never supervised my homework before. He had no idea what my subjects were — what I was good or bad at — until Mr Kearny, my form teacher, had contacted him about my poor performance in class. Dad kept saying, "Really? I see," into the phone. He'd never met my teachers, and had only ventured once into school when Mr Bazrai from the allotment had said it would look bad if he didn't watch his daughter's solo flute performance. I found him wandering aimlessly along a corridor, as if he'd wound up in my school accidentally when he'd meant to go to the butcher's.

"You're not concentrating," Dad snapped, tapping his desk. He snatched my sheet of hazy calculations and ripped it in two.

"I am," I protested. "I just can't do it." Charlie was hiding in his bedroom, surrounded by anatomical diagrams and the slender arms of Sarah-Jane, the school beauty, who loved him so much she'd made him a tape of moon songs: "Blue Moon", "Moon River",

"Fly Me To The Moon". Sarah-Jane was so lovely, with flowing fair hair and caramel skin, that Dad had relaxed his no-visitors rule.

I drew the long-division shape: the upright and the line across. It looked like a wobbly diving board. "Now," Dad said, "thirty-four into two thousand, one hundred and twenty-six."

Small number, big number. The little one had to fit into the big one. This would probably involve an extra bit, an untidy leftover, which meant that the answer was point-something. Nothing fitted exactly. My left eye had developed a tic, as if an electrical current was running through it. Warm tears dripped on to Dad's leather-topped desk.

"Look at the state you're in," Dad snapped, spinning round on the swivel chair to face me. "Take a look at yourself."

I couldn't. There wasn't a mirror in Dad's study. Just the dark wooden desk, the typewriter and adding machine, and a shelf bearing coin jars and an old Blue Band margarine tub filled with cheap plastic Biros.

I stared down at a fresh sheet of white paper, wondering if the gold locket was still hidden in the drawer. I wanted to take out the box, and lift out the necklace — dangle it in front of Dad's face, like a pendulum. I could hypnotise him into forgetting about maths and bumbling off to attend to his sweetpeas at the allotment.

Long bloody division. It sounded like some kind of torture. The top buttons of Dad's shirt were undone, and curly grey hairs peeked out. He was rapping on the desk with his fingernails. "Why won't you pay attention?" he thundered. "You're just like —" Then he pushed back the swivel chair, sending it clanging against the filing cabinet and flounced out of the room.

Just like who? I wondered.

From Charlie's bedroom came Sarah-Jane's sparkly laughter. "*Stop* it," she cried, smothered with giggles. I was pretty certain that she didn't have a problem with long division.

I wiped my dribbling nose on my sleeve. Then I rested my head on my folded arms, gazing sideways at the spindly diving board, and the clumsily formed numbers queuing up on it, poised to leap into the deep.

CHAPTER
SEVENTEEN

The Orange Tree

"I feel awful," Ed says, "for making you do it." I had frozen there, mesmerised by the sunlight that hit the pool's surface like fragments of mirror. I'd stepped down and gone to get changed. I hadn't expected to find Ed waiting for me outside Aquasplash.

"You didn't make me," I tell him. "I just panicked."

We're sitting on battered wooden chairs amid the rubble in what will eventually be the Orange Tree Café, owned and run by Ed, and offering the finest lattes and cakes, but which currently amounts to a semi-derelict launderette. Dad used to come here. Rather than bother himself with our temperamental washing-machine, he would drop off his laundry for a service wash, thus avoiding being spotted using the machines (I could imagine the article: "TV has-been whiles away twilight hours watching his socks go round").

"I'd hoped to be open by Christmas," Ed says, handing me not an expertly brewed latte but a chipped mug of weak instant, "then the friend I moved down with changed her mind . . . got cold feet." The way he says it, I know he means a girlfriend.

I glance into the back room where Lil, the launderette lady, used to smoke skinny roll-ups and watch old black-and-white movies. "What made you leave Glasgow?" I ask.

"We — she — just wanted . . ." He pauses.

"An adventure?"

A flicker of a smile. "That's right. Her idea, really. And I wanted to come. We were going to set it up together, until . . ." Fat droplets of rain start to streak down the blue lettering on the window, which still reads: "Fully Attended Coin-operated Washeteria". "The café thing," Ed adds, "was just a phase she was going through."

"Sounds familiar," I murmur. "So, did she go back to Scotland?"

"No, she's travelling around Europe — I get the occasional postcard."

"When will she be back?" I ask, trying not to sound as if I care.

Ed shrugs. "When she's over the travelling phase."

"So you're setting up this place by yourself."

He nods, edging forward until our knees are nearly touching. I glance at the piles of cracked plasterboard and ragged holes where the machines were plumbed into the walls, and remember Alex's notion of opening an American-style diner in town, before he decided that his future — *our* future — lay in figure-of-eight-shaped water features.

"Think a café will work in this part of town?" Ed asks. His green eyes remind me of a pale dessert, like sorbet. *Anyone can dive,* he'd told me. *Just let yourself go.*

"Of course it will," I say firmly. Then another dessert, sweeter than sorbet, pops into my head.

Jelly. I promised Midge I'd make jelly. "What's wrong?" Ed asks, as I leap up from the chair.

"I told Midge I'd give her a special tea to make up for not taking her swimming. I said there'd be jelly. God, Ed —" I check my watch. Six forty-five. An hour has flashed by without me noticing.

"Is Midge your little girl?" Ed asks.

"No, just my neighbour, nothing to *do* with me, really — it's ridiculous that I feel bad for forgetting but —"

"And it's too late for tea?" he asks, amusement flickering across his face.

"I think," I tell him, "the jelly's off."

To avoid detection I scurry up my path, unlock my door with a swift turn of the key and close it quietly behind me. There's no note from Midge, no answerphone message. No "Stella, where *are* you?" Those girls — they make me feel hounded. Nervous in my own home. Through the wall I can hear giddy laughter, and the whine of something like a hairdryer. Maybe Dad was right. They should learn to respect other people's privacy.

I dump my bag of swimming things in the hall, wondering why I didn't ask Ed for his number or offer him mine. I'm out of practice, that's the trouble. I'd never imagined, before Alex left, that I'd find myself in a potential number-swapping situation again.

I head upstairs, run a hot, deep bath and climb in to wash away the chlorine smell that never seems to swill away in the changing-room showers. "Hello?" calls a thin voice through my letterbox. "You there, Stella?"

"Leave me alone," I mutter. Diane has only come round to make me feel bad for forgetting Midge's jelly. Why doesn't *she* make jelly?

"Ste-*llaaaaa*," Diane sing-songs, then bangs the letter-box shut. There's a sharp rap on the glass, then just the doleful squawk of a gull. I sink deeper into the water, thinking about my disastrous dive, and how next time I'll swoop beautifully into the water, watched and applauded by Ed.

I come downstairs to find a note on my hall floor. It's smeared with something greasy and red, as if it's been used to blot lipstick, and bears the message "Stella, can you babysit later, about 8.30? I am going out. Luv Diane". The letters are painstakingly rounded, like an early attempt at joined-up writing.

I could pop round and say, "Of course, I'd be delighted — what time do you need me?" Diane's singing now, to a Phil Collins record. "Groovy Kind Of Love". Not a favourite of mine. Her voice wavers on the long note: *luuuuurve*. She's probably dancing. I've glimpsed her swaying in front of the gas fire, not caring that lit rooms are easily seen into.

I screw up her note. I don't want to babysit tonight. In the living room I curl up with a newspaper, but can't

204

concentrate. I keep expecting to see Diane's pink-cheeked face looming at the window as she announces, "Ha! I knew you were in. I need you to babysit. Jojo, Midge — I've found her."

In case she comes knocking again, I creep upstairs to my bedroom. There are hairs — Surf's long, pale ones — on my duvet. The room still smells of Jean Patou, with canine overtones. Dad has left a book, *Beautiful Gardens In Difficult Places*, on the bedside table. The handwritten message on the inside cover reads, "To my darling Frankie, from your Maggie xxx".

Outside, a gang of children wobbles down Briar Hill on silver scooters. I draw the curtains and lie flat out on the bed with Dad's book. I'm vaguely aware of Diane's front door banging, and the clop-clop of her heels growing fainter as she strides down the hill.

A cartoony burble floats in from the TV next door. Perhaps she asked a friend to look after them, or some relative. The girls have never mentioned any family apart from their dad. "The thing about George," Diane once told me, as she pegged shredded dishcloths on to her washing-line, "is he liked the *idea* of a family, but wasn't prepared to look after us." The girls, she added, hadn't seen him since they left the Midlands. "He's the one with the fancy car," she muttered, stomping across the cracked flagstones, "but can't be bothered to get off his fat arse and visit. I've always been drawn to useless lumps of shit."

Music filters through now. It's not Phil Collins but something with a relentless bass and bouncy chorus that's sung over and over again. Midge is squawking tunelessly. It's nearly ten o'clock — why aren't they in bed yet? There's a small cry and a clatter, like something metallic hitting the floor. I want to check that they're okay, but what if they do have a babysitter? "Of course everything's fine," she'll say, looking up from a multi-choice quiz in her teenage magazine. "The girls are just mucking around, that's all." Anyway, I'm not even dressed.

There's another noise, thin and strained, like a small animal needing Harry Sowerbutt with his kind words and gigantic syringe. Maybe they're playing one of Midge's war games. She's blammed Jojo with the torpedo-shooter, or pinged her in the eye with the spud gun. Jojo's been blinded, and it's my fault. The packaging said it was fun and safe but I still shouldn't have bought it. Diane remarked, rather tersely, that she was sick of her vegetable rack being ransacked, and having to Hoover up pellets of mouldering spud.

Someone's crying now — heartily, from the diaphragm. It could just be pretend, some dramatic accident game. I pull on a sweater over my pyjamas, hurry downstairs and step out.

I bang on their door — no one answers — then peer through the living room window. The TV's on, but no one's watching. Fairy lights blink dolefully. There's a scattering of toast on the carpet, beside an empty plate, as if someone has been trying to fling their crusts on to it and missed every time. The crying is fainter now, coming from the back of the house.

I try the door and push it open. Jojo tumbles from the kitchen, crying, "Stella, please help us!"

206

"What's happened?"

"Midge is hurt." I hurtle past her and find Midge in the kitchen, clutching her wrist. There's a large welt there — livid pink and wet-looking, in the shape of a slug — with an angry glow round it. "Where's your mum?" I ask.

"She went out."

"What were you doing?" I pull her in for a hug, feeling sick, helpless.

"I touched that," she whimpers, pointing to the black enamel grill pan, which looks like it's been pulled out in panic and flung on to the floor.

"Wait," I say, "I'll get something." What's best for burns? Butter, cold water, magic cream? I'm totally unequipped to deal with an injured child. Melody did a better job at dealing with Charlie's bleeding arm, the day he cut himself in the Beetle.

"It really hurts!" Midge squawks.

"Don't panic, sweetheart, I'll find something —" I delve into the everything-drawer, sending bills, takeaway menus and ripped-open buff envelopes fluttering to the floor.

"I think there's magic cream," Jojo offers, "but maybe it's all used up."

"Here it is." I grab a crushed tube of Savlon and some of the grubby off-white fabric that Diane uses for bandages. Midge grips my sweater sleeve with her good hand as I dress the wound.

The worktops are scattered with grated cheese. The pan is heaped with baked beans and edged with slabs of something pink and fleshy — some kind of tinned meat. The beans are partially covered with a burnt crust. "You were cooking," I say, "all on your own?"

"It would have been all right," Jojo snaps, "if she'd let me do it, but she pushed me and snatched it —"

"I didn't," cries Midge. "She *made* me do it."

"It doesn't matter whose fault it was."

"I was hungry," she protests.

"Couldn't you have had a biscuit or —"

"You never made my special tea," she adds accusingly. "You said you'd make jelly. And you didn't."

"Well, I'm sorry."

"Can we have jelly another day?"

I sigh, gathering up the papers that had fallen to the floor and stuffing them back into the drawer. "Yes, I suppose so."

"Promise?"

"Promise."

We wait in the living room, away from the food and the burnt smell. Jojo sucks a strip of greying lace that's come loose at the neck of her nightie. Someone has snaffled all the chocolate decorations from the tree without untying them: remnants of foil still hang from the branches. An opened box of dates lies beside the lipshaped ashtray on the coffee table.

Midge keeps rubbing her eyes with her knuckles. "Does your mum often leave you alone at night?" I ask.

"Not much," Jojo mutters.

"What were you trying to cook?"

From her pyjama pocket Midge extracts a crumpled square of paper — onionskin paper. I take it from her, unfold it, and it's Dad's writing: "*Baked Beano: Take a can of luncheon meat, slice thickly and spread with French mustard. Fry until* . . ." The rest is illegible, smeared with bean sauce.

"She stole it," Jojo whispers.

CHAPTER
EIGHTEEN

Steak Diane

From the hall she yells, "You girls still up? Didn't I say bed by half ten?" There's a clatter of heels on floorboards, then the smell of her — perfume, smoke and good humour — as she strides in. "Oh!" Diane says. Her gaze drops to my striped pyjama bottoms.

"Hi," Jojo murmurs, without turning round. I'm sandwiched between the girls on the sofa. It feels as if we've been positioned like this for weeks, waiting morosely for someone to storm in and take away all the furniture. On TV a choppy-haired woman flips crustaceans across an enormous flat pan on a barbecue.

"Everyone all right?" Diane asks, casting off her denim jacket and dropping it on to the mustard armchair.

"I came round," I say, "when I heard —"

"You're in your pyjamas," Diane says, laughing through her nose. "Not that I mind, Stella. I like friends to feel comfortable in our house." She is wearing a deep purple top and a tight above-the-knee denim skirt. Her cheeks are glossy like pink snooker balls.

"Midge," I say, "show Mum your hand."

Midge drags her gaze from the TV and reluctantly offers her wrist. Diane lowers herself unsteadily and touches the bandaged hand. "Oh, my baby," she cries, "what happened?" She unfastens the bandage and peers at the injury. Her eyes dampen instantly.

"It got burnt," Midge whispers.

"They were cooking," I snap. "Midge hurt herself on the grill pan."

"My poor darling!" Diane lurches forward and wraps Midge in a fierce hug. Midge continues to gaze at the crustacean lady over her shoulder.

"They were on their *own*," comes my voice, as I remember Charlie — who was much older, of course, but still scared, still hurt, with bloodstains on his T-shirt from cutting his arm on the Beetle's shattered window. We needed Dad then, not to administer magic cream or fix on a bandage — Melody did that — but just to be there, because we were kids.

Diane glares at me. "Jojo was supposed to be in charge," she states flatly.

"She's only ten." I hate my new voice: superior, accusing. *I'm astounded, really, that you can't long divide!*

"I wrote you a note," she says, gathering herself up from the floor, "asking you to babysit."

"Are you suggesting it's my fault?"

"I do have a life, Stella —"

"So do I!"

"Just went for a drink with a few girls from work. Birthday do. Why shouldn't I have some fun?"

211

"But they're children, it's night time, anything could have —"

"What do *you* know about children?" she asks, shouting now.

"I know they shouldn't have been left by themselves." I stand up, aware of the space I've left on the sofa. Jojo winds a length of tinsel tightly round a finger.

"Who are you to judge me?" Diane rages. "What do you know about my life, Miss Perfect?"

"Nothing, I —"

"I thought you were a friend," she says, sounding helpless now. Her lips are tightly gathered like the opening of a drawstring bag.

"They're not my girls, Diane."

I want to be out of here, away from the beleaguered tree and the cards shoved wonkily on to the mantelpiece. Midge hiccups into her hands. Jojo's middle finger is entirely encased in tinsel.

Diane follows me into the hall, thrusting her face into mine as she hisses, "Damn right they're not."

January skulks forward, milky and misty as if a fine veil has fallen over the town. My private pupils start to leave like migrating birds. Katy's mother calls to announce that they're moving to open a chip shop in Yorkshire — chips are gold bars in edible form, apparently — and shows up for the final lesson with a bouquet of cream lilies, which look mournful wherever I place them. Finally I position the vase on my bedside table, hoping they'll mask the smell that lingers there, but I can still detect Mum's spilt perfume. It's impregnated itself in my nasal passages, and will stalk me, even if I move house.

Amy, a sullen thirteen-year-old who's had only a handful of lessons, explains, "My dad can't afford it any more. Says it's not worth the money." A new starter fails to show up. When I call her house there's just her mother's bleak voice on the answerphone, and no one ever rings back.

Although she still comes to group lessons at school, Jojo has stopped turning up for her Thursday-night lessons. The first one she missed, I wanted to go round to remind her that these are proper lessons, that we have an *arrangement* — but couldn't face Diane's pinched mouth and hostile eyes. I saw the three of them one Saturday, marching through the market. Diane kept her gaze fixed straight ahead as if her life depended on it. The girls scurried behind her across the puddled ground.

Some mornings I see them marching to school in their oversized Christmas coats. They walk purposefully, not looking back.

My evenings are longer now, longer than days. They start at around five and yawn onwards through the dull thump of Queen and the occasional squabble. The girls' fights are brief, compressed into seconds of squawking, as if someone has trapped all their hate in a tin.

Things happen so quickly when children are involved. They come from nowhere with their missiles and antennae umbrellas and creep under your skin without you noticing. They pop round to tell you about their day, or to lie on your rug and demand Party Hoops — none of your rice cakes or organic oatcakes, which they complained tasted like cardboard. You find yourself collecting cartons and plastic bottles for the little one to bind together with Sellotape. You start buying chocolate fairy cakes with chunks of Flake jabbed into the butter cream, and gigantic bottles of lemonade. The big one says, "We wanted to come round earlier but we know you teach Lisa till a quarter past eight," and their intimate knowledge of your weekly schedule fails even to surprise you.

An unfamiliar sensation settles uneasily in your chest. You feel needed. You don't even mind when they try on your slippers, doing lumbering flat-footed walks around your house. Some evenings the little one falls asleep on the sofa with her head on your lap. Her hair is pale blonde, soft as pillow stuffing. The older one swoops through Fauré's "Sicilienne", and when she's all played out she draws at the table. She knows where felt tips are kept without having to ask. Some roll on to the floor. They are lidless, and will probably stain your cream rug. You didn't notice the point at which you stopped fretting about minor damage to your home.

Then something happens. The girls stop coming. Your home, your life and your slippers — they're all yours again. You're left with a grocery box stuffed with missile components, and flat lemonade in the fridge.

"What I'm making tonight," Dad says, "is Steak Diane — a quick, easy dish for an informal get-together."

Dirk, the presenter, lurks behind him, rocking from foot to foot. He looks mildly agitated, like a child forced to behave nicely during a visit to a tedious uncle. "I'm tenderising the meat," Dad continues, "to make it —"

"Tender," Dirk cuts in.

"That's right. Makes a big difference to the finished result." One side of Dad's shirt collar is poking up, jabbing his chin. Contemporary chefs don't wear shirts and ties. They wear T-shirts and lob a meal's components into a pan, slosh on olive oil from a great height and slam the entire thing into the oven. "Now I'm briefly frying the mushrooms," Dad says, "and in a separate pan I'll cook the steak, adding lemon juice, Worcester sauce —"

"What's interesting," Dirk butts in, "is that I didn't think anyone made Steak Diane any more."

"It's very popular," Dad protests, flipping the steak and mushrooms on to a plate.

"Who *was* Diane?" Dirk asks.

"I've no idea. The chef, perhaps, who invented —"

"Is Diane your wife?"

"No," Dad blusters, "my wife —"

"What?"

"She . . . she . . ."

My stomach flips. Dad's wearing a tight, static smile. He's not required to be witty — it's too raucous now to decipher what anyone's saying — but just to stand there, grinning wildly, being Frankie, a sixty-one-year-old joke.

He's started to appear in magazines again. I'd found one on the table in Paul Street's staff room that reported he'd been tracked down in his cottage at Penjoy Point. The article was accompanied by a blurred snapshot of Dad in his garden, his face a boulder of fury glowering over the wall.

Friday Zoo's credits are rolling now. The camera closes in on the messy remains of Dad's Steak Diane.

"The comeback king," the magazine called him, "who has turned his naffness to his own advantage, regaining a place in the nation's hearts."

That's preferable, perhaps, to being forgotten. Or being no one.

It's the coldest winter I can remember — too cold, even, for dipping so much as a toe into the sea. I fill after-school spaces by swimming powerful lengths at Aquasplash, always keeping an eye open for Ed, and becoming suddenly aware of my pulse when I glimpse someone who looks like him. The right height, right skin colour, right hair length and shade. Wrong man. I alternate between breast stroke and crawl, thinking, One more length, and he'll stride out of that changing room. Just one more length. I swim on and on, further than I've ever managed before. My limbs feel strong, powerful, tireless.

Other days after school I go shopping — I've devised my own charity route but still can't see beyond the pottery owls with gold-painted beaks and the sandals adorned with plastic crocuses. I walk home past the old launderette. Its window has been covered with a canvas sheet to stop people like me peeking in.

One Monday evening after school, I join Jen and a cluster of teachers at the Anchor to celebrate Claudine's return to work after maternity leave. Claudine runs the nursery at Paul Street; endless patience streams through her like blood. "Anyone know what happened to Toby Nichols's eye?" she asks, sweeping scattered peanuts into a small pile.

"I'm not sure," I tell her. "When I asked about the bruise, he said he'd lain under his sister's bed with his dad's old tape recorder. You know how they sound when the battery's worn down? He played it really loudly, scared the life out of her . . ."

"And she punched him?" Claudine asks.

"So he says."

"I wouldn't be surprised," Jen cuts in. "We know what a bully he is. How old's his sister, Stella?"

"Six."

"Some punch," Claudine murmurs, "for a six-year-old."

I spot Robert at the bar, dipping his hand into a bowl of nuts. He's wearing a dark grey suit and his hair looks freshly combed — ironed, even. I've never seen him spruced up and workish before. Everything about him looks older.

I go up to order drinks, and startle him by saying, "Hello stranger," right into his ear.

"Stella, hi! I've been meaning to call you." His elbow collides with a glass dish of pretzels on the bar.

"That's okay. You told me you'd be busy for a few weeks. How are things at home?"

"Got a letter from Verity's lawyer. We're in lawyer territory now."

"What does she want?"

"A divorce, of course." He glances towards the table where the teachers are sharing ripped-open packets of crisps.

"I'm sorry, Robert."

"Hey," he brightens, "those kids from next door still plaguing you?"

"Had a bit of a fall-out with their mother. She went out one evening, left the girls at home on their own —"

"That's terrible. Some people aren't fit to be parents."

"Everyone makes mistakes," I murmur.

"Not like that, they don't. Did anything happen while she was out?"

I think for a moment. It feels wrong, discussing Diane's shortcomings with Robert. "They just got scared," I tell him.

I carry our drinks between after-work crowds, intending to go back and ask him to join us. But when I look, he's already gone, leaving a half-finished beer on the bar.

"Who's your friend?" Claudine asks.

"Just a guy I teach —"

"And make lunch for," Jen adds, "but the sod didn't turn up."

"Cute," Claudine says. "Worth forgiving, I think."

I smile, shaking my head. "He's about to go through a divorce and has two-year-old twins."

"God." Claudine laughs. "I can't imagine you, Miss Sorted and Organised, taking on someone else's kids."

After the pub I stride along the promenade. Yellowish light filters through the canvas at the launderette's window. Behind it I see moving shapes, and hear urgent hammering. The area outside is cluttered with skips piled high with shattered plasterboard and rusting radiators. I wonder if Ed's a little like Alex, with a headful of dreams and schemes that come to nothing. The Orange Tree's grand opening seems as distant as the tanker that forms a thin line on the smudgy horizon.

I come home to an answerphone message from Lori Pearson's mother, explaining that she'll be taking a break from lessons. "So many activities to fit into the week," she exclaims, "what with gymnastics, Brownies and tap. Sorry we couldn't give more notice, Stella. We'll keep in touch, in case Lori ever wants to start lessons again." She speaks as if music is just something else to be *fitted in*, another task on the to-do list.

I erase the message and lift Midge's pad from the bookshelf, flicking through pages and pages of intricate drawings of robots. Some have clusters of cogs nestling in cut-away sections in their bellies; others have springs sprouting from their rectangular heads, like crazy hair. I tear out a blank sheet, trim it to a neat square with round-ended scissors and write:

FLUTE TUITION OFFERED
IN YOUR OWN HOME OR TUTOR'S HOME
ALL AGES, ALL STAGES TO GRADE EIGHT
PLUS MUSIC THEORY
NO BLOCK BOOKING REQUIRED

My handwriting is immaculate; it just comes out that way. I used to hope that the praise heaped upon it would cancel out bad stuff like long division. I'd practise at Dad's desk in his study, looping my beautiful letters until I reached a plateau of neatness.

I reread the ad. It sounds like someone who'll do anything for anyone. It sounds desperate.

There's the click of my front door opening, and a small noise in the hall. My chest tightens. Someone's there — in *my* hall. Another click. I sit rigidly, aware of the hairs prickling on my arms, and my silent, shallow breathing. Jangling music drifts and fades from a passing car.

I shift position, flinching as the chair legs scrape against the floorboards. "Hello?" I call softly.

Nothing. I pad across the living room and peer round the door into the hall. And I see it: the slender black case placed on the floor close to the front door. I crouch down, rest it on my knees and click it open. The flute is in perfect condition — looks recently polished, in fact. I fit the pieces together, turning the instrument in my hands. It feels different, no longer mine.

Earlier this week Jojo's class teacher hurried after me as I left school. "About Jojo," Polly said. "Had her mother on the phone. Rather . . . forthright, isn't she?"

"I don't really know her," I said.

"She wants Jojo to stop music lessons," Polly continued. "Says she's worried it's interfering with her core subjects." Polly smiled brightly, as if relieved to have got this over and done with.

"Is that what she said? Core subjects?"

"She said her main stuff, like reading and writing."

I forced a smile and said, "Well, that frees up a place for someone else."

I stand now, lifting the flute to my mouth, ready to play right there in the hall. I run through scales, playing through the blasts of a horn as a car struggles up Briar Hill, its occupants roaring their delight at Plymouth's victory.

Then I take the flute to pieces, place them in the case and shut the lid firmly. It feels like an old friend who's strolled back into your life when you've forgotten how to be with them.

CHAPTER
NINETEEN

Ready Or Not

My ad on the newsagent's glass-fronted board is surrounded by for-sale cards depicting bunk beds, a Barbie scooter and a fully adjustable dog lifejacket with grab-handle "to stop you losing a beloved pet at sea". A few callers have responded to my card. When I told her my fee one woman announced, "Good Lord! We could only stretch to lessons once a month," and I heard myself say, "Fine, we can set something up."

An elderly man asked if I teach bassoon — I don't — and was I the music teacher who had worked at St Mary's in the late fifties? Another man quizzed me thoroughly on my teaching credentials, and said he'd consider whether I was "right" for his daughter. I wondered if I should cut-price myself.

"Good response to your ad, Stella?" asks Joyce. She has owned the newsagent's for as long as I can remember. Charlie and I used to come here for the sherbet lollies and crisps that constituted our school lunches.

"A few enquiries," I tell her, "but I'd like to pay for six more weeks."

She leans over the counter and murmurs, "I'm sorry to hear your dad's news, Stella."

"What news?"

Her eyes flick down to the small stack of *South Devon Echos* on the counter. A headline above a narrow column — beside the main story, about flooding at the new housing development — reads: "TV Frankie Sacked After Dramatic Scuffle".

"You didn't know?" Joyce asks.

I pick up a newspaper, folding it over to hide Dad. "One of those stupid exaggerated stories," I tell her. "You know what the papers are like." I pull out my purse from my bag to pay for my ad and the paper. Coins scatter over the neatly arranged copies of *Surfing World* and *Yachting Today*.

"I didn't think it sounded like your dad," Joyce adds kindly. "Absolute nonsense, that *Friday Zoo*. Never watch it."

"Neither do I."

"TV programmes aren't what they used to be," Joyce says.

Outside the newsagent's I open the paper and read:

TV has-been Frankie Moon has hit the headlines for all the wrong reasons — by slugging Dirk Turner of *Friday Zoo*. Turner, who suffered a fractured jaw, told the *Echo*: "The whole point of the slot is to make fun of Frankie in a kind and affectionate way. After all, lots of our older viewers remember his shows from the late seventies and are very fond of him.

"What he did was out of order, particularly as *Friday Zoo* has revitalised his career and brought him to a whole new generation of viewers." The heartthrob's lawyers are pressing charges against Mr Moon, 61, who lives in north Cornwall. Frankie's agent, Coral Dawson, and Mr Moon himself, have declined to comment.

Maggie says, "Frankie can't come to the phone, dear. He's resting upstairs. He's been very tired, after all this fuss. Not himself at all."

"Will they prosecute?" I ask.

"We're taking advice," she says carefully, then adds, "He was provoked, of course. That wretched man, soon as they came off air — jibing at him . . ."

"What did he say to Dad?"

"I don't want to repeat it. It's so unjust, when you think of your poor father, with his experience and professionalism . . ."

I start to tell her that Dad's not a violent man — there must be some mistake — but my voice is drowned by Surf's fretful barks.

Midge stands in my hall like a stranger. "Does your mum know you're here?" I ask.

She shrugs and says, "She's having a sleep."

"Are you allowed to come and see me?"

Midge gnaws a snag of skin by her thumbnail. "No, we're not." It's always "we", even when she's on her own, as if the spectre of Jojo hovers over her.

The front of her hair, which is too long to be called a fringe, clings to her face in damp clumps. There's been a light flurry of snow. I saw her, out in the street, trying to catch meagre flakes on her tongue. "Maybe you should go home," I suggest.

"Don't want to. Don't care what she says."

"You should, she's your mum —"

"I hate her."

"Don't say that."

She pulls off her damp coat, strides into the living room and tosses it on to the rug. "I *do* hate her," she announces. "She shouted at me just 'cause of my glitter."

"What did you do with it?"

"Nothing! Just sprinkled it in the toilet to see if it would float."

"Does glitter float?" I ask, smiling.

"Yeah. But it won't flush away. So every time Mum goes to the loo it's all glittery and she remembers what a bad girl I am." She curls up on the rug, where I left the *Echo*. I nudge her coat with my foot to cover Dad's startled face. "Want to play a game?" she asks suddenly.

"Okay, just for a few minutes. I don't want you to get into trouble with your mum."

"Hide and seek?"

"Want to be hider or seeker?"

"I'll seek," she says firmly, and slaps chilled-looking hands over her eyes.

One. Two. Three. Four. I hurtle upstairs and into my bedroom but remember her ruining Mum's makeup and head for the bathroom instead, where no bad things have happened. There are no real hiding-places — only behind the door — so I duck into

225

the small bedroom where my spare mattress is propped against the window.

Eleven. Twelve. Fourteen. Fifteen. She always skips thirteen. It's unlucky, like walking under ladders or leaving up your Christmas decorations beyond the sixth of January (although Diane, I noticed, only got round to taking hers down three weeks after Christmas; I really can't see why she takes such issue with glitter in the toilet).

Nineteen. Twenty. Coming, ready or not!

I have squeezed behind the mattress. The back of my head is pressed against the cold glass. Midge thunders upstairs and makes straight for the bathroom: there's the clank of the toilet lid being flung back, as if I might have stuffed myself down there. She bounds on, humming, to explore my bedroom. There's a slithering sound, as if she's worming under my bed.

She's on the landing now, breathing coarsely. "Stella?" comes the tentative voice. I cough, a small clue. She clomps in, sniffing, then scampers downstairs, roaring, "Where are you?"

Cough.

"Stella!"

Cough-cough.

"Where *are* you?"

"Up here," I call out, and we collide on the stairs as she flings herself into my belly, sending me toppling backwards. "Midge," I say, "what on earth's wrong?"

"I thought I'd lost you," she cries.

I pull her towards me and hug her. Her heart beats frantically through her Tank Girl T-shirt. "It was only a game," I say softly.

"I don't ever want to lose you," she whispers.

"You won't lose me, sweetheart. I'll always be your friend."

"Promise?"

"Promise," I say. "Come on, let's dry your face, and I'll take you home."

We find Diane reclining in her glossy apricot dressing gown and puppy slippers on the sofa. "Hi," she says, idly flicking the pages of *Woman's Life*.

"I went to Stella's," Midge mutters.

"So I see," Diane says, poring over an article entitled "I Lost Five Stones and Wasn't Hungry Once". The woman in the picture is grinning fiercely, next to a blurry snapshot of her former self.

"Just wanted to see her," Midge adds defiantly.

"It's up to you where you go."

I shift uneasily, aware of Diane's hostile vibes, even though I can only see the back of her head. "Diane," I say, "I wondered if you still have any boxes or tea chests from when you moved in?"

"Mmm, probably."

"Could I borrow some?"

"What for?" Reluctantly, she tears her gaze away from the magazine.

"I'm packing up my ex-boyfriend's stuff. It's driving me mad, seeing all the things he left behind every time I open a cupboard."

"Oh," she says, softening. "Yes, of course you can. I'll bring them over later, when I'm dressed. You can make me some tea."

This, I figure, is the closest Diane ever comes to saying sorry.

"Alex, I want to drop off the rest of your stuff."

"Hey," he says — his don't-hassle-me voice, "what's the problem?"

"Your things. Can I bring them round?"

"I'll pick them up some time. Hey, I saw your ad in the newsagent's — not taking on more pupils, are you? How d'you find the time?"

"I work, like most people have to."

"Well, I work too."

"Faking crop circles, Alex, and that was last summer. So, will be you in later if I come round?"

"That urgent, is it?" he asks, sounding hurt.

Yes, it is. You're still here, all around me. Like Mum's spilt perfume, you won't go away. "I'm just trying to tidy the place up," I tell him.

"It was tidy the last time I looked."

"Around eight, will that be okay?"

Alex sighs. "I'll be ready and waiting," he says.

In the bathroom cabinet I find three unopened tubes of Alex's eucalyptus toothpaste (why had peppermint suddenly become so unpalatable?). It made his morning kisses taste medicinal, although that might not have been just the toothpaste.

228

His fishing rod is propped up and impossibly tangled at the back of the wardrobe. Behind my boxed shoes — he laughed at my habit of keeping them in their original boxes, like precious things — is the stack of encyclopedia he bought from an ad in a Sunday supplement. I flick through the P-T volume.

Rainbow.
A series of arcs caused by the refraction and reflection of sunlight falling on water droplets. The common primary bow results in arcs of the following colours . . .

Beneath it,

Rainbow trout.
Member of the salmon family, with an ability to leap dramatically and fight hard in an attempt to resist capture. Species: *Oncorhynchus mykiss.*

Mykiss, I like that.

I pile the encyclopedia into Diane's boxes and haul them downstairs. I drag down the bags of shirts, the zip-up bag of his summery things and a carrier bag of his creams and lotions, plus the fishing rod.

In the cupboard under the stairs, I find his rake, spade, an implement to drill small holes in the ground, and knobbly gardening gloves with a brittle soil crust. I'll keep these as Alex no longer has a garden. He'd had big plans to grow things, for all of one fortnight in May, and placed a row of tomato plants on the shelf at the kitchen window. They grew fervently, sprawling across the glass and leaving me shrouded in shadows. My sea view had gone. Alex had chosen a variety called "Big Boy" to make me laugh. Despite the abundance of foliage, the plants produced a total of three orangy pearls, which he dressed, ceremoniously, with olive oil and vinegar, carefully cutting the third tomato in half so we could share it. I watched his mouth as he ate, wanting to kiss it.

I carry the boxes and bags to the car and fill the boot. In one carrier bag I can see Alex's checked pyjamas, bought when he'd decided to stop sleeping naked and required a thin layer of cotton between us.

Jojo appears, ghostly pale in her pink nightie at the window, and watches me drive away.

Alex's dingy stairlight ekes through the rippled-glass rectangle above the door. I have unpacked the boot and piled everything on the damp pavement. It's all his now, which means it really *is* over. I look down at the boxes and carrier bags, swallowing hard. At least I folded his shirts carefully, nestling fragile items between layers of faded cotton. I've taken a lot more care than those Movers & Shakers men.

The door opens. Alex seems slightly bewildered, as if he's just woken up. "So much stuff," he says quietly.

"You did leave a lot."

He crouches to unzip the bag and pulls out the battered Birkenstocks, wincing, as if they've been fouled by a stranger's feet.

"I'll help you carry them up," I say.

"You needn't bother."

"I'd like to, Alex."

We haul up the bags and dump them in the middle of the living room. His flat feels cool and sparse and is painted all white. The small pale grey sofa and the metal shelving unit — housing a portable TV, stereo and small pile of books — look as if they've been brought in to make it seem as though someone actually lives there. The living room is carpeted in an oatmeal colour, the kind you find in offices. Everything about the room feels temporary.

Alex peels the tape from a box and starts to unpack magazines: *Trout and Salmon, Caged and Aviary Birds, Poetry Now*. There are reminders of his eco-warrior phase: *Green Living, One Planet*. I sit cross-legged on the carpet, watching him sort them by title and heap them neatly, like mini tower blocks, on the floor all around him. "Don't know where I'm going to put everything," he says.

I glance round the room. It feels pleasantly simple, like the kind of budget hotel room frequented by salesmen. "Do you like living here?" I ask.

"It's okay. I'm getting used to it." He has his back to me as he piles the magazines on to the shelf.

"Are you planning to stay?"

Alex turns to face me and says, "That depends."

"On what?"

He just smiles.

I wake up entangled in pale yellow sheets in a small room that overlooks the bedding factory behind Dock

231

Lane. There are no curtains. The sky is mottled grey, smeared with purple. Alex stirs behind me and rests a warm hand on my stomach.

I glance down at it, at the fingers turned ochre by the light filtering in through the sheets. He breathes softly into my neck. His hand trails between my legs. I lift his arm, and slide away from him, then lower it into the space I've left. He has no job to go to, no need to wake up yet. I wonder if he's still living off the crop-circles money.

It's eight thirty. Not enough time to drive home, wash, get changed and pick up my flute and music for school. I'll have to call Jen, tell her I overslept, which she'll know isn't true. I *never* oversleep.

I pull on my knickers, socks, sweater, jeans. In the bathroom I splatter my face with cold water, then use his toothbrush and eucalyptus paste. I check the bedroom again.

Alex is still sleeping, flopped over on to his back now. Last night he said he'd made a mistake, realised it as soon as he'd left me. As he was leaving, in fact, in Mo's clapped-out van. "That girl," he said, "she was nothing to me. It only happened a couple of times."

"Why did you do it?" I asked.

He said, "I was swept along by her," making her sound like a wave.

"So you'd been seeing her when we were still together."

"It was nothing," Alex insisted. "Please believe me."

I study the softness of his face now, the pale pink of his parted lips. Spending the night with him wasn't my smartest move; not what the magazines recommend. "Accept that it's over," is the advice they trot out. That day at the doctor's I noticed "Sex With Your Ex" screaming in fluorescent pink lettering from a magazine cover.

I touch Alex's forearm. He shifts and murmurs, thinking I'm still in bed. But it's over this time. I'll never come here again.

"Bye, Alex," I whisper. Then I kiss him, and run.

CHAPTER
TWENTY

Running Away

My college place was secured. In six months' time, I'd be free. The urge to turn and run bubbled inside me every time I rounded the corner and our house came into view. Then, just as freedom gleamed like a pearl in the distance, Dad came up with his Great Idea.

"What I need," he said, tearing off his corduroy jacket, "is a new format."

I looked up from my geography revision and stared at him through the over-long fringe I'd cultivated to try to make myself at least look *laissez-faire*. I was seventeen, but appeared two years younger, with my gawky frame and apologetic breasts. I hadn't even known he'd been thinking about formats. I'd assumed he'd given up, and that we were getting by on his earnings from occasional articles he wrote for an Australian food magazine. "What . . . *format*?" I asked.

The clock on the mantelpiece ticked hollowly. Dad grasped my hands — I flinched, unused to his touch — and said, "You."

I knew, before he uttered another word, that my answer was "No."

"It's a father-and-daughter show," he explained. "Who better than an ordinary, *very* ordinary girl, who doesn't know the first thing about cooking, has never shown the slightest interest in my work, to demonstrate how easy my recipes are?"

"No!" I snapped, slamming my folder shut.

"Listen —"

"I can't do it. You'll have to find someone else."

He seemed to sag then, as if some of the air had gone out of him. "I don't have anyone else," he said.

"I'm sorry." I wanted him to leave the room, to stomp off to the allotment to cuddle That Woman, or whatever it was he got up to. Although I performed in concerts without the faintest flutter of nerves, I had an aversion to being filmed or photographed. I was still recovering from being photographed for the *Echo* after winning an inter-schools solo competition. The photographer, a greasy-faced man with dense sideburns, had insisted on taking my picture in front of our house, in full view of the street, rather than in the back garden as I'd begged him to. He'd dragged his tripod about, gouging up grass and waggling his light meter flamboyantly. Lynette came sniggering down our street and watched us, her kohl-rimmed eyes mocking as the shutter clicked over and over, freezing my smile.

I hoped that Dad would forget about *Frankie's Girl* — as he had decided to name the series which would, undoubtedly, wreck my young life — or at least conclude that I was the wrong shape for TV. My elbows were too pointy, my feet long and narrow like canoes.

"It's not about your feet," Dad insisted. "It's about the interaction between the two of us."

"But we don't," I protested.

"Don't what, Stella?"

"Interact!"

"Well," he said quietly, "we'll just have to try."

I slumped upstairs and lay on Charlie's bed, staring at the shark pictures which had been pinned up haphazardly with fluorescent drawing pins. Instead of the band posters favoured by most boys of his age, he'd opted for great whites and hammerheads shifting eerily through dark oceans. I wanted to turn into a shark, and spend the rest of my life under water. Or, better still, I'd be one of those gnarled-looking fish that lurk on the sea-bed, five miles deep.

Over the next few days Dad remained in his study, emerging only for snacks and the bathroom. He'd still be clattering urgently on the typewriter when I went to bed. Finally, he emerged with a sheaf of paper worryingly entitled. "The Script".

He had us read our lines. Mine came out stiff and ill-fitting, as if someone else's teeth had been jammed into my mouth. "Can't Charlie do this?" I protested, slouching at the kitchen worktop and handing Dad an empty bowl, which was supposed to contain breadcrumbs, chopped apricots and raw egg.

"No, he can't."

"Why not?"

"He's got *university*."

"I've got exams, and if I don't get the grades I won't be accepted into —"

"You need a haircut," he snapped. "It just sort of . . . hangs there."

"I'm not doing it. I'm *not* going on telly." I was shouting now, clutching the glass bowl to my chest, as if it might protect me.

"We're only talking a pilot," Dad said calmly. "One show, Stella, two or three days' work is all I'm asking."

Dad had already been in touch with his old production company. Enough time had elapsed for them to forgive his small tantrums, his outrage at *Frankie's Feasts* being cancelled. They were keen, he told me. Very keen. "Please, Stella," he said, desperation shining out of his milky grey eyes.

My entire body wilted. "Okay. Just a pilot, a one-off."

He didn't thank me or exhibit any emotion that might have resembled gratitude. He just fished a crumpled fiver out of his trouser pocket. "That's for your hair," he muttered.

Despite shambolic rehearsals at a run-down studio near the docks in East London — I'd had to miss a whole week of school, with exams looming — the pilot would be filmed. "I'm not ready," I hissed, on the morning when *Frankie's Girl* was about to become horribly real.

"Of course you are," Dad insisted. We were staying in a twin room in the cheapest hotel he'd been able to find. The huddled terrace had a partial view of King's Cross station and reeked of the resident Alsatian. Someone had drilled a tiny hole through the wall of our room. I'd lain awake, convinced that a camera lens or a real human eye had been peering at me through it.

Frankie's Girl was filmed before an assortment of technicians in grubby T-shirts and oily drainpipe jeans. The producer, whose cigarette intake had accelerated throughout the day, said, "Thank you, Frankie, Stella. It's been quite an experience." I knew I'd come across as doleful, flat as a raft. Dad had tried to overcompensate by bounding about energetically, which had made him look marginally out of control.

The day it was broadcast, I met Jen after school. We drifted around town, eating vinegared chips, and I flinched each time we passed a shop with TVs in its window in case I glimpsed my horrified face. Even though no one would be watching some tragic low-budget cookery show — at least, no one who mattered — a worryingly high proportion of my schoolmates happened to see it. The following day Kenny White made vile slurping noises behind me in the dinner queue. Someone chalked a picture of me on a blackboard, grinning madly while I nibbled the end of a phallic-looking éclair.

For the rest of the week I feigned illness, lying beneath bobbly nylon sheets with the radio mumbling. I'd creep down for water or biscuits and find Dad at the table, spooning Ambrosia Creamed Rice into his mouth from a tin. He said, "I'm sure it'll be commissioned, we'll be talking a six-show series at least," but the flatness of his voice suggested that even he didn't believe this. *Frankie's Girl* had died before it had properly come into the world.

"If it does," I said, "you'll have to ask Charlie. Call it *Frankie's Boy*." Dad pretended not to hear. My brain — suddenly grasping the concept of mental arithmetic — figured out, instantly, how many days would pass before I, too, would be able to leave home and be free, like Charlie. Six months = 182.5 days. I hadn't even needed to use Dad's adding machine. I ran upstairs and scrabbled under my bed for the bulky grey calculator Elona had bought me for Christmas: 182 days (I skipped the half, couldn't be fagged with fractions) = 4368 hours = 262,080 minutes. Six months sounded better.

I left school that June and spent the summer shampooing heads at Shear Brilliance in Bay Street. As my hands swirled through sudsy hair, I'd spirit myself away to music college where I was due to take up my place in September. Something strange had happened to Dad: he seemed to wilt, like a plant no one had bothered to water, as if he really minded me leaving. Mum had gone, then Charlie. No series of *Frankie's Girl* had been commissioned. The pilot had been forgotten, like an unpleasant but mercifully brief illness.

One evening, when I'd come home from a late shift at the salon, I caught Dad watching me over the top of his newspaper. "What's wrong?" I asked.

"Only a week now," he said.

"Four days. I'm moving into the flat on Saturday." I tried to sound suitably grief-stricken.

His eyes were gleaming like opals. "You're very like your mother," he added.

"People often say that. I don't see it myself." I didn't like being observed over the top of his *Daily Express*.

"Would you like a special meal before you leave?"

"Not really, Dad."

"Why not? Charlie would come — I'd *insist* that he came. You could invite a couple of friends — that Jane you're so fond of."

"Jen," I corrected him. The idea of being cooked for by Dad — all of us eating together, having a jolly family time — was so alarming and alien that I hoped he'd forget, and wind up spending my last day in Devon at the allotment. I wondered if Mr Bazrai, or even That Woman, had put the idea into his head.

Then I realised. He didn't want me to go. It wasn't that he liked me particularly, or cherished my sparkling company, just that I was all he had left.

The meal happened. Dad made a cheese and cider fondue, long after fondue sets had been put into hibernation in attics and charity shops. Jen politely dipped cubes of French bread into the oval-shaped orange pot, but I could tell that the cider, or maybe the cheese, wasn't sliding down easily. Charlie, who was conducting a short-lived experiment as a vegan, ate only the bread. Carole, a friend from the school orchestra, dipped and swirled with enthusiasm, but later complained of an ache in her gut. "It's the cheese, Carole," Dad announced, "mixed with all that cold beer you've been drinking. It solidifies, you see, forming a ball in your stomach."

This was Dad's attempt to cheer up the proceedings. Carole was laughing but her eyes had clouded with fear. "We're probably talking hospital," Dad continued, spooning piped cream from a slab of gâteau into his mouth. Carole had stopped laughing. Charlie marched upstairs, saying that he needed to pack, although he'd come home from uni with no change of clothes.

The girls and I cleared up. We waited until Dad had fallen asleep in the frayed brocade chair and crept out to the Jolly Roger where old wine bottles contained dribbling candles and underage drinkers were warmly welcomed with snakebite and black. "Your dad's weird," Carole announced, slurping her drink.

"He was just trying to be nice," I said lamely.

She knocked back the rest of her purplish drink. She had to go home then: her tummy was hurting too much. I pictured her lying unconscious on a hospital bed having the cheeseball removed. It would be hosed down and photographed for health education posters warning: "FONDUE IS BAD FOR YOUR HEALTH."

Just as well, I decided, that I was leaving.

Next day I moved into the maisonette near London Bridge. I hadn't known what a maisonette was when I'd answered the ad. My only visits to London had been the long-ago school trip and the *Frankie's Girl* disaster. I'd imagined a cottage with a well-tended garden in front, and was quite shocked when it turned out to be a two-storey block of stained concrete sandwiched between a kebab shop, in which some gigantic meat product rotated and dripped in a sinister manner, and a tattoo parlour called Prick 'n' Pix. Beneath the maisonette's windows there were reddish smears where the metal frames were slowly rusting, like the cars on the Slab.

The first recipe arrived a week after I'd moved in. My flatmate Lennie, a runner for a film company in Wardour Street, peered at the onionskin square in my hand and said, "Worried about you, is he? Isn't that sweet?" She wore oxblood DMs and tie-dyed dresses from Camden Market. My Devon accent was, she declared, also "sweet". She read over my shoulder: "'*Blend one can tuna, a finely chopped onion, one tin kidney beans and five tablespoons mayonnaise. Use to fill a jacket potato or eat on its own as quick, nutritious snack. I hope you're eating properly, Stella. I know what students are like, drinking too much and not looking after themselves.*' How sweet!" Lennie squealed, laughter tumbling from her burgundy-painted mouth.

I tried to change my voice as the months passed, and become a real Londoner like Lennie. I pored over the Tube map as if it were an exam subject, and started eating falafel. I turned briefly vegan like Charlie, a dietary experiment that coincided with the arrival of a recipe for Brazilian Beef, requiring cubed cow — Lennie referred to meat varieties by their animal names — to be stewed for several hours in strong coffee. Lennie owned a T-shirt with the slogan "Meat Kills".

Occasionally Charlie would write to me, jumbling together anecdotes from uni that would have me laughing and crying simultaneously. Lennie was surprised to learn that I had a brother. "I'd just assumed," she said, "with your dad doting on you so much, you must be an only child."

Lennie never found out about Dad's TV years; neither did the succession of subsequent flatmates, who always left something behind when they moved out — a broken lamp, a bottle of Clairol shampoo, a pair of tights with the knickers left in, lying under a bed. I liked it that I could talk about Dad as if he were ordinary — as if I, like the new friends I'd made at college, had grown up in a nice, normal home filled with porcelain ornaments and well-dones.

For the first time, I was just me.

Mrs Bones, my flute teacher, wrote to me, her sentences strung across the blue airmail pages like delicate necklaces.

> Dear Stella,
> I saw your father in town last Wednesday. He looked well but was concerned that you hadn't been in touch for some time despite him writing to you. I reassured him that you're happy and settled in London, and that you have a lovely flat in a respectable part of the city.
> He mentioned that he is thinking of leaving Devon. In fact, when I passed your house recently I noticed a for-sale sign. I do hope he's happy, Stella — it can't be easy for him now that you've gone, even though there's that ladyfriend who seems extremely nice. I think he misses you very much.

I'll sign off, now, Stella, and hope that you'll pop by if you're home for Christmas. Perhaps we could play the Mozart duets together.

With best wishes,

Lorna Bones

I hadn't intended to go home for Christmas, but then I fell in love. Thomas, the brother of my current flatmate, moved in, ostensibly until he found a permanent place to live. Then my flatmate left, and it made sense for Thomas to relocate from the dented sofa-bed in the living room to her room. We liked to joke that I'd stumbled, mildly drunk, into his bedroom after a particularly arduous shift at the pizza restaurant where I worked three evenings a week. He'd tell our friends, "If Stella hadn't had to deal with that bunch of prats throwing garlic bread, we'd never have got together." The way he told it, that it had just *happened* — a happy accident, devoid of stress and embarrassment — was how it felt to me.

Thomas worked as a sound engineer. I'd wake at odd hours, before the Tube trains had begun to judder beneath the flat, and hear him undressing. I'd feel his warm arms round me, his soft kisses on my neck. Of course I told Thomas about Dad. We spread out the onionskin squares on the mud-coloured carpet and constructed make-believe menus. "Tonight, my darling," Thomas said, "I shall cook for you . . . let's see . . . stuffed eggs, followed by *gratin au fruits de mer*" — Thomas ladled on a French accent, which made me

244

giggle — "and, to finish, *ma petite filou, le soufflé de Grand Marnier.*"

For a split second, it was no longer Thomas and me in our London Bridge maisonette. It was Charlie, lurching into exaggerated French, making me laugh, making everything all right.

One night, as we slipped towards sleep, Thomas said, "You must go home for Christmas. We can't have him sitting there with a sad little meal for one."

The "we" surprised me. "He won't be on his own," I told him. "There's some woman, according to Mrs Bones. And why shouldn't Charlie go home? Why should it be me?"

It was what I'd said when Dad had forced me to participate in *Frankie's Girl*. The truth was, Charlie pleased himself.

Thomas shrugged and rolled over in bed to face me. "I think you'd make him happy. I'll come with you, if you want me to."

I knew then that we'd go.

The first thing I saw was the sold sign. "Estate agent said there wasn't a hope," Dad said, shaking Thomas's hand briskly, "not at this time of year. It was sold in a week. I told him, I've found a place, got nothing to hang around here for."

We followed Dad into the house with Thomas agreeing that his new home — Dad flashed us a rumpled picture of a ramshackle structure teetering on a cliff's edge — was indeed the perfect place for a man whose children never came to see him. It was called

Silverdawn Cottage. I wondered if he was considering renaming it Home for the Unloved.

I pulled out a kitchen chair for Thomas, and Dad landed heavily in the opposite seat. "So, Thomas," he said, "what do you do for a living?"

"I'm a sound engineer. I work with bands, musicians —"

"Real, professional musicians?" Dad asked, immeasurably more impressed with my boyfriend's credentials than any of my music-related achievements. Thomas nodded. "Tell me about some of the people you've worked with," Dad prompted him.

Thomas talked about the former page-three model who'd required sixteen hours of recording to put down her vocal, and still sounded as if she was having a limb amputated with no anaesthetic. In turn, Dad hauled out his press cuttings and the reams of pages he'd written for *Woman's Life*, now gone pale brown and brittle. You couldn't walk across the living room floor without treading on Dad's beaming face.

There was no mention of the woman friend Mrs Bones had talked about in her letter. When I asked, Dad glanced up briefly from his life spread out on the carpet and said, "There's no one special, Stella, no one special at all."

I left them in the living room, discussing Dad's greatness and Thomas's burgeoning career. I would have rescued Thomas — suggested we watch a film on TV or go out for a drink — but he didn't sound as if he wanted to escape. There were rumbles of laughter, and the tinkle of the top being removed from the crystal decanter. I peered into kitchen cupboards, looking for signs of someone — unfamiliar teacups, perhaps — but found only our chipped Royal Doulton plates, and shelves jammed with tinned soup.

Upstairs I lay on the single bed in my old room, which hadn't been decorated since I was a child. The walls were papered with a violent pattern of spiky orange flowers with brown centres. There were faults at the joins: the lengths of paper hadn't been hung properly.

Thomas was heading upstairs now, tracking me down. "You okay?" he asked. "Frankie says dinner's almost ready." He had fitted in so easily. One brief afternoon and he was part of my family already, relaying messages from Dad — sorry, *Frankie*.

"I'll be down in a minute," I said. "Have you found your bedroom?" Dad had made it clear that Thomas would sleep in Charlie's old room.

"Yes, thanks. Interesting posters. Think I might have a shark nightmare."

"I'll come in and rescue you if I hear you screaming."

"Don't worry," Thomas said. "I'll find *you*." My own bedroom was filled with too many flowers, all fake and fading: mixed blooms on the flannel curtains, grimy plastic tulips in a vase on the windowsill. Later that night, Thomas crept through from Charlie's room into my bed. I slid my arms round him, and was poised to kiss his mouth. He pulled away from me and said, "Stella, this must have been a wonderful place to grow up. You're a lucky girl."

247

★ ★ ★

Next morning I reached out for him but found only snagged nylon sheets. I pulled on my pyjamas and rumpled them up so it would look as if I'd been wearing them all night, and padded barefoot on to the landing. The olive-green carpet felt sticky and gravelly. When I inspected my feet, bits of grit were trapped between my toes.

Dad and Thomas were huddled over the kitchen table, too engrossed in the matter at hand to notice me wander in. "Use the palette knife," Dad was instructing him, "to smooth it."

He was showing Thomas how to ice a cake. I had never known Dad bother to make one before. I wondered why he'd gone to the trouble when only Thomas and I were spending Christmas with him.

They stood back and admired their joint creation. "Not bad," Dad pronounced.

"It's still lumpy," Thomas said. "Maybe I didn't beat the icing enough."

"For a beginner you've done a good job."

"If I wet the knife, could I smooth it over again?"

"You could try."

Thomas ran the knife under the tap and swiped at the cake but the icing was setting already. A thin crust had formed. It looked like a shattered ice rink. "Oh, hell," Thomas said. Flecks of icing clung to the front of his sweater. He looked horrified at the damage he'd inflicted on an innocent fruitcake.

"Just leave it," I suggested. "You're making it worse."

"No, he's not," Dad protested.

248

"I've wrecked it," Thomas said.

I tried to take hold of his sugary hand but his fingers hung limply. "Come on," I said, "let's go down to the beach." I loved the back beach in winter when there were no day-tripping hordes. I wanted us to roll up our jeans for a paddle. We could wade out, daring each other to brave the icy water. I thought it might bring him back to me.

Dad was already mixing something in a Pyrex bowl: a new batch of icing, which he started to smear over the cake with the palette knife. "What are you doing?" Thomas asked.

"Whipping it up into peaks," he said. "Now, Thomas, you take over. Don't worry about trying to be perfect." Tentatively at first, then becoming freer with sweeping strokes, Thomas sculpted the icing until the cake looked like one of the spiky flowers on my bedroom wall, but in dazzling white.

"What do you think, Stella?" Dad asked.

I looked down at the cake. They'd made it, the two of them. Thomas was grinning proudly. I remembered the horror of *Frankie's Girl*, how I'd cocked up Dad's chance of a comeback, how he'd said a series would have been commissioned if only I'd not looked so bloody self-conscious.

"It's perfect," I said.

On the train back to London I flipped through *Garnishing Made Easy*, my Christmas present from Dad. I couldn't have been less likely to carve a mango hedgehog ("a beautiful adornment for many dishes, especially curries").

I felt Thomas's eyes on me as I skipped over pages of butter roses and swans carved from apples, wondering who Dad thought I was.

Thomas said, "Frankie's not like I imagined. Not a bit like you described him."

"What did you think he'd be like?" I asked.

He swirled his cardboard cup of coffee. "Much sterner. Pretty horrible, actually. He's a lovely guy, Stella — so kind and interesting. You should give him a chance."

I watched the sweeping fields and the Canada geese flying in a ragged arrow, heading south, escaping. I wished we'd visited Mrs Bones, paddled at the back beach, done things together. Thomas was sitting in the opposite seat. He'd pulled off his boots and kept teasing the side of my leg with his toe.

I edged away from him and said, "It's too late."

CHAPTER
TWENTY-ONE

Love Heart

"What's that you're wearing?" Toby's voice has a cruel singsong edge. He and Jojo are huddled at the far end of the girls' cloakroom.

"A badge," Jojo says. I'm poised at the door. He shouldn't be here; neither should Jojo. Afternoon lessons have begun. In the small gaps between the coat rails, piled high with damp jackets, I see flashes of their red sweatshirts.

"You wear it all the time, don't you?" Toby asks casually.

"Yes, I like it. It came free with a comic."

"Comic?" he sneers. "You still read comics?"

"Sometimes."

"It's a love-heart badge, isn't it? You in love with someone, Jojo?"

I don't catch her response. Maybe she just shakes her head. Claudine hurries past me, ushering a desperate child from the nursery class to the toilet.

"Give me it," Toby says suddenly.

"What?"

"Your badge. Take it off."

"I don't want to." Jojo's voice is soft and breathy, like a younger child's. Sometimes I wonder if she puts it on to remind adults that she still needs looking after.

"I said, give me it, Piggy."

I stride past the coat rails to the end of the cloakroom. They swing round to face me. "Shouldn't you be in class?" I ask.

"We're just talking," Toby says airily.

"Really? You weren't trying to take something from her?"

He shakes his head vigorously, as if astounded by my outrageous suggestion. Jojo has already unpinned the love-heart badge and is gripping it fiercely. "What did you call her?" I ask.

"Jojo. I called her Jojo."

"No, you didn't." I can feel my cheeks blazing.

A bubble of snot appears briefly at Jojo's left nostril. Inflate, deflate, like a tiny balloon. "Off to your class now," I tell her.

She swipes her nose with the flat of her hand and clomps across the glossy wooden floor. Toby turns to follow her. "Just a minute," I snap.

"What?" His dark eyes narrow. The bruise has faded, but the area under his left eye still looks swollen.

"I heard what you said. You called her Piggy. I won't have you bullying her, Toby."

He wafts his eyelashes at me, as if to say, *And who are you? Just a music teacher. Not a real teacher at all.* "I wasn't bullying her," he says.

"Don't lie to me." My voice is too loud, verging on a shout.

252

"Everything okay here?" Jen calls across the hall.

I step back quickly. "Toby's just off to his classroom," I say, like a machine that's managed to put random words in the right order.

We watch him stroll across the hall. Something dull thuds inside me. "Well," I say, "I'd better get over to St Mary's."

Jen nods, and it's the same old Jen, but her smile is slightly askew, as if it doesn't quite fit her.

That evening, standing in her grubby fallen-down socks, Jojo swoops through "Gymnopédie" as if she hasn't had a break from playing at all. "That was lovely," I tell her.

"Thanks," she mutters.

"Shall we start your Thursday lessons again?"

"Can I?"

"Of course you can."

She grins, snatching a biscuit from the plate on the table.

"What was going on with Toby today?" I ask.

"He was just being friendly."

"He didn't sound friendly to me."

She turns the biscuit slowly, grinding its edge with her front teeth. "Hey, guess what! We're going to visit my dad."

"Will that be okay?"

"Yeah. No. He likes Midge best. Everyone does 'cause she's clever and I'm thick."

"Jojo, of course you're not thick. Midge struggles too, with her maths. Everyone's good at different —"

"Mum gets mad," she cuts in, brushing crumbs from her lips. "Says I'm lazy and don't try hard enough."

"It was like that in our house. My brother's really clever, and I wasn't brilliant at school — with maths especially. Dad would lose it with me. That made it worse. I'd get so het up I couldn't think straight."

"Did you hate him?" Jojo asks brightly.

"Of course not," I say, picturing Charlie huddled over his biology notes, which showed all the layers of skin, hairs sprouting from the epidermis like reeds. "He was my brother, I —"

"I mean your *dad*."

"No, I didn't hate him." My stomach twists uncomfortably.

"What about your mum? Did she shout as well?"

"Mum died when I was thirteen. I'm sure I told you that."

"Oh, yeah." She says this as nonchalantly, as if I've reminded her that I once lost a handbag. "What happens when you die?"

"Well, no one knows for sure. It depends on what you believe."

"Midge will go to hell," she murmurs.

"She's your sister, Jojo."

She blinks at me and asks, "Did you cry when your mum died?"

"Yes, lots," I say, although I can't really remember: wet or dry face, what does it matter?

"How did she die?"

"She fell into a road and was hit by a car." I didn't mean to tell it so graphically. I meant to say, "She had an accident."

Jojo removes a sock and scratches a troublesome spot on her sole. "Think I've got athlete's foot again," she murmurs. "Mum got me some cream for it. So, she fell? What — like tripped over?"

"She was in a hurry. She wasn't thinking." This is how I've played it, filled in the gaps. Of course, I wasn't there. I was in Mrs Bones's living room, with the faded rose-patterned walls and the glinting carriage clock, trying to breathe with my diaphragm.

"My dad got ill," Jojo continues, "and we thought he might die. He was drinking a lot, doing stupid stuff like falling over and banging his head on the cooker."

"Oh, that's terrible."

"He had a big, bloody bandage. It was embarrassing."

"And he's okay now, your dad?"

She smiles, and a flicker of real happiness — like clouds parting, and the sun beaming through — lights up her face. "Yeah," she says. "My dad's all right."

I pass the old launderette, which is now, officially, the Orange Tree, with its freshly painted white and tangerine sign. The canvas sheet has been taken down from the window. I've glimpsed Ed, bringing out a wheelbarrow of rubble or blending in with the assortment of builders and fitters. Even if I had the courage, it has never seemed like the right moment (the right moment to do what? Ask him for a drink?

"Look, Ed, I can see you're busy carrying — what's that? Shelving? — but would you like to come out with me some time?"). It's been years since I've given a man my number or asked him out. Like playing a wind instrument, you need to practise these skills. I fear that my breathing will falter, that the phrasing will come out all wrong.

No one's working in the Orange Tree this evening. When I peer in I see that the floor has been stripped, and the walls painted, awaiting tables and chairs and pretty young waitresses who'll flit round Ed, eager to please him. *Beautiful woman savaged by bonkers hound?* Bet he says that to all the girls.

There are no tables free in the Anchor so Jen and I perch on high stools at the bar. Workers from a nearby construction site keep reprimanding each other for swearing. "There's ladies present," one says, as if bad words might cause our ears to dissolve.

Jen is describing her son Elliot's shared flat: amazingly neat and organised, considering it's home to four eighteen-year-old boys and several pet rats. "And he's finished with Ruby," Jen continues. "Said they'd drifted apart. Doesn't that make him sound so *old?*"

"That's scary," I say, and it really is. I remember being astounded by the sheer power emitting from the three-year-old Elliot in a Batman costume as he swung, monkey-style, from his bedroom doorway. He fell off, split his ear on the sharp edge of a radiator and had to be rushed to A and E. "I was being Batman!" he cried, as Jen's mother bundled him into the car. Jen took to motherhood with remarkable ease, even when dealing with injury. She said it was what she'd been made for, which I tried to understand, but couldn't. I wondered if I'd been made to do anything other than play the flute.

I want to tell her that I hadn't really overslept on Monday but had spent the night with Alex. That I'd crept out without waking him up, the ultimate in rudeness. A very drunk man with a veiny face keeps wafting an open packet of powerful-smelling pork scratchings between us. "No thanks," Jen says, turning her back to him. This is the calibre of man I attract these days.

"Elliot's decided he's not coming home for Easter," Jen continues. "He and Rachel — that's his new girlfriend — are going touring in a friend's camper van. I told him we *always* spend Easter at Auntie Caroline's . . ."

I try to listen, as if I know how it feels to have a son who no longer wants to spend his holidays with me. "It's not a lot to ask," Jen adds, and Dad's words flood back: "Is it too much to ask, Stella, that I might see you at some point during your holiday?" And I rattled excuses: studying, work — I was still waitressing at the pizza restaurant; too many commitments to visit him, even for a couple of days. *Sorry, Dad — maybe I'll be down in the summer, or at Christmas. I'll see how things go.* I was aware of the space I'd left, even then.

"So," Jen says, "what was going on with Toby and Jojo yesterday?"

"He called her Piggy in the girls' cloakroom."

Jen sighs deeply. "That's awful. I'll have a word with him."

"And he was trying to take her favourite —"

"Stella," Jen cuts in, "don't you think you're getting too involved with those girls?"

"What d'you mean?"

"You said they're always coming round, plaguing you."

"They don't any more. It's calmed down."

"Jojo's dropped out of your group lesson, hasn't she?"

"Just . . . just a blip. I think she'll come back. I'm hoping she'll perform in the spring concert."

Jen laughs, waving away the persistent man and his pork scratchings. "Are you sure? She's only been playing since . . . what? September?"

"She's picked it up so quickly." I sound limp, embarrassed.

"Don't tell me you're allowing her back into the group?"

"I want to give her a chance."

Jen smiles kindly and says, "You're too good to them."

"I don't do much," I say. I haven't told her it's my flute that Jojo's learned to play, or that her rapid progress is largely due to free lessons at my house.

She drains her glass, kisses my cheek and says, "Better get home. Simon's cooking tonight." As she threads her way through the crowds I realise I still haven't told her about Alex.

★ ★ ★

The taxi driver turns sharp left, past Aquasplash, his wipers battling against insistent rain. In Main Street he stops at a red-and-white barrier and flashing amber lights. A police officer directs him down a narrow side street. Main Street is flooded, some trouble with drains. "Christ-on-a-bike," the driver mutters. "Can you imagine what it's like, dealing with this kind of situation every day of your life?"

Assuming he means the flooded road, or perhaps just the rain, I say, "It must be terrible."

"Sorry I ever got into this game. No respect, that's their trouble. Cheeking their elders."

I can't figure out whether his thoughts are filling the gaps, or chunks of his sentences are flying out of the open driver's window, which is allowing fine spray to douse his right shoulder. "In my day," he adds, "people had time for each other."

Perhaps I'm more drunk than I thought. I've only had a couple of drinks — on an empty stomach, which is now aching hollowly. The lane snakes between stern-looking buildings shrouded with twiggy plants — Virginia creeper, I think, but still leafless. A seagull squawks from a rooftop, as if lost. The street is full of cheap shops — Bargain Bazaar, Quids In, Everything Under A Pound — the kind that make you wonder how many cottage-shaped tea-light holders people really need.

I think about Jen, and realise she's right: Jojo might be able to play simple pieces in my house, and even in group lessons, but in front of gawping mums and dads she'd freeze. I can't put her through that. Toby will play a solo, as he did last year, and we'll do a group piece. With the choir, guitar group and the Mad Dogs — a band formed by three boys in year six — there are plenty of acts for a concert without torturing Jojo.

The lane ends at a T-junction. I'm about to ask the driver to turn left, but he swings right so dramatically I'm sent slithering over the peeling back seat. We're heading back towards the seafront — to the furthest end, the Orange Tree end. Something stops me telling the driver he's going the wrong way.

"Dodgy pub," the driver observes, as we pass the Lorimer Arms. "Those punters, you have to ask for fares upfront. You can tell them, the type that's going to do a runner. You can see it in their eyes." The driver keeps making eye contact in his rear-view mirror. He looks as if he's had his fill of the rain, the roadworks, the customers who dodge their fares. "You, young lady," the driver adds, "you're not the type, I can see that."

"Not what type?" The café comes into view. There's a light on inside, an orange glow.

"The type to do a runner," the driver says.

"No, I'm not." I wonder what Alex thought when he finally woke up. If he really imagined I'd skip work to lie there with him.

There are two people in the Orange Tree. Ed and a woman. At first I think they're working — painting, perhaps, the final touches. The driver's voice drones on, like the mumblings of a radio I've stopped listening to.

Dancing is what they're doing. His arms are round her as she leans into him. She has a powerful body, a swimmer's body. It's the traveller, who isn't travelling at all. Or another girl — a girlfriend he omitted to mention, and why should he have told me anyway?

Of course they don't see me, or even the passing taxi. They don't see anything because they're holding each other. I turn away to face the sea, which usually looks vast and inviting but now seems endlessly flat. "Come the wrong way," the driver mutters, performing a rash U-turn and speeding away from Ed, his girl and my stupid ideas.

Staring through other people's windows is a habit I really must stop.

CHAPTER
TWENTY-TWO

Nothing To Wear

"You all know about the spring concert, don't you?" I ask at the end of the Paul Street lesson.

The kids bob their heads eagerly, apart from Toby, who's gazing at the acetate drawings. "Willow," I say, "I think you're ready to play a solo this year, and Toby, of course . . ."

Willow glances at the others excitedly. Toby wrinkles his lips — an I-don't-think-so face. Something about his guarded expression says he doesn't want me to cajole him, not in front of the other kids. I try to make eye contact but he's peering at the clump of children crouching on the dusty tarmac outside. Each class is taking its turn to line up coppers on the ground. A mile of pennies for St Vincent's Hospice, that's what Jen's aiming for. A photographer is coming from the *South Devon Echo* to take pictures of the kids and their snaking lines of coins.

Jojo looks up from her scales book and says, "I'd like to play in the concert, Miss Moon."

I'm startled by her use of my teacher name. She usually avoids referring to me by name at school, and at home, of course, I'm just Stella. "Are you sure?" I ask.

I picture her reading aloud in front of her old class, and being so scared that she had an accident.

"I'd be all right," she says.

"It's just . . . you've never played in front of an audience before."

"I don't mind. I want to do it, Stel — *Miss Moon*."

"Maybe you'd like to think about it."

"Okay," she says flatly. As the other children leave for lunch she hangs back, slowly putting away the flute. She doesn't seem to have made friends at Paul Street. Most breaktimes she drifts around the playground, flipping through the gaudy pages of *Planet Girl* or *World of Fairies*. Other girls of her age have graduated to magazines filled with pop-star interviews, posters and makeup tips.

"Hadn't you better hurry off to lunch?" I ask.

"Euch," she says, shuddering. There's been a drive to improve school meals, to offer more vegetables and fruit, and include all the food groups. Since the scheme started Jojo and Midge have nagged Diane to make them packed lunches, but she's not a bloody catering company.

"I know I could do it," Jojo announces, before sauntering off to brave something disgusting with broccoli in it.

When the *Echo* comes out, Jen pins up the picture of the pupils and their mile of pennies on the noticeboard in the main hall. The huddle of red-sweatshirted kids beams between the anti-bullying poster, and the flyer inviting children to audition for the spring concert.

Midge has parked herself at the front, hands planted firmly on hips, and is grinning triumphantly, as if she'd collected all those pennies herself. A dark-haired boy, possibly Toby, is gazing down at the tarmac like someone dragged into a wedding photo by his embarrassing parents. There's a small gap between Jojo and the rest of the children, as if the person who was standing next to her has been erased.

And I realise why she wants to play in the concert. She wants to matter.

The days slide into spring with endless, unblemished blue skies. Diane buys a white plastic table and four matching chairs, bringing them home from Discount DIY in a taxi. She drags them through the house and arranges them on the patio at the back where they're soon splattered with seagull droppings. No one bothers to clean them. Since Diane increased her hours at the bedding factory, the girls have taken to preparing their own breakfast to be eaten outdoors. The moment they've finished and gone back inside, gulls swoop down to feast on spilt Coco Pops.

My meagre back lawn starts to sprout. One Sunday I haul out the dilapidated lawnmower from the dank shed at the bottom of the garden. Alex despaired of the way the rusting blades tore hopelessly at the grass and would stagger back inside bathed in sweat. I suggested buying a new one but he retorted that he couldn't bear to turn into "the sort of person you see in garden centres, staring at mowers".

"You stare at pictures of water features," I said.

264

"That's different." Lawnmowers, I decided, were just too damn *useful*.

Diane ambles out to observe my mowing endeavours from a patio chair. She's wearing her apricot dressing gown and the puppy slippers. Some kind of pearlised white lotion is swirled thickly over her chunky bare legs. "Need some help?" she calls over the fence.

"No thanks. I'll be done in a minute."

"You want a big strong man for that," she adds, with a cackle that disintegrates into a rattling cough.

I'm trying to pretend she's not there but the apricot blob glows in the periphery of my vision. A blur of cigarette smoke drifts over the fence. Sometimes I wish it was higher; I've even considered planting a hedge. Certain types of willow, I read, grow at the impressive rate of up to twenty feet in one season. But you can't put up barriers after new neighbours have moved in. You'd be making a point, literally shutting them out — like slamming a door in their face.

Diane flings her cigarette butt on to the patio and flattens it with her slippered foot. "Come over," she says, "when you're finished. I can't promise a big strong man, but I'll make you a cuppa that'll put hairs on your chest." She swans back inside, leaving the cigarette end still smoking on the fractured paving slab.

"I'm making a hamster swing," Midge announces, kneeling on a precarious stool at their kitchen worktop. I wince as she attempts to pierce a half coconut shell with an old-fashioned hand drill. Diane seems

265

unconcerned by the real possibility of her severing a finger. "Careful," I say. "Those things are really sharp."

"I'll manage," Midge retorts, but the drill bit keeps slipping and the shell rolls off the worktop and bounces across the floor.

"You hold the shell," I suggest, "and I'll drill the holes."

She frowns and asks, "Know how to use it?"

It's just like the one that Charlie used to attack Black Forest gâteaux. "I'll try," I say, and start to drill holes as Midge cuts lengths of wool to hang up the swing.

Diane is using a child's plastic spade to shovel rank-smelling hamster bedding from the cage into an open carrier bag at her feet. "Want to hold him?" she asks, dumping the filthy spade on the worktop. She picks up the hamster, which trembles in her cupped palms.

"No thanks. I'm not good with rodents."

"It's not a *rodent*," Diane retorts, thrusting the hamster into my face. Jojo's minor scales ripple downstairs.

"Has Jojo told you she wants to play in the spring concert?" I ask, with my back pressed into the microwave to distance myself from the quivering animal.

Hamburger makes the small leap from Diane's hand to the table. "I think she might have mentioned it."

"Will she be okay, playing in front of an audience?"

She shrugs. "If *you* think so."

"Well, I think she'll be fantastic."

"Done it!" Midge cries, dangling the coconut swing by its wool.

"Lovely," Diane says. I'm not sure whether she means Hamburger's new plaything, or the fact that her daughter is preparing to play Debussy's "Syrinx" before three hundred pairs of gawping eyes.

Diane and the children spend half-term in Birmingham with George, the girls' father. Without them around, my house is eerily quiet. There are no bangs on the door, no squeals filtering through in muffled form, no Queen's *Greatest Hits*.

Charlie has been ill, and from one brief phone conversation I can diagnose his condition as lovesickness — a mysterious, shadowy period during which he divides his time between work and staying in at the lodge with the object of his affections, leaving him with little inclination for swimming with me, or even a five-minute chat on the phone. "I think we should go down to Dad's," I say, "and see how he is."

"Not sick or anything, is he?"

"I mean after the *Friday Zoo* stuff."

"I thought you said that Lance guy had dropped charges. That it was just some dumb publicity stunt."

"Dirk. He's called *Dirk*. And he let it go because of his mum — she's a huge fan of Dad's, apparently. Has all his books from the seventies. Didn't you read the interview with her in the —"

"I don't read gossip columns," he says airily.

I pull a face into the phone. "He's out of a job, Charlie. With the bad publicity he's had lately, I doubt he'll ever work in TV again."

"He hasn't worked for years. He has to face it — it's all over for him."

Somehow I've turned into the One Who Worries About Dad. "And that's okay, is it?" I ask, banging down the phone before Charlie can answer.

I drive to Dad's by myself. The first thing I notice is the new Silverdawn Cottage sign, its lettering embellished with spindly curls as if it has been carefully painted by Midge. The NO TRESPASSERS sign has gone, and the garden is already abundant with flowers — just tamed enough, unlike Surf, who is recovering from eating poisoned meat that a farmer must have put out for foxes.

Dad is giving the small back lawn its first cut. He waves, but doesn't turn off the mower to greet me. "You won't believe this," Maggie says as we head indoors, "but the *Penjoy Bugle* has run a piece on your dad."

"What did they say?"

"Good things, all about the lovely job he's done on the garden. Here, let me show you." She leads me into the musty kitchen. She's been making dumplings, which will loll like small boulders in the kind of vegetable casserole that makes Dad profess to being not-hungry-at-all.

Maggie wipes her floury hands on a tea-towel, opens a drawer beneath the kitchen table and pulls out a newspaper cutting. I take it from her and read:

FRANKIE'S COMING UP ROSES

Life's bloomin' marvellous for local celebrity Frankie Moon. Since his scandalous sacking from popular show *Friday Zoo*, Frankie, 61, has thrown all his energies into transforming the unpromising grounds of his cottage at Penjoy Point. Although Frankie has worked steadily in the garden since moving to Penjoy in 1987, it's only this spring that his efforts have come to fruition with astonishing effect.

The garden has attracted visitors, who are keen to discover how the soil has been improved to produce the abundant display. When asked for his secret, Frankie told the *Bugle*: "Creating the garden has taken a huge amount of work, plus a special ingredient to improve the poor soil, which I am not prepared to divulge, for personal reasons."

Visitors are welcome at Silverdawn Cottage between 10a.m. and 3p.m. on Sundays. No dogs please.

There's a picture of Dad, affecting a casual pose by leaning on a fork in the garden. Behind him — like my first glimpse of the allotment — there is an eruption of colour.

Dad is now pruning the pyrocantha, which hugs the far wall. "Maggie showed me the article," I tell him. "It's looking lovely out here."

He frowns, and I wait for the barbed comment about Charlie not coming or caring. But his eyes soften, and he looks at me levelly. "Nice to feel you're good at something, isn't it, Stella?"

"Yes, Dad," I say. "It really is."

Something wells up inside me. I think it's called pride.

I come home to a message from Robert: "Stella, I know you're away at your dad's, but I was passing your place and saw this *thing* in your front garden — a kind of play tent. Those two girls were running around it. The little one had a weapon — a tomahawk, I suppose you'd call it. Do you mind this going on while you're away? Just thought you should know. Oh, and let's have a drink some time."

I find the girls in their back garden, slashing at an ageing Buddleia with Midge's light sabre and a long-handled brush. "You're back!" Midge yelps, as if we've been separated for months.

"How was your trip to your dad's?" I ask.

"Great!" She rearranges her face to an expression of seriousness. "Mum was meant to sleep on the bed that's a sofa."

"You mean a sofa-bed."

"Yeah. She got into it — I saw her in her nightie — but in the morning when I went in to see Dad she was in bed with him."

"Midge!" Jojo elbows her in the stomach.

"With her nightie off," Midge adds. "Can we come over?"

270

"Later."

"Aww, when?"

"When the jelly's ready to eat."

On the first day back at school Jen and I audition singers and musicians, plus Dylan Storey, whose act involves having his arms taped to his sides, then being bundled into a large cardboard box from which he bursts out, Houdini-style. We're not expecting virtuoso performances. We're just trying to minimise the risk of acts stumbling on for too long, and suggesting cuts where necessary.

After auditions I go to the music room, which becomes the after-school club at three twenty, to pick up some sheet music I need to photocopy. A cluster of girls is painting at the main table. Most of the boys are installed in chairs, riveted by a PlayStation game. Toby is gripping the controls. "We've just finished auditions," I tell him. "Sure you won't play in the concert?"

"No. Yes. I'm not playing." His eyes are fixed on the screen. The swelling has gone now, but there's a small, burgundy-coloured cut on his cheek. I want to ask if he's okay, whether he's been winding up his little sister again, but he's reached the next level — the other boys are cheering him on — and I have ceased to exist.

Diane is rarely at home when the girls return from school. They have their own key now, which Jojo wears on a string round her neck with her fairy necklace. They let themselves in and make sandwiches (Diane has banned cooking: the first thing she does when she comes home is rest a hand on the hotplates).

Midge invites me in to see her design for the cover of the concert programme. She's drawn the school with notes soaring over its roof, like homecoming birds.

"It's fantastic," I say.

"Yeah, I know."

Jojo's gaze is fixed on the TV. "Let's run through your piece for the concert," I suggest.

"No thanks." She stares at the screen.

"Not nervous, are you?"

"I've changed my mind. I'm not doing it."

"Why?"

"Shush, I want to watch this."

"What's wrong, Jojo? You were right — you *can* do it. Think how proud your mum will be when —"

She gathers herself up from her cushion on the floor and stomps out of the room. I find her hunched, knees pulled up to her chin, on the top bunk in her bedroom. "What's wrong?" I ask, scaling the ladder and perching on the edge of her unmade bed among a scattering of tights and knickers. She looks milky, unwell. "Don't want to do it," she whispers.

"Why not?"

"I've got nothing to wear."

"But you have loads of lovely clothes. Come on, let's look through your wardrobe."

"I'm too fat."

"That's ridiculous —"

"No, it's not. That's why I've got nothing to wear. I've tried everything on — *everything*."

272

Her mouth trembles. I touch her bare, goosepimply arm. She lifts her pillow, under which she's stashed a Marmite sandwich. She takes a tentative bite, then flings it on to the floor.

"Have you talked to your mum about this?"

Jojo glares down at the carpet, where the room-dividing masking tape has started to come unstuck. "She doesn't care," she says quietly.

"Of course she does."

"She says she can't afford to buy me new clothes."

"We could go shopping," I suggest, "and choose something. I'll treat you. It's your birthday in May, isn't it? We could make it an early present."

She lifts the key that's strung round her neck and presses its thin end into her palm, making an indent. "Don't know what to go as," she says.

"It's not fancy dress," I say, laughing.

The *Scooby Doo* theme tune drifts upstairs. "I should wear something loose," Jojo announces, "so I can breathe properly, with my diagram."

"*Diaphragm.*"

"Yeah, and I could pin up my hair with my sparkly clips." She grabs her hair in handfuls and lifts it, mock-pouting.

"You'll look fantastic."

"Think so?"

"I *know* so."

She grins at me, her cheeks flushed as her Marmite kiss lands smack on my lips. "What was that for?" I ask.

"Everything," she says.

CHAPTER
TWENTY-THREE

Stage Fright

Dear Stella

Lovely to see you at the weekend. I'm glad to report that Surf has made a full recovery and is his usual exuberant self.

Stella, I'm really writing to tell you about something very exciting that has happened to your father (you know how modest he is — he'd never tell you himself). A TV researcher saw the article about our garden and came to talk to your dad about it. The girl was too young to have seen *Frankie's Favourites* but was very interested when he showed her all his cuttings and books. In fact, she was here for several hours.

This girl has put together a proposal for a gardening programme with your father as presenter. The production company she works for is keen to get started as soon as possible. They're beginning filming — here at Penjoy — in two weeks' time, and the series will be broadcast from the middle of May. I'll check the exact date for you as I'm sure you won't want to miss it. They're calling it *Frankie's Flowers*, which I hope you'll agree has a certain ring to it. Of course, your father is working all hours now, making sure the garden is looking its absolute best. I have even found him weeding by torchlight.

Isn't it funny how things turn out?

With love,

Maggie

I reread the letter, fold it into a tiny square and slip it among the onionskin squares in the red-and-gold box. And I relay the news, via answerphone, to my brother's love-nest.

Jojo chooses a lilac halterneck dress, and after shopping we stop for drinks and fat slices of chocolate cake at the Beachcomber. At the counter a man with dishevelled hair is buying a takeaway coffee. Jojo has pulled the dress out of the carrier bag and draped it across her lap to admire it. The man turns, and it's Alex. A piece of cake sticks in my throat. "Hi," he says, approaching our table.

"Hello, Alex." I can feel Jojo's eyes burning into me.

He glances down at her. She's rammed the last lump of chocolate cake into her mouth. "Who's your friend?" he asks.

"This is Jojo. She's playing flute in the school concert. We've been choosing something for her to wear."

"Very pretty," he says, then lowers his voice and adds, "I was a bit upset that you didn't say goodbye."

275

Jojo keeps glancing, wide-eyed, from Alex to me. "I had to go to work," I tell him.

"Well, I was really hurt." He picks up his paper cup of coffee from our table, turns and strolls out of the Beachcomber.

"Who was *that*?" Jojo asks, as if a film star she vaguely recognised had just walked by.

"That was Alex, my ex-boyfriend."

"The one with those funny magazines about fish?"

"That's the one."

"What did you do to him?" she asks. I don't get it. "He said you hurt him," she adds, frowning.

"It was just his feelings I hurt," I say, as if that doesn't count.

Jojo mulls this over, smearing wet cake from her mouth on to her wrist. "Still love him?" she asks suddenly.

"No," I say, "I'm over him now," and it's no word of a lie.

The evening before the concert Jojo wants to skip her lesson. She knows I'll ask her to run through "Syrinx" again and doesn't want to play it until her performance. She's had her hair cut — the fringe falls heavily over her forehead, like an awning — and badgered Diane to buy her silver sandals to complement her new dress. "You look fantastic," I tell her, as she models her outfit in my living room.

"Not fat?"

"Jojo, you're not fat."

She musters a smile, almost believing me.

★　★　★

Friday. Concert day. I set off at five thirty — the concert starts at seven — having shaved my legs and chosen a floaty black calf-length dress, which Alex said made me look "a bit witchy" but feels lovely on. I don't usually make such an effort for school events. And it's silly to dress up, when the hour before the concert involves helping to place three hundred plastic chairs in neat rows in the hall.

I drive to school, passing Robert's block. A familiar car is parked outside. It's Verity's, crowded with car seats. The back window bears a sticker that reads, "Twins On Board". I wonder if she and Robert are having a heated discussion about custody and money while he rakes back his hair with his hand, hating every minute.

Or if she's come back to him.

Before a concert performance some kids hide in corners and play with their hair. Others draw unflattering pictures of each other on the whiteboard, or fool about with the baskets of percussion instruments. Willow is stomping around and jabbering as if she's been fitted with super-charged batteries. The Mad Dogs are trading Yu-gi-yo cards as if it's an ordinary evening. Dylan Storey is embellishing his escapologist's box with a silver pen.

Jojo gazes up at the board games, which are meant for the after-school club; they are all missing vital components and never played with. "Feeling okay?" I ask her.

277

"Uh-huh."

"Are you sure? You look upset." She reaches up to adjust the halter neck of her dress. "You'll be fine," I add. "The waiting's always the worst part. The second you start to play, you'll forget about all those people watching."

"Mum hasn't come," she murmurs.

Jen has appeared at the door to wish everyone luck. Stephen, the deputy head, is shushing the children, slowly wafting his hands with fingers outstretched, as if that might dampen the insistent chatter. "Still fifteen minutes to go," I whisper to Jojo. "The hall's only half full. Didn't she bring you and Midge?"

She shakes her head. "We got chips and went home and I ironed my dress. Then we came back by ourselves."

"Where *is* she?"

She shrugs. "Dunno."

"I'm sure she'll be here in a minute. I'll check the hall if you like."

Jojo smiles weakly and says, "Thanks."

I was fibbing when I told her it was only half full. All the seats are occupied — rows of plastic chairs are jammed together — and a bunch of parents leans against the radiators at the back of the hall. Some have their video cameras ready. There were no videos when I performed as a child, just hundreds of expectant faces — all those eyes — which I'd scan as I walked on to the stage, looking for Dad. I never expected him to be there, not really, but I knew, having discovered the heart-shaped locket, that he was capable of hatching

278

surprises. I couldn't help wondering whether he might surprise me.

I'd see Jen's parents — smart people in expensive knitwear — eagerly awaiting her viola performance. Younger children would be wriggling in their seats, already yawning and demanding to go home, or at least be allowed to go out into the playground. Sometimes I'd spot Mrs Bones in her pale blue twinset and dice necklace. Charlie would rush in when all the seats were taken. He had this look, this way of saying, "It'll be okay," with a split-second glance. Maybe I imagined it, and it was just his ordinary face. But it worked every time because it always *was* okay. I'd take a breath, and the first note would come, and all those faces would fade to nothing.

Midge sees me checking the hall and waves her light sabre excitedly, accidentally clonking Toby, who's sitting stiffly beside her, on the shoulder. I hurry out, past the year-six girls who are selling programmes bearing Midge's soaring-notes design from a table in the corridor.

Someone is smoking a cigarette in the playground. For a moment I think it's Diane, but the woman turns and nods in recognition. Toby's mother. His dad marches across the tarmac towards her. "Shame Toby's not playing," I say, still glancing around for Diane.

"We're very disappointed," his father agrees. "We've tried everything with that boy — every damn thing. We're at the end of our rope with him."

His wife gives him a sharp look, throws down her cigarette and strides into school, leaving a glowing tip on the ground. Still no Diane. If she doesn't show up, Jojo will refuse to play. I run towards the staff car park, unlock my car, take my special flute from the boot and pelt back into school.

The hall lights are dimmed now. Under the spotlight the stage looks enormous — quite terrifying, in fact, with all those cameras and eyes. It's the first time I've ever looked at a stage and felt nervous.

In the after-school room Jojo is sitting cross-legged in a corner, dipping her hand into a packet of sweets, which look like veiny eyeballs. "I can't see your mum," I tell her. "It doesn't matter, Jojo. She's probably just running late."

"It *does* matter." She crunches a sweet. Hot patches, like small pink clouds, have sprung on to her cheeks.

"Think how hard you've worked, all these months —"

"I'm not playing." A fragment of eyeball is stuck to the front of her dress.

I sit on the floor beside her with the flute case on my lap and open it. "Want to try it?" I ask.

Jen's voice filters into the classroom as she thanks the parents for coming and supporting Paul Street PTA. She sounds so grown-up, infinitely capable. There's a swell of applause, and the Mad Dogs tear into their first song.

"It's your special flute," Jojo says.

"Yes, it is. Have a try."

She frowns, takes the open case from me and runs her fingers tentatively across the silvery keys. "It makes me nervous," she says.

"Just play it, Jojo."

280

She pulls herself up, brings the flute to her lips and plays an A. "Stop that, Jojo," Stephen hisses. "They'll hear you in the hall."

"Want to play it tonight?" I whisper. It's a stupid idea. You don't perform with a different instrument. You get to know it, slowly befriending it, until it's as familiar as your own skin.

"What about Mum?" Jojo asks.

"There are lots of other people who are dying to hear you play."

"Like who?"

"Like me."

She grins, showing shiny pink gums. I take the ordinary flute from her and stuff the bag of eyeballs into my pocket. The Mad Dogs have finished, and Georgia Buckley is about to perform her guitar solo. Jojo is on next.

She stares down at the special flute, which she's gripping fiercely with both hands. "It makes me nervous," she says.

I laugh and say, "It's only a flute."

Georgia strides off-stage with the honey-coloured guitar still strung across her small, skinny body. From the fire-escape door I watch as Jen announces the next performer. ". . . been playing flute for less than a year . . . I'm sure you'll all agree that she's exceptionally talented. Ladies and gentlemen, boys and girls, a big hand, please, for Jojo Price."

She treads gently on to the stage. One of her socks has fallen down and left a pink indent round her calf.

281

Her silver heels glint under the spotlight. The applause dies away, and her eyes flit anxiously across the audience. I'm sure I can hear her thudding heart.

She lifts the flute, takes a breath. The first note — the B flat — cuts like ice through the hall. Jen is standing very still at the opposite side of the room. She catches my eye across rows of parents and raises an eyebrow.

Jojo is swaying slightly, relaxing into the piece. She could be playing just for me, in my living room. I glance round the hall, looking for Charlie, but of course he's not there. We're grown-up now, and it's Jojo on stage, not me.

As she holds the final note I think, *She could be me.*

The note fades and there's a surge of applause, which seems to go on and on. The smile breaks like a great, gushing wave across her face.

And someone shouts, "Piggy! Hey, Piggy!"

She seems to shrink in the oval of light. Her hands, which are still gripping the flute, fall to her knees.

And she runs.

In the corridor I crash into the table, sending unsold programmes bearing Midge's bird design fluttering to the floor. I scream Jojo's name. She's outside now, clattering across the playground in silvery heels, through the gate, pelting onwards with her hair flying behind her. "Jojo!" I shout.

She doesn't stop. There's a flash of silver — the flute reflects streetlights as she reaches the pavement — then no lights. Just black. My hands are all over my face, and I can't look.

CHAPTER
TWENTY-FOUR

Accidents Will Happen

I was a qualified teacher and a proper grown-up when Charlie told me what had really happened to Mum. I hadn't intended to come back to Devon after college, but Jen had heard of a peripatetic teaching job, and Dad had moved to Cornwall by then, so it was safe.

Charlie had also moved back. The lodge was ridiculously cheap to rent, and he could take the train to the university where he'd been offered a lectureship. We'd both been sucked home, but pretended we'd made our own choices, that we really could have lived wherever we liked.

We were walking alongside the old harbour before the marina was built. There were only fishing trawlers then, none of the fun boats — no cruisers or yachts. Charlie had brought his camera and a sheaf of mind-boggling notes, which he'd intended to read on the back beach. But it was too chilly to sit. The air was damp, and listless grey clouds spilt across a vacant sky. We walked, stopping occasionally to pick up beads of seaglass, which we stuffed into our pockets. "Let's go out for dinner tonight," Charlie said suddenly.

"Okay," I said. "What's the occasion?"

"I need a porcelain crab to help a student with his thesis. If you find one, it's my treat." He described its nutty brown shell, adding, "It's tiny — fits under a penny." We spent the rest of the afternoon peering among bits of frayed rope and lobster pots. He was teasing me, game-playing. "Come on," he called finally, "let's give up." I stalked over to him and uncoiled my hand.

Charlie smirked, ready to tell me it wasn't a porcelain crab but an ordinary sand crab, of which there were millions — but it really was the right kind. He fixed the close-up lens to his Nikon, and later, in Antonio's restaurant, he flipped through his notes and showed me a drawing captioned "Porcelain Crab, *Pisidia longicornis*". Beside it, in soft grey pencil, he wrote, "Found by Stella at 4.20p.m., low tide, at Lorimer Harbour, South Devon, 17 August 1989."

I said, "This is the first time we've been out for a meal together."

"I hope you're appreciating it."

"Mum used to take me to that Italian café," I added, "after my lesson on Saturdays."

"Yes, I know."

"Did you?" I'd assumed it had been our secret. A smaller secret than the special flute, but still a secret.

"You smelt lemony," he said, "when you came back."

"Were you jealous?"

"Hugely," he said, with a small laugh, so I couldn't tell if he was joking.

"Charlie, she loved us equally."

"Of course she did." He was looking down at his plate. He'd stopped laughing. I wanted to hug him then, but the waiter had reappeared at our table and was dragging breadcrumbs towards its edge with a scraper device.

Charlie took a sip of wine and fixed me with cool grey eyes. He said, "You have to know. It wasn't an accident."

"What wasn't?"

"What happened to Mum."

My breath caught in my throat. *Please don't tell me,* I thought. *Let's talk about your troublesome students, or porcelain crabs. Let's not spoil this.* "You don't know," I said. "You weren't there."

"I heard Dad talking with Uncle Tom and Uncle David late at night, after the funeral. I sneaked out of my bedroom, crept downstairs and listened at the living room door."

"What were they saying?" The words seemed to drift above us, as if they'd floated from someone else's mouth.

"She ran out of Mrs Bones's building, along the path and into the road. She meant it, Stella —"

"How do you *know*?" The waiter approached with dessert menus depicting lurid sundaes, then quickly retreated to the kitchen.

"The woman who lived downstairs saw her. She saw it happen."

Music filtered into the restaurant. Something bland, vaguely jazzy, the kind you don't usually notice. "Why," I managed, "did she do it?"

Charlie shrugged. "She could have told the doctor she needed more pills — you knew about her Valium, didn't you? Those little yellow tablets on the top shelf of the bathroom cabinet?"

"Yes, I think so."

He reached across the table to hold my hand, knocking over a small vase of wilting cornflowers. "She was sick," he said.

"Someone should have helped her."

"Like who?"

"Dad. Us. We could have done something."

"He was so wrapped up in himself, trying to be *famous* again."

"But we —"

"We were just kids, Stella. It wasn't our fault."

I tugged away my hand and started to pull on my jacket. "That's not the way it happened," I insisted.

"You don't know."

But I did know. She'd been running, and kept on running, down Mrs Bones's road to the point where it joins the wider main street, not stopping at the kerb, not reciting the Green Cross Code, as she'd often told us to do when we were little: *Look right, look left, look right again. When all's clear, quick march.*

The part of her brain that should have screamed, "Stop!" hadn't worked that day. The car hit her. It wasn't travelling fast but still sent her flying right over its roof like a doll. I knew that one of her slingbacks was found in a child's sandpit in someone's garden. Elona had taken a different route home so I wouldn't see where it had happened.

286

It had been an accident, just as I'd been told all those years ago. She hadn't made it happen.

I stared down at Charlie, who was picking at fragments of wax that had spilt over the edges of the glass candle holder. The bag that rested at his feet contained a small plastic box with a perforated lid in which he'd placed the porcelain crab with strands of damp seaweed and sand. Crabs were lucky, I decided. They kept shedding their shells, but a new one always grew to protect the tender insides.

"I'm sorry," Charlie said.

"I never listened at doors like you did."

He stood up, wiping my face with his sweater sleeve. "You were a good girl," he said.

Jojo sits with her fingers laced together on her lap in the staff room. The man who grabbed her, who stopped her being hit by the car, was Mr Chambers, Willow's dad. He was running late at work, and delayed even further by the roadworks that have churned up Main Street, turning our town centre into an eyesore. He'd parked as close as he could to school and run towards it, desperate not to miss Willow's performance. She was hurtling into the road — the girl in lilac — and he'd grabbed her dress and flung his arms round her.

He hadn't stopped to consider that you don't grab children.

"When you think," Jen says, "what could have happened."

Mr Chambers waves away the mug of tea she offers him. He has a well-worn face and windblown sandy hair. The skin round his eyes looks paper-thin. "Terrible shame about your flute," he tells Jojo.

"It's Stella's," she whispers, sucking a mousetail of hair. She dropped it when he grabbed her. It was run over — destroyed — by the car that could have hit her. As soon as he knew Jojo was safe, and not likely to do anything stupid, Mr Chambers stopped an oncoming van and retrieved the crushed flute from the road.

"Is it really yours?" Jen asks, perching on the arm of my chair.

"Yes."

"God, Stella —"

"It doesn't matter." It's all I can say.

"Of course it matters!"

"It's just a cheap one," I insist, because I want Jen and Mr Chambers to stop gazing mournfully at it, as if they could possibly understand.

"When you think what could have happened . . ." Jen says, touching Jojo's arm.

"I'm okay," Jojo mutters.

"We know who shouted," Jen adds. "I'll be contacting his parents. Picked on Jojo before, hasn't he, Stella? He's a difficult child, a real problem."

Mr Chambers pats Jojo's shoulder and follows Jen into the main hall. The concert is nearly over. Stephen and the other teachers have kept it running to schedule. The only small mishap was one of the Mad Dogs breaking a guitar string, and no one seemed to notice. There are cheers as Dylan bursts out of his escapologist's box.

288

"Wonderful performers . . ." Jen is saying ". . . huge effort . . . your fantastic support . . . very proud of our talented children."

My special flute sits on the low table in the staff room, which is usually littered with unfinished crosswords and coffee cups marred with brown drips. The solid silver headjoint is unharmed. I could pass it round a beginners' class, encouraging them to blow across the mouthpiece. It's the best way to begin, with none of the keys, which look impossibly complicated when you're starting out.

It doesn't look complicated now. The middle section has been flattened, its keys pressed into the barrel. I wonder if Mr Grieves at the music shop knows anyone with surgical instruments and delicate fingers with which he performs complex operations on flutes.

"I'll buy you a new one," Jojo murmurs.

"Don't be silly."

"He called me Piggy," she adds, dabbing her nose with a scrap of moist tissue.

"Sssh, forget what he said."

Car doors are slamming, children being called to heel. They mustn't run off like that in the dark. Look how busy it is, with all this traffic.

I pick up the flute and try to separate its parts, but the end section won't come away from the main body. "Where's its case?" Jojo asks.

"Still in the after-school room."

"Shall I get it for you?"

"No, don't bother. Go and find your sister, bring her here. I'll drive you home."

She stands up and smoothes the front of her dress. "Here," I say, digging into my pocket and fishing out her bag of sweets.

She takes the bag, pops an eyeball into her mouth, and stares down at the crushed silver. "At least you've got another one," she says.

Diane flings open her front door and says, "You're all back at last. I was starting to worry."

I try to find the right words.

"Where have you been?" she asks, as the girls push past her into the house.

"The concert," I say, "was tonight."

"Oh. I think I saw a bit of paper about it in Jojo's bag. Want to come in?"

"No, it's getting late."

"Something wrong, Stella?"

She really doesn't know. "Why didn't you come?" I ask.

Her mouth shifts uncomfortably. Her eye makeup is heavier than usual. Too much black liner, which makes her eyes look like tiny pieces of gravel. "Had my hair done after work," she explains. "Model night — only cost me a tenner. Normally the colour alone would be thirty. Sure you don't want to come in?"

I stare at her freshly dyed hair, which looks inky blue in the streetlight. She has remodelled her makeup, tried to make her face fit. "No, thanks," I say.

She really doesn't get it. The months of practising, the fretting over what to wear, the bubbling excitement

290

and fear, which evaporated instantly as Jojo drew breath to play that first note. None of it means a thing.

I'm still holding my special flute, which I wrapped like an injured thing in a sweater I found in the car. I didn't bother collecting its case from the after-school room. Diane peers down at it quizzically, then pats her unyielding hair. "You might as well say it," she says finally.

"What?"

"You don't like it. I knew I should've gone blonde."

"That might have been better," I manage, though she could have opted for bubble-gum pink for all it matters. In fact, she could be someone else entirely: a middle-aged washed-up TV chef, barely glancing over the newspaper as his daughter comes home from her end-of-year recital. Worse than not caring — not even noticing.

And, for that moment, I hate her.

Robert has left a message: "Wondered if you'd like to meet up. We could take the kids to the beach, have a picnic. I'd like a chat, Stella."

Jen has called to say that a flute, plus an empty case, were left in the after-school club. "Not sure if they're yours or Jojo's," she adds, "but I've brought them home for safekeeping until Monday. I hope Jojo's feeling better."

Without unwrapping it, I place the jumper parcel on top of the bookshelf. I can still see her, deathly pale in the oval spotlight, her hands fallen to her knees. She hadn't wanted to play when Diane failed to show up.

Why hadn't I left it at that? She could have had a future in music. Now I doubt that she'll ever play in public again.

I climb the stairs and slide into bed, watching the darkening shadows creep into my room. Much later I dream of eating lemon sorbet with a crushed silver spoon, and can still taste it, sharply sweet, when I'm woken by bleating gulls.

CHAPTER
TWENTY-FIVE

Frankie's Flowers

"One of nature's clever tricks," Dad says, "is to ensure that most plants look right together. What we're looking at here is the overall blend of colours — the wider picture."

The camera closes in on a rogue crop of poppies. "I didn't plant these," he continues, wafting large hands over the blooms as he strolls along the cobbled path towards the camera. "They appeared in just the right place." His voice is gentle: it's not his long-division voice. He's wearing rumpled brown cords and a rust-coloured polo-necked sweater. Surf keeps lolloping into shot, a grubby grey blur.

"I didn't like him at Christmas," Midge announces from her seat at the table. "He's nicer on telly. How does that happen?"

"What, Midge?"

"How does being on telly make someone different?"

Scarlet petals, laden with bees, crowd the screen. "I think he's happy," I tell her.

★ ★ ★

I unwrap the flute and place it on the shop's glass-topped counter. Mr Grieves bends to examine it. "What happened?" he asks.

"It had an accident."

He touches the worst part, the flattened part, where the keys have been squashed into the barrel. The backs of his hands are patterned with raised blue veins, like dribbles of wax. "I'm very sorry to see this," he says.

I wish I hadn't brought it in. I want to snatch it from the counter, bundle it back into its sweater and leave. Mr Grieves runs an index finger along the silver. Gleaming, undamaged flutes are displayed on plush velvet in the locked case on the wall. Mr Grieves is offering 30 per cent discounts, easy-payment plans. The shop is struggling.

"As you know," Mr Grieves says, "springs can be replaced, as can keys. Flutes can be completely overhauled." He talks slowly, like treacle pouring. "I have serviced this instrument several times," he adds.

"Yes, I know."

"If it were just a dent, or even a bend in the body . . ."

A bend in the body, like a person damaged in a road accident: serious, but fixable. A narrow escape.

Mr Grieves gathers up the corners of the sweater and folds them over the flute, as if he is wrapping a gift. "I'm sorry," is all he can say.

I pass the hardware place with its gaudy display of silk anemones in the window. That's what happens to shops in Bay Street. There's not enough passing trade, so they try to diversify. Feathers 'n' Fur has a display of dusty-looking porcelain fairies, their skinny limbs protruding from gauzy skirts. "I *want* one," a little girl bleats, rapping the glass until her tight-lipped mother hauls her down the street like a pull-along toy. I follow them as far as the steps to the beach, where I have arranged to meet Robert.

And I wait, sitting on the seafront's concrete edge, with the jumper parcel nestling in my lap, like a damaged pet. He's ten minutes late. This doesn't count as properly late. Ten minutes can be lost while you peer behind radiators, searching for a toddler's toy monkey, or gaze at antique yogurts in the fridge, trying to assemble the promised picnic.

I flip through a celebrity magazine that someone has left on a bench. It's filled with Hollywood stars and less glamorous British soap actresses: pages of faces bleached by camera flash. Rings have been drawn round dimpled thighs and peculiar knees, showing that the rich and famous are just as flawed as ordinary people.

"Dad!" a small boy yells on the beach. "Want a go on the grabber machine?"

"Shut up," the man snaps from behind his newspaper. It's warm enough now to lounge on the sand. Most of the green-and-white striped deck-chairs are occupied by parents half watching their children.

"I want a prize," the boy whines.

The man throws down his paper, weights it with pebbles and says, "For God's sake, come on, then."

295

The kid pelts up the steps towards the machine. His dad delves into trouser pockets for change and lets the boy post in a coin. The silver claw moves forwards, then down, and I'm expecting it to come up empty but it's gripping the tiger, which drops into a chute and the boy's quivering hands. The dad glances at me and says, "Haven't been stood up, have you, lovely girl like you?"

"No," I say, trying to appear as if I'm just sitting, not *waiting*.

"I've seen you swimming — in winter sometimes. You're either brave, or barking mad." He grins, showing a gold front tooth. The boy is chatting intently to the tiger. "We could swim together some time," the man adds.

"Thanks, but I usually swim by myself."

He frowns and says, "I'm sure I know you. You from around here?"

"I grew up here, yes."

"Which schools?"

"Paul Street Primary, Lorimer High."

"That's it. Lorimer. Stella, right? Flute player, TV chef dad. That old guy who was sacked from *Friday Zoo*, got into some kind of fight with one of the —"

I turn away from him to see Robert hurrying along the seafront, his too-big T-shirt flapping in the breeze. "Boyfriend?" the man asks, as Robert waves to me.

I fix on my broadest smile and say, "Yes."

Robert hasn't brought the children. "Verity's taken them to Aquasplash," he explains, which I translate as

296

"She didn't want them to spend the afternoon with you."

"Where's the picnic?" I tease him.

"I thought we could pick something up."

"I'm not hungry yet. Let's just walk."

We jump down to the sand and pass the deck-chairs where the tiger boy's dad is pretending to snooze. I don't recognise him from school. Occasionally people say, "Don't I know you?" They might vaguely remember the sole episode of *Frankie's Girl*, or one of my performances in a school concert. Sometimes I pretend it wasn't me, that Stella Moon isn't someone I've heard of.

We climb over rocks that are smothered with jagged limpets. At the furthest cove the sand is creamy-white, soft as a child's hair. I tell Robert about the concert, and my run-over flute. I unwrap it and watch him handle it. It looks like part of a car engine, or something to do with plumbing. "That's terrible," he says. "Will she pay for a new one?"

As if that would fix everything. "Of course not. She's just a kid."

"Her parents should pay. How much did it cost?"

"It was a present. I have no idea."

"It doesn't seem fair," Robert says.

My sandals are digging into my heels so I pull them off. My pale, skinny legs are stretched out in front of me. Diane was angry when I shunned her offer of thirty pounds, which she pushed through my letterbox in a grease-stained envelope. "I pay my way," she protested, when I handed it back. She'd darkened her eyebrows with black pencil so they'd match the new hairdo. They looked like pieces of liquorice.

"You can use my flute," Robert says.

"It's okay, I have another."

"I'm thinking of selling it," he adds, grinding a finger into the sand. "I don't really play any more. Stella . . . Verity's come back. I'm not sure what'll happen with us, but I —"

"I know she has," I say. "I saw her car, and I assumed —"

"We're trying to work things out."

A girl and a boy have waded out of the sea. The jewel in the girl's belly-button glints in the sun. The boy wraps a towel round her hair, rubs vigorously, and when he takes it away her hair's frizzy and mad-looking, which makes him laugh.

"I'm pleased for you," I say.

Robert says, "I think I am too."

We clamber back over the rocks in search of food. There's a new French restaurant, La Grenouille, on the seafront. We peer through half-drawn ivy-patterned curtains. A waitress is hunched over a table, ladling soup into her mouth.

"We could try that other new place," Robert suggests. "Orange something, where the old launderette was. Ever been there?"

"No," I lie.

"It looks okay. Can't help thinking, though, another café's the last thing we need around here."

"Let's just go to the Beachcomber."

"Come on, Stella," he says, tugging my hand. "Let's try somewhere new."

The Orange Tree smells of paint and hard graft. An agitated girl with her hair secured in plaits is wiping tables and asking customers, who keep trying to attract her attention, to place their orders at the counter.

Ed is manning the till and fetching orders from the back room where Lil, the launderette lady, used to smoke and watch black-and-white movies. Now, of course, it's a kitchen. The only free table is next to the counter. Ed's too busy to see me. Robert picks up the tangerine-coloured menu and says, "They only do sandwiches, cakes, snacky stuff."

"That's okay." If I hadn't seen Ed and his girl, I'd feel comfortable in here. The image of them, with their arms round each other, beams into my brain.

Ed is explaining, "No, it's not vegetarian cheese. It's organic, yes — everything is — but not vegetarian."

"And don't you have a high chair?" the customer asks.

"We'll be getting some. We've only been open a week." His voice is steady, ever patient. His anyone-can-dive voice.

"You should have baby-changing facilities," the woman barks on, "I'm sure it's the law, and somewhere for breastfeeding."

"You can breastfeed in here if you like," Ed says, sounding weary now.

"You need better facilities," she retorts. "Next time I'll go to the Beachcomber."

299

She marches back to her table and rams a buggy, containing a mewing child, out of the door. "Good," Ed says under his breath.

I get up to order our food. Ed brightens and says, "Stella, it's not usually like this . . ."

"It looks fantastic, Ed."

"We need to . . ." a flicker of a smile ". . . improve our facilities. What would you like?"

"Two lattes and . . . I can't decide."

"Something sweet?" he suggests.

I gaze into the display cabinet. There are strawberry tarts like you see in French *pâtisseries*, and something part-way between chocolate cake and mousse. The kind of dessert that involves making a mess of yourself.

And there's something with pastry and caramelised apples. An upside-down apple tart, like Charlie chose on holiday in France.

Dad couldn't forget the *tarte tatin*. It was as if the taste had impregnated his tongue. He tried to re-create it at home but the apples dissolved in our mouths like indistinct clouds, and the pastry wasn't right. He blamed substandard British flour, and me for buying the wrong kind of apples. He started to use words like "caramelisation". Like a wayward child, it wouldn't behave the way he wanted it to.

"Who's your friend?" Ed asks, loudly enough for Robert to hear.

"That's Robert, my —"

"Boyfriend?"

"No," I say firmly. The waitress pushes past me on her way to the kitchen. I'm taking too long, dithering at

300

the counter. I ask for two slices of *tarte tatin*, aware of Ed watching me as I head for our table.

Robert looks up and says, "Verity isn't happy about you and me spending time together." He gazes through the window at the long-limbed girls flying back and forth on rollerblades, their hair wafting behind them like aerosol spray.

"Why?" I ask.

"You don't know, do you?" He smiles, blushing slightly.

I shrug, confused.

"She was convinced I had a thing about you. Even accused me of having a fling."

"That's ridiculous!" I decide not to confess about the toothbrush stashed in my bag, the day we went to Butterfly Land.

"She wanted me to stop my lessons," he continues, "but I wouldn't. And she was right, you know. Verity's very perceptive."

"Right about what?"

Robert squeezes my hand. A fragment of pastry melts on my tongue. "I did have a thing about you," he says, as Ed appears to take away my empty plate.

CHAPTER
TWENTY-SIX

Missing Person

Diane brings dense floral perfume into my hall. "Could the girls sleep over on Friday night?" she asks.

"You mean *all* night?" She hasn't mentioned the concert. She's either deeply ashamed for not being there, or has forgotten it ever happened.

"They won't be any trouble."

"I'm not sure —"

"I've got tickets for Wicked Queen," she says. "Normally I wouldn't bother with a tribute band — bloody diabolical, most of them. But we've booked a hotel. Room at the top, fantastic view of the whole of Wolverhampton."

I don't ask who the other part of the "we" might be. I'm more concerned at the prospect of being in sole care of her children at weird hours like four thirty a.m.

"Okay," I say, "if you're sure they'll be happy staying here."

"They'll love it," she says, awash with relief. At that moment, Wolverhampton seems as distant as Adelaide.

Friday, five twenty-eight p.m. The girls are picking at chips and watching SpongeBob, an animated yellow

302

sponge who inhabits an underwater city called Bikini Bottom. I bought oven chips and studied the instructions on the bag: "Preheat oven to 200 degrees. Spread chips thinly on a tray and place near top of the oven. Bake for around twenty minutes until crisp and golden."

"My dad's show's on in a minute," I tell the girls.

"But we watched it last week!" Midge protests. Jojo lets herself slide, as if she's been liquefied, on to the floor. She has already removed her silver sandals and socks and lined up ten nail polishes — a different colour for each nail — which Diane bought for her birthday. Before the girls crept into my life I wouldn't have let anyone place lidless bottles on my floor: I'd have laid down newspaper, and insisted that only one bottle was open at a time.

Dad ambles into shot. One paper described him as "affable and modest, with a relaxed style and infectious enthusiasm" but in fact he's barely noticeable among erupting flowers. He doesn't look like a dad any more but a granddad: the kind who'd help a child with her homework, not rip her worksheet in two.

He's been commissioned to write a book, *Frankie's Flowers*, to accompany the series. A photographer spent three days at Silverdawn Cottage. Maggie sent me colour photocopies of the pictures: irises, like long purple tongues, and blazes of poppies and cornflowers.

Maggie can pay for more help in manning the car park. She has cleared out the spare bedroom and surprised Dad by repainting it. He complained that the white she'd chosen was too harsh for his eyes. She

303

bought a self-assembly desk, which neither of them has got round to building yet. "I've tried to persuade him that he needs a computer," she told me, "but you know how he is with technology. Who else still uses an adding machine?"

When *Frankie's Flowers* has finished I clear away the girls' plates and lift down Midge's box of missile components from the bookshelf. "Would you like to play my flute?" I ask Jojo.

"No, thanks," she mutters. Since the school concert she's had no instrument to practise on. I've offered mine when she's been with me, but she's always found something better to do, like picking the icing from Party Hoops and scattering pink and green crumbs on my rug.

"It must be your bedtime," I suggest.

"We don't have one," Midge chirps, from her missile workshop at the table.

"You mean you never go to bed?"

"I'm not tired," she says, widening her eyes to demonstrate her alertness.

She has constructed a weapon capable of blasting the top bunk through their roof, and Jojo with it, to some distant planet where they do unspeakable things to girls who love pink and fairies.

Two twenty-seven a.m. A muffled noise, like hiccups. I laid out the spare mattress in the small bedroom, covering most of the floor and creating a padded-cell effect. Jojo lined up her fairy dolls in sitting positions so they could watch her as she slept.

More hiccups. I swivel out of bed and creep through to the spare room. There are dark shapes of the girls' faces, swathes of fine hair on pillows.

A pair of eyes gleams wetly. "Jojo?" I whisper.

A damp sniff.

"Are you okay?"

"I'm asleep," she whispers hoarsely.

I step across the parts of the blanket with no limbs beneath and crouch beside her. "What's wrong?" I ask. "Are you missing your mum?"

Fierce shake of the head.

"Can't you sleep?"

"I'm okay," she hisses.

"Come in with me so we don't wake your sister."

She untangles herself from the blankets and lets me lead her by the hand to my room. She's wearing the pale pink nightie with the lace coming undone at the neck. We sit on my bed's spongy edge. "Tell me what's wrong," I say, putting an arm round her shoulders. She feels cold, slightly clammy, and is clutching a startled-looking doll.

"It's Toby," she murmurs.

"Forget about the concert. It was awful, but he's just —"

"He's hurt," she cuts in. "Someone punched him and gave him a pain in his tummy."

"Hasn't been fighting again, has he?"

She turns to me, and her eyes gleam like marbles. "You know how Mrs Summer said he wasn't allowed to talk to me ever?"

"Yes." The Monday after the concert, Jen called Toby into her office and laid down strict rules. She had already spoken to his mother on the phone. One more step out of line and his parents would be brought in for a meeting. She won't tolerate name-calling in her school.

"He came up to me at breaktime," Jojo continues, "on Thursday, I think, and I was going to say leave me alone, but —" Her voice splinters.

"Jojo, what did he do to you?"

"Nothing. He started crying. I've never seen a boy cry — only Dad when we moved out. And he's not a boy. He's a man."

"Was Toby sorry? Is that why he cried?"

"He didn't mean to say it. He was just upset 'cause his mum and dad had made him come to the concert."

"That's no excuse," I tell her. "He's just a horrible bully."

"He was already in trouble for not playing in the concert. His dad was even madder 'cause of what he shouted at me. So he hit him. That's why his stomach hurt."

Jojo wipes her wet face on her nightie. "Are you sure about this?" I ask.

She nods, and I lead her by the hand back to her makeshift bed. When I peek in later there's a faint smell of sweets, even though teeth were thoroughly brushed. Jojo is breathing steadily. But I know she's not sleeping.

Diane has revised her opinion of tribute bands. "Lead singer," she announces, the following evening, "had his teeth fixed so they'd look like Freddie's. Twelve grand it cost him." She goofs her front teeth to demonstrate the kind of dental handiwork she's talking about. She's brought the programme to show me — "Unforgettable, Unadulterated: A Night Of Pure Showmanship!" — plus bubble-bath sachets and a hefty octagonal glass ashtray embossed with "Plaza Hotel". "Thanks," I say, "but I don't smoke."

"Use it for nibbles," Diane insists. "Come on, girls, get your stuff. Stella will be glad to see the back of you."

Midge stuffs her weapon into a carrier bag. Jojo pulls on a matted yellow cardigan. We haven't discussed Toby since last night. I need to talk to Jen; there are guidelines on how to deal with these situations. Words like "guidelines" and "policies" are reassuring.

As they leave Diane adds, "Met the lead singer, Martin. Lovely bloke, no airs about him, even though he's played all over the world — London, Paris, Wolverhampton, Coventry . . ."

"What did you talk about?" Midge pipes up.

"The day Freddie died. What we were doing. I remember it like it was yesterday — working in that bee place, couldn't bring myself to open up. Visitors hammered on the window. Couldn't face their bloody questions. I just sat there, stone still, hoping they'd think I was a wax dummy."

She smiles unsteadily and ushers the girls home. I retrieve a stray chip from the floor and go to call Jen, who always knows what to do. But my phone rings, and

Maggie blurts out, "Sorry to disturb you, Stella, but —"

"What's wrong?"

"I don't suppose you've heard from your dad?"

"No, not since his last letter. Why — has something happened?"

"He went out four or five hours ago when I started building his new desk. I got into such a muddle with the silly instructions — all these crucial bolts and things missing — that I didn't notice the time. He hasn't come home, Stella."

"Where was he going?"

"Just the usual, walking the dogs."

"He's probably run into Harry and gone to the Smugglers."

"I've already phoned Harry."

"I'm sure it's nothing, Maggie."

"It's so unlike him to do this. There's bound to be some explanation, isn't there, Stella?"

"Of course there is," I say, trying to keep the trace of doubt out of my voice.

I call her back an hour later. Still no Dad. "I've been up to the village," Maggie says, "and checked the Poachers — Kevin says no one's seen him since quiz night last Wednesday." Her voice is high-pitched and breathy, like a child's.

"I wish I could do something."

"I've phoned the hospital," she adds, and the words fracture.

308

"Maggie, don't get upset. Maybe he's visited someone, lost track of time."

"It's nearly midnight," she protests.

My hand strays to the red-and-gold box on the bookshelf. I trace its carved curls with a finger. "Do you think you should phone —"

"The police? I already have. Grown man, out walking his dogs — they pretend to be concerned but it's not a priority."

"And there's no sign of the dogs."

"No."

I run a finger along the sharp edges of the folded-up recipes. "Maybe you should try to get some sleep."

"Yes," Maggie says softly.

"Call if you need me," I say, feeling powerless and small.

Instead of sleeping I watch my alarm clock's blue glow: 12:37, 12:38. I try holding my breath for a minute but can't even manage thirty seconds. It feels like my diaphragm's not working properly.

Faint music drifts in from next door. "We Will Rock You". I slide out of bed, pull on my dressing gown and head downstairs to check the answerphone again, although I would have heard the phone ringing, even over the music. I try Charlie's number — he's been out all evening — but it just rings and rings.

People go missing. They go out for a newspaper or a short walk, as if it's an ordinary day, and are never seen again. Some have another family, another life. Others, I suppose, are desperate.

I lift the colour photocopies of Dad's flowers from the bookshelf and flick through them. In the cool streetlight they look eerie, as if they belong in a forest where wolves live. Round-ended scissors, a glue-pot and pieces of ripped cardboard litter the table from Midge's recent craft session. I've stopped putting things away when she's finished. Sometimes the table is cluttered with her stuff for days on end, and I eat my supper from my lap on the sofa. It no longer seems important to be neat.

Diane is singing now, at one seventeen a.m., and Dad still hasn't come home.

Charlie phones just after eight a.m. "Dad still hasn't shown up," I tell him.

"You're joking. I assumed —"

"He's missing, Charlie. Maggie's been to the police station. They said most people who go missing turn up safe and sound in a day or two."

He says, "Please don't cry."

"I'm not crying, Charlie. I'm just scared."

"I'll come over."

"I'll meet you on the back beach later. I can't stand being here, staring at the phone."

"Okay," Charlie says.

On my way into town I ring Maggie on my mobile. "They asked me what he was wearing yesterday," she says. "How would I remember? I said brown trousers." Her throat catches as she repeats, "I think it was brown trousers."

★ ★ ★

Charlie is sitting with his knees pulled up to his chin on the wooden walkway that runs alongside the beach huts. "We should go to Dad's," I tell him. Beach-hut owners are sharing picnics and drinking beers on folding chairs. There's no sign of Phoebe, Charlie's ex. I've never known him have a relationship that lasted more than a few months. Mum once said she couldn't reach him. I wonder if that's how his girlfriends feel too, that he shuts them out — his hermit-crab position.

"I don't think it'll help," he says.

"We could go looking for him, be with Maggie. She sounds frantic, Charlie."

"He's only been gone for, what?"

"Nearly twenty-four hours."

"There must be a reason," Charlie says, looking past me towards the flat, washed-out sea.

"Like what?"

"They had a row, she's too embarrassed to admit it . . ."

"Relationship expert," I snap, then wish I hadn't.

He stares down at the wooden walkway that's gone silvery, smooth as steel.

"You don't care," I murmur.

"Of course I care," Charlie says.

I fling a sweater, jeans and my toothbrush into a bag, and leave a message for Jen to apologise for being unable to come to school tomorrow. "There's a family problem," is all I say. I can't bring myself to tell her what's happened — to put the words out there.

I carry my bag to the car, dump it on the back seat, turn the key — and nothing. A couple of boys in hooded tops rattle down Briar Hill on skateboards, making long, late-afternoon shadows.

I turn the key over and over again. Something's died in the engine. I wait before trying again, as if my car is a battery-operated toy and might rouse itself, if it's given time to recover.

Diane is watching me through her window, clutching a mug. The headboard still rests against the front of her house. Midge has turned it into a den. Most of the salmon-coloured velvet has peeled away from the wood, and what's left has gone mottled from being rained on. I've found Midge behind it, lounging on a small mound of satin cushions filched from the living room.

The door opens and Diane comes out. "What's the problem?" she shouts, through the driver's window.

I climb out, and hear myself saying, "My dad's gone missing. He's on some police computer, which means he's *really* missing. I just need to get there."

"Where?" Diane asks gently.

"Cornwall. My dad's."

"Come in," she says. "Your car's going nowhere." She sounds like someone in a film, someone who makes grand statements. I follow her into the house.

The remains of the girls' tea — fish fingers and beans — have congealed on plastic plates on the coffee table. "Has he gone missing before?" she asks.

"No, of course not." I don't tell her that they've found his dogs. Turf showed up late last night and barked to be let in. It was the first time Maggie had ever heard him bark. Surf was found chasing sheep two miles from Penjoy Point. There's been a campaign to stamp this out — irresponsible owners allowing their dogs to worry livestock. He was lucky not to be shot.

"There'll be some explanation," Diane says. The skin beneath her eyebrows is puffy, as if she's been vigorously plucking stray hairs.

"Something's wrong, I just know it —"

"Where was he going?" she asks.

"Just the usual places, Maggie thinks — across the fields. There hasn't been a proper search yet."

Maggie told me she'd never realised that Dad had so many friends. They all know him — the bakery brothers, Kevin from the Smugglers, the elderly man from the post office, the couple who do B-and-B in Penjoy village. They've all been out searching, but nothing's been found. I didn't ask what they were looking for.

I fish out my mobile from my bag and call Maggie again. "I was going to come," I babble at her, "but the car won't start — battery, I think — and I don't know how —"

"Don't worry," she says, being the calm one now. "It'd be dark when you got here anyway. There's nothing we can do in the dark."

"I'll catch the first train tomorrow."

"He'll be home by then," she says bravely.

"Yes, of course he will."

The rumbling voice of a storytape narrator comes from upstairs. A girl's brothers have been turned into swans. Diane's living-room floor is strewn with snippets

313

of synthetic fabric. "For my rugs," she says. "What I do when stuff's getting on top of me is get my rug things out. Keeps my mind occupied."

She opens a drawer in the sideboard and pulls out a metal hook with a curved wooden handle. "I'll show you," she says. "It's offcuts they sweep up from the factory floor. We're allowed to bring bags home. You find all sorts in the bags — ciggie ends, bits of sandwich. Last time I found half an orange."

From under the sofa she extracts a piece of rug backing. One corner is tufted with nylon strips in jarring colours. She snags a piece of nylon on to the hook, performs a twisting motion with her wrist and says, "You try."

The storytape man sounds like he's talking into a cardboard tube. The sister is weaving nettles to make coats, which she'll throw over the swans to turn them into her brothers again. Diane presses the hook, the backing and a fistful of nylon strands into my hands. I hook a piece through, come up and catch the loop — soon I've made small purple lawn.

"Good girl," Diane says, as if she's acquired an additional child.

The swans' sister has one coat to finish. But the king is angry because Elise — that's the girl's name — won't speak. If she does, the spell will never be broken. He doesn't understand that she has something important to make out of weeds, out of nothing.

"I should go home," I say. "I hardly slept last night."

Diane squeezes my hand and says, "It'll be a fuss over nothing. You know what parents are like."

No, I think. *No, I don't.*

Next morning I take my coffee from the plaited girl at the Orange Tree. "Stella?" Ed says, behind me. "You're early today." I have started to pick up a coffee each morning to take to school. It's better coffee than I make at home, that's all.

"I'm going to Cornwall," I tell him. "Catching the eight-twenty train."

"Not school holidays, is it?"

"No, I'm going to see my dad." My vision mists as I correct myself: "I'm going to *find* Dad."

"Something's happened," he says gently.

I can feel the steam from my coffee rising through the hole in the lid. "He's missing. There's probably some explanation. He'll have taken himself off on some trip, worrying us stupid . . ."

"If there's anything I can do —" he starts, then scribbles a phone number on a paper napkin. "You can call me any time."

"Thanks. I'm sure he's *fine.*" I stuff the number into my jeans pocket. It feels so right, the very opposite of awkward, when he pulls me into the warmth of his chest.

I don't care about the girl I saw him with. All I care about is Dad.

Ed's coffee has gone dishwater cool before I remember to drink it. I watch lush, rolling hills sweep past the carriage window. When I get off this train I'll take a taxi from the station to Penjoy Point. Maggie tried to insist on collecting me from the station, but I didn't want her driving anywhere in case something happened, in case she was needed.

There are only five other people in the carriage. It's an ordinary Monday morning, not a holiday. I buy another coffee but by the time I've carried it back from the buffet car, half of it's slopped down the side of the cup and the rest looks too muddy to drink. The woman sitting opposite is patiently filling in a crossword with green Biro. *Beware the green Biro*, Dad said. The woman glances up at me. Her mouth is heavily smeared with oily-looking lipstick.

I call Charlie again, and his voicemail tells me to leave my name and number. "Where *are* you?" I bark into the phone.

The woman opposite gives me a brief, prim smile. Then my mobile rings, and I assume it's Charlie, finally taking an interest in our father's disappearance.

There's a hollow crackle. A voice pauses, not daring to speak. "Hello?" I say.

And Maggie says, "They found him."

CHAPTER
TWENTY-SEVEN

Falling

I know from her voice that she doesn't mean they've found Dad but Dad's body.

My phone feels light, plasticky in my hand. The woman looks up, then turns back to her crossword and fills in seven across. I've never been able to do cryptic crosswords. I don't have the right kind of brain. She's written so firmly that her pen's dug through the paper: BEWILDERED.

"Stella?" comes Maggie's faint voice.

"Where?" I ask.

The cliff where he walks the dogs — or, rather, beneath it — is where they found him.

I don't ask who found him, or whether he landed on rocks, or water, or missed his footing and fell or anything else. The woman gnaws the end of her pen. She's wearing dangling coppery earrings, which are trapped like twigs in her hair.

"Oh, Stella," Maggie cries.

My phone falls, and I drop to my hands and knees to try to retrieve it, but it's slid right under the seat. When I come up the woman rests her pen on the table and her eyes meet mine. "My dear," she says, "has something happened?"

I don't know what I tell her. Only that there's a swoop of dress, patterned with garish fuchsias, and the stickiness of her lipstick on my cheek.

A police car and two ordinary cars are parked outside Silverdawn Cottage. A uniformed officer is guarding the door. "You must be Stella," he says. I nod, feeling not quite awake, as if I'm covered with gauze.

In the living room Maggie is sitting close to a woman whom I assume is a friend — Maggie's hand is resting loosely in hers — but it turns out that she, too, is a police officer. Not just a police officer, a *family liaison officer* — as is the man in a pale grey shirt and dark trousers who's talking in a hushed voice on the phone.

We need these people, apparently. They have been assigned to us.

Maggie tries to get up to greet me, but can't coordinate her feet and legs and sags back into the sofa. I bend down to hug her. Her hair smells of cooking and dogs, the house-smells.

The man on the phone says, "Your sister has arrived." He's talking to Charlie. He finishes the call, turns to shake my hand. The backs of his brown hands are bumpy, like the batter on fish.

"I'm Helen," the woman says, also gripping my hand. I feel as if I've walked into a terrible party. She has an ordinary, healthy young face and is wearing a plain navy sweater and trousers. "We're very sorry," she says, and I find myself nodding and thanking her, trying to behave well.

"The press have already been here," Maggie says shakily. "Two reporters from the nationals, one from the *Penjoy Bugle* — he was the worst. Persistent." She spits out the word. It's these police officers' job to keep them away, to look after us. We're being cocooned.

I squeeze into the space beside Maggie. "Matthew, my colleague, can collect your brother from the train," Helen says.

I think, It's just your job to be here when things like this happen. You've probably done this dozens of times. This is ordinary for you.

Matthew is in the kitchen now, turning on taps, opening cupboards, making tea.

"What happened?" I blurt out, which is stupid because nobody knows. There were no witnesses, only the dogs.

"It's a dangerous path," Helen says. "It had been raining heavily, there was mud . . ."

"You think he slipped?"

"We don't know," Helen says.

Then Maggie cries out, "Twenty-five years I've loved him," and smothers her face with her hands.

Twenty-five years.

She knew him when Mum was alive.

She knew him when I was a child.

Dad sat with her at the allotment, drinking in the last of the sun, not knowing that Charlie and I were watching.

Her thin shoulders start trembling. I should comfort her but I can't do a thing: I'm frozen here, trapped on a dog-hair-strewn sofa with the woman Dad really loved.

And I'm sickened. A traitor to Mum, simply by being here, breathing in the stale air.

Maggie turns to me, her lips moving tentatively as if rehearsing words: "It's not what you think," she whispers. Then her tears come again, and the sound she makes is so awful, I just want her to stop.

Charlie has arrived too soon. Matthew couldn't have driven to the station and back again so quickly. Then I realise we've been sitting here for hours — it's gone nine p.m. — and time has slipped away. Charlie is saying, "I'm sorry," with an arm round Maggie, although I don't know what for, because he got here as quickly as he could. Matthew had tracked him down at the university. Charlie doesn't believe in mobile phones. The last thing he wants, when he's lecturing or scraping around in rock pools, is to be interrupted. His face looks bleached, his eyes as empty and dead as a shark's.

Helen is fielding phone calls. Her voice is curt, like that of a company director's secretary. I'm glad the phone keeps ringing. It feels as if things are happening around us.

Harry arrives with his wife Jean. "This is terrible, terrible," Harry keeps saying. They have soft, rounded bodies and are wearing ageing sweaters. Jean wraps her arms round Maggie, and Harry stands against the wall, as if he is waiting to be told what to do. "I've heard a lot about you, Stella," Harry tells me. "Your father was very proud, I hope you know that."

It's after midnight when Charlie says, "We should get some sleep." I follow him upstairs. There's no longer a bed in the spare room, or even pillows on the roll-out mattress on the floor because it's Dad's office now, with framed photos of poppies and irises on the walls — a gift from the photographer who shot the pictures for *Frankie's Flowers*.

The walls are white, and there's a white desk that wobbles when you lean against it. It hasn't been assembled properly. On the desk there is a marmalade jar filled with pens, and a pad of onionskin paper — I didn't know the sheets came from a pad — and the grey plastic adding machine with its chunky keys and pulldown handle.

Of course there's no bedding put out for us. We weren't expected. No one knew this would happen.

In the cupboard on the landing I find thick brown blankets, which smell of dust, and two damp, sagging pillows. They're all talking downstairs: Maggie, Harry, Jean and the family liaison officers. Maybe Matthew and Helen will stay all night. That's their job — to comfort, to be there. I carry the bedding into Dad's study and find Charlie crouched on the floor, running flattened hands over his face and hair.

He didn't care who saw him when we came out of the cinema after *The Railway Children*. Mum kept shushing him. By the time we reached home her patience had withered and she snapped, "For God's sake, it's only a film." It occurred to me even then that she never spoke to me so sharply. I was so ashamed by her blatant favouritism that I escaped to my room and pretended not to hear when she called me for dinner.

The day he was trapped in the Beetle, I was shocked at how quickly my big brother dissolved into sobs. He stared, horrified, at the scarlet splashes all over his white T-shirt.

This is the third time I have seen Charlie cry, and I still don't know how to help him.

An hour, maybe two hours later, I wake up and hear his deep, steady breathing. The room is stiflingly hot. I push off the covers and watch as shapes slowly form: the sharp angles of Dad's desk, the small rectangular window-panes. I pull myself up and tread lightly across the room, aware of sweat trickling down my temples.

The window won't open. The harder I try to pull it up, the more determined it seems to remain firmly shut. I need air in here to breathe properly. Charlie shuffles a limb, trying to kick off the blanket.

I crouch next to him, so close I can smell the coffee on his breath. "He lied to us," I murmur. "Did you know that, Charlie? The nice things he did — taking us to the studios and to France — he felt guilty, did you know that?"

A tear glides down my cheek and lands on Charlie's forehead. In the moonlight it gleams like a bead of seaglass, waiting to be picked up and stuffed into a pocket. Gently, I wipe it off.

"So those things meant nothing," I add, as raindrops start to pat against the window.

"Go to sleep," Charlie whispers.

"He was having an affair, Charlie. While Mum was still alive."

The door creaks open. Maggie stands there in her velvet dressing gown, clutching a china teacup. I didn't even hear her coming upstairs.

"Whatever you think," she says into the darkness, "your father was a good man."

Although Matthew has gone by the morning, Helen appears to have stayed the night on a makeshift bed in the faded living room. Sheets and a blanket are neatly folded on the sofa. "I loved *Frankie's Flowers*," she says, as Maggie stuffs bread into the toaster. "Never missed a programme. He was so unaffected, so *natural*."

"Are you a gardener, Helen?" Maggie asks with exaggerated brightness.

"Well, I try."

"Take some plants, anything you want from the garden. Take it all." She fills the sink with water, intending to wash up, even though there are only two dirty mugs. She peers into the toaster and realises she hasn't switched it on at the wall.

"Perhaps you should leave things as they are for now," Helen says.

Maggie cuts thin slices of butter for toast. "Forgot to take it out of the fridge," she scolds herself. "I keep doing this, forgetting little things. Don't know where I am half the time." She flits round the room like a bird that can't find its way out.

"You're doing fine," Helen says. "You all are."

I think, How would you know?

Maggie starts scrubbing out Surf and Turf's brown earthenware bowls at the sink. "Harry's taken the dogs," she announces.

"That was good of him," I say.

"Yes — isn't everyone good to us?" She turns from the sink, her eyes glimmering, her face as pale as vanilla icecream.

There will be an inquest into Dad's accident. That's what we're saying, "the accident", like we did with Mum. Maggie is questioned for more than an hour, with Helen present, and two officers talk to me in Dad's study. One has wiry ginger hair, which is turning fawn above the ears. The other is younger, with a dark crop and the kind of mouth that moves too much as he speaks. They want to know about Dad's state of mind, how he was feeling before it happened.

"Was he happy, do you think?" the younger one asks.

"I think so," I say. "He had a new show and was starting to write a book. He was fine, I think — things were going well for him."

I'm making stuff up.

"And you last saw him . . ." he prompts me.

"I was here at half term and they spent Christmas with me. They'd had trouble with the house, plumbing problems."

The man nods, as if this might be significant. "And he often went out on his own with the dogs?"

"Yes, most days. Maggie takes them out occasionally. Dogs need to be walked, especially Surf."

"A creature of habit," the older policeman says. The skin round his eyes is crinkled, as if he smiles a lot.

"He had a favourite place on the cliff. He took the dogs there. He liked looking down at the rocks, being higher than birds."

The older man nods. "A nature lover."

I wish they'd stop summing him up in phrases. I know what they're doing — trying to find out what sort of man he was. They want to know if he fell from the cliff, mistook overhanging grass for something solid that could bear his weight. Or if it wasn't an accident.

"He liked being alone," I tell them.

"Of course he did," the ginger man says, as if he knows the first thing about him.

Each night Maggie insists on carrying up the sofa and armchair cushions for Charlie and me. He sleeps soundly, having spent the best part of the days dealing with the funeral director and church minister at St Cuthbert's in Penjoy village. There are cars to arrange, Dad's friends to contact, flowers to be ordered, reams of paperwork to be sorted through. He is tackling the aftermath of Dad's death with the dedication and efficiency I assumed he reserved for his final exams.

I let him do everything, which makes me feel slightly guilty and immensely relieved. "It's better," Charlie says, "than the two of us stumbling over each other."

When I question the graveyard burial, he says, "It's what Maggie wants. She needs a place she can go to."

She could go to the cliff, I think, where it happened. That's what Dad would have chosen. He wanted to be cremated, like Mum was, and scattered — carried away by the wind.

I hear Maggie at night, padding from kitchen to living room, clicking lights on and off. Sometimes there's Matthew's voice, or Helen's. One morning I find Matthew admiring the barometer on the kitchen wall. "I've always wanted one of these," he says.

"You can have it," Maggie says. "It's never worked properly. Perhaps you could take it apart and fix it."

"There's no need to start getting rid of his things," Matthew says gently. "It's too soon. You might change your mind."

Harry Sowerbutt shows up frequently and busies himself by hoiking out bindweed and dandelions from the borders for want of anything better to do. I go out to help him. "Don't do that," Harry says, examining the muddle of plants in my hand.

"Why not? I thought —"

"They're peonies, Stella. They were Frankie's favourites."

"Sorry," I say, and try to jam them back into the ground.

There will come a point when Charlie and I will go back to Devon. Harry will stop popping in so often — he's the only vet for miles around and won't have the time — and the family liaison officers will stop answering the phone, making tea, fending off stray reporters. We have decided that none of us wishes to speak to the press.

At night I wrap myself in a coarse brown blanket and stand at the window, gazing down at the garden. The climbing roses are beginning to flower now, like tight, bunched little fists.

The funeral happens four days after the accident. It does that — just *happens*. I wonder how all these people have arrived at the right place, with all the right things happening in the right order. Of course, Charlie fixed everything.

We're greeted by strangers with anxious faces, who seem to know who we are without being introduced. Bill from the post office surprises me with a real hug. He has gentle eyes, the kind that cry at sad endings. "Your father lit up this area," he says, as if Dad were a firework or a comet.

"What he did with that garden," his wife adds, "is nothing short of a miracle. No one can understand it — what he did to the soil. He's taken his secret to the grave."

Bill pats her arm and says, "Shush now."

"Maggie wants to keep the garden looking good," Charlie says, although we know this isn't true. Every time someone phones, she's offering plants, threatening to go out there and dig them all up herself. It's as if she wants to erase him.

"We'll all help her to keep it looking nice," Bill tells him.

The minister, a short, bulky man with swept-over silvery hair, says, "Maggie's in good hands here. It's a wonderful community."

I am the resurrection and the life, says the Lord.

Those who believe in me, even though they die, will live.

And everyone who lives and believes in me will never die.

Charlie's hand feels sturdy and capable. A big brother's hand. I don't know what Dad believed. As far as I'm aware, he never went to church. We didn't have a Bible at home.

Weak sunshine filters through jewelled windows. The colours should clash but somehow work together like a fistful of gems from a treasure chest.

The minister talks about Dad, a man known by many, who had found happiness here at Penjoy Point. "An intelligent man," he says, "and a caring man, who will be greatly missed by our community here at Penjoy."

I grip Charlie's hand tightly, not wanting ever to let go.

Helen drives Charlie and me to the station. "You both have my number," she says. "Call me any time."

We thank her as the train slides to a stop, and find a vacant table close to a couple with fair-haired twin boys who are engrossed in *Superman* comics. The sea looks perfectly still, like an enormous blue plate. The train follows the coastline, then veers inland where everything looks freshly rained-on.

328

Charlie goes to buy coffee from the buffet. While he's gone I delve into my pocket for my train ticket, and pull out the scrap of paper napkin with Ed's number. I could roll it into a ball, flick it under the seat. It's not as if I'll ever use it. Instead I fold it over and over until it's a tiny square, and push it back into my pocket.

Charlie walks unsteadily down the carriage and dumps our coffee on the table. "It wasn't what he wanted," I tell him.

"Who?" Charlie asks, gazing out at the swooping hills.

"Dad, of course. To be buried like that."

"Like what? In a cemetery?"

"He didn't want a burial. He wanted it to happen like it did with Mum."

"It was important to Maggie," he says.

"So she got what she wanted," I snap.

Charlie frowns, and his eyes cloud as he says, "Let it go, Stella. It doesn't matter now."

"No," I say, my heart racing, "of course it doesn't."

CHAPTER
TWENTY-EIGHT

Learning To Dive

There's a scuffle of kids all around us in the main hall but still Jen hugs me for a very long time. "Take more time off," she says finally. "You shouldn't be here. I didn't expect you in today."

The noise dampens as children filter into their classrooms. "I just want to be normal," I say.

She studies my face and adds, "You can stay with us for as long as you like."

"I'll be okay at home, Jen."

"Let's have a drink after work."

"Yes, I think I'll need it."

I teach my morning groups, drifting from Paul Street to St Mary's as if I'm wearing a veil, and can't remember a single thing we covered in the lessons.

At lunchtime I stop off at the Orange Tree and stare at the chalked blackboard menu on the wall. Ed is in the kitchen discussing a vegetable order that hasn't shown up. "Can I help you?" asks the skinny-plaits girl.

I can hear Ed saying, "When did they say they'll deliver? What good is that to us, Caroline?" Even his cross voice makes me smile.

The plaits girl sighs heavily. "I'd like . . ." I begin. I have to choose something. I don't even have to eat it. I could take it out, fling it into a bin for the gulls to gorge on. 'Can you decide?' the girl's expression says.

Another waitress with cropped silver hair sweeps up pitta bread from beneath a table. Two teenage girls are spooning marshmallows from their hot chocolate. And I say it: "Can I see Ed?"

The plaits girl gives me a surprised look and shouts, "Ed, your friend's here."

He marches out, and when he sees me he says, "Stella, was everything okay?"

I blink down at the *tarte tatin* in the cabinet. "Ed," I say, "my dad died."

He comes to me, past the silver-haired girl, who's clutching two glass bowls filled with pale yellow icecream or maybe sorbet, and says, "I'm so sorry."

"I don't know why I'm telling you. I should be at work. My next lesson's at —"

"It's okay," he says softly, "everything's going to be okay." I'm aware of the marshmallow girls' stares as I bury myself in the warmth of him.

Jen is waiting for me after school at a corner table in the Anchor. To avoid talking about Dad I ask, "What happened about Toby?"

"Had the mother in for a meeting," she says, "in the guise of 'What can we do about his disruptive behaviour? Is everything okay at home?' She says he's coping well, considering that she and his dad are splitting up."

"So there's nothing we can do."

She sighs, peeling a thin paper layer from a beer mat. "You know how it is. You can be around when they're changing for gym — see if there's any bruising or marks. I asked Polly to keep an eye open when they did PE on Tuesday. Toby seemed okay." She pauses and says, "You don't think Jojo made it up?"

"Of course not. Why would she?"

"An attention thing, maybe. Or she has a crush on Toby, and is kidding herself that he tells her things he hasn't told anyone else . . . that they have a special rapport."

You don't know her, I think. You didn't see her that night in my house. "She was telling the truth," I snap.

"I'm not saying she lied . . ."

"Jen, I'm sorry. I just miss him. You know all those recipes he sent me, the ones I stuffed into a box?"

She nods, covering my hand with hers.

"I can't believe I won't get any more." I want to leave now, to get on with the business of calling my private pupils to apologise for missing last week's lessons. According to Diane, a couple of girls turned up at my house with their mothers, one on Tuesday, another on Thursday, she thinks, although she's prone to muddling days. They banged on my door until Diane stomped out and told them I'd phoned from Cornwall and my dad had fallen off a cliff. Put that way, it sounded like a joke.

The parents who sidle up to me outside school avoid words like "died" or even "accident". They say, "I'm so sorry to hear your news, Miss Moon. Terrible tragedy. We're all thinking of you."

"Come back to mine," Jen says now. "I'll make you some supper."

"Thanks, but I just want to go home."

I come in to find a hand-delivered card from Alex depicting loosely sketched sailing boats at a harbour. Inside it reads, "So sorry to hear about your dad, darling. Hope you're OK, call me anytime, A xxx".

I'm surprised that he knows — but, then, everyone does. There's been TV coverage — a cobbled-together montage of clips from *Frankie's Favourites* and *Frankie's Feasts* — plus obituaries in all the newspapers. People writing about Dad as if they knew the first thing about him. So many "friends" being quoted, you'd think he'd had a jam-packed address book. Even Dirk from *Friday Zoo* has said kind things about him. "I regret what happened now," he told some trashy magazine, which I found in the Paul Street staff room. "He was great fun to have around. We just had a small misunderstanding. I'd found some old photos on the Internet — him and his wife and their kids, looked like they were on holiday. I had them up on the screen to show him when we'd finished filming. All I said was 'Is it true your wife was a bit of a crackpot?' and Frankie went for me. I wish I hadn't said it. Obviously touched a raw nerve. It was so long ago, her accident and that, but I guess Frankie was a deeply sensitive guy."

★ ★ ★

Diane gave me a newspaper with an obituary for Dad. I bring it up to bed now, spread it out on my pillow and read:

TV Chef Dies at 61

Frankie Moon, celebrated TV-chef-turned-gardening-expert, has died near his home at Penjoy Point, north Cornwall. Throughout the late seventies his top-rating show, *Frankie's Favourites*, encouraged housewives to create lavish dinner parties using simple ingredients. Yet as well as creating four-course menus — often culminating in desserts liberally doused with alcohol and set alight — Moon devised speedy recipes for working mothers, often requiring little more than tinned luncheon meat and baked beans.

By the early eighties Moon had failed to keep in step with the nation's changing eating habits. He once announced, "Salads fail to excite me," and dismissed vegetarianism as a passing fad. His show was cancelled, and his books languished in bargain bins. Personal tragedy struck when his wife, Eleanor, was killed in a road accident. A recent attempt to resurrect his career on popular show *Friday Zoo* resulted in a highly publicised scuffle between Moon and *Zoo* presenter Dirk Turner.

More recently, however, Moon enjoyed brief success as presenter of *Frankie's Flowers*, the low-budget gardening show that has proved a surprise hit.

Moon is survived by a son, Charles, a daughter, Stella, and his long-term partner Maggie.

Helen calls to check that Charlie and I arrived home safely, whether I'm back at work, how I'm *feeling*. I'm unused to someone — especially a stranger — checking up on my well-being.

"How's Maggie?" I ask, even though we spoke only yesterday. Her voice crackled as if I'd woken her from a deep sleep.

"She seems to be managing," Helen says, "but she's insisting on packing away his things and hauling them up to his study. I suggested that it might be too soon, that she should give herself time, but she's determined."

"What's she planning to do with his stuff?"

"Give it away, I think, to anyone who wants it. Says she can't bear it all around her."

I keep asking about Maggie to avoid talking about me. "I'm glad you're spending time with her," I add.

Helen says, "I'm doing what I can."

Diane has instructed the girls not to come round. I need space, she explained, and not to be bothered with demands for empty cereal boxes, Pritt Stick and Party Hoops. She has appeared at odd times with hot meals: a Tupperware carton of solidified lasagne, a slimy burger in a dented roll from the chip shop, and half a cooked chicken on a foil-covered plate, none of which I could stomach. I feel dizzy and light, but oddly energetic, as if my body's being fuelled by fresh air.

335

"It's okay, come in," I say, when Midge appears at the door.

Diane stomps in after her, saying, "Remember what I told you. You mustn't stay for long. Stella's *bereaved*."

Midge picks up a newspaper clipping from the table and reads the caption: "'Moon killed in trag . . . tragic accident.' How can it be killed?"

"Your reading's really coming on," I tell her. "Accident's a long word."

"Still can't do sums, though, can you, Midge?" Diane remarks. "What about your subtraction, those extra worksheets they sent you home with on Friday?"

Midge screws up her face and says, "Who killed the moon?"

"It's not *the* moon, Midge. It's my dad."

"Was that his name?" she asks, incredulously.

"That's his surname, like mine. It's what they do in newspapers. If you were famous they'd call you Price. They'd say, 'Price has invented an incredible spacecraft capable of soaring to Venus.'" When she laughs, it's like the sun splitting rain into all of its colours.

Maggie says, "We've just come back from a lovely barbecue at Harry's."

"We?" I say, before I can stop myself.

"Me and the dogs. Everyone's *so* kind, even when Surf runs off over the fields, comes back drenched in disgusting stagnant water and rolls over Harry and Jean's cream suite. Honestly, Stella, you wouldn't believe the smell." She babbles on about Surf, her words running together, leaving no spaces for breath.

* * *

The parcel arrives a week later, smothered with shiny brown tape and my address written smudgily in fat black marker. I rummage in Midge's craft box for scissors — she's purloined all my pairs — and hack open the box.

Inside there are yellowing press cuttings, interviews and book reviews, their edges ragged and holes forming in their folds. There are dozens of Café Crème tins with rectangular white labels, and a videotape bearing a printed label on its side, which reads, "*Frankie's Girl — Pilot.*" On a black hard-backed notebook Dad has simply scrawled "Notes".

The writing inside is chaotic, like tangled wire. I pick out phrases: ideas for TV shows, books, regular magazine columns. A book of failure.

The final page, which is more carefully written, is headed "Tarte Tatin". Beneath a recipe, in tinier script, he has written:

Hôtel Tatin, in the Sologne region of France, was owned by the Tatin sisters. The elder sister, Stephanie, was distracted by other chores, or perhaps the attentions of the butler, as she threw apples, butter and sugar into a pan and left it on the heat. A rich aroma filled the hotel. Stephanie had overcooked it. In panic she covered the caramelised concoction with pastry, popped it in the oven to brown, and turned it upside-down to serve to her guests.

The tart met with such acclaim that the owner of Maxim's in Paris sent a spy, in the guise of a gardener, to discover Stephanie's secret.

I close the book and pile everything back into the box. On the floor lies a note from Maggie:

Please do what you will with your father's things. Also, while I am able to take care of Turf, Surf is proving too much for me to cope with at this time. Harry has been very helpful but he too has limits. I am planning to visit friends in Devon in two weeks' time — and to drop in to see you and Charlie, of course. I wonder whether I might leave Surf with you.

I think, I can't have a dog.

"For God's sake," Charlie says, "how can I take care of a dog?"

We're on the back beach, like any normal Sunday afternoon. He pulls off his clothes to his swimming trunks and strides towards the sea. "Well," I say, "someone has to. She can't manage him. We know what he's like."

"What about you?"

"You're saying I should have him?"

"I've got my job, Stella."

"So have I!" I storm away from him, fixing my swimsuit straps as I march towards the jetty. I'm sick of being the good girl, the one who worried about Dad, who insisted we visited, who tried to do the right thing. It's just assumed that I'll do this — take in Surf on top of everything else.

"Where are you going?" Charlie calls after me.

I keep walking, my heels landing heavily on the rough stone of the slipway, then the smooth wood of the jetty. A tight ball of anger burns inside me. So, I'm to look after a dog now, am I? In a small terraced house with an even smaller back garden? What about Charlie, at the lodge, with access to the vast grounds of Hurleigh House? He's the wildlife man. The one who's devoted his life to the study of the animal kingdom.

The trouble is, Surf isn't a crab.

I stop at the end of the jetty, aware of my thudding heart. The cool breeze skims my body, steadying my breath. Glimmering water shows through gaps in the planks.

"Stella!" Charlie shouts again.

I stare across the rippling sea. It looks vast, even though it's cluttered with fishing boats and faraway jet skis, which hum like fast-flying insects.

I stand tall, bend at the knees, spring up —

And I fly.

CHAPTER
TWENTY-NINE

Jewel Cakes

Sift together 5 oz self-raising flour with 2 tbsps cocoa powder. Cream 5 oz soft margarine and 5 oz caster sugar. Beat two eggs and fold into the flour mixture. Bake in a moderate oven for around twenty-five minutes.

Instead of the chocolate sponge, which is perched on a cut-glass cake stand in *Frankie's Family Meals*, I use the mixture to make buns in corrugated paper cases. If they go wrong and turn out looking like biscuits, I can sandwich them together with buttercream and pretend they were meant to be that way. There's very little, in cooking, that can't be rescued.

Also, small cakes are easier to eat on a big wheel.

"I'm *not* rocking the basket," Midge protests, lurching forwards to peer down at the quivering shapes, which are actually people. I grip the girls' hands — it's terrifying, being in temporary charge of someone else's children 75 feet above ground — plus the plastic box that contains the cakes. I bought Chewy Jewels to decorate them. I thought they'd gleam like gems but the butter-cream smeared all over the sweets. The girls licked off the topping, passing the cake part back to me. I had to admit, for my first attempt at baking, they were pleasingly *spongy*.

The wheel slows down and stops as we reach the top. "We're the highest basket!" Midge announces. I wish she'd stop calling it a basket, which sounds horribly fragile — like something in which you'd put tangerines or a pot plant. Not people.

"Why couldn't we bring Surf?" Midge asks, rocking wildly.

"He'd get too excited, run off and go crazy." Too much noise and colour are triggers for Surf — as are running taps and music (particularly the higher octaves). He can cope with Queen, unless it's "Bohemian Rhapsody", which makes him snappy and irritable. Passing traffic causes anxiety. I hope he's behaving, left at home alone all afternoon. On work days I pop back during breaks between lessons. Dogs are meant to greet their owners with bounding enthusiasm. Surf looks deflated when he sees me, as if I'm a blind date who's failed to meet with his high expectations. Or maybe he's disappointed that I'm not Dad.

Jojo wants to get off the wheel and ride on the ghost train, but we're trapped at the top, in this quivering basket. Midge smears buttercream from her lips on to her camouflage T-shirt. "We're going back," she says suddenly.

Jojo jabs her with an elbow.

"What?" Midge mouths.

"We're not going anywhere," I tell her. "Maybe it's stuck."

"No," Midge murmurs, looking down at the crowds, "I mean we're going *home*. To Birmingham. We're moving back in with Dad."

My stomach lurches. "You mean all of you?"

"Yeah," Midge says dully.

"But why?" *You can't*, is what I mean. *You can't leave, not now.*

"'Cause Mum's fallen in love with Dad again," Jojo says, without looking at me.

"That's great," I manage.

"Suppose so," Midge murmurs.

"So you'll be going back to your old school?"

"Yeah."

"And your old house."

"Uh-huh." They're probably making this up. Kids have wild imaginations, like kaleidoscopes twirling too fast. They crave happy endings, like in the wild swans story, when Elise threw the nettle coats over the birds and had brothers again.

"Are you pleased," I ask, "about going back?"

"Of course," Jojo says. "He's our dad."

The big wheel starts turning, bringing the three of us slowly to earth.

I drop off the girls at their house and drive to the supermarket where I gaze at the shelves of pet food. Phrases like "natural juices" and "gently cooked quality meat" crop up over and over again on the lurid labels.

There are varieties for small dogs and big dogs. As Surf comes somewhere between, I choose Bouncer Lamb With Vegetables For Large Breeds because he has a large-breed personality. I have stopped minding the pungent smell when I open a tin, or perhaps don't notice it any more. My house probably reeks of mutton laced with Jean Patou, which might explain why a new pupil switched from weekly to fortnightly lessons with no warning. Her mother said, "Melissa's finding it hard to fit in her practising, with all her other activities."

"That's fine," I said, figuring I'd take Surf for a walk instead. I no longer feel as if I should fill every spare minute with teaching.

I check my shopping list. My handwriting, which once merited school prizes, has deteriorated to a lopsided scrawl. I pick up the fruit I'm forcing myself to consume, to keep up vitamin levels, and fill the boot with my shopping. My car has been fixed but is, according to the garage man, nearing its end. I used to check its oil and water and clean it regularly, inside and out. Its interior has acquired a dusting of crumbs and pale dog hairs, and smells oily, of Surf. I even let children eat candyfloss in it. Jojo, whose turn it was to ride in the front on the way home from the fair, dropped tufts of pink fluff at her feet.

At home, Surf has gnawed a cushion, dragging out its white stuffing like lumps of fake beard. I snatch the *Yellow Pages* from the bookshelf, and find dog-related services — Boarding Kennels, Dog Breeders, Dog Grooming — but no foster homes for unruly hounds, no canine adoption services.

I coax Surf from the sofa and into his fraying basket in the corner of the living room. He settles himself on its grubby green cushion and gives me an accusing stare. Before I became a pet owner I hadn't realised that dogs can glare. And it does smell in here — of Surf's fur and breath. I have tried to bathe him but the sound of the tub being filled had him barking frenziedly and scurrying downstairs, away from my bottle of Glossy Doggie shampoo. Nothing would placate him — not even a pig's ear from Feathers 'n' Fur — and he calmed down only when the water had swilled down the plughole.

Diane told me that Jojo still freaks when she's having her hair washed. They've tried the shower, the bath with a towel over her face, even dry shampoo which accumulated in floury lumps and made her hair look even dirtier. "You've just got to keep at it," she said, "and show them who's boss."

"It's okay," I told her. "I'm used to his dog smell."

Back in Birmingham, Diane and the girls had a dog: a stout yellowish thing with wiry fur and a permanently dribbling nose. Diane had wanted to call him Flash, like the Queen song, but he was too idle to flash anywhere. Midge had insisted on Zack, a space-age name. Their new landlord didn't allow dogs, so they had to leave him with George. According to Diane, Zack is the most well-behaved animal you could ever encounter.

After feeding Surf I rap on her door. She appears with her hair trapped beneath a shower cap, possibly gleaned from that Wolverhampton hotel, and wine-coloured dye smeared on her forehead. "Stella," she says, "come in — can I help you with anything?"

I watch, transfixed, as an inky dribble descends towards her left eyebrow. "Yes," I say, "I think you can."

Maggie wants to move out of Silverdawn Cottage to a smart, modern bungalow in Penjoy village. She wants people around her — *amenities*. Without Dad she feels isolated. The garden, like Surf, is proving too much to cope with. She can't bear to see it running wild, after all the work he put in.

I think: he's been gone for less than a month.

"So you're selling the house," I say, cradling the phone in bed.

"No, dear, Silverdawn's only rented. I'll give four weeks' notice." She says this as if I should have known. None of it — not even the garden — was really Dad's.

"Have you started packing?" I ask.

"Nearly done, no need for you to come and help," she says, even though I haven't offered.

"You sound pretty organised."

"Getting there, Stella. Just a few bits and pieces now, which I'm hoping to sell — kitchen table, chairs, your dad's desk . . ."

"I wish I'd known."

"I've kept some things I thought you'd like," Maggie rattles on. "His books, all his cookery things — the implements . . ."

She set this in motion, without telling me, in case I asked her to stop.

"You don't want me to come, do you?"

"Visit me when I've moved, got the place looking nice. I'm very busy at the moment, breaking up the house . . ."

It sounds like she's snapping bits off, like Hansel and Gretel at the witch's house. "I wish you weren't doing this," I say.

"Well, I'm sorry, but I have to move on."

I start to say he was my dad — she can't do this without my permission, without *asking* me — but it comes out as "He was mine."

And Maggie's voice wavers as she says, "He was mine too."

"What we're talking about," Diane says firmly, the following Saturday, "is an unruly kid. When it comes down to it, there's little difference between children and dogs."

The five of us — Diane, the girls, Surf and I — have arrived at the grassy expanse in the park where the Slab used to be. She has ordered Jojo and Midge to sit quietly on a bench, not to cause any distraction. "I want to help," Midge whines, but Diane wants no interference.

"I need to work with the owner," she announces, as if she's forgotten that she knows me, "and establish some ground rules."

Her newly wine-coloured hair looks like a wig she's wearing for a joke. Surf bounds around my shins, trying to shut out her strident voice. It must be her training voice. "Often," she says, "discipline problems start at home. Surf can't be told off for begging at the table, then offered titbits. Consistency's what we're talking about." I think of the countless times I've caught Midge flicking Party Hoop crumbs from the table in the direction of Surf's snapping jaws.

"Is there any point in this?" I ask. "Dad said Surf's untrainable."

"No dog's untrainable, Stella. It's good for him to learn to respond to instruction. We're strengthening the bond between dog and owner."

Owner. I am Surf's owner. He licks my hand tentatively. Given time, he might actually like me.

I must walk with him as I normally do so that Diane can identify problems. There are so many — he strains forwards, then tries to snap at the lead, finally plonking his rear on the damp grass — that she looks quite exhausted, and we haven't begun to teach him anything yet.

Patience is vital. I must never lose my rag, never shout at him. "You'll put him off," Diane says, as we hurry home through proper rain. "We can mix in some games for him — lots of praise and affection. Learning should be fun. But you'll need a proper Haltie instead of this ragged old lead. Next lesson, we'll help him achieve a successful sit."

I repeat her mantra as Surf lurches indoors: *I am the boss around here. Leader of the pack.*

Alex turns up as I'm finishing a lesson. Melissa is showing potential, even though her previous teacher — a shouter, apparently — nearly put her off music altogether. I'm trying to be extra-patient, as I am in Diane's obedience classes.

"I'm sorry," Alex says at the door, "you're busy . . ."

"Come in, we're nearly finished. You can wait in the kitchen." I wave a hand in its direction, forgetting that he lived here, that it was once his kitchen too.

The instant she's gone he ambles through to the living room and slides his arms round me. I'm conscious of the roughness of his sweater, how unfamiliar his body feels now. I pull away, and offer to make coffee.

"How are you doing?" he asks, lacing the words with concern.

"I'm okay. Sometimes I forget and think he hasn't sent me a recipe for ages. I'll even check my post for his handwriting. You know how he was — I'd get three in a week, then nothing for months."

"Like buses," Alex says, trying to lighten the atmosphere.

He won't sit down properly but perches on the table's edge. Surf growls irritably from the basket. "And you've taken on his dog," he adds.

"I haven't taken him on. He's just mine now."

"You're not going to find him another home?"

"Why? Are you offering?"

He laughs and says, "It's not really the right time."

I look at him. He hasn't come to check on my welfare but to tell me something. "So," I say, "what's happening with you?"

"That girl I was seeing," Alex says. He looks levelly at me. I feel nothing.

"You're still seeing her," I venture, to fill the space. "It doesn't matter, Alex. You can do what you like."

"She's pregnant."

"Lucky you." There's a thud inside me. Surf bounds out of his basket and nuzzles against me, then lies on his side with his legs flexed, wanting a belly scratch. I crouch beside him, grateful for the distraction.

Alex sighs, choosing the words that won't make him seem like the bad guy. "We're not together any more, but I'll still be around, involved. I thought you should know."

"Thanks for telling me." So that's his latest project: a baby. Unlike a fishing rod, it can't be hidden at the back of a wardrobe and replaced with an acoustic guitar.

"I'm not ready, you know, to be a dad," he continues. "I'm just trying to make the best of it. It's not as if the baby was planned . . . we didn't *mean* it." Didn't mean to do it, like Midge burning herself on the grill pan.

"What's her name?" I ask.

"We haven't decided on names yet," he says, thinking I mean the baby and not the long-legged girl from the market.

"And when's it due?"

"She's got four months to go." He gives me the big-eyed look that once turned me butter-soft, and made me promise I'd spend more time with him, play my flute less often.

This time it doesn't work.

He tries to hug me again but I turn away and press firmly on Surf's back, the way Diane showed me, to

349

help him achieve a successful sit. "I've never held a baby," Alex adds. "Don't know what to do with them."

"I'm sure you'll think of something," I say.

Diane isn't using a cowboy company like Movers & Shakers because George, the girls' dad, and his two brothers are bringing a van in which their possessions will be lovingly loaded and transported back to Birmingham. "He's insisting on doing the removal himself," Diane tells me. "I think he's scared I might change my mind." She stuffs cushions into a bin bag and knots it firmly.

"I could take the girls out," I suggest, "so you can finish packing in peace."

"Please," she says, "they're doing my head in," even though they're quietly watching a Scooby Doo video. Diane won't disconnect the TV and video until they're ready to go.

"Could you let me have their swimming things?" I ask.

She exhales, figuring: another job to add to the list. "Give me five minutes," she says, untying the bin bag and gently placing the toaster on a cushiony nest.

"Stella," Jojo says as she climbs into the car, "I'm not keen, you know, on going in the sea. All that stuff round your legs."

"It's called seaweed, Jojo."

"Yeah. It's disgusting."

"We're not going to the beach," I tell her. "We're going to Aquasplash."

★　★　★

Midge leaps into the pool and careers to the far side by means of her unique crawl/doggy-paddle hybrid. Jojo swims steadily, her jaw set in fierce concentration. I'm aware of a rippling shape beneath the surface, of someone swimming powerfully towards me, and move to the poolside to let him pass.

He surfaces, shaking water from his hair like a dog. "You've got company today," Ed says. He grabs the rail, kicks out his legs.

"They live next door," I tell him, conscious of the smile spreading across my face. "Midge, the younger one, has been badgering me to bring her here for ages."

"How have you been?" Ed asks.

"Okay. Sometimes I'm just getting on — you know, teaching, shopping, ordinary stuff — then suddenly I'll remember. And it's so strong, this feeling, it really shocks me. It's not as if I saw him often. We weren't close — he could be so grumpy, belligerent . . ."

"Yes, mine too." He laughs softly.

"Your dad . . ."

"Disappeared when I was twelve. We eventually found out that he'd gone up the Highlands, met this woman, was living in caravans, scraping a living selling scrap."

"And he's still around?"

Midge is lying on one of the lilypad floats, using her hands to propel herself towards us. "I wasn't sure," Ed says, "until Kate, my friend from back home, came down to see me. Said my dad had been spotted around Glasgow."

351

"I think I saw her. I was passing the launderette — the *café* — one night . . ."

"Known each other since we were babies," he says.

"Whose baby?" Midge squawks, lunging towards me and flinging skinny arms round my neck. I can't tell if they're splashes of pool water or tears on her face.

"No one's. Ed was just —"

"I'm going to really *miss* you," she cries.

"Are you moving?" Ed asks, as Midge peels herself off me.

"No, it's the girls — they're going back to Birmingham to be with their dad." I think, hope, he looks pleased.

I watch the girls swimming their widths and lengths, aware of Ed watching me. And when I dive into the lagoon from the board, it's to show off to him, like a child. He's clapping when I come up for air, and I flip under again to hide my burning face. I surface beside Midge on her lilypad.

"You're not scared any more," Ed says, as the girls and I head for the changing rooms.

"You like him, don't you?" Midge yells, through the speckled blue cubicle wall.

"Who?" I ask, feigning innocence.

"The one you were staring at."

"Midge, I wasn't —"

"Yes, you were. D'you love him?"

"I hardly know him!"

"Well," she says, "he's nicer than that cross man you went to the butterfly place with."

352

Our last supper is a feast of prawn-cocktail crisps, Chewits and insipid hot chocolate from the pool's vending machines. We occupy three sides of a flimsy white plastic table in the café. "It's *him*," Midge hisses, as Ed strolls through the reception area and steps outside.

"Go after him," Jojo commands.

"What — you mean chase him?"

"Yeah, why not?"

"Grown-ups don't do that! They don't chase people."

"So what *do* you do?" she asks, leaning towards me, as if awaiting a potted lecture entitled "Growing Up For Beginners".

"I've forgotten," I say helplessly.

She sniggers, tipping the remains of her hot chocolate into her mouth. "Hey," she adds, "there's this scheme thing at my old school — my *new* school — where you can borrow instruments for no money, and they've got flutes."

"That's brilliant. I really hope you'll keep playing." I busy myself by fixing the love-heart badge, which is pinned to her fleece and had worked its way round to an upside-down position.

"Are you sad?" Midge asks, examining my face.

"No," I manage. "I'm really happy for you."

"Can we have more crisps? And one of them peppermint Aeros?"

I post more coins into the machine. Our spoils slip down a whole lot easier than Dad's farewell fondue.

★   ★   ★

George is apologetic-looking with fading hair that straggles down his back. He shakes my hand weakly, and his eyes moisten as he says, "Great job you've done with our Jojo and that piccolo, Stella."

"I only helped her along. She's a very talented girl."

His eyebrows shoot up in delight, as if this is the first time anyone's said something positive about his daughter.

Jojo and I head upstairs to tissue-wrap her fairies (one fractured a leg during the previous move and she's keen to avoid further casualties). Midge's weaponry, craft supplies and most of the girls' toys have already been loaded into the van. Their clothes have been stuffed into clear plastic sacks, which Diane brought home from the bedding factory and has piled up in the front garden like sandbags awaiting a flood.

Jojo places the fairies in a cardboard box, which we carry between us downstairs to the living room. Diane is rolling up the hand-tufted rug on the floor. Its randomly chosen colours are jarring; the purple patch, which I contributed, butts against crocus yellow. There's even a streak of burnt orange. "Like it?" she asks.

"It's lovely," I say — and, in a bewildering way, it is.

"Have it. Something to remember us by."

"No, I couldn't. It's taken you weeks to finish."

"It's yours," she says firmly, tying it up with a pair of burgundy tights. "I always said your place could do with cheering up."

"Thanks, that's so kind."

"It's nothing," she blusters.

Outside George is trying to direct operations by telling the sprightlier of the brothers how to pack the van correctly. He keeps sighing and asking, "How did so much stuff fit into that tiny house? It's like a bloody Tardis."

"Midge," Diane yells through to the kitchen, "have you peeled that tape off your bedroom carpet yet?"

No reply. I find her hunched at the kitchen table with the hamster cage on her lap. Her face is shining with tears. "Oh, Midge," I say, "it's going to be okay. You'll love being with your dad. And you'll have your dog back."

"Yeah," she whispers. "I'll be great."

I lift the cage on to the table, take her hand and lead her through to the living room. "Come and see your presents," I say.

For Jojo I've bought a sinister-looking fairy from the hardware shop. "She's lovely," she gushes, planting a noisy kiss on splodgily painted lips.

Midge rips the tissue paper from her gift, exposing buff plastic, then the pull-down handle and numbered keys. "What is it?" she asks.

"It's an adding machine. You tap out your numbers, pull down the handle and your answer comes out on this roll of paper."

"Wow, how does it know?"

"It just does."

The girls jump into the van and sit next to George, who's driving. Diane clambers in last and blows a kiss through the open window. Her other hand clasps Hamburger's cage, which sits on her lap.

George's brothers will follow in a battered Ford Fiesta. "I'll send you letters," Jojo shouts. "I said I'd write to Toby too. He's moving to Liverpool with his mum. We've swapped our new addresses."

Then the engine splutters, choked and uncertain, and I'm hoping it behaves like my temperamental car and they'll have to unpack everything again. George turns the key repeatedly. There are yelled goodbyes, and I'm batting away hot tears as their hands flap like sycamore leaves.

The van rouses itself, and they're gone.

CHAPTER
THIRTY

New Improved Surf

The Crook Inn stands alone and stranded on Bodmin Moor. Delphie, its owner, glides back and forth behind the polished front desk as if on castors, her golden hair tied back with a chiffon scarf. "Single room, isn't it, Miss Moon?" she says, checking the reservations book while Surf laps at the water bowl in the foyer.

"Yes, that's right." The Crook Inn welcomes dogs — it's a "dog hotel", the website said, which made me wonder at first if it wasn't a place where people could stay but upmarket boarding kennels. Delphie hands me a photocopied map, showing dog-friendly walks that start from the hotel grounds.

"Would you like a table for dinner?" she asks.

"Yes please, at around eight."

"You were lucky to get the last room," she adds, "with the schools breaking up last week. Are you on holiday or travelling through?"

"Just a short break."

She glances at Surf, who has settled himself on the rug by the water bowl. "Lovely dog," she says. "Nice to see one so well behaved."

★   ★   ★

My room is pale lemon and filled with a soupy smell that filters up from the kitchens. A wicker dog basket inhabits one corner, and tentative pastel drawings — of a spaniel, a dachshund, and some breed I don't know with a sleek black coat and speckled white snout — are not quite aligned on one wall. On the scratched dressing table lies the dog artist's card: "Capture Your Dog's Beauty and Personality with a Unique Portrait. Head Studies, Group Portraits Also Cats, Rabbits, Hamsters and Any Domestic Animal. Prices on Request." I leave Surf in the room, dozing in the basket, and head down for dinner.

A sharp-nosed waitress shows me to a small table by the window so I'll have something to watch, to occupy myself. Clouds stir anxiously above undulating moorland. To emphasise my single status the waitress scoops up the other place setting and carries away the other chair. She lifts a small vase of white carnations from another table and places it in the space where my companion's plate should be. "There," she announces. "That's better."

Each evening I bring things to read — a newspaper or *The Visitor's Guide to Bodmin and Around* from my room — but more often gaze out at the shifting sky with its startling colours.

Dear Charlie *[I write in the lemon room]*,
Decided to come to Cornwall — not sure for how long. Tried to visit the Eden Project but dogs aren't allowed, and Surf started going crazy when he thought he was being left alone in the car.

We've visited some botanical gardens, but he
seems happier out on the moors. It's magical,
Charlie — just endless space and these massive
skies.

We, he: I'm talking about Surf as if he's a person.
Dog as boyfriend substitute. I finish with

Hope you're taking good care of yourself, will call
as soon as I get back. Love, Stella.

There's a scuffle of paws as I click off the light. Surf
leaps on to the bed — strictly Not Allowed at the
Crook Inn — and settles around my feet.

On the fourth day, I call her. Maggie says, "You're on
Bodmin Moor? You must come and see my new house.
Do you have the address?"

"Yes, you sent it."

"Stay with me," she says. "Make it a holiday."

I tell her, "I'm just passing through."

Maggie's cheeks are powdered, her mouth freshly
lipsticked and eyes shining determinedly. Her brave
face. She hugs me, then ruffles Surf's neck and says, "Is
this really the same dog?"

He no longer jumps up, or zooms away when let off
the lead. "He's been obedience-trained," I tell her, as if
it were that simple. Diane put hours into working with
Surf. She said, "Look at all the time you put into *my*
kids," making it sound as if Surf was my child, and this
was her way of repaying me.

Maggie's new bungalow is sparsely furnished with plain, modern furniture in creams and pale greys and none of the old things from Silverdawn Cottage. I don't recognise a single thing. "New people have already moved in," she says cheerfully. "The outside's been painted — looks so much fresher — but the garden's not what it was. Would you like to see it?"

"We could walk over, I suppose. Surf needs to let off some steam." Turf ambles into the living room and sniffs at Surf, showing no sign of recognition.

We head out, with Maggie telling me, "It's to be expected, of course. Those herbaceous borders — they'll never be the same now. You see, Stella, no one's digging your dad's soil improver into the ground any more. They're probably using chemicals and whatnot."

"What did Dad use?" I ask, unhooking Surf's lead as we turn down the narrow lane that leads to Penjoy Point.

"Don't you know?" Maggie says, with a small laugh. "All those vegetable casseroles — don't think I hadn't cottoned on."

I still don't get it.

"His little game," she continues. "Thought I had no idea. I'd go up to bed — I always needed more sleep than your father — and by morning the leftover casserole would be gone."

"You mean he dug it into the ground, like fertiliser?"

She smiles, but her jaw is set firm. "I never minded," she says. "It made me chuckle. And it showed that your dad wasn't quite as clever as he thought he was."

★ ★ ★

Silverdawn Cottage looks too white — too new — although the garden doesn't seem any different. I wonder if Maggie is seeing things clearly. We walk on, taking the path that runs close to the cliff's edge. Neither of us speaks as we stop at the place where it happened.

I gaze down at the rocks and the splashes of surf far below. "Maggie," I say, "what was Dad like, when he was younger?"

"You know," she says quietly.

"I mean, from your point of view. What was he like when I was a little girl?"

She watches the gulls circling and weaving, yellow-beaked and fearless. "I think your dad did what he could," she says, "for his family." Her voice is gentle, as if she's reading the sensitive part of a children's story: Hansel and Gretel lost in the woods, holding each other.

"Do you remember his allotment?" I ask.

"Yes, I do."

"I saw you once. Me and Charlie spied over the wall."

She bends to fuss over Surf for something to do. Turf has curled up at her feet. "Your mother had someone too," she says suddenly.

"What do you mean?"

"A man. A boyfriend, I suppose."

I stare at her, at the tiny gold earrings she always wears. They're shaped like hearts. I'd never noticed that before. And her necklace, too, is a gold heart — the one I found in Dad's desk drawer when I was fiddling about with his Biros and adding machine. "Who?" I ask, aware of the blood rushing in my ears.

"Some man in Somerset. It had been going on for years, your dad told me. Devastated him at first. Eleanor was his life, you do know that?"

I shake my head, unable to speak. *No, I didn't know that.*

"I'm sorry, Stella."

"Does Charlie know?"

"No, only you."

"So when —"

"She was seeing him before your father and I met."

Your father and I. Her words sound so formal as they cut through the breeze. I turn away and start walking along the narrow path towards the village, holding Surf's lead as he trots obediently beside me. I don't want to hear any more. I want to leave things just as they are, undisturbed. "I never met your mother," Maggie continues, some way behind me, "but saw pictures, of course — do you know how like her you are?"

"People say that," I murmur.

"It was painful for him, having you in the house."

"But I'm his daughter!" I cry, turning to face her. We stop on the path.

"He tried, you know, to get closer to you. That time he took you to France . . ."

"And banned me from playing my flute!"

"And the TV show, Stella — *Frankie's Girl*, was it called? He did his best, don't you realise that? But you pushed him away, just like your mother did. He said that being left with you, after Charlie had gone, was like having Eleanor around. Then *you* left him."

"Of course I did! I went to college — what was I supposed to do? Spend my life looking after him?"

"He wouldn't have wanted that," she says.

"And that man, Mum's *boyfriend* . . ."

"Patrick someone."

Patrick Lowey, the Christmas-tree man. He had flinty eyes and a solid jaw and his dark, cosy kitchen smelt of mulled wine. I felt uncomfortable being there, as if he and Mum didn't want me and Charlie around. He'd hardly speak to us. I was too nervous to ask where the toilet was. Charlie would offer to help him load the tree into the back of the car, but Patrick never let him. We'd wait in the car — me, Charlie and an outsized pine — while Mum went back into the farmhouse to pay.

As soon as we arrived home she would vacuum the pine needles out of the car, erasing any evidence of our excursion. She said we weren't to bother Dad by telling him about it. He had more important stuff on his mind, like the tax man.

Even as a kid, I used to wonder why Mum had taken us to choose a Christmas tree — all the way up in Somerset, for God's sake — when we were old enough to stay at home by ourselves. I felt as if we were being used as some kind of protection. "Why didn't she leave Dad?" I ask Maggie.

"Because of you, of course."

"And Charlie."

"Well, yes, Charlie too . . ."

"Maggie, what was it with me? Why did she treat me differently?"

"She was proud of you. Of your music."

"Lots of parents are proud."

"I think it was what she wanted for herself," Maggie says, walking briskly beside me. "Did you know she played the harp when your father met her?"

"No, I didn't."

"He asked her to stop. It wasn't the lessons — they weren't the problem — but the practising for hours on end."

"He objected to that?"

She sighs, as if I haven't a hope of understanding. "His career was at its peak then. Do you know how successful he was, how it drained him? He needed her support."

"So he made her stop playing." I remember it now: Mum and me, standing outside Grieves and Aitken, the day we bought my special flute. Her admiring the harp in the window, trying to keep her face in order.

"Not stop," Maggie continues, "but tone it down. Keep it as a little hobby." I could laugh, almost, if I didn't feel so angry for her.

"Your mum wouldn't have that," Maggie continues. "She sold her harp, and I don't think she ever played again."

"I can't believe he did that to her."

"His career was very —"

"Important. Yes, I know."

"Especially when she was expecting Charlie. He had a family to support. And, of course, your mum threw herself into bringing up you two. She got over it, your father said. Music wasn't important to her any more."

Yes, it was. That was why she carried on taking me for lessons with Mrs Bones, even when we could no longer afford them. And bought me the special flute. No wonder she'd never told Dad.

Back at the bungalow, Maggie makes tea that remains transparent, even with milk in. "That man Mum was seeing," I tell her, "it makes me feel as if I never really knew her. I had no idea."

"Why would you, dear? You were only a child." Her cup makes a tinkling noise as she places it on its saucer on her lap.

"I blamed Dad for everything, Maggie. Did he try to stop her seeing him?"

"Of course, dear."

"How could she —"

"Shhh." Maggie pats my hand.

"She was a wonderful mum, you know that? I thought she could do nothing wrong."

The smile warms Maggie's face, smoothing away the years. "No one's perfect, dear," she says, ruffling Turf's neck as he settles at her feet.

The new tenants' things are carried into next door by efficient men who don't dump everything on the pink gravel. They bring in the tables and chairs, which might have come from Habitat, and cardboard boxes (each is labelled "bathroom", "kitchen", or whichever room is its final destination). It's a very smooth, organised house move.

Luisa, my new neighbour, is beautiful in a fragile-vase way, and pregnant. She and Mark are planning to set up a therapy centre towards the end of the seafront — near the Orange Tree. "The rents are still reasonable," she says over coffee in my kitchen, "but you feel it's an up-and-coming area."

"The café's doing really well," I tell her, as Surf charges in from the garden.

Luisa flinches. "I've been scared of dogs since a Labrador bit me on the way to school." She shows me her left hand. The tip of her little finger bears a tiny comma-shaped scar.

"He has his mad moments," I say, "but he's never bitten anyone." I don't mention the scratching incident.

Luisa tells me that her ex, the baby's dad, nagged for a dog, but she knew it was just a phase he was going through. "I thought Mark —" I begin.

"Mark's just a friend. Known each other since we were kids. The baby's dad and I broke up — the prospect of being a father scared the wits out of him."

"Oh, I'm sorry." I think of Alex, not ready for fatherhood.

"He's no loss," Luisa says, smiling bravely.

"Hope you don't mind me calling," Mr Grieves says, "but I spotted your card in the newsagent's window, made a note of your number. Something's come into the shop. It's not a replacement, dear — nothing could replace your original flute — but I've put it aside for you. No obligation, of course."

I head over to the shop after school. The window is filled with a fluorescent orange sign: CLOSING DOWN SALE.

"Are you really closing?" I ask.

"Finishing up," Mr Grieves says, as if the shop has been a meal he's been slowly consuming for twenty-five years.

"I'm sorry. I'll really miss you."

He clears his throat and pulls out a case from a drawer behind the counter. "It needs work," he says, fitting the sections together, "but there's nothing here that an MOT wouldn't put right. Why don't you try it?"

The flute feels heavy and cold in my hands. "It's lovely," I say.

"The headjoint's solid silver, which accounts for the price, but I can offer a substantial discount, Stella, seeing as it's you."

"Thank you."

"Really," he adds, "it just needs the right home."

I bring the flute to my lips and hold a note until my breath's all gone, and I'm empty and eleven years old. Mum's writing the cheque and saying, "Remember, it's our secret." I can't replace the special flute. I don't even want to.

I place it on the counter. "Are you all right, my dear?" asks Mr Grieves.

"I'm sorry, I won't take it."

"I just thought I'd ask," he says.

Dear Stella
We miss you lots my riting is getting better midge
doing well at sums with yor machine. It is nice to
see our dog dad is all right mum says hi
Jojo xxxxxxxx

With the letter comes a red card, blotchily printed with
black flecks spinning off the letters:

George Cribley and Diane Mercury Price
request the pleasure of STELLA PLUS GUEST
at their wedding

at 11a.m. on Saturday, 17 October

St Barnabas', Church, Dale Road, Brats Hill,
Birmingham, and afterwards at theVie en Rose
Hotel, Davenport Road.

"Want to come with me?" I ask Charlie. "Be my
guest?"
He pulls his leave-me-alone face.
"Please, there's no one else I can ask."
"So I'm your last resort," he says, then peers through
my kitchen window and asks, "Who's your new
neighbour?"
"There are two — two and a half, really. Luisa's
pregnant. She lives with her friend Mark."
"How modern," he says, and keeps looking.
"Stop staring, Charlie. You'll scare the poor girl."

He grins and picks up the videotape that's lying on the worktop. "What's this?"

"Just some of Dad's stuff that Maggie sent me."

He frowns, reading the white label stuck on its side. "*Frankie's Girl*," he says. "Is that the show —"

"Give it back, Charlie."

He laughs, waving the tape before my face, then pelts through to the living room. "Let's watch it."

"No!" I yell, prompting Surf to scramble out of his basket and bark madly.

"Come on, I've never seen it."

"Give it *back*."

He crouches at the video-player, stuffs it into the slot and presses play. Dad's face flickers on to the screen. And mine, set rigid, a small but clearly discernible twitch playing at the left side of my mouth.

My usually abundant hair has been chopped into a sharp line. The face is thinner than I remember, with a long, prominent nose. A less graceful, bigger-nosed version of our mother.

And I'm not bad. In the realm of hugely self-conscious teenagers being forced to utter coherent sentences before an army of technicians, I put in a competent performance. Maggie was right: Dad really *was* trying, not just to make that wretched show work but to connect somehow with me. He wanted us to be friends.

When it's over, Charlie can barely speak for laughing. What I *think* he says is "God, Stella, you were bloody atrocious."

★　★　★

369

Summer slides into autumn and I see more of my brother than I have since we were teenagers. Every Sunday we swim off the back beach, and Charlie usually comes to my place for supper.

Armed with a plump folder of papers, he installs himself in the last remaining sunny patch on the back lawn. At first I was flattered that he was spending so much time here — since Dad's accident he seems to need me more — then realised that his desire to Spend Time With Stella coincided with Luisa and Mark moving in (or, specifically, Luisa).

She's talking to him over the fence now, her hair shining in the syrupy sunshine. When he comes in for supper, more than an hour later, he is wearing *that look*. "Nice time out there?" I ask him.

"Yes, thanks."

"Enjoyed chatting to Luisa?"

"She's a lovely girl."

"Isn't she, Charlie?" I set my fork down.

He blinks at me, and the grin is smeared all over his handsome face as he says, "What?"

"I'm just pleased, that's all."

"What's there to be pleased about?"

"If something happens with Luisa," I tease him, "at least I'll know what's going on with your love life."

He doesn't deny it, or tell me to mind my own business. He doesn't even shrug me off as I come round and hug him, for no reason at all.

"What shall I do?" he asks suddenly.

"She's just had a baby, Charlie. That's quite a distraction."

"For how long?" Outside, the faintest hint of a rainbow smudges the sky.

"About eighteen years," I say, laughing.

CHAPTER
THIRTY-ONE

Scattering Dad

Ed has expanded the Orange Tree's menu and now offers home-made savoury tarts with melting pastry and luscious blueberry pie. I make a point of introducing Charlie to Ed as "my brother Charlie", which comes out so awkwardly I feel like a bad actress stuttering through her script.

"It's got egg in it," a woman protests at the counter.

"I know," Ed says. "I made it myself this morning."

"I'm allergic to eggs," she continues, and I realise it's the woman who complained about there being nowhere to breastfeed and figure that Ed's right, she wants attention — *his* attention.

And I wonder why this makes me feel strange.

The woman is balancing on spindly heels. Ed rattles off every egg-free item on the menu. Although I'm not looking — not staring — I'm aware of the curve of his brown arms, the skin which looks as soft as a child's. I want to say something to Charlie — to confide in him — but then he'll know, and he'll *look* at me like he knows, and then Ed will know and I won't be able to come in here for *tarte tatin* any more.

"You should ask him out for a drink," Charlie whispers, popping a sliver of caramelised apple into his mouth.

"Charlie," I hiss.

"You know you want to. It's obvious, Stella."

I have Ed's number. I could call him, any time. "Maybe," I murmur, turning my attention back to my plate.

"Why not invite him to that wedding?"

"A wedding? Don't be crazy —"

"Well, I'm not going," he says, folding his arms firmly.

"Charlie, you promised!"

"Ask Ed."

"No!"

"You're hopeless," he retorts, as if he's teaching me to surf and my feet just won't do as they're told.

Diane marries George on a blustery Saturday morning in a plunging blue dress that is split to her thigh and adorned with tremulous frills. "Like it?" she asks in the windswept churchyard. "It's called Cascade. It's meant to look like water flowing."

"You look gorgeous," I say, and she does.

George lingers behind her in a suit that looks borrowed from a larger person. "Proposed to her in the Plaza Hotel in Wolverhampton," he says. "Couldn't believe it when she said yes."

Midge hurls herself into my belly and says, "You haven't written."

"Midge, I have! I wrote to you last week."

"Only one page." Her eyes settle on Ed, who's standing a little behind me. She frowns, trying to place the face.

"Hi, Midge, we met at Aquasplash," Ed prompts her.

"We thought Stella was bringing —"

"My brother couldn't make it," I cut in.

"Second choice," Ed says, shrugging. "Better than nothing, I guess."

"Like my dress?" Midge asks, tweaking unyielding apricot taffeta.

"You look gorgeous," Ed tells her.

"Like a princess," I tease.

"*Ugh*. Can't wait for this to be over and I can get the bloody thing off."

Ed and I follow the throng of outrageous straw hats from the churchyard towards the hotel. "What made her marry him now?" he whispers.

"Because he finally asked her," I whisper back.

"I'm glad you asked me. To this wedding, I mean."

"So am I," Midge trills behind us. "You're loads better than that boyfriend with the dumb magazines about fish."

The wedding cake is shaped like a pink Cadillac, in homage to Freddie Mercury's cake, which was stolen from his fortieth birthday party. Instead of "FREDDIE" the number-plate reads, "DIANE & GEORGE", black lettering on white.

Music comes courtesy of tribute band Wicked Queen. I dance with Ed and George's brothers, and the girls who are hot-cheeked and leaping across the slithery floor.

"I feel sick and I want to go home," Jojo cries later, when the band's finished and it's just disco music. When I look over her shoulder Diane is smooching with Martin, the singer whose Freddie-style teeth cost more than this wedding. She sways her hips, her eyes tightly shut, a delighted doll in his arms.

It's gone ten when we say our goodbyes and wander out to my car. "We could stay," Ed says, climbing into the passenger seat.

I start the engine, and turn to study his face. "There's the dog, I can't really —"

"And I'm on an early shift tomorrow," he cuts in.

I touch the bracelet Midge made for me. She was right, I did lose the first one. The second, made from green Chewy Jewels, nearly ended up down Surf's throat when he spied it on the living room table. Diane didn't get round to teaching Surf not to steal food.

"Let's go home," I say, turning out of the car park and waving at Jojo, who stands, silhouetted, in the doorway of the Vie en Rose Hotel.

We're deep into the night when Ed picks up the Mexican box from the floor of my car. He lifts off its lid, unfolding one recipe at a time. " 'Baked Apples with Raisin Filling'," he reads. " 'Deep-fried Fish Balls. Sausage and Bacon Plait'. Why are these in your car, Stella?"

"They're from Dad. He sent them for years — kept on sending them, even though I hardly cook, really —"

"So why . . ."

I glance sideways at Ed, seized by an urge to turn off the motorway at the next junction and see where it takes us. "It was Dad's way of showing he loved me," I tell him.

It's one twenty a.m. when I pull up at the far end of the seafront. The area looks smarter now with the Orange Tree's freshly painted windows and sign, and the therapy centre that Luisa and Mark have opened. "Come in, if you like," Ed says, still holding the Mexican box.

I glance up at the tiny flat above the Orange Tree. "I'd love to, Ed, but there's something else I'd like to do tonight."

He looks quizzical as I reach over to the back seat for our slices of wedding cake, handed out by Midge in pink net bags with gold ribbons. I suspect she filched fragments of icing — of red bonnet, or black-and-white number-plate — because my piece looks ravaged by mice. We wolf our cake, suddenly ravenous. "So, can I come too?" Ed asks.

I open the glove compartment, lift out the jumper parcel, and climb out of the car. "Let's go," I tell him.

We walk past the café where Luisa, her baby and I stopped for coffee two days ago. The Orange Tree is favoured by young parents: it's the only child-friendly café around here where you're not presented with slimy burgers. Luisa leaned towards me over the silvery table and said, "I like your brother. I like the way you're so close, the way he's always hanging around at your

376

place." I had to pretend he'd always done this. "Bet you were thick as thieves as children," she added.

I remembered us delving into the freezer for gâteaux, and stalking Dad to the allotment, and how things changed when Charlie and I spiralled off. "I used to worship him," I told her, "but then I saw sense."

"What were your parents like?" she asked, spooning coffee froth into her mouth.

"Just ordinary," I said.

Ed and I walk onwards, my hands filled with jumper parcel, the Mexican box weighing down the bag that's slung over my shoulder. He doesn't ask again where we're going, just walks with me, his arm resting lightly round my shoulders in the indigo night.

We're passing the marina now, and the Anchor, where chip papers fly in the cool, dry air. We pause at the jetty, then tread carefully over the boards as if we're playing a game — not stepping on gaps. The wind is more forceful now, swirling my hair round my cheeks. "Know something, Stella?" Ed asks, as we reach the jetty's furthest point. "That day we first met, at the doctor's, I'd followed you in. I just wanted to talk to you."

The wind catches the pale green dress I chose for Diane's wedding, flapping the fabric against my bare legs. I smile and say, "I'm glad you did."

I place my bag on the slippery wooden slats, then peel away the jumper from the flute. Ed touches the crushed keys, the twisted threads that were once delicate springs. "What is it?" he asks.

"It's a flute. At least, it *was* a flute."

"What happened to it?"

"I'll tell you some time."

"That's awful, Stella —"

"I don't care any more," I say, and I really don't. Then I just do it — throw it as hard as I can, like a stick for a dog. It falls in a perfect arc, cutting into the sea with barely a splash. I feel light and free, and a smile as wide as the horizon floods my face.

From my bag I pull out the Mexican box. "Take off the lid, Ed," I say.

He does, and we stand there, waiting. Finally the wind lifts a folded onionskin square, then another, until they're all flying into the inky sky where Mum is, and where Dad wanted to be.

We watch the pale shapes twisting and flying, like children's hands waving, until they're all gone — Mum, Dad and their tangled past, which no longer matters. It's just us at the end of the jetty now, our salty lips meeting in a kiss that takes my breath away.

Just Ed and me.

Afterwards

A recipe for blackcurrant cheesecake is carried across barren ground close to where Surf ate the poisoned meat, and catches on hawthorn branches. A young woman unhooks it gently. The writing is smudged — it was written with an old-fashioned fountain pen — but she can still make out the words. It reminds her of Frankie Moon, the TV chef who died nearby. She had changed her walking route after that. Being close to the cliff's edge made her nervous.

The woman remembers eating cheesecake as a child, how it coated her tongue. She slips the recipe into the zip compartment of her bag. She knows where wild blackcurrants grow.

Mrs Bones didn't want to leave her flat but the stone stairs were too steep and it became too difficult to go out. She moved to a sheltered bungalow near the match factory, and for most of the summer she can smell sweetpeas from the allotment. She's on her hands and knees on the shared front lawn now, trying to find the beads from her snapped necklace. They are little black dice. She needs to find them all — there should be thirty — so they can be rethreaded.

379

She's picking through grass when a scrap of paper flutters to the ground. It's a recipe for asparagus fondue. Mrs Bones made a fondue for her daughter Christine's twenty-first; everyone fried pieces of steak in bubbling oil. Christine lives in Coff's Harbour, Australia. They fell out when she moved. Christine said she'd made her feel guilty for moving, that Australia wasn't so far away.

Mrs Bones decides to write her a letter. It upsets her, the thought of losing people for ever — like the pupils who promised to keep in touch, or her daughter Christine. You can't lose a child, not your own flesh and blood. She stops hunting for dice because, she decides, a necklace doesn't really matter.

Frankie's Sole Véronique recipe is carried on a north-easterly wind, finally landing on St Agnes, Isles of Scilly, where it's pecked to shreds by a ravenous gull.

An onionskin square comes to rest in Bay Street, a beleaguered corner of town where Mr Grieves is packing away the last of his stock, which he hopes to sell privately. Certain instruments, like the flute with the solid silver headjoint, he's decided to keep.

He is carrying a cello to his car when he spots a small square of damp paper stuck to the windscreen. He peels it off, and sees that it's a recipe. "Lemon Sorbet", it's headed. Lemon, water, sugar. He remembers the Italian place, Dino's, that used to be next door. And Stella, who used to have lemon sorbet in there with her mother.

380

Mr Grieves slips the recipe into the pocket of his brown jacket. He eases the cello on to the back seat of his car and wanders into the shop. All that's left now are the oboes. He opens a case, fits the parts together and puts the reed to his lips.

He's not really an oboist. The flute is his first instrument, clarinet a close second. He starts to run up and down scales, and it feels right, fluid, but he doesn't know if it sounds any good.

It doesn't matter, because no one's listening. The notes keep coming, from some place deep inside him, and all he's doing is sending them out.

ISIS publish a wide range of books in large print, from fiction to biography. Any suggestions for books you would like to see in large print or audio are always welcome. Please send to the Editorial Department at:

ISIS Publishing Limited
7 Centremead
Osney Mead
Oxford OX2 0ES

A full list of titles is available free of charge from:

Ulverscroft Large Print Books Limited

(UK)
The Green
Bradgate Road, Anstey
Leicester LE7 7FU
Tel: (0116) 236 4325

(Australia)
P.O. Box 314
St Leonards
NSW 1590
Tel: (02) 9436 2622

(USA)
P.O. Box 1230
West Seneca
N.Y. 14224-1230
Tel: (716) 674 4270

(Canada)
P.O. Box 80038
Burlington
Ontario L7L 6B1
Tel: (905) 637 8734

(New Zealand)
P.O. Box 456
Feilding
Tel: (06) 323 6828

Details of **ISIS** complete and unabridged audio books are also available from these offices. Alternatively, contact your local library for details of their collection of **ISIS** large print and unabridged audio books.